CW00421205

To MARK
ENJOY
Pete

Peter Mark May was born in Walton on Thames Surrey England way back in 1968; he still lives nearby in a place you've never heard of called Hersham. His first novel *Demon* was released in January 2008 Vanguard Press and no one has thrown any back at him yet. He has read at BFS Fantasy Con 2008 and appeared as a special guest author at both Gamesfest 3 & 4.

His short story *Blood & Guts* has appeared on the *Horror Bound Magazine* (Volume I, Issue I) website in Canada in 2008. His story *Into the Endless Sea of Night* appeared in Issue 6# & 8# of the US pulp magazine *Astonishing Adventure* in 2009.

He is currently working on several projects including a follow-on from *Demon* and two short story collections and several other novel ideas. 2009 also saw the inclusion of his first short story to feature in a horror anthology. He has also co-founded the *Novelblog.com* with his American friend Dan Boucher.

Official Website   http://darkside6869.webs.com/

Other sites   Thenovelblog.com

Sweet is war to those who know it not...

Pindar

KUMIHO

Peter Mark May

KUMIHO

Vanguard Press

A CIP catalogue record for this title is
available from the British Library.

ISBN 978 1 843865 89 6

Vanguard Press is an imprint of
Pegasus Elliot MacKenzie Publishers Ltd.
www.pegasuspublishers.com

First Published in 2010

Vanguard Press
Sheraton House Castle Park
Cambridge England

Printed & Bound in Great Britain

Dedicated to my late father:

Private Raymond John May

1ˢᵗ Battalion The Middlesex Regiment
National Serviceman ~ BAOR Germany 1949, Korea
1950,Hong-Kong 1951

Mentioned in Dispatches:

(Two uncles I never got to meet)

Gunner Frederick (Peter) May
312 Battery, 90 Lt. A.A. Regt. Royal Artillery
Died 29th October 1944 Italy

Private Albert Edward (Brudgie) May
2ⁿᵈ Battalion East Surrey Regiment
Died 8th February 1942 Singapore

Katie Meer for typing my scribbles into New Times Roman

All those who bought *Demon* and believed in me.

Also to my Mum, who has suffered so much loss in one lifetime.

Also by the same author

Demon

HORROR FICTION:

ISBN No: 978 1843863 98 4 (Vanguard Prss)

Contents

Foreword

The Korean War

In 1945, after the end of the Second World War, Korea, after the Japanese occupation, was divided into two countries (a little like East/West Germany): the communist North and the US friendly South (or Republic of Korea).

In 1950, the communist North led a surprise and devastating attack on its Southern counterpart. The Republic of Korea (ROK) forces were overwhelmed and within days the capital Seoul had fallen. The newly formed United Nations sprang into action, led by the United States of America. They had the most troops on the ground during the war, with the British Government finally sending the *'Woolworth Bridge',* made up of the 1st Battalion the Middlesex Regiment (hastily beefed up with National Servicemen) and the Argyll & Sutherland Highlanders.

By the end of October 1950 the invading North Korean army had been forced back over the 38th parallel (the invisible dividing line between the two countries), nearly to the Chinese border. The end of the war and victory were almost imminent, or so the United Nations forces thought...

This book is a work of fiction, set during a real war, using the correct regiments and places. A little artistic licence has been used on troop movements, dates and HQ locations, including the fictional Yŏu Plateau: that and the fictional horror content of this book should not detract from the sacrifice in lives and minds of the brave men, from many nations, who fought the Korean War.

Prologue

Lil set the huge turkey down on the Christmas festooned dining table, with its red tablecloth, and more cutlery than you could ever use. Robert London rose from his seat at the head of the table and looked round at his small family and smiled with hungry anticipation.

He picked up the long carving knife and fork and began to carve the brown roasted skin of the bird as his family drooled and young Paul shook his cracker in his high-chair to Robert's left. He cut long precise slices with his sharp carving knife and placed them on plate after plate offered up to him.

He as usual, saved himself for last as Angela cut up two-year-old Paul's turkey into bite-sized pieces, as well as his roast potatoes and vegetables. Robert cut away the last pieces of stubborn fowl from its ribcage and then stopped and moved his head closer to the large bird.

Through the ribs of the turkey he could see something inside the bird that should not be there. It wasn't stuffing that was cooked separately; surely Lil had not left the giblets inside. Then it twitched looking like a small pink chicken breast inside the turkey's cavity. Then to Robert's shock it turned, revealing tiny arms and bent legs and a small snout and mouth. His wife and son-in-law rose now to see what he was staring at, but Robert just watched in morbid amazement as the thing inside the bird grew as he watched, sprouting course ginger hairs.

Robert stepped backwards, his legs bumping into the back of his chair; as he still held the carving knife and the fork before him.

There came a crack, then the turkey exploded like a firework had been let off inside, showering the family and the

table with its fowl debris. Lil screamed and Robert looked at her and saw a fox cub at her neck biting into her artery and sending blood shooting off onto the nearby real Christmas tree. Lil fell with the ever-growing fox creature on top of her. Colin, his son-in-law moved forward with his dinner knife to stab at the thing, but it was upon his head now twice cub-size biting off his nose. Colin fell back over his chair and disappeared from Robert's sight below the table.

Angela, his daughter screamed for her husband, but only the fox jumped from the floor, onto the table. It was a full adult vixen now, with a snout covered in red blood of his family. Robert seemed rooted to the spot, paralysed with fear as the fox leapt off the table at his daughter and tore off her face.

Suddenly he could move and rounded his crying grandson's high-chair and stabbed the creature in the back with the carving knife and fork as it feasted upon his daughter's innards.

The fox howled and rose to a height not too far off his own stocky frame; she pulled the knife and fork from her back and plunged them deep into his lungs, causing him to crash to the carpet in breathless agony.

*Then he could only watch on helplessly as the fox creature approached his grandson Paul and whispered **"Pok-Kku"** and then in English, **"restoration."***

Robert London woke from his nightmare, gasping for breath that would not come from his cancer-laden lungs. He finally grasped his oxygen mask and took a small breath into his airways, sobbing from yet another evil dream that had plagued the past few months of his terminal illness. He knew time was running out now and death was not far from catching him. He knew he had to talk to his grandson Paul, soon before it was too late.

Chapter 1

Journeys

"Paul, there's a call for you," Ruben said, poking his head round the door.

"Who is it?" Paul asked rubbing his tired eyes. God knows how he was going to survive Uni, with all the booze, birds and partying going on.

"Your mum, I think," Ruben Cohen replied in his all too cheerful voice.

"I'll be there in a min," Paul replied swinging his naked legs out of the single bed of his room. He yawned, pulled on his jeans, standing up and tucking away his privates as he zipped up.

Grabbing a black 'Doors' T-shirt, he pulled it over his mess of dark hair. He reached back and smacked the covered figure hidden beneath his duvet.

"Time to go, erm, whatever your name is." A pretty, but obviously worse for wear young woman appeared from under the duvet.

Paul didn't wait for small talk and left the girl to dress as he entered the corridor and headed for the communal wall phones.

Ruben Cohen was standing guard by the telephone like some old faithful family hound. He handed over the phone with a proud gawping smile.

"Cheers, Rubes." Paul grabbed the black receiver and flicked his head to tell Ruben to leave, pronto.

"Hello," he croaked, then cleared his throat. What had he been eating last night?

"Oh darling, I'm so glad to hear your voice, it's been far too long," his mother enthused down the phone.

"Hi Mum, why didn't you ring my mobile?" Paul smiled wickedly, suddenly remembering what he had eaten last night.

"I've tried for the last two days, but it's either off or engaged," she scolded.

"You could text," he bluntly replied. The whole point of going to Uni so far away from home was to escape his nagging mother and useless father.

"Text! You know I can't do all that technological stuff Paulie, I wish you'd call me now and again or even write," Angela Harvey pleaded to her only child.

"Blimey, Mum, no one writes anymore, it's the 21st Century, it's e-mail or nothing now," Paul shook his head and sniffed. "Anyway, what you calling for?"

"It's your grandfather." Her voice grew grave and monotone. "He's very ill, Paul, and he wants to see his only grandson before...he..." Mrs Harvey did not finish, her sentence descended into a trail of sobbing.

"It's okay, Mum, don't cry." Now even he felt a lump rise in his throat. "I'll catch the next train home, okay."

"Thanks, son," she managed, "bye."

"Yeah, bye mum." Paul put down the receiver and ran his fingers through his short raven hair. Why do events always conspire to stop him having a good time?

Paul exhaled and slowly ambled back down to his room, deep in thought. Why couldn't it be the 'old man' who was ill, not Granddad? He had got his height and steely grey eyes from his granddad on his mother's side. Thankfully he had skipped past most of his father's genes except the liking of loose women and booze. Two things Paul could live with.

As he reached his dorm room door he realised he had never loved anyone as much as his grandfather; only his late grandmother (Granddad Robert's wife) came close. Granddad Robert was his silent role model, from an age where real men acted on, not spoke about, problems. Small talk was for the wives and you worked hard and stayed true to your family and marriage vows.

Paul opened the door to find the rather sexy blonde bed-cohabitee from last night, pulling on her jeans.

"Who said you could get dressed?" Paul smiled wickedly, his dimples showing and his grey eyes taking in the view.

The girl licked her lips, held his gaze for two seconds; then let her jeans slowly slide back down her fake-tanned legs.

"What you got in mind, pet?" She tried hard to match the authority in his voice, but quivered in the end.

"It's not your mind I'm interested in at the moment." Paul closed the door behind him and slowly closed the gap between himself and the half-dressed Geordie beauty queen.

SURREY, GUILDFORD: PRESENT DAY.

Colin Harvey opened the front door and entered the house, just as his wife put down the telephone receiver in the hall.

"Chin-wagging again, my dearest wifey?" Colin made the question sound like a taunt as he closed the door behind him.

"No, I was talking to Paul; about his granddad," Angela replied, wiping the tears from her forty-three year old eyes.

"The blue eyed boy eh," Colin said taking off his coat and throwing it over the stair banisters. "So is he coming home to see Granddad Bob pop his clogs?"

"Don't speak about my father like that," Angela spat, "and yes he is as a matter of fact."

"Okay, keep your hair on, love. I was only joking." Colin reached into his coat pocket and pulled out a folded *Daily Star* and some betting slips.

"You've been down the betting shop again, seeing her!" Angela Harvey moved a step towards her husband in anger.

"Who's her, the cat's mother?" Colin asked reaching back once again into his coat pockets to retrieve his cigarettes.

"You know perfectly well who I mean, that ginger-headed bimbo you've been seeing behind my back!" Angela spat at him, wishing it was venom that could kill and not just spittle.

"Nah, she don't work there anymore," Colin smiled, one of his best features on his handsome and young-looking forty year old face. "'Cause you see, some frumpy blonde housewife came into the bookies giving it some of all that," Colin mimed speaking with his left hand, "and now she's got the old tin-tack."

Angela just stared at her husband, her face red with anger and years of frustration.

"Ring any bells, Angela my love?" Colin tilted his head and gave his best sarcastic grin.

"Why don't you just fuck off and die Colin." She screamed in his face, burst into tears and ran off upstairs.

"Come on, Ang, don't be like that," he called up after her, "Ang, huni."

Her only reply was to slam the master bedroom door so hard it rattled the glass in the front door.

"Suit yourself," he said to the empty hall and he walked into the front room to watch the racing from Sandown.

"Anyway," he chuckled to himself, "the blonde that's replaced her is much tastier." Colin pulled on a cigarette from his pack and changed the television to *Channel Four Racing*.

A few streets away in a two bed bungalow, the Macmillan nurse let herself in with the key the patient's daughter had given her. The house was old, tired and, like its owner, it had seen better days. She took of her coat and hung it up on the sparsely occupied coat rail. Tightening her grip on her bag she entered the second room on the left, the patient's bedroom.

She was glad the curtains were open for once and the old, tall, but withered man lay on his clean cotton sheets. An oxygen bottle and tubes led to a mask, that was sitting on the pillow next to the man's head.

"Mister London," the nurse touched the man's shoulder, "it's Lorna, the Macmillan nurse."

Robert London turned his head and opened his eyes with a wide grin.

"Surely I've died and gone to heaven, to have such an angel looking over me," his voice was sincere and mellow.

"You say that every day, Robert," Lorna Da Silva replied softly, "but I never tire of hearing it."

"So are you well, my dear?" Robert asked pulling himself up on the pillow a bit more.

"Tired," she replied, "overworked and underpaid," she laughed lightly.

"It doesn't show," he smiled back.

"Stop with the flattery, Mister London, I'm here to ask you how you are, not vice-versa."

"Still dying," he replied honestly.

"Robert, ssh now," she rummaged in her bag to get his prescription out. "So did you pull the curtains then?"

"Nah, my daughter did it earlier when she did me some porridge. Made it to the loo on my own last night though, major achievement, eh?" Robert London reached for his glass of blackcurrant as Lorna handed him his pills.

"You have your bedpans you could use, save those wobbly legs of yours for dancing and romancing." She watched kindly as he dutifully took each colour pill one at a time.

"The day I can't shit on my very own bog, is the day I give up and die." He smiled even though swallowing the pills caused a pain in his chest.

"If you say so Robert, now let's give you the once over before I leave, eh." Lorna rose and pulled down his sheets.

"My cheap thrill of the day, eh, lucky me." Robert London closed his eyes and his thoughts drifted off to another nurse, in a hospital he had been in many years before.

BRITCOM GENERAL HOSPITAL, KURE, JAPAN.
17TH OCTOBER 1950

"Wake up Private London," came a crisp voice out of his troubled dreams.

Private Robert James London opened his eyes and breathed in deeply through his nose. The Japanese winter sun streamed through the blinds of the window next to his hospital bed. He smiled at the sight of his favourite nurse attending to his crumpled sheets. Nurse White was the most beautiful woman he had ever seen in his life: all nineteen years of it. The sun's rays made her uniform shine like she was an angel. Robert had been to hell and this certainly seemed like heaven to him. Lilies in a glass vase next to his bed, lent the air a musk, like from the Garden of Eden.

"Surely I've died and gone to heaven, to have such an angel looking after me," his voice was young and excited.

"What rubbish. You say that every day Bob London," she replied in her Liverpudlian accent, "and it still isn't true."

"Beauty is in the eye of the beholder, Nurse White," Robert smiled back at her.

"Oh ssh," and she pushed the thermometer into his mouth to shut him up.

"Let's check that wound of yours." Nurse White moved closer to him, taking off the bandage and gauze from his left ear.

Robert couldn't help but stare at her large but well secured bosom as she changed his dressing.

"Mmm, looks good, Private," she nodded in agreement, "healing nicely. How's your hearing?"

"Mardom," he said through his thermometer-clenched teeth.

"Oops," Nurse White whipped out the thermometer and studied it. "Normal," she said then shook it in the air and popped it back in her breast pocket.

"The doctor will be round later," she fluffed his pillows, "looks like you'll get the all clear."

"Will you miss me, Lillian?" he asked softly to her right ear.

"I miss all my boys, Bob, but that's what we're here for, to make you better." She smiled brightly at him, her teeth seemed too white, her hair too golden blonde beneath her hat.

"You make me better, Lillian White," he spoke with deep emotion, a lump in his throat.

"Go on with ya," she blushed, but held his gaze. He had lovely grey eyes, that told her all she needed to know about him.

"Nurse White, can you help me lift Corporal Polley here please?" ordered an older looking nurse in a darker blue uniform.

"Coming sister," and with a last warming smile she turned and hurried across the ward to help out Sister McDermott.

Private London closed his eyes once more and sunk back onto his pillows. He wondered how he would cope returning to the war and never seeing her again.

BRITCOM GENERAL HOSPITAL, KURE, JAPAN.
19TH OCTOBER 1950.

Private Robert London sat on his kit bag outside the busy hospital waiting for his transport to arrive. He adjusted his beret for the twentieth time, wherever it sat it seemed to rub on his scar and annoy him. Finally he had enough and pulled it off, folded it and pulled it through his left epaulette. He stared around the place, wishing he had a roll-up at hand.

Japan, his third new country in six months; not bad for a boy whose furthest trip before that had been to the seaside at Bognor Regis. He'd soon be back on the hospital ship HMS *Maine* and on his way back to Korea: and the war.

He wondered how he would ever describe all these exotic places, sounds and smells to his family at home. It wasn't like home at all nor was it like the jungles described by his brother, in his letters from Burma during the Second World War. The hustle and bustle of Hong Kong, its acid beers and erotic temptations. The bleak rolling hills and valleys and woods of Korea, and now Japan, different again.

He glanced at his fake gold watch, nearly half-past ten: how long would he have to sit here? Then he stared at the strange trees across the road, resisting the urge to scratch his scar.

"Still here Private London?" came the sweetest sugary voice from behind his left ear.

Robert London rose and turned in a hurry, a huge smile beamed across his face.

"It's good to see you, Lillian, I thought I wouldn't see you again before I left." Robert spoke from the heart again, simple honest and true.

She came down the steps to join him, her hands behind her back. She had a mischievous pixie look on her face and two perfect dimples to match.

"I don't normally do this you know," she said mysteriously, her eyes on his polished boots.

"Do what?" he asked, moving closer.

She grabbed his hands and pushed an envelope into them; then pulled him closer and kissed his cheek.

"Stay safe, Bob," she whispered in his ear, "for me." Then she turned and ran up the steps and disappeared into the busy hospital before he could even mouth a word.

He didn't know what to think or do; his hand went to his slightly wet cheek. He put his foot on the first step, oblivious of the world around him.

A large blast of a horn woke him from his thoughts. He turned round to see a troop truck had pulled in beside him.

"You Private London?" a rat-faced corporal with a moustache yelled out the passenger window at him.

"Er yes, Corporal," Robert stammered.

"Well grab your kit and get your nasty little National Service arse into the back of the bleeding truck," the corporal yelled louder.

Robert London took one last look at the hospital entrance then bent down and grabbed his kit. He ran to the back of the truck and pushed his gear on first then aided by two other soldiers got on the back of the vehicle and sat down. The truck lurched off for its next destination, before heading back to the docks.

Robert watched the hospital disappear behind a line of trees, then carefully opened the envelope that Lillian had given him. Inside was a single handwritten piece of paper folded in three. Robert opened it up carefully and slowly and read what it said:

> *Dearest Bob,*
> *Please keep in touch, now and after the war.*
> *Love your Lillian xxx*

At the bottom of the page were her address at the hospital and BFPO (British Forces Post Office) number and her home address in Liverpool.

If he had been alone in the truck he would have whooped for joy. Instead he carefully folded the letter and put it back in its envelope. Then he gently pushed it into the right breast pocket of his battledress.

SURREY, GUILDFORD: PRESENT DAY.

"I'm off now, Robert," the nurse touched his right shoulder to wake him, "do you need anything else before I go?"

"No love, I'll be fine here with my thoughts," he replied remembering where he was and the frailties age had put on his once strong body.

"Okay, I'll catch you tonight, Robert," with a genuine smile of warmth Lorna left him to his thoughts again.

He stared out the window watching the white clouds move across the bluest of skies. His eyes darted to the picture frames on the window sill. He smiled at the picture of him and his wife from 1953, then settled on a picture of his only grandchild, Paul. He loved Paul, just as equally as he despised his son-in-law, Colin. Paul though had the advantage of London blood in him. He hoped his grandson would visit him soon: his time was getting short. He needed to talk to Paul urgently and he was the only person he could trust to help him.

TRAIN: PRESENT DAY. SOMEWHERE BETWEEN NEWCASTLE AND LONDON.

Paul Harvey shifted from one buttock to the other to curb numbness. He had been cat-napping with his head against his coat, which was lodged against the train's dirty window. He blinked and stretched and looked across the table he sat at to find a woman in her mid-thirties had replaced the previous occupant, a balding businessman, as he dozed.

He picked up his bottle of water which had been next to his copy of *FHM* on the table and smiled at the woman.

The chestnut haired businesswoman, smiled back at the handsome young man opposite. Then she looked down at the seminar papers she had been glancing at, a little embarrassed. Embarrassed, because she had been watching the handsome young man as he slept. Wondering what colour his eyes were, what his smile was like, how he spoke. In fact she had thought up quite a little fantasy about the lad while he had slept. They had both visited the loos together and things had started to get steamy: but then her fantasy toy boy had woken up.

31

Oh well, she thought, *back to the boring seminar papers, her suburban house, paunchy husband and three kids, nice fantasy while it lasted.*

"That looks a bit boring, fancy a look at my *FHM* mag?"

Shona looked up from the page entitled 'Creative Thought Processes and Logistics', to stare into the young man's smouldering silver-grey eyes.

Shona looked down to see a busty female star of *Hollyoaks* showing off her body on the cover of the 'Lads' Mag' he held across to her.

"I'm more of a *Woman's Own* girl myself," she replied with all the bluster she could manage: *Girl! Who was she kidding?*

"Shame," he sneered with his nose, not losing his cocky grin at all. "'Cause there's a cracking social article on page seventy-two."

Shona looked from her papers, to the magazine, to the handsome guy, who must be twenty years old, tops. She wasn't used to these flirty type situations; everyone knew her husband and his hard-man reputation and stayed respectfully clear.

"Go on then," she reached over and took the magazine, "page seventy-two you say?" Shona Lyons couldn't believe what she was doing, but it was unexpected and exciting: unlike her life.

"Yep," he replied sucking his bottom lip under his top one and leant forward over the table towards her.

She finally found page seventy-two, a colourful, picture-filled, two page spread entitled 'Sex on Wheels'. It had various stories from couples about sex on trains, motorbikes, bikes and even moving cars.

She read a few lines about a teenage couple going at it on a train from Waterloo to Portsmouth. It was very much down the lines of her fantasy before the handsome young man had woken up.

"Mmm, very informative," was all she could muster, looking up into his gorgeous grey eyes again.

"So you going all the way?" he paused, "to London?"

"Yes I am," she replied licking her lips, without even realising it.

"Long trip eh," he said.

"Very long, very boring," she replied, leaning closer. God she felt like she needed to go and ring out her knickers soon.

"I've got hours to spare too," he said rising from his seat, heading round the table to lean across her. "If you fancy keeping me company, follow me now?"

His last words were a husky whisper, as he stood and slowly walked down the train to the nearest set of loos. She looked around; no one was taking the slightest interest in her or the young man: their heads buried in books or papers, or they were asleep.

Grabbing only her purse she slid out of the seats and as nonchalantly as possible followed the man down the length of the carriage.

Cockily he didn't even look back to see if she was following; he pressed a button to open the sliding door to move out of the passenger part of the carriage to where the automated loos were. He jammed a thumb on a green open button and as the loo door slid open; so did the carriage door.

Paul turned and smiled at the woman and entered the loo: without thinking of her husband, children or reputation, she quickly joined him. Paul pushed a button inside the loo to close the door, then pulled the nervous woman to him before the door had even fully closed. Years of pent-up passion from her and youthful virility from him exploded, as they urgently French kissed. They tore at each other's clothes, as their kisses continued. Her blouse was unbuttoned by his eager young hands as her hands roughly unbuttoned his trousers.

Paul kissed down her neck and pulled her left breast free from its bra cup and sucked on her already hard nipple. Her right hand had dived into the tropical pubic jungle inside his boxer shorts. Already he was stiff and ready for action, as she wanked his long hard cock, loving the feel and hot warmth of it.

Shona hadn't felt so excited and scared at the same time since her youngest daughter had been born. The young man's penis pulsed with youth, vigour and blood, *God she was so wet!*

Paul put his hand on her hips and gently coaxed and turned the older woman around; until she was bent over the toilet, her hands resting on a basin on the wall for support.

He slowly pulled up her skirt inch by inch, revealing shapely legs, then thighs and then her knicker-covered behind. A red flush ran from Shona's cheeks to her chest, God why hadn't she worn a thong or cami-knickers today, not her normal big-arsed knickers.

But those thoughts dissolved into oblivion as the teenager hooked his thumbs into each side of her black knickers and pulled them slowly down to her ankles. Paul knelt as he pulled down the woman's underwear; the wet stain in the gusset did not go unnoticed to his gigolo eyes.

He savoured the sight of her exposed vagina, her tufty brown mound, her moist inviting wet lips. Opening his mouth and extending his tongue and dived in.

Shona gasped in pleasure as his hot breath, tongue and lips met her exposed parts. She found herself unknowingly grasping at her own exposed breast and nipple in lust. The young man's tongue and fingers were exposing and exciting her wet vagina to perfection.

Suddenly she took a sharp intake of breath, her mouth forming a silent 'O'. Here she was, thirty-six; good job; married with three lovely kids; half naked in a train's loo, with a man half her age who was licking her with his wet tongue.

SURREY, GUILDFORD: PRESENT DAY.

It felt so good. He lay back in his bed, his eyes closed in appreciation, as she rode his cock for all its worth. Her soft small hands were on his chest, as her perfect thighs rose up and down on him, sending waves of pleasure through both of their bodies.

He couldn't keep his eyes shut any longer. Astride him was his beautiful wife, her blonde locks covering her back and shoulders. She stared down at him and bit her bottom lip, a secret smile of love on her lips. His eyes devoured her elfin beauty, her pink lips and her silvery-blue eyes. He was a lucky chap alright, closing his eyes again he reached up to cup her bouncy breasts.

He pushed up his penis going deeper into her as her pace increased. Hard and harder her downward thrusts became, 'til it became even a little painful. An ache began to form in his belly as her wild thrusts began to painfully bend his penis forwards and backwards.

"Hey calm down, Lillian," he whispered and opened his eyes again. Yet the eyes that met him were brown not blue, and looked feral. Suddenly Lillian's body from the eyes outwards changed, her skin stained, her hair darkened and a once familiar Asian face now sat on top of him.

The woman cackled in his face and spat "Gusel!"

Robert London awoke from his first erotic dream in seven years with a yell of terror. He tore at his bed sheets, his eyes wild, gasping for breath and fumbling for his oxygen mask. Tears rolled down his cheeks as a fit of coughing hit him; at last he managed to put the mask over his pink face. Yet it was half an hour before the coughing would stop. His wife had been dead five years and the other woman's face he hadn't seen in his dreams for over fifty more.

A few streets away Angela Harvey stamped downstairs, her lips pursed; a hint of anger only a twitch away from her cheeks. She fetched her bag and coat; it was time to visit her father again.

She had managed to cool her anger with her second power-shower of the day and a bout of serious masturbation. Now as she heard the sounds of the racing coverage from the front room, it had been brought to the surface again.

She frowned then turned to the front door, pulling at her collar.

"Need a lift?" Colin's voice behind her made her jump.

"No thanks; that's why we have two cars, so I don't have to rely on you." Angela turned to face her wayward husband. "'Cause face it, Colin, you ain't reliable."

"More reliable than your Saab out there, hun," he replied with one of his winks.

"That supposed to be funny?" she bit back, but looking at his cheeky grin and green eyes, her resolve was wavering.

"Barely," he admitted, "How about we go out to dinner tonight?"

"What about Paul?"

"He can come too," he said, "give us time to catch up as a family."

"Where?" she asked suspiciously, "Superfish?"

"I was thinking of the San Marco," he raised his eyebrows looking for approval.

"You feeling flush then," she asked, "or have you got off your arse and got a job?"

"Private Pleasures!"

"Eh?"

"Private Pleasures, she's just won the 4.05 at Sandown, twenty-five to one," he explained taking a step closer.

"How much you win?"

"Two hundred and fifty smackaroons, my little blonde bombshell." Colin sidled up to her and took her in his arms.

"So I'll drive you to your dad's, then stop off at the bookies, then pop into the Italian to reserve a table for tonight. How's that sound?"

"Better," she admitted, "but you don't get round me that easy."

"Wouldn't be us if it did." Colin chanced his luck and moved in to kiss her.

Angela resisted at first, but that was Colin's charm, he was irresistible. She kissed him back, hating herself on behalf of all womankind, as she succumbed to his passionate advances.

Soon they were tearing one another's clothes off in lust, because without lust the only thing they would have in common was Paul and the same address.

"You got time for this?" Colin asked his left hand finding its way into her knickers.

"Only a quickie," she panted, "now shut up and fuck me!"

The train from Newcastle finally pulled into King's Cross Station at around six.

"So where you off to now?" Paul asked Shona as he helped her off the train with her things.

"Home," she smiled, but showed no teeth, "and you?"

"Home to see the folks," he replied.

After their sex session in the loos, there hadn't really been much to say.

Shona grinned, Paul grinned politely back.

"Oh, here's my card, if you wanna?" she offered him a card from her suit jacket pocket.

"Oh thanks," he smiled, held up the card to her, "shall we?"

Shona followed his extended hand and they headed off down the platform, towards the ticket barriers.

"This is where we part I suppose?" Shona said a little sad, but also dying to get home to hug her kids and possibly shower before dinner.

"Yep I'm off down the tube." They stood facing one another in an embarrassed silence; apart from their love-making they were total strangers.

"Better say goodbye eh," Shona said, feeling like a teenager at the end of a first date.

"Yeh," he leant forward and kissed her cheek, "you were the best ever," he whispered.

Shona's cheeks went scarlet, but before she could reply he turned and hurried down the escalator, with only one look back.

Shona stood and watched him until he was out of sight. "Come on you silly cow, pull yourself together," she slowly moved off heading across the station concourse towards the exit and taxi ranks.

Paul walked down onto the tube platform and took the card out of his pocket. He looked up and checked the time of the next tube, three minutes. With a last look at the name on the card, he flicked it out of his fingers and watched it fall onto the track below.

HMS *MAINE*: HOSPITAL SHIP. SOMEWHERE IN THE KOREAN STRAIT.
22ND OCTOBER 1950.

Robert London put both hands on the rail of the starboard side of the ship and breathed in deeply. The air was softly cool and refreshing; any smell apart from the stench of bleach and infection was welcome. He hadn't noticed as much on his first trip, but the smell of disinfectant and disease was overpowering below decks.

"Not long now, eh laddie?" a thick Scottish voice bellowed from behind him.

Private London turned to see one of his fellow passengers, Regimental Sergeant Major (RSM) James 'Jock' McConnell approaching. The sergeant major was an imposing man even though he was only five foot five in his boots. He had the look of a bulldog and the experience of a veteran of three campaigns during World War Two. For some reason he had taken a shine to Robert, even though they were from different regiments.

"No Sergeant Major," Private London replied, straightening up as he replied.

"Getting some fresh air eh?" The sergeant major came to stand next to the young National Serviceman.

"Yes, Sergeant Major," Robert replied, "I wanted to get away from that smell."

"Aye son, it smells worse than a prostitute's fanny after a visit to the crabs' clinic."

Robert London laughed out loud and the sergeant major guffawed at his own words also.

"Soon be back to Pusan and the war," Robert said after a few minutes of silent wave watching.

"In the morning aye," McConnell replied, the conversation had waned a little.

"I'm scared, Sergeant Major," Robert said softly, his eyes felt watery.

"I would be worried if ya weren't, laddie."

"But last time I shipped out with the boys, I was excited, didn't have a scared bone in my body," Robert turned to explain. "Why am I like this now?"

"'Cause when you shipped out you were a boy. Ya had ya mates with ya, spurring you on and now you've seen the action; blood and guts and death," the sergeant major smiled kindly. "Now you've been out of the war, laid in a warm, dry bed, tended by nurses and ate three warm meals a day. With no shells coming overhead, no orders, no fear. You've experienced life again and now it's bloody precious to ya."

"What do I do, to go on?" Private London asked.

"Don't fear that bullet with your name on it, laddie; 'cause if ya freeze on the battlefield you're a dead man." The sergeant major clapped his shoulder.

"Thanks, Sergeant Major, shame I ain't in your regiment." Private London sniffed, his thoughts drifting to Nurse White again.

"I would-nay have ya, you southern Sassenach Nancy boy." Sergeant Major McConnell looked back at him and turned to leave the young National Serviceman with his thoughts.

SURREY, GUILDFORD: PRESENT DAY.

Robert London awoke from his daydream sitting on the sofa in his living room. He wondered why he had bothered to let his daughter get him up in the first place, if all he would do was fall asleep again. He pulled his dressing gown across his pyjamas as they had gaped open while he had forty-winks.

On the television Sean Connery played an immortal Spanish swordsman, while some French actor played a Scotsman in the Highlands. Maybe that was where his daydreams of good-old Sergeant Major McConnell had drifted into his subconscious, from hearing their accents.

Robert looked left to a set of three interlocking tables, that descended in size. On top of the larger one was a round white doily with a black and white picture of his beloved wife in her nurse's uniform on it. The tears began to well up in his eyes, as he stared at her in her beautiful youth.

"I miss you so much, dear," he sobbed to himself, "but I'll be with you soon." He reached out a trembling hand and lightly touched the edge of the frame.

He hated the cancer so much, it had taken his father, and his wife five years ago: now it was eating away at his lungs. He didn't want to die like this, a skinny scarecrow shell of the immense man he had once been. The soldier, amateur footballer

39

and county cricketer for Surrey for three years, after his National Service had ended. A career he gave up at twenty-three to run his father's Coalmongers' company, after his father had passed away. He looked up at a fading picture on the wall, of him standing in his cricket whites next to his fellow players including Peter May, Alec Bedser, Jim Laker and Tony Lock. They had been great Surrey and England players, while he had been an okay fast-medium bowler and number eight batsman. He would have loved to have carried on, but his pay as J. London's and Sons Coalmongers had been three times that of a county cricketer.

Robert felt a tickle in the back of his throat and he began to cough. He hoped Paul would come home soon because he had things to resolve before he died and a story to tell.

PLATFORM TWO, WATERLOO STATION. 7.09 PM.

Paul got on the second carriage of the train and set his belongings down between his legs before he sat down.

A couple of young girls of sixteen/seventeen sat opposite him and smiled warmly at him. Paul wearily smiled back and pulled his mobile from his front jeans pocket. He flipped it open and speed-dialled his parents' house.

He looked out the carriage window to avoid looking at the whispering puppy-fat peroxide twins opposite. The phone was answered on the third ring.

"Hello, Battersea Dogs' Home," a posh male voice answered.

"Dad, put Mum on the phone," Paul asked ignoring the old man's humour.

"Paulie, son; hope you're nearly home, we have a table booked at San Marco's at eight," Colin said, ignoring his son's request.

"Yes nearly, now get Mum; I need her to pick me up at the station." Paul could feel the old hackles rising on his back again.

"Fair enough," his father replied and Paul heard the phone being put down.

"Ang, it's golden boy, he wants picking up from the station," Colin said walking into the kitchen.

Angela Harvey put down the tea towel and mug she was holding and hurried to the phone.

"Hello Paul," she answered excitedly a beaming smile on her face.

"Hi Mum, can you pick me up at the station in about forty minutes?" Paul asked as the doors to the train hissed automatically shut ready for departure.

"Not a problem, son." Angela was glad her only child was nearly home. "Did your father mention he's taking us out for dinner tonight?"

"Yeah he said," Paul snorted, "what he find a wallet in the street or did he win at the bookies for once?"

"Don't spoil it, Paul, for my sake eh," Angela asked remembering all the arguments and huffs that had gone on in their house over the years.

"I won't if he don't," Paul replied, "anyway, catch you in forty mins, Mum, okay?"

"I'll be waiting, Paul, and thanks for coming back so quickly."

"Bye Mum," he clicked off his mobile, cutting her goodbye in half.

He glanced around the carriage as the train started slowly out of Waterloo station. The peroxide twins were still eyeing him up, while applying another layer of slap. Paul delved into his pocket and pulled out his silver iPod, popped the earpieces in and let his thoughts be blasted by the latest Indie-Rock band. Outside the sun went behind a layer of clouds, so he could stare out the window, without being blinded by the rays of the early evening dusk.

GUILDFORD, SURREY. 7.20 PM.

Robert London shuffled into his kitchen in his dressing gown and pulled a frozen chicken meal for one from his freezer. A call from his daughter Angela, telling him Paul was on his way home, had put renewed vigour into his dying body. He felt hungry for the first time in months and he even set the table in the kitchen, instead of his usual tray in bed.

When Lorna Da Silva came in at eight o'clock to check on him and give him his pills; she found him halfway through a chicken dinner. His sallow skin even had a touch of pink in it and a glass of bitter stood half-empty next to his meal.

"Having a dinner party are we, Mister London?" she smiled.

"Just felt a bit peckish, my dear." He saw her looking disapprovingly at the beer glass, "And a mite thirsty."

"Good to see you in such fine fettle, Robert," she said putting his pills on the table. "You better wait a couple of hours and take these with a nice glass of water, okay."

"Yes Nurse," he joked, a twinkle back in his grey eyes.

"So what's put you in the culinary mood, been watching *Ready, Steady, Cook*?"

"My grandson is on his way home from University to see me," Robert said, popping some stuffing and potato into his mouth.

Lorna smiled inwardly, so that was it, amazing how the body can respond when it has something to look forward to. She was worried also, she had seen this hundreds of times with cancer patients. Many times she had witnessed patients experience a brief oases of improvement, before the end. It often gave false hope to relatives, but Lorna, a regular churchgoer, saw it as a final gift of clarity from God. A brief spell to make your peace with the world: set your affairs in order and say your goodbyes.

Ten minutes later Lorna Da Silva sat in her car outside Robert London's bungalow, when she suddenly burst into tears. Her experience, training and faith told her, Robert London would be lucky to live to see the end of the week.

SAN MARCO RESTAURANT, GUILDFORD. 8.30 PM.

The three diners chomped away at their main courses in near silence. Paul made sure he had loads of everything, dining out at posh Italian restaurants was way beyond his usual student fare.

"This is nice, isn't it?" Angela Harvey smiled. The two men nodded, but only Angela meant what she had said. She had missed Paul so much over the last eight months: Newcastle was so far away. When he did come home (with a suitcase full of washing), he ate her out of house and home and stayed out 'til all hours with his old mates.

She felt sad, lonely and frumpy most of the time. Colin was a waste of space, either out, down the pub, bookies, racecourse, football, snooker rooms or chasing skirt. He must have cheated on her over ten times in their twenty-one year marriage; it may even have been double that.

She had matched his dalliances in her thirties with love affairs with her salsa teacher and two tennis coaches: now that was a doubles match to remember!

Whereas Colin's affairs made him happy, her affairs just made her feel sad and unfulfilled. She should have left him years ago, but deep down he loved her, their fights and wild sexual make-ups. He was still as handsome as the day he started at her dad's coal depot and he knew it. She still looked good for her age: her hair bottle-fed now, her tummy tucked last spring.

Now her dad was dying, her hero. He gave her a purpose now as she visited him twice or three times a day. What would she do with her days after he had gone; she dreaded his passing, like it would be the end of her life also.

"So Paul, got yourself a girlfriend at University yet?" Angela asked quickly before her melancholy thoughts turned to tears.

"No one special," he replied tucking into his Bolognese.

"Bet you've got a string of girls, eh Paul," his father chuckled, "I hear the Geordie birds are right dirty."

"Colin, do you have to bring everything down to your gutter level?" Angela protested, putting down her cutlery.

"Sorry, Ang," Colin replied quickly, seeing the look on his son's and wife's faces.

"When we gonna see Granddad then, tomorrow morning?" Paul asked, before he took a sip of fizzy Italian beer.

"I'll take you over there at about ten if that's okay with you?" Angela replied, picking up her cutlery from the table.

43

"Ten!" Colin spat through his seafood linguine, "He's a student, Ang, he won't be out of his pit 'til noon."

"When's the last time you got out of bed to do an honest day's work, Dad, ten years ago?"

"Stop it, please, can't we have even a civilised meal together without you two kicking off!" Angela reprimanded.

"He started it," Paul jabbed a fork in his father's direction.

"He started it, is that the best you can do with your University educated mind?" Colin retorted.

"Okay, you're a work-shy, parasitical, somnolence; you're also a fallacious, duplicitous, predatory git!"

"Don't mince words, son, tell me what you really think eh," Colin took a sip of his red wine and smiled, "and for Christmas, buy me a thesaurus."

Paul smiled in spite of himself, Colin grinned back and Angela looked on relieved, peace had broken out once again in the Harvey family.

ROBERT LONDON'S BUNGALOW: GUILDFORD. 9.49 PM.

Robert London sat in his bed, propped up on pillows with the light off. The curtains were pulled, only a small portable television, brought any illumination to the room. He was suffering from his earlier exuberance and his old body felt every part of three quarters of a century old tonight, and more.

He was normally asleep by now, his illness had put paid to his late nights months ago. He had the television on to keep him awake, because for the first time since Korea, he felt afraid to go to sleep, in case he never woke up.

He tried to concentrate on the television; there was a documentary on BBC 2 on the decline of the British shipbuilding industry. The sight of the ships and docks sent his mind wondering back to the events of 1950 again.

HMS *MAINE*: HOSPITAL SHIP, PUSAN, KOREA.
23RD OCTOBER 1950.

Private London watched from the deck rail as HMS *Maine* slowly reached port in Pusan again. The 'Welcome United Nations Forces' banner, which was white and clean in August, was now dirty and slightly ripped in one corner. There was no huge crowd today, no bands to play them ashore.

Private London grabbed his gear and moved down the deck, as the gangplank was swirled into position by rope. He looked up to see regimental Sergeant Major McConnell walking towards him from the other side of the deck. His battledress and trousers had been replaced by a thick commando type pullover, kilt and stockings with all the trimmings. He had a cane under his arm, with a silver top, inscribed with the badge of the Argyll and Sutherland Highlanders. An unfortunate green looking private called McClaren followed, carrying not only his gear, but the sergeant major's.

"Ready to get back to the war, laddie?" he bellowed from only two yards away.

"Ready, Sergeant Major," Robert lied.

The sergeant major gave him a squinty eyed look down his nose, then simply said, "Good."

Five minutes after a few officers and medical staff had disembarked, they followed. Private London was back on Korean soil, back as a front-line infantry soldier during a war.

The other private, huffed and puffed behind them as they made their way over to the adjutant's office for transport instructions.

"What's the matter, McClaren, can't your girly arms take the strain?"

"It's a bit heavy, Sergeant Major, maybe the other private could help?" Private McClaren grunted, looking a bit pink in the face, to match his piggy countenance.

"No he can't, Private McClaren, because there is one difference between you and he," the sergeant major stopped and spun neatly round on the spot.

"We're both privates, Sergeant Major," McClaren replied, which was his second mistake.

"Incorrect, Private McClaren, he is a soldier who has faced battle at Middlesex Hill and got wounded in action. You, on the other hand, are a piece of dogshite, that somehow survived

45

Paisley backstreet abortion, was dressed up like a soldier and sent over to Korea as a replacement for some brave dead laddie." The sergeant major was now turning the colour of the private he was reprimanding. "Now you two stand easy here, while I find out our travel plans." The sergeant major marched off to the adjutant's office at a quick march.

"You his adopted bunk boy or summat?" Private McClaren asked, peeved at the dressing down he had received.

"Shut up, Piggy," Private London warned as he towered over the Scotsman.

Just then, as Private Piggy McClaren backed off, a girl appeared beside Private London with a bunch of blooms.

She had a pretty face, round black hair and was dressed in white and black.

"For you," she bowed and handed a flower to Private London. He reached out to take the flower, only for it to change into a small glowing ball. "Gusel!" the girl spat.

Robert London screamed himself awake, somehow he had fallen asleep during his daydream and she had invaded his mind again. He reached for his oxygen mask as his cancer-riddled lungs gasped for air.

ROBERT LONDON'S BUNGALOW, GUILDFORD. 3.03 AM.

Something woke Robert from his sleep in the wee hours of the morning. His breathing was fine and his airways surprisingly moist: the use of the oxygen mask usually dried his mouth to a desert-like state. His bladder didn't need emptying, so why had he woken up? Any sleep without pain or for long periods was a bonus now, soon he'd sleep forever.

Somewhere in the trees of his back garden, a squirrel screeched a warning to its friends and family to stay off the lawn.

Robert's eyes were adjusting to the dark, so he decided to reach over and take a sip of water. As he pulled the cold glass to his lips and drank, he thought he heard a sound outside. Lowering the glass to rest on his chest, he strained his ears, to see if the sound was repeated. He waited anxiously for ten seconds (which seemed like a minute to him), but the sound did not recur. Robert put down his glass on the bedside cabinet and the sound came again.

Robert cursed silently, as the sound of his glass on wood had masked the sound once again. Robert London lay still on his propped up pillows, and tried not to breathe hard.

He closed his eyes to help concentrate, then he heard it! A faint scratching coming from his back garden against his back door. The scratching sound grew louder, sounding like some feral animal was trying to get in. Robert and his wife had never had a pet between them in their nearly fifty year marriage. Robert disliked dogs and cats and Lillian hated the mess they caused.

The scratching grew louder and more intense now, like the animal wanted to find a.way in through the heavy, wooden backdoor.

"Go away, leave me in peace!"

Robert's cry brought a cessation to the attack on the back door. He waited silently in the darkness: once a soldier and sportsman, now a frail old man hiding under his bedcovers. Robert London prayed for the dawn and for him to be there to see it.

Chapter 2

Beginnings

ROBERT LONDON'S BUNGALOW 8.30 AM.

"Is he really coming?" Robert asked his daughter as she opened the curtains in his bedroom to reveal a wonderful sunny day.

"Yes Dad," she smiled back at him, "I'll bring him, round about ten-ish, okay?"

"Yes, as long as I can talk to him alone, Angela," he stated, pushing his bedcovers aside.

"If you wish, Dad," she sighed, "now what are you up to?"

"Well you don't think I'm going to greet my only grandchild wearing pyjamas and laying in my deathbed do you girl?" he scolded, making her feel ten years old again.

"Dad, Paul won't mind," she moved forward and took one of his large rough hands in hers.

"I have my pride, Angela," he coughed, while swinging his legs slowly out of bed.

"Know what pride goes before?" she frowned and reached down to unbutton his pyjama top.

"'Pride goeth before destruction, and an haughty spirit before a fall'." Robert quoted staring out the window at the cloudless blue sky.

"Blimey, where's that from?" she asked, moving over to the wardrobe to get him a clean shirt to wear.

"Proverbs sixteen: eighteen," he replied pulling his arm out of one sleeve.

"Didn't know you were into the Bible, Dad?" Angela asked knowing her father was a strictly births, marriages and deaths visitor to a church.

"There's lots of things hidden away in this old head dear, some I wish I could forget," he mumbled to the floor and his bare feet.

48

"Like Korea?" Angela asked, pulling a yellow shirt from the wardrobe and closing it.

"Like Korea," he nodded, "come on girl, chop-chop, let's get me dressed for my grandson." He brightened up again, the sun streaming through his windows giving him renewed vigour.

"Anything for my dad," Angela beamed, with love flowing from every pore towards him.

ROBERT LONDON'S BUNGALOW 9.15 AM.

Lorna Da Silva pulled up as Angela Harvey came walking down the rose-lined path of her father's front garden. Angela recognised Lorna and her car and approached as Lorna got out with her bag.

"Hi, Lorna," Angela smiled and waved.

"Morning, Angela, how are you keeping?" Lorna asked, moving round the bonnet to stand next to Robert's daughter.

"You know," she shrugged, "so-so."

"And how's the patient this fine morning?" Lorna asked putting her heavy bag down on the pavement.

"Dad," Angela involuntarily craned her head back to glance at the bungalow, "he's full of the joys of spring."

"Ah yes, the return of the prodigal grandson," Lorna clicked, "he told me last night."

"Yeah it's cheered him up to have Paul back from Uni." Angela found a smile came easy to her face when she thought of her only child. The glorious morning and the perfume of her father's roses also helped.

"Is he staying long?"

"I'm not sure. Dad wanted to see him urgently for some reason," Angela looked down at her shoes, "to say goodbye I suppose."

"Angela, I don't want to upset you, or speak out of turn, but he hasn't got long left. Have you discussed taking him to hospital, since last time we spoke?" Lorna pursed her lips, because you never knew how families could react in her job.

"He's adamant he does not want to die in unfamiliar surroundings like Mum did and I back him one hundred percent." Angela could feel her throat contracting with emotion as she spoke.

"That's fine, we'll help you as much as we can." Lorna touched Angela's arm to reassure her.

"Lorna, tell me honestly, how long does he have left?"

This is the question that Lorna and her Macmillan colleagues heard the most and absolutely dreaded. She stared into Angela Harvey's eyes, trying to suss out if she could handle the truth.

"Angela, I could be wrong, but I think we are looking at days rather than weeks." Lorna exhaled a long sigh. "I'm so sorry."

"It's okay," Angela sniffed, "you're just confirming what I was already thinking: thanks for your honesty."

"You're welcome," Lorna replied humbly.

"Well," Angela brightened, "I better let you get on with the pill-popping duties; I'd better get home and get my son out of his pit and ready to visit his grandfather." Angela wiped her eyes and turned towards the car. "See ya later," she managed.

"Yeah, goodbye Mrs Harvey," Lorna picked up her bag and headed through the open front gate.

THE HARVEY'S HOUSE. GUILDFORD. 9.45 AM.

"You ready to go, Paul?" Angela stood in her long hallway, nervously twiddling her car key on her index finger.

Paul and his father appeared from the front room.

"Just got to get me trainers on," Paul replied moving past her to sit on the stairs to put his Converse Allstars on.

"What about you, Colin, you coming too?" she asked, hoping his reply would be negative.

"Sorry dear, I've got football today." He gave her a great teeth-filled fake grin.

"On a Sunday, what time are you leaving?" Angela hated football, as well as golf, athletics, racing, snooker, rugby and darts.

"I got to be at White Hart Lane for noon, I'm leaving in a min."

"God you love that football team more than me."

"Ang dear, I love Arsenal more than you," he joked.

Paul cracked up, even though it was a cruel retort. Luckily Angela saw the funny side too and only gently clipped her husband around the head.

"Right you two shits, I'll drop off Paul then head off to the tennis club for lunch with the girls then," Angela pouted; maybe the club pro could take her mind off things.

"Good for you, love," Colin nodded, as Paul stood up, his bumper boots now on and tied up.

"Let's go then," he said, wanting to see his granddad again.

ROBERT LONDON'S BUNGALOW. 9.46 AM.

After his Macmillan nurse had left, Robert had got the tea things ready and then went into the living room to sit down. He'd switched on the television just for background noise and pulled a large book from his bookcase. He gingerly sat down and opened the book: it was one of Michael Palin's travel books. Paul had got it for him at Christmas; he'd never looked at it before today. Yet he had been born to a politer generation, so he got it out today and opened it halfway to appear that he'd at least attempted to read it.

He found a chapter about a train journey the writer had taken, so he read that part. As he read about the cramped conditions it reminded him of a similar journey he had taken from Pusan to Pyongyang, well over fifty years ago.

SEOUL RAILWAY STATION, KOREA.
25TH OCTOBER 1950.

"Ch'a, ch'a?"

Private London awoke with a start to find a round-faced Korean man, only inches from his face, a metal cup in his hand.

Robert sat up in his train seat, to find the man was standing in the open doorway of the train and that they had stopped at a large train station.

"Aniyo," Sergeant Major McConnell replied gruffly to the man, waving his hands in front of his face and shaking his head.

Seeing the look of the red-faced, large moustached sergeant major, made the tea seller retreat from the carriage and find easier business elsewhere.

"Where are we?" the noise had woken Private 'Piggy' McClaren from his snoring slumber.

"Seoul," Sergeant Major McConnell replied, "we might be here a while."

Private London rested his arm on top of the muzzle of his No. 5 .303 rifle and peered out onto the busy station. The rumours they had heard on their train journey north through South Korea, was that the North Korean army was on the run and the war would be over in weeks. Robert London hoped so; it would be great to join up with his D-company chums again to celebrate the end of hostilities.

Just then an officer appeared at their open door, with a porter behind him, with a trolley overloaded with two kitbags and a brown suitcase.

"Officer!" sergeant major barked and shot to his feet stiff as a board. Private London followed a half-second later and Private McClaren another two seconds after that.

"Hello chaps," the young captain smiled enthusiastically, "bit of a full train, any room for a small one?"

"Aye sir," McConnell saluted, "acres of space, sir."

"Good show." The captain grabbed his suitcase from the trolley and climbed in. "Could you lads help with my gear? I don't travel light, you see."

With a glare from the sergeant major, the two privates helped take the kitbags off the porter's trolley and into the overhead luggage compartments.

The porter shut the door and the officer threw a coin through the open window for him. Finally they all sat down again and within a minute a whistle blew to signal the train's departure.

52

"Off we go," the plumy-voiced captain enthused, "so you boys all going to Pyongyang?"

"Yes sir," all three of them replied, the privates now on their best behaviour.

The captain took off his cap and cast it on the seat beside him, revealing golden blond hair underneath. Private London reckoned he must be only five years older than him, but worlds apart.

"As we're going to be travel companions for a while, we better make introductions." The captain leant back in his seat. "I'm Captain Ashley Woodholme-Browne, Royal Engineers, Fifty-Fifth Field Squadron. They want my expertise up at the front line for some reason."

"Regimental Sergeant Major James McConnell. First Battalion, The Argyll and Sutherland Highlanders. Twenty-seventh Commonwealth Brigade; rejoining my men after being wounded in action assaulting Hill 282 near Sangju, sir." Private London noticed how the sergeant major puffed out his chest as he spoke with pride.

"That horrible wee oik is Private McClaren, a replacement for the Argyll's from the Scottish Border Collies." The sergeant major pointed at Piggy McClaren, who opened his mouth, then had a think and closed it again.

"And who are you, Private, not with this lot I see?" the captain asked Private London.

"I'm Private Robert London, First Battalion, The Middlesex Regiment, Twenty-seventh Infantry, I mean Commonwealth Brigade." Robert London spoke fast only tripping over his tongue once.

"Got a nasty scar by your ear, seen a bit of combat in Korea have we?" the captain probed.

"Yes sir, I've just shipped back from Japan, sir." Private London nervously replied.

"Another one wounded in action, while his company took Middlesex Hill, sir, got Mentioned in Despatches didn't you sonny?" the sergeant major added with pride.

"I believe so," Private London mumbled. He was unused and uncomfortable with praise, even if it was deserved.

"Good show boys, no wonder the war's nearly over with you three stout chaps on our side." The captain slapped his hands on his knees and smiled widely.

An hour went by as the train puffed and chugged its way north. The conversation became sporadic, usually instigated by the jovial captain.

"And what really surprised me was the flora and fauna. I didn't expect to see pine, ash, birch and apple trees here," the captain enthused.

"And poplar trees, we have a poplar tree in our back garden at home," Robert added, having relaxed into conversation now with Captain Woodholme-Browne.

"So what did you do before National Service Private London?" the captain asked, taking a hip-flask from his left breast pocket and unscrewing the hinged top.

"I worked for my father in his coal yard, driving the lorries and delivering coal," Robert London explained, his thoughts drifting back to his family at home.

"And you, Private McClaren, what did you do?" the captain asked, taking a swig of his brandy.

"I worked for a removals firm in Perth, driving the pantechnicons and loading furniture," the private replied.

"Bit of a driving theme going on here, what about you, Sergeant Major, done any heavy-goods driving or you a career man?" The captain extended his arm and offered the flask to the next highest-ranking soldier.

"Oh, don't mind if I do, sir." The sergeant major took a respectful swig of the brandy, then passed it to Private London. "I've done a fair bit of driving, from half-tracks to lorries in Africa and Italy during the last war."

"Eighth army man eh, I have a cousin who was wounded at Monte Cassino," nodded the captain respectfully.

"My brother George died there, he was in the Royal Artillery," Private London said, then took a good slug of brandy and resisted the urge to cough.

Private McClaren took the flask from his limp hand, before the captain took it back and also had a sip. Coughing slightly he returned the now half-empty flask back to the officer.

"We lost a lot of good men there," the sergeant major mused and the conversation slipped into thought and silence again. Robert London watched as some paddy fields rushed past and wondered what awaited them all at the end of their journey.

GUILDFORD: PRESENT DAY. 10.00 AM.

The doorbell shook Robert London out of his daydream and his legs twitched, sending Paul's book onto the floor. Leaving it where it was he shuffled off towards the hall and front door. This had been the fastest he had moved in three months.

Opening the door inward, a beaming smile underlined his sunken cheeks as he saw his daughter and grandson standing before him.

"Paul, I'm so glad you're here!" Robert's eyes moistened slightly at the sight of his only grandchild.

"Me too, Granddad." Paul moved forward to gingerly hug his grandfather. Trying not to let the shock show on his face, at how withered and shrunken his once powerfully-built grandfather had become.

"You okay, Dad, do you want me to stay?" Angela asked as the two men in front of her released themselves from their embrace.

"I'm very much okay, now Paul is here, you get off, love, we'll be fine." Even though he looked frail, his voice had recovered some of its old resonance.

Angela kissed her father's cheek and rubbed at Paul's shoulder at the same time. "Okay, but call me if you need me," she fussed, "and Paul, don't tire your grandfather out okay."

"I won't, Mum," Paul promised and they watched her retreat down the garden path and back to her Saab.

"Come on, Paul, come inside and I'll let you brew me a cup of tea," his grandfather smiled, which relaxed Paul a little. The cancer seemed to have shrunken his once powerful grandfather and jaundice sallowed his eyes and skin.

He followed him slowly down the hall which turned right into his grandfather's twenty-five years out of style kitchen. Paul suddenly felt six years old again, because the old Formica tops hadn't changed since before he was born. He could almost visualise Granny Lil at the sink peeling spuds for his fish finger, chips and beans tea. He used to love to stay here, while his mum and dad jetted off on their extra holidays; excluding the fortnight he went with them to Tenerife, during summer hols.

"Can you brew up the Rosie-Lee, son? I'm always so bloody weak these days," Robert asked, slumping into a chair next to the breakfast table.

"Sure, Granddad, it will be my pleasure." Paul busied himself with the kettle and teapot, with real tea leaves in it.

"There are custard creams in the cupboard and don't forget one for the..."

"...pot," Paul finished, "I do remember."

"Good lad." Robert managed a smile even though his lungs felt like two firebrands in his chest.

"So why did you want to see me so urgently?" Paul asked, getting the cups and saucers turned up the right way.

"Later, let's have our tea first."

"Okay."

Later, Paul had helped his grandfather into his favourite, near hallowed, armchair in the living room and Paul perched himself on the edge of the sofa.

"Paul, I need your help before I die." Robert's old eyes stared straight into his grandson's matching irises.

"Anything for you, Granddad." He meant it too, nothing was too much trouble for such an immense man as his grandfather.

"Good lad, first I need you to get something for me, something hidden in my shed," Robert asked, wringing his hands together without realising it.

"Hidden, okay, where and what is it?" Paul asked, intrigued.

"It's a Cadbury's tin. Go to my shed, right at the end where my workbench is. Under it are two cupboards, under the cupboards is a four inch trim; use my crowbar to pull it away. Under there you'll find the tin, bring it to me please."

For the first time in his life, Paul saw that his grandfather seemed nervous and agitated. "You want me to go and get it now?"

"Yes please, son." Robert nodded solemnly.

Paul stood up and left the room, making his way through the bungalow, to the kitchen backdoor. He wondered what was so important about the tin and what treasures it held inside. It was a rather pleasant sunny day and his grandfather's garden still seemed to be well tended to. Maybe his mother got someone in or Tobias from next door lent a helping hand.

Paul followed the winding concrete path as it led though a line of willow trees to the back of the property which had both a garage and a large shed/workshop beside it. Paul pulled at the shed door, but it was locked.

"Oh fuck it," Paul swore at the door, thinking he would have to walk back to the bungalow again, to get the key. Then he saw Droopy the Dwarf and smiled. Paul walked over to the ancient rockery and lifted Droopy from his resting place, half lost in a covering of pink phlox. Underneath it in the dirt and next to two worms that had made it their abode was the spare key.

"Yuck," he said as he touched the worms to retrieve the key. Shaking off as much excess dirt as he could, Paul put the key in the shed lock and opened it.

The place was as he remembered it, yet seemed dirtier and mustier than memory served. He moved inside, only to get a face-full of invisible spiders' webs.

"For fuck's sake." Paul batted at his face and hair as he walked to the end of the shed and his grandfather's workbench. Paul searched the tool racks and workbench for the crowbar, but it was missing. Instead he found a hammer and used the other end to start to force the trim at the bottom of the bench off.

It was well hammered in place and took Paul a full five minutes to get the entire length of five foot trim away from the base of the workbench.

A few more "fuck"s and "er"s followed as he reached into the dirty woodlice dwelling and used an old shammy leather from the workbench to clean off the tin.

It was twelve inches by six inches and three inches high. Some sort of army webbing belt was fixed firmly around its middle and the words Cadbury's could still be seen in blue on the yellow painted tin lid. Paul pulled at the strap buckle and was surprised when it fell apart in his hands, in three mildewed lengths. He dropped them on the floor and walked out of the shed, not wanting to spoil his grandfather's thunder by opening it.

Paul looked up and was surprised to see that the sunny spring day had suddenly clouded over. There was a metallic smell in the air, like you get with humid June thunderstorms: yet it was only the end of April. A stillness had come to the garden, the earlier breeze had departed and birds in the surrounding trees sang and chirped for all their might.

"Funny weather," he mocked in a funny Dudley Moore-like voice and then headed back to the bungalow. Paul had an uneasy feeling at the back of his neck, like he was being observed as he traversed the concrete path. Once back in the kitchen he shut the door and stepped away: then stepped back and locked it.

Gripping the box in both hands like a royal courtier holding a pillow with a crown on it, he walked into the living room again.

"Got it, Granddad," he announced.

"Quickly, put it on here!" his grandfather urged, his hands were hovering over an occasional table he had pulled in front of him since Paul had left the room.

"It's a bit skanky, want me to put a newspaper underneath it?" Paul suggested, looking at the lacquered top of the mahogany table.

"Sod the table boy, just put it down!" Robert angrily raised his voice with his nineteen-year-old grandson.

Paul put the tin down quickly, a little hurt by his grandfather's voice and shocked as he hadn't raised his voice to Paul in years. Putting it down to the pain and cancer, Paul knelt down on the other side of the table and waited.

Robert's hands were trembling badly, was it old age, the cancer, trepidation? No, Robert knew what it was: fear! His hands grabbed the lid of the tin, warily like it might give him an electric shock. As his fingers touched the tin box for the first time in a quarter of a century, he felt only the cool grimy lid. This wasn't the time to become a coward, so late in life: he was dying anyway what harm could it do to him? But he knew from his time in Korea, there were things worse than death.

He pulled at the lid and was surprised at how easily it came off, to reveal its treasures; or firstly some sort of once white cloth, that seemed to Paul like it was made out of the same stuff as cotton wool.

Robert pulled back the cloth and dropped it on the floor, revealing his personal treasures that no one, bar Robert London himself, had seen all together in the same place.

"F-f-far-fuck, Granddad, that's a bloody gun!" Paul's eyes had darted to the most startling object the tin held.

"It's an Enfield number two, mark one revolver to be precise," Robert corrected his grandson, but his eyes were fixed on another object in the box.

The revolver took up most of the space and lay on some old envelopes, a few bullets (seven) were scattered around the box. There were two military medals, two sporting medals and in the corner a small black lacquered oriental looking box, inlaid with opal and jade.

Paul's eyes were as wide as they could get, no wonder his grandfather called him home to show him the contents of the tin.

"Can I hold it?" Paul asked, a thousand war and crime films flowing through his mind at once.

"If you want to, it's not loaded." Robert could see the excitement in his grandson's eyes and he picked up the revolver. Robert London had no desire to hold it again, even if his ill health would let him. He'd handled such weapons and used them half a century or more ago and caused pain and death with them.

The revolver felt heavy when he picked it up, but now properly gripped in his hand it felt well-balanced and powerful. Robert watched his grandson, letting him get the gun out of his system; glad that Paul wasn't in the armed forces.

"So what else is in there?" Paul asked holding the revolver in his lap, as his interest peaked again.

Robert reached in and picked up the two small sports medals, tarnished with age to a grey/black colour. "These are my cricket medals, when Surrey won the County Championship in 1953 and 54."

"Cool," Paul enthused, staring at the medals in his grandfather's trembling hands, "you never played for England then?"

"No, but half the Surrey team did, I may have done if I had continued." This was one of Robert London's regrets in life, but he had to do his duty and take over the family business.

Paul nodded, knowing how his great-grandfather had died and granddad's two elder brothers had been killed in World War Two: leaving only him to run the company. He had to put his youthful dreams away, but at least he had Granny Lil by his side.

Robert London had done his duty and worked hard in the coalmongers, building up the business for thirty years. His mother finally died in 1980 aged eighty-one and seeing his family duly fulfilled he sold the business for a tidy profit and retired aged fifty. He bought the bungalow and a great swathe of land near the town centre. In 1990 he sold the land to a property developer for £750,000 and bought his daughter and her lazy husband a new house and put half a million in a special account for her, and her only. The only things he got out of the money were a debencher at the Oval and a holiday in Egypt for him and the wife.

Robert London always had a solid head on his broad shoulders. He sold the family business before the coal industry went into decline, he invested in property and bided his time and sold wisely. It also meant Lillian and he had had twenty years of carefree life and adventures before she passed away a couple of years into the twenty-first century.

"These are some love letters from your grandmother, better not look, she was quite the saucy young thing, you know," Robert smiled, remembering the things he and Lillian had got up to inside and outside the bedroom.

Paul smiled too, then reached in to pick up the two brightly ribboned medals. "These your war medals then, Granddad?"

"Yes, that one is the British Korea Medal," pointing to a round, silver medal with a yellow ribbon with two yellow stripes. "The thin blue and white striped one is the United Nations Korea Medal."

Paul took the medals off his grandfather, slightly reluctantly exchanging them for the revolver. Paul really liked the colours of the ribbons and wondered why his grandfather had hidden them away for so long.

"So what's in the little black box?" Paul put down the medals on the table and reached inside the tin for it.

"Don't touch it, Paul!" Robert London bellowed even though it sent an excruciating pain around his chest and back.

Paul flinched back, as his grandfather swiped the box up in his large hands, followed by a fit of coughing.

"What's in it?" Paul asked a little hurt, "is it a grenade?"

"No," his grandfather coughed, "something far more deadly than that."

Robert London held the black lacquered box in the palm of one hand. Paul noticed the jade leaves and opal flowers inlaid on the lid and side shone like it had been produced yesterday. Robert inhaled the largest breath he could without coughing and slid a small section of the bottom of the box out. His finger, shaking like he'd been sitting in the snow for an hour naked, had pushed a secret release mechanism inside.

There was a precise click inside and slowly the lid began to rise, by expert design. Robert moved the metal tin to the sofa and gently placed the box on the table, before his shaking hands stopped. Inside on a cushion of real velvet was what looked like a marble or a large pearl. It looked white at first to Paul's eyes, but then he saw that the colours were swirling inside. Like crystallised pink, various hues of blue and shades of jade, it changed and swam like there was also a glow-worm of miniature pastel coloured lights inside.

"What is it, Granddad?" Paul asked, slightly mesmerised by the swirling and the changing colours of the opal. He wondered what it could be made of. It didn't look glass or plastic, it had a more organic look to it.

Seeing his grandson reaching out for it, Robert snapped the lid shut. As Paul looked up a little dismayed and confused, Robert answered him.

"It's a Gusul," Robert London said softly, fear shaking at the edges of his voice.

"Oh," Paul mused and considered if he should know what a Gusul was, and concluded that he didn't, "what's that then?"

"It's alive and it's pure evil, Paul, and it cannot die." Paul had not seen his grandfather this down and disconsolate since Granny Lil had died.

"How can it be alive? It's been hidden away in your shed for donkey's years." Paul was getting a bit stressed now, as his grip on reality was being loosened finger by finger.

"I know you have many questions, Paul, and the only way of answering them is to tell you the full tale," Robert sighed and rung his hands together.

"Can't you just tell me what it really is first?" Paul probed, he wasn't renowned for his long attention span. That's why his longest relationship had lasted a month, yet deep down he yearned for the love his grandparents had shared.

"A wise Korean man once told me: to understand where your destination is in life, first you have to understand the journey." Robert London smiled a little, remembering those words and the man who had spoken them to him with lingering admiration.

"So you better get us a couple of beers from the fridge before I get started. 'Cause once I've started I won't want to stop, because this is one part of my war adventures that no one has heard, not even my late and lovely Lillian."

Paul got up and handed the revolver over to his grandfather again and headed off to the kitchen. This was one weird day and things looked to be getting weirder. He glanced outside as he pulled two cold lagers from the fridge. A movement in his peripheral vision caused him to look out the kitchen window.

The garden was empty, *'must have been a cat,'* Paul thought as he looked up at the darkening clouds above. A storm was brewing and by the smell and humidity of the air would hit within the hour. Pausing only to open the bottles, Paul headed back to the living room...

Chapter 3

Land of the Morning Calm

"Should you be having this?" Paul asked handing over the bottle of beer to his grandfather.

"I am over twenty-one, Sonny-Jim," Robert faintly smiled, the cold bottle felt good in his hot palm.

"I mean with all the pills you're taking?" Paul added sitting down on his sofa, one seat away from his grandfather. Paul was saddened to see the contents of the tin had been put away and the lid placed on again.

"The pills can't stop me dying Paul, so the beer won't matter will it really?" Robert replied; then had a swig, savouring the sensation. How long did he have left before he felt, saw or breathed no longer?

"I won't grass you up to Mum," Paul winked and took a long slug of beer. "So tell me about the pearly marble thing then!"

"In time, Paul, we'll get to that eventually, but to really understand it you'll have to hear the full story, okay," Robert London stared deep into his grandson's eyes.

"I'm ready," Paul nodded. Usually he loved to hear about his granddad's life, how he met Granny Lil, the war, his cricket career, coal mongering tales: now he wasn't so sure.

"It all started when I returned from being wounded in Korea. I had just met your grandmother for the first time. Now I was travelling to our joint British/American HQ at Sinanju. We'd travelled in US army trucks from Pyongyang; I was hoping to rejoin my company somewhere north of Kasan. It was a sunny day, but a bitter wind was blowing down from the hills to the north. Lucky I had been given some winter gear: jumpers, hat with flaps and a coat before we had left Pyongyang. The black drivers dropped us off at a blown up bridge outside of town with happy smiles, turned their trucks around and headed back to the rear echelons. We had to walk in single file over a half-constructed US engineered bridge and got to camp at about eleven o'clock on the 30th October 1950."

US 24TH DIVISION. FORWARD HEADQUARTERS/27TH COMMONWEALTH BRIGADE. SINANJU, NORTH KOREA. 11.01 AM.

Captain Woodholme-Browne led the way across the half-constructed bridge, enthusing over the speed and workmanship of the construction. Regimental Sergeant Major (RSM) McConnell followed, pack on his back and his Sten gun half at the ready. Private McClaren followed huffing and puffing, his rifle slung over his shoulder. Two bemused North Korean locals followed, having been conscripted into the pay of the British Army, to carry the captain's bags and suitcases. At the rear came Private London, his rifle in his hands, hearing all the wisecracks from the US engineers that the captain seemed oblivious to.

The US 24th Division Forward Headquarters lay on the outskirts north of Sinanju; in fact only five days earlier it had been a North Korean position. There were only four buildings, nabbed by the top brass and medical staff. Otherwise it was a town of tents, sandbags and American personnel. The 27th Commonwealth Brigade was now under the command of the 24th US Division and the base was buzzing with activity.

The British contingent, led by the captain, passed through a couple of dug in .50 M2 machine gun nests and into the camp. A signpost stood nearby with a 24th US Army sign and a smaller one below it telling you the exact distance to Jacksonville, Seattle and the latrines. Another part of the camp seemed like a vehicle depot housing two and a half tonne trucks, ambulances, tanks and artillery.

Now further into the camp, the green khakis were interrupted by the odd Australian, British or R.O.K (Republic of Korea) soldiers walking by. Finally they reached a building with a huge tent attached to one side; it had a lot of officers and men buzzing around it.

"This looks like the place, chaps," the captain said loudly, taking of his cap to wipe his brow on his shirt sleeve.

Regimental Sergeant Major McConnell scanned the area and fifty feet away was a small brown tent with a small '27th Commonwealth Brigade' sign hung from the open flap. A Small foldable desk and a chair occupied by a bored-looking British staff sergeant sat in the opening to the tent.

"And that's us, sir," McConnell pointed at the tent. "Well goodbye sir."

The RSM and two privates snapped to attention and saluted the captain. The captain whose hand had been about to shake the RSM's hand, moved it up to his temple and returned the salute.

"It was great fun travelling with you boys," the captain smiled, looking from face to face. "Now don't get yourself killed eh and London, keep your head down next time."

"Yes sir," Private London replied smiling at the happy-go-lucky handsome captain.

"Well carry on," he waved and trudged off to the camp commander's tents, fishing his orders out of his breast pocket as he did. The two bemused North Korean (conscripted) batmen followed carrying his gear.

"I wish Captain Woodholme-Browne was my C.O., he's so…" Private London struggled to find the words.

"Nice," Private McClaren offered.

"Down to earth, one of the boys?" The RSM offered.

"Yes, Sarge," London beamed at the older Scotsman.

"Good job he's an engineer and not your commanding officer, Private London," McConnell warned solemnly. "Because nice, one of the boys, dandy officers like him on the battlefield will get you killed, laddie."

"Sergeant Major?" Private London questioned, he thought the charismatic captain would be followed by his troops anywhere. He was tall, handsome and sculpted like a Greek Adonis, blond and brave, wouldn't every soldier flock to his banner?

"I've seen his type before, lead from the front, putting his life before the men," McConnell mused thinking of his time in World War Two. "His problem is he needs a bit of the auld bastard about him. He'd be afraid to order his men to die, that would cause him to delay and in war delay means your whole bloody platoon gets mowed to butcher's slices."

"I understand," London replied, but he didn't really.

"Right, let's get over to that tent and see how we get back to our regiments." The sergeant major pointed at the tent with the small desk outside.

"Sergeant Major," McClaren interrupted, "I need the latrine."

London watched the RSM's cheeks turn from rosy pink to raging red.

"I could do with seeing a man-about-a-dog myself Sergeant Major," London butted in to save McClaren an ear-bashing.

RSM McConnell looked at the two privates and gave in, exhaling his anger. "All right, off ya go, but meet me by the tent in ten minutes sharp!"

"Yes Sergeant Major," both privates replied, dumped their gear and hurried off to find a latrine.

It took three minutes to locate the latrine and only then on the directions of a friendly Australian artillery man. The latrine was a large foul-smelling tent with two entrances at each end. Both privates were glad that they didn't need to defecate, because the smell of excrement and chemicals was vomit-inducing. Instead, out behind the tent were old shell casings, wedged into a bank of earth as makeshift urinals. The two wasted no time in unzipping their flies and relieving themselves, almost with looks of ecstasy on their faces. They had nearly finished, when they heard several footsteps behind them.

"Hey guys, never fear, da limeys are here!" a thick New York accent cried out behind them.

The two privates with hands on their privates, turned to find five G.I.s standing behind them.

"Someone has to get this war won," Private McClaren replied as he finished pissing and turned around.

Robert London closed his eyes in despair, then looked skywards hoping for God to save him from 'Piggy' McClaren's big gob. Robert wished his full bladder would hurry up and empty.

"You couple of English queers are under US military command here, so you better keep your limp-wristed opinions to yourselves," a dark-haired and hairy corporal spat back with venom, sounding like a gangster from a Jimmy Cagney film.

"You tell him, Teddy," a ginger-headed thin soldier goaded and his three sheep-like companions grunted in agreement.

"Ah ain't no fucking Sassenach, you arse-faced yank! I'm Scottish and I'm gonna wipe the floor wid ya!" Piggy McClaren retorted angrily, he was a bully and a coward normally, but no one on God's good Earth called him English.

The two bullies squared up to each other, fists up at the ready; but there are no Marquis of Queensbury rules where bullies are concerned.

"George, Liam get him," the corporal ordered and two of his goons, including the thin ginger one, rushed forwards and grabbed Private McClaren's arms. The corporal smiled a yellowed-toothed grin, and rabbit punched Piggy McClaren in the stomach.

"Leave him alone," Private London warned as he still waited for his pee to stop.

"Or you'll do what?" A voice sneered in his left ear; one of the other American soldiers had moved round to stand behind him.

"Turn round," Private London turned and pissed all over the G.I.'s crotch, legs and boots.

"Urgh!" the small balding American cried and jumped back out of urine-range. "He fucking pissed on me, Teddy."

As the G.I. looked down at himself, Robert London took the opportunity to shake off and retreat his weapon.

"Maybe we cut off his water supply," sneered an olive-skinned soldier who had been hanging at the back of the group. He came towards London after pulling a cut-throat razor from his boot.

"Put da blade away, Guido!" the corporal ordered, "you wanna spend the next twenty years in the stockade?"

"Put it away like the good corporal said, laddie," a loud Scottish voice boomed from behind them. There stood RSM McConnell, standing at ease with his Sten gun resting on his right shoulder.

"Come on you slouches, let's get back to work," the corporal smiled out the side of his mouth. He left the area with

67

his henchmen behind him, one of them shaking at his piss-drenched fatigues.

"I cannae leave you two alone for a minute, can I?!" the RSM barked, after the American soldiers had left.

"They started it, Sergeant Major," Piggy whined, "they called me English!"

Regimental Sergeant Major McConnell roared with laughter, bursting from his chest like a damaged drain pipe.

"If I was London here I'd be insulted that they called ya English!" The sergeant major's laugh slowly died away. "Come on, let's be having ya, we've got to find our billets for the night."

The RSM turned and the two privates followed behind, jogging to keep up with the sergeant major's fast strides.

"So what's happening then, Sergeant Major?" Private London asked, as the RSM led them back to their weapons and gear.

"We've got three cots tonight, in with the Third Royal Aussie Regiment. Then in the morning, Private McClaren and myself ship out with their artillery boys to rejoin the glorious Argylls," the RSM explained as they wandered through the camp to their gear; which was now in sight.

"What about me?" Private London asked, knowing that this was when the travelling companions from Japan parted ways.

"I got you a lift on the back of a Yank M4A3's tank tomorrow, so you'll rejoin your company at some place called Taechon." The three soldiers reached their gear and weapons.

Private London just stood there staring at the Command Post tent that the captain had entered, he felt at ease here. He had one night left in the company of Piggy McClaren and the formidable RSM McConnell. He had the unshakeable feeling that after tonight he would never ever feel safe again.

"London!" The RSM screamed, "grab your gear soldier, this isn't a tea party at the Palace. Pull your finger out, man!"

"Yes, Sergeant Major." Robert London bent down and retrieved his pack and rifle, as Piggy McClaren smirked behind the RSM's back.

"And you can shut up an' all, McClaren," the RSM barked, lending to the myth that at the rank of sergeant all soldiers are fitted with an extra pair of eyes in the back of their heads.

US 24TH DIVISION FORWARD HQ CP. 11.30 AM.

Captain Woodholme-Browne sat on a fold-up chair in the large tent fixed to the side of an old farm building, his legs crossed, sipping strong American coffee. He'd already been waiting for twenty minutes and had read a copy of *Stars and Stripes* that a Lieutenant US staff officer had offered him.

He sat fiddling with his cap in his hands and wondering what the war held next for his travelling companions.

Just then a US captain stepped out of the building and walked across the hard ground, under the canopy and right up to his sitting position.

"Captain Woodholme-Browne?" the young-looking captain asked.

"Yes," he replied, standing and putting his cap back on his blond-haired head.

"Come with me please, the Colonel is ready to see you now." The US army captain turned and then Captain Woodholme-Browne followed, dropping the magazine on the lieutenant's makeshift desk (four ammo crates on an old cupboard door) as he passed.

They entered the building which was a hive of industry, folding tables, desks and chairs were everywhere and every inch of wall space was covered with orders and maps of Korea. In the centre of this maelstrom of activity was a table littered with all sorts of maps of the local and surrounding areas. Round it stood three officers, who looked up from their map pouring as the two captains approached the table.

"Captain Ashley Woodholme-Browne, Fifty-Fifth Field Squadron, Royal Engineers, reporting for duty, sir." The captain snapped to attention and saluted the officers in front of him.

The US colonel did a loose salute, while the other officers, a US lieutenant and a British major saluted back with more precision and vigour.

"That will be all, Captain Peters," the colonel said and the captain whom had escorted him in, headed off to sit at a typewriter at the far end of the room.

"Good to have you here, Captain," said the major, a liaison officer from the Middlesex Regiment, offering a handshake which the captain quickly accepted.

"Glad to be here, sir," Woodholme-Browne replied, moving to shake the lieutenant's hand also.

"Good show," the moustached major nodded, "let me introduce you to Colonel Yorke, the Commanding Officer of the Twenty-First Infantry regiment, Twenty-Fourth Infantry division." The colonel, who had the shortest and tightest haircut the captain had ever seen, did not look up from his map.

"I'm Major Davidson, the First Battalion Middlesex Regiment Liaison Officer and this is Left-tenant Samuels from the Twenty-Fourth's, Third Engineering Battalion." The major had pointed to the young and green looking lieutenant, who nodded and grinned back.

"Captain, come closer, son, so I don't have to shout and you can see what I'm on about." The colonel looked up while jabbing his finger onto a map he was scanning closely.

"Yes sir," and the captain went around the table to stand on the colonel's left. The lieutenant stood to his right, while the major stood across the table.

"We are situated here, north across the Chongchon River at Sinanju." The colonel pointed to a round spot on his map on a river with a north, south and eastern road leading from it.

"The Twenty-First have taken up positions here in Pakchon and have relieved the Argylls and Australians here at Chongju." The colonel pointed out two more towns, Changju and Kasan, both along the western road from Pakchon.

"While the 'Die Hards', my Battalion, have had the North Koreans on the run to the north and are taking up defensive positions at this village here." Davidson pointed to a small dot north of Kasan and Pakchon, marked 'Taechon'.

"Thank you, Major," the colonel continued, "our next objective is Kusong, north of Chongju and north-west of Taechon. This is where it gets tricky, gentlemen, the road to Kusong is some of the most god-awful mountain terrain you'll see west of the Rocky Mountains." The colonel pulled at his slightly stubbled jaw.

"Patrols report that the roads, such as they are, are like ambush alley; running through canyons before they rise to the objective," the major added, pointing at a line on the map.

"Add to that the Korean winter, which seems to be getting worse by the day, and we could be in for a tough time," the colonel continued.

Captain Woodholme-Browne nodded, understanding the situation, but not the reason for his or Lieutenant Samuel's presence.

"You're probably wondering why the hell you're here, aren't you, son?"

"Yes, Colonel," the captain frowned; he was a Royal Engineer and had been a civilian architect and bridge engineer for two years after he had left University.

"Then I'll explain," the colonel smiled. "We have R.O.K intelligence that there is another route up through the mountains that circumvents Kusong. Aerial reconnaissance has confirmed this, as well as some of the Die-Hards' forward patrols."

The colonel leant over the map and jammed a stubby finger at an area on the map north-west of Taechon and east of Kusong. "Here between Taechon, the mountains and Kusong is a plateau, independent of the other mountains. The place looks like God himself has come along and cut off the top with a butter knife." The colonel looked up and both the major and the lieutenant smiled.

"We are led to believe that the only access to the plateau is a rope bridge on the Taechon side and another on the Kusang side. If we could get our boys across this plateau in sufficient numbers we could surprise the Gooks and take Kusang with minimal casualties." The colonel stood up now, hands on his hips, waiting for the major to continue.

"Captain, we want you to go with Left-tenant Samuels and his men and find these bridges, see what shape they are in and if we can replace them with something more military friendly," the major beamed.

"I can do that, but why pick me, sir?" the captain asked the colonel and major.

"Colonel Yorke wanted the best and your commanding officer said you could construct a bridge across the Thames with only two jerry cans, a length of rope and a plank," the major explained with a fixed smile on his face.

The captain looked from one officer to the next; a more plausible explanation was his father, the general, had pulled a few strings to get him closer to the action. Which he didn't mind if it was part of the job, but if he'd wanted to be an infantry man like his father had wanted, he would have signed up for it.

"Colonel, can I ask why aren't the North Koreans entrenched on that plateau? It seemed like an excellent place to fortify and defend," the captain asked, examining the map.

"We thought the same damn thing, Captain, apparently there's some god-damn Buddhist temple on the plateau and the Gooks are scared stiff of the place for some reason; which is fucking odd behaviour for a load of Commies," the colonel explained, his only religion being the 21st Infantry, US army.

"Do we have any maps of the plateau sir?" asked the young dark-haired lieutenant, speaking for the first time.

"No Loo-tenant, only aerial recon photos, but we do have something better," the colonel replied, then waved to his subordinate, "Captain Peters, send in the Sergeant!"

"Yes sir," the US captain replied and moved off through a door into another part of the building. He returned a minute later with a Republic of Korea sergeant, in his mid-twenties, following behind.

"Gentlemen, may I introduce your guide, Sergeant Kim Jun Ho of the R.O.K. Second Corps." The sergeant, who was five inches shorter than any of the officers, approached the table and saluted and then bowed.

"We were very lucky to get him," the major explained as they all returned his salute. "He and his family lived in Kusang back in the forties and fled south when the country was divided in 1945."

"And he speaks English better than I do according to Major Davidson here." All the soldiers around the table chuckled at this. "You will lead our little survey, Captain Woodholme-Browne, leaving here in three days," the colonel explained.

"Can I ask the Colonel why we aren't leaving sooner, isn't the area secure, sir?" the captain asked, intrigued by the plateau and its temple and eager to get started.

"It's a front line, Captain, the situation is always fluid. But that's not the problem, transport is," the colonel explained in usual military terms. 'Situation is fluid' meant 'Hold onto your hats boys: anything could happen'.

"Don't we have any transport, sir?" the captain asked.

"Trucks we have, sir, drivers for the little enterprise we don't. We can't spare them at the moment; a shell hit the drivers' tent yesterday, killing ten of them. You'll just have to hold your horses, Captain, until we can replace them. Unless you have any better ideas?" The colonel put the captain in his place and the picture simultaneously.

"Left-tenant, how many drivers do we need?" the captain asked the young lieutenant beside him.

"Just three drivers for three two and a half tonne trucks, sir," the lieutenant replied quickly.

"Then Colonel, I might just know where to get my hands on three drivers, if you'd give me carte-blanche," the captain beamed back at the colonel and major.

"Captain, if you can get those trucks outta here by 07:00 tomorrow morning, you got my full authority to darn well fucking break any of the Ten Commandments you deem fit."

The temperature at the Forward HQ had fallen rapidly as the day had gone on. Robert London had naively hoped that the temperature might have risen. A draughty old Australian billet tent did nothing to warm the blood either.

The only thing that had put a smile on his face, and a bigger one on Piggy McClaren's, was chow time at the US Army mess. Robert fancied trying something called a 'hot dog', but found that a long line of somewhat disappointed R.O.K soldiers had polished them all off before they had got there.

Piggy had pushed into a line of grumbling G.I.s, but Robert apologised and pulled him by the ear to the rear of the chow-line. Private McClaren then got the hump with him and, to Private London's joy, gave him the silent treatment for the next quarter of an hour. As they queued, Robert scanned the huge pavilion-sized tent for the rowdy Yanks they had encountered earlier in the latrines. If they were there, he couldn't see them, but kept a wary eye out anyway.

Piggy went off and squeezed himself onto a table full of very green-looking young American soldiers, with the tightest crew-cuts Robert had ever seen. Robert himself went and sat with some of the Australians and enjoyed himself. He brought up the subject of cricket, him being a keen cricketer and former Surrey Colt player. The chatter was robust, but friendly even though they referred to him as the 'Bloody Pom' all the way through dinner. A dinner which he rather enjoyed, with soup, chicken, spuds and something called 'cornbread'. He missed his cup of Rosie-Lee and had to settle for a dark, throat-burning coffee, his first ever. It put him off coffee for life, but it warmed the cold from his body for a while. Lucky for him on the tea front the Aussies were going to have a brew up when they got back to their billets.

Robert's travels had led him to try different teas in Hong Kong, then Japan and Korea, like cricket it would become a lifelong passion.

They had been back at the draughty tent an hour and it was dark outside when Piggy strolled in. Robert was glad he'd missed the Aussie's 'brew-up', but Piggy was back to his obnoxious chatty self after fleecing the young G.I.s at their own game: something called 'Craps'. Robert's meaning of the word 'craps' and the US version were rather different and he tried not to imagine what the game entailed. Robert reckoned that Piggy was full of the stuff, so that's what must have made him an instant expert.

Feeling the cold, Private London pulled his sweater over his battledress and tried out his new cap with flaps, which made him look fourteen years old the Aussies told him, but with their hats leaving red raw ears, Robert though that they were just jealous. He reached for his baccie tin, intending to roll up a fag.

"You boys all cosy and well-fed?" came RSM McConnell's voice from the entrance to their tent. They hadn't seen the sergeant major since he disappeared three hours ago with a Sergeant McNulty from the Aussies, to drink and talk about the 'Auld Country'.

"Yes, Sergeant Major," the two British privates replied, standing by their beds. The Australian soldiers looked up and seeing that it wasn't one of their NCOs went about their business.

"It seems that we have new orders, laddies," the RSM explained. "We are to report to the truck depot at 06:00 and await further instructions."

"What's going on, Sergeant Major?" Private McClaren asked.

"Aren't we rejoining our units?" Private London added.

"This is the army," the RSM growled, "we have our orders signed by one of your lot, London, a Major Davidson, to report to the truck depot at 06:00 tomorrow morning. End of message, now sort out ya kit and get to ya fucking beds, we have an early start tomorrow!" The loudness of the RSM's voice stopped any further questioning and he did a wheeled-turn and marched out of the tent.

"Looks like you two Pommie boys have just been volunteered for something," one of the Australian lance corporals called Donald jeered.

"First thing ya bloody learn in the army, mate, never, ever fucking volunteer for anything!" another Aussie called Stan added.

"But we haven't volunteered for anything," Private London replied, bemused, then looked at Private McClaren, "did you?"

"Fuck no," Piggy McClaren shot back; he'd be after the blind, crippled, women and children before he volunteered for anything.

"You poor bastards," Stan said shaking his head, "means you've been recommended for duty and you know what that means, boys!"

"No?" Private London shook his head.

"What?" Private McClaren asked.

"Bloody suicide mission!" half of the men in the tent of the 3rd Royal Australian Regiment shouted at them with glee.

ROBERT LONDON'S BUNGALOW, GUILDFORD: PRESENT DAY.

"You okay, Granddad?" Paul asked as Robert London's slow stream of small coughs escalated into a dry coughing attack.

"Bit dry that's all," Robert gasped, taking a suck on his oxygen mask beside him.

"Can I do anything?" Paul asked, concerned for his granddad and what he could do if things got worse.

"Cup of tea will sort me out, son," Robert wheezed between coughs and gulps on his air mask.

"Okay, no problem." Paul stood up not sure if he should leave the room at all.

"Earl Grey I think," Robert's chest tightened like a vice with every cough and wheeze.

"You want it now?" Paul asked, but didn't know why, he was worried and babbling.

"Paul, hurry up," Robert winked at his grandson, who left the room and headed for the kitchen at a brisk pace. Once the kettle was boiling he could pop back in to check on his granddad.

When Paul left the room, Robert opened a small drawer in the top of the occasional table that stood next to his chair. He pulled out a silver pill box and took out two white strong painkillers and washed them down with the only liquid he had, his warm beer.

He had saved up these morphine pills for months, for this very time. He had to tell his story to Paul before he died; he knew he was on borrowed time now. He had to tell Paul what had happened in Korea over half a century ago, or he wouldn't be the only family member to die this year!

Chapter 4

More Brown Hills

Private London wished he hadn't bothered to polish his boots as
the October frost had ruined the shine in minutes. RSM
McConnell, Private McClaren and himself had been at the
vehicle compound for fifteen minutes already and it was freezing
cold. A wind, blown south from the snowy mountain tops cut
through the soldiers like shards of glass from an exploding
window.

"Jesus Christ! If they think it's cold in Scotland they should
try it here, it's freezing," moaned Piggy McClaren.

Both McConnell and London gave him dark looks, they all
knew it was cold; talking about it wouldn't warm them up.
McConnell was stamping his feet when a group of American
soldiers sauntered into the compound.

London and McClaren's hearts sank as they recognised two
of the Yanks from yesterday's latrine incident. The corporal,
who had been the obvious leader of the gang, and the ginger
headed G.I. They were led by a short, dark haired, grimy looking
sergeant, and another two privates made up the group.

The RSM and the sergeant, both deemed World War
veterans, nodded to each other out of professional respect, but
Anglo-American relations ended there. The two British and
American groups kept their distance, and the corporal, who was
chatting to a tall pale private, didn't seem to have recognised
them.

Two minutes passed before two officers entered the
compound and approached the groups. A few hundred yards

away a couple of G.I.s were revving up a 'deuce and a half' truck.

"Attention!" the RSM barked and the American sergeant copied two seconds later as the British captain and American lieutenant approached.

A broad smile appeared on Private London's face as he recognised it was their old travelling companion Captain Woodholme-Browne. He glanced at McClaren, who smiled back; maybe this wasn't going to be such shit detail after all.

"At ease men," the young lieutenant ordered, "and close up the ranks, we are all in this together."

The two sergeants looked at each other a bit concerned, then sideways shuffled to close the two groups. Just then a R.O.K. sergeant entered the compound, saluted the two officers and went and stood to the right of Private London.

"Right men, I am Captain Woodholme-Browne of the Royal Engineers and this is, as some you may already know, Left-tenant Samuels from the Twenty-Fourths, Third Engineering Battalion." The captain, hands on the hips of his long trench coat, paused for effect. "The Left-tenant and I have been ordered to take a little jaunt up the road a bit to A, find a rope bridge across to a plateau and B, evaluate the bridge and possible construction of a more permanent, military one." The American soldiers to a man looked at each other and groaned.

"As soon as our kit is stowed we will set off down the road through Pakchon to Taechon. Sergeant Kim from the Republic of Korea Second Corps will be our guide from there." The captain pointed at the sergeant whom bowed in response.

"I will be in command of this little expedition, with Left-tenant Samuels as my subordinate. We and you chaps from the Third Battalion will bring the bridge expertise, while the RSM and his privates will be our chauffeurs so to speak." The captain smiled and pointed towards the RSM.

"Sir," the RSM responded, acknowledging his part in the expedition.

"It also helps to have a few battle-hardened infantry support along, don't you think so, Left-tenant Samuels?" The captain turned to his subordinate.

"Glad to have them along for the ride, Captain," the young lieutenant beamed. He, like the two young British privates, was under the captain's heroic spell. The lieutenant had studied ancient history at college and the dashing captain reminded him of Alexander the Great, with a dash of Pericles thrown in.

"Right, we'll leave in fifteen minutes, that will give the drivers time to familiarise themselves with these three lovely two and a half tonne trucks over there, and for you all to stow your kit and extra rations," the lieutenant both explained and ordered at the same time.

"First I would like a five minute confab with the NCOs over here." The captain pointed at RSM McConnell and Sergeant Dempsey trudged over to the two officers.

"Sergeant Kim?" the captain said to get his attention.

"Sonsaengnim?" the sergeant replied, not too sure of British/US protocols, but saying it in Korean all the same.

"That includes you too," the captain smiled.

The R.O.K sergeant hurried over, his rifle at his side, all these United Nations officers seemed so tall and like matinee idol actors to him.

Privates London and McClaren stared at each other a little lost, then grabbed their gear and followed the Yanks to the three waiting trucks with stars on their doors.

"Driven by Limeys and led by a Gook, this is gonna be some fine picnic, boys." the US corporal muttered as the four remaining US engineers headed for their trucks.

"Too fucking right, Teddy," chirped in Private O'Keefe, the corporal's well known parrot.

Behind them, Private First Class (P.F.C.) Perez and Private Hartnell said nothing; they had heard it all before.

A couple of buck privates who had been revving up the trucks earlier, gave the two British soldiers the run down on the 'deuce and a half's' as they referred to them. They showed them how to start 'em up; make 'em stop; change gear and the best way to make 'em start again if they stopped for mechanical/gremlin type reasons.

All the while the American engineers stowed gear into the back of the canvas-covered trucks; the corporal mainly stood around and blew onto his fingerless gloves.

Across the compound the officers' and Non-Commissioned Officers' (NCOs') brief briefing was coming to a close.

"So to sum up, Sergeant Kim is in charge of navigation, Sergeant Dempsey is to help the engineering side run like clockwork, and the Regimental Sergeant Major will advise on security and transportation matters," Captain Woodholme-Browne summed up.

"Any questions?" Lieutenant Samuels asked the small group, "before we set off."

"No sir," Sergeant Kim readily replied with a mini bow.

The captain looked at the two veteran sergeants' grim, blank expressions and realised anymore words would be wasted on them. "Okay chaps, let's stow our kit and move out," he smiled even though the cold wind made his teeth hurt. The officers and NCOs made their way over to the three trucks all lined up bumper to tail and ready to go.

"How we doin', Corporal Baker?" Sergeant Dempsey asked in his normal, but loud, New Jersey voice.

"The deuces are all loaded, Sarge." the corporal thumbed behind him. "First truck has stores, kit and some bridge equipment; second is all the long bridge stuff and the last one is empty."

"Thank you Corporal," the young lieutenant said sharply, noticing the man always reported to the veteran sergeant and not to him.

"Right then let's get onboard." The captain clapped his brown leather gloves together.

"Can I ask which vehicles we are travelling in, sir?" the sergeant major asked, adjusting the strap of his Sten gun.

Captain Woodholme-Browne looked up and saw that privates London and McClaren had already taken up their driving positions in the first two American military trucks.

"Well it's simple enough, old man, Sergeant Kim and I will join Private London in the first two and a half tonner. Left tenant Samuels will have the pleasure of Private McClaren's company and Sergeant Dempsey will ride with you, RSM," the captain ordered and then moved around the truck with the South Korean sergeant at his heels. One thing the 'General' had taught him was to give an order and move on quickly, giving no time for debate. This was the 'Army', not a democracy, debating in war caused hesitation and hesitation caused death.

The others, having no reason to delay, made their way to their vehicles; anyway it was too damn cold to hang around. A tall, thin soldier with thick-rimmed glasses gave the RSM a run down on the truck as he and the US engineers made their way to the last vehicle of the small convoy.

Private London looked to his right and wondered how he got here. A lad from Guildford, doing his National Service with the Royal West Surrey Regiment's, seconded with a hundred plus other men into the 1st Battalion Middlesex Regiment, shipped to Hong Kong, taken by Her Majesty's navy to Korea, where he was wounded in the head charging a North Korea machine gun post on 'Middlesex Hill', medically evacuated to Japan, fell in love, then shipped back and volunteered to drive a left-hand drive US truck, with a Republic of Korea sergeant next to him, and a British Royal Engineer captain, on the same double seat hanging out the window. It was a long way from his dreams of playing cricket at the Oval for Surrey and England.

The captain who had been looking back down the line of trucks got a thumbs up from Sergeant Dempsey and then a wave and thumbs up from Lieutenant Samuels. The captain returned the thumbs up and pulled himself back into the cab of the idling truck and pulled up the window.

"Okay, Private, let's go," the captain smiled and pointed to the way out of the vehicle compound.

Private London turned to see the captain and sergeant beaming at him. "Right you are, sir." He replied crisply and yanked the beast of a vehicle into gear; the truck rolled five feet then came to a stalled halt.

Private London flushed bright red, which warmed his cold cheeks, but did little to cover his embarrassment.

"In your own time, soldier," the captain said sarcastically, his head fixed out the front window.

"Sorry, sir."

Private London re-started the truck, then remembered something the Yank G.I. had said and went with that. The truck lurched then set off again steadily out of the compound gates. The other trucks followed, Private McClaren smiled at both

London's cock up and his ease at driving the US two and a half tonner. The third truck followed with the RSM at the wheel, driving different vehicles was second nature to the Regimental Sergeant Major. He had driven half-trucks in North Africa, British trucks in Sicily, US Jeeps in Italy and old German trucks in Berlin. The left-hand drive was a bit of a pain, but he wasn't going to let the Yank sergeant sitting next to him know that. In the back of the third truck the men shivered visibly; unfortunately they had no engines in front of them to warm them. The canvas canopy and wooden sides did little to keep out the icy winds. After five minutes of banter, led by the corporal, the only sounds audible were the chattering of teeth and knocking of knees.

They were soon waved out of the forward HQ and were on the road north towards some brown hills and the debris of recent combat. The drive through the hills made the RSM nervous, it was perfect ambush territory. Halfway through they passed a row of US tanks parked to the left of the road. It raised everyone's morale in the convoy and took a full fifteen minutes to drive past. In the lead truck a brief chat about cricket had tapered off into silence and the R.O.K. sergeant was hardly a chatterbox.

"Shame we don't have a wireless eh, London," the captain mused as the brown hills ended for a while to be replaced by more brown, battle-scarred hills.

"Yes sir," the private nodded. He liked the captain, but had little in common with the Oxford-educated officer.

"Know any good songs then?" the captain ventured, leaning back on his seat and putting a boot up on the dashboard.

"Blimey," the private exclaimed, racking his brains for something suitable, but only rude songs his brother on leave had taught him came to mind.

"Well, any luck, Sinatra?"

"Okay sir, you asked for it." Private London grinned then began to sing, or shout more like, at the top of his limited vocal range. "Bless 'em all, the long and the short and the tall." The captain laughed heartily and joined in. "For we're saying goodbye to 'em all. You'll get no promotion this side of the ocean. So cheer up my lad, fuck 'em all…!"

"Join in, Sergeant Kim if you can," the captain smiled and sang, as the bemused South Korean tried to catch the words as they repeated.

A bemused Lieutenant Samuels frowned as he heard singing coming from the lead truck. Piggy McClaren giggled and joined in the 'British Army's Soldier Song'.

RSM McConnell joined in after hearing Piggy McClaren's dulcet tones and Sergeant Dempsey, who had fought with the British at 'Market Garden', joined in also. In the back of the last truck, no one joined in, their lips were too numb.

"More bloody brown hills," the RSM muttered as he drove the last truck in the convoy.

"All it seems to be in the north of the thirty-eighth parallel, brown hills and more brown hills," the American sergeant added.

"Least in the last war I got to see deserts, beaches, most of Italy and half of Berlin," the RSM added, as the truck bumped over a large pothole.

"I know what you mean, Mac, with the Eighty-Second Airborne I got machine gunned at Utah, sniped at in Holland and shelled in Germany," Sergeant Dempsey smiled, "but at least the fucking scenery was ever-changing!"

The two sergeants looked at each other and burst out laughing: the two veterans of the rag-tag group.

"So how are we progressing, Sergeant Kim?" the captain asked as a river came into view to the left of the road.

The small but wiry sergeant bowed slightly and broke his silence, which he had maintained for half an hour.

"We are progressing well, Captain," he began, "any minute now we will see a road leading west, which we must take to cross the river, sir."

"Then what, Sergeant?" Private London asked, keeping his eyes half peeled to the left on the lookout for a turn-off.

"We head along the western road for thirty minutes and then turn north towards Taechon," Sergeant Kim continued speaking in clear, professional English.

"I see, good work, Kim, when do you reckon we will get to Taechon?" the captain asked stretching out his back.

"By the middle of the day, sir," the sergeant smiled for the first time. All his time working as an English teacher in Seoul before the war was paying off. Now sitting conversing in the Queen's English, with proper Englishmen, was one of his dreams come true. Another was to return to the area where he was born, before his family had fled the separation of Korea in 1945.

"There it is," Private London pointed out the window, as a turn-off came into view up ahead, heading west.

In the second truck they drove in silence. Lieutenant Samuels couldn't understand half of what the thick-accented Private McClaren was saying and didn't really care either. He just wanted to be in the front truck with the enigmatic Captain Woodholme-Brown, so they could talk history or discuss the war. Lieutenant Samuels came from a wealthy Boston family, the nearest thing to the upper class America had. They could trace their family tree back to Agincourt and were very proud of their English heritage. How long would they go on without stopping? In the next half an hour he would have to stop for a latrine break whatever the convoy or war was doing.

The small United Nations convoy drove on, meeting American tanks and a truck of Australians as they turned from the western road north before they reached Kasan. Signs of battle were evident as they headed north across another river. Apart from the RSM, Sergeant Dempsey, Sergeant Kim, Corporal Baker and Private London, it was the first time that half of the group had ever seen a corpse. Or in the case of some of the burnt out North Korean tanks and vehicles, burnt bodies or just pieces of people.

They cheered up as they passed some supply trucks heading south, then sobered ten minutes later when a fleet of ambulances drove by.

By the time they reached a friendly road-block set up between an old ox cart and a burnt out T-34 tank, the whole convoy was bursting for a latrine break and their stomachs rumbled louder than an enemy tank. The road ahead had slimmed to a muddy single road. Private London could see the peaceful thatched cottages of Taechon ahead, with more brown hills encircling it. As they slowed to a stop at the makeshift barrier, to his joy Private London recognised the men at the checkpoint were from his own Middlesex Regiment.

A sergeant that Private London didn't recognise came round to the passenger's window, with a lance corporal he knew from sight, from A company.

The sergeant saw the captain leaning out of the passenger window and saluted ceremoniously like only the British can.

"Can I help you, sir?" the sergeant asked noting the captain's Royal Engineer's cap badge.

"I hope so, Sergeant, my band of troubadours are heading north to build a bridge. I wonder if we can impose ourselves on you and stop for a picnic and a piss?" The captain smiled down at the fatigued Sergeant.

"Can I see your papers first, sir?" the sergeant asked, following army procedure.

"Here you go," the captain beamed, pulling some folded card from inside his coat.

The sergeant shifted his rifle to his shoulder and opened the papers and orders with fingerless gloved hands.

Private London exhaled, his cold breath billowing towards the windscreen. Why was the sergeant taking so long? He wanted to get into the village and find some of his old mates.

"That all seems to be in order, sir." The sergeant handed back the documents. "If you follow the road, the Major has set up shop in a large hut by the cattle pen, you can't miss it." The sergeant saluted again and the captain returned it.

"Come on then, London, let's go break bread with your chaps," the captain ordered and Robert London was happy to oblige.

The small convoy pulled up in line over a former vegetable patch of bare earth. The temperature was so cold it was like parking on concrete rather than soil.

The soldiers really noticed the cold when they left the trucks; even the engineers who had been in the back of the

85

draughty third truck. The men assembled, or rather, huddled in country-segregated groups by the side of the vehicles.

"Right men, let's get to work before our bits freeze off." The captain tried to sound jovial as the biting north wind turned his soft cheeks pink. "Sergeant Dempsey, could you organise the refuelling of the vehicles, while the RSM seeks out the latrines and chow for our hungry, full-laddered bunch," Captain Woodholme-Browne continued. "Left-tenant Samuels, Sergeant Kim, with me." The two subordinates jumped at the handsome, tall captain's commands. They briskly followed the captain as he headed past a few bemused British soldiers to find the officer in charge.

"Okay you lazy bastards, you heard the man, let's get those gas barrels outta the second deuce. Hartnell, go get the siphon outta the first truck," the veteran sergeant bawled, clapping his padded mittens together, to get them moving and keep his extremities warm.

The American engineers moved off about their business, with a certain amount of grumbling.

"Looks like we landed in Limey-land eh, Teddy?" Private O'Keefe joked as the group headed for the second truck.

"Yeah it's a real shit-hole, that's why they look so at home," he spat on the ground in front of him.

P.F.C. Perez laughed next to him and O'Keefe laughed louder, like his life depended on it.

"Irish! Shut up and get in the back of the deuce!" the sergeant ordered, rounding the side of the truck.

"What about us, Sergeant Major?" asked Private McClaren, hopping from one foot to the next, bursting for a slash.

"Well as you look like you're gonna wet your nappy any second, you better find where the latrines are, McClaren," the Regimental Sergeant Major ordered, with a hint of his own amusement.

"And me, Sergeant Major?" Private London asked excitedly.

"I know, London, you're excited to be back with your mates, just try and secure some chow while you're about it!" The RSM smiled in spite of the freezing wind attacking his lips.

"Yes, Sergeant Major," London dashed off, stopped and spun on his heels, "thank you."

The RSM waved him forward, shaking his head, "I must be going bloody soft in my auld age."

Private London jogged through the small hamlet, not feeling the cold at all. He passed a few faces he recognised from A-Company, even noted where a fire had been set up to cook, next to some mess tins and wooden boxes, with C7 rations etched on the side.

He was about to admit defeat, thinking D-Company must be deployed outside the village somewhere, when he heard a familiar voice coming from a hut beside him.

He burst through the half open door to find eight men crowded around a burning oil drum, trying to roast a chicken over a metal sieve.

"Hello, wankers!" he greeted them with the usual D-Company friendly welcome.

"It's a bloody ghost," joked Private May from the far side of the drum.

"Wotcha doing here?" Private Troughton asked in shock.

"We thought you were a bloody goner, Bob," beamed Lance Corporal Wainwright, Robert London's best mate.

The two of them shook hands and patted each other on the backs.

"Getting shot in the head couldn't keep us apart, Nobby, me old mate." Private London let himself be led back into the bosom of his comrades, if only temporarily.

"Robbo's caught a bleedin' hen, fancy a bit when it's cooked?" Nobby asked.

"Not if Robbo's cooking it as well," Robert laughed and so did all his old D-Company mates. It felt so good to be back among men he could trust with his life again. He pushed to the back of his mind the fact he had only one or two hours in their company.

Three quarters of an hour later, Robert London was standing next to the three deuce and a half US army trucks, with Nobby, Robbo, Ray and Mooro.

"So you're babysitting some Yank sappers," Mooro stated. "Rather you than me," he added.

"Big bloody lorries ain't they, how do they drive?" asked Robbo, who was the platoon's car and vehicle nut.

"Like an elephant, with no head, on an ice rink," Robert London explained with a grin.

The group chuckled at the description; the officers, Americans and Sergeant Kim were all over the other side of the village having a warm meal. Private McClaren was in a hut, sitting in on a card game and the RSM was in the latrines.

"So how the hell did you get yourself volunteered for this game of silly-buggers?" Nobby asked, lightly punching his old schoolmate on the arm.

"Usual, wrong place at the wrong time," Robert answered.

"So you got an F-G and two Jocks along for the ride as well. You must have peed God off in a previous life is all I can think, Bob," Mooro went on.

"F-G?" Robert London asked bemused.

"Friendly Gook," Robbo explained.

"You've missed too many briefings from Sergeant Shitbag, so you have," Ray joked, mocking their sergeant's Northern Irish accent.

"How long you gonna be driving for Uncle Sam's lot then?" Nobby asked. He had missed the strength of his best mate beside him.

"Dunno, we gotta head north-west from here, scout about, sort out a bridge or two, then bring the buggers back again. Two, three days," Robert London ventured.

"Betcha it'll be a week," said Mooro, who would bet on anything.

"Then they'll get you to drive General MacArthur, join the parachute regiment, then drop into Russia and single-handedly destroy the Commies," joked Robbo who was rarely serious about anything.

"Shut up, Robinson," Private London retorted.

"Make me then, big guy," Robbo skipped about, his fists up ready for a Marquis of Queensbury boxing match.

"I'll give you a bunch-of-fives in a minute." Nobby raised his fists and smiled.

Just then RSM McConnell appeared from behind a hut on his way back from doing his bog business.

"Just seen the Captain, London. We bug out in fifteen minutes." The RSM walked past the close-knit group of combat-weary 'Die-Hards' and headed for the last truck in line.

"That your Sergeant then, that hairy lipped Jock?" Ray asked, when the RSM was out of earshot.

"Yeah, but he's all right. The Captain is a good bloke an' all." Robert defended his travelling companions, well some of them.

"Frig me, it's cold," Robbo moaned and it was getting colder by the hour.

"I reckon it's gonna snow before too long," Ray, the avid gardener and allotment holder back home in Surrey, prophesised.

"It's bloody cold enough," Mooro added.

"Great," said Robert, "all I need is to drive in a blizzard at night, things couldn't get any worse." They did, just then Sergeant Dempsey and his men turned up. Private Robert London knew he didn't have long with his platoon, before setting off down the road again. He knew he had to go, grey clouds were forming over the grey/brown hills and in two hours the countryside would be pitch black.

"Okay, yous guys," Sergeant Dempsey yelled, "let's stow our gear and mount up." The American engineers set about their tasks with gusto, if only to quickly get out of the icy chill wind.

"Mount up? He sounds like John Wayne, Bob," Mooro commented, flapping his arms at his sides.

"Nah, more like Jimmy Cagney," Ray said stomping from one foot to the next to bring any friction warmth to his feet and legs.

"Well they act like a bunch of gangsters sometimes," Robert joked in a low voice.

"Hey London, just took some of your soft Southern lads for ten pounds!" Piggy McClaren shouted and waved on his return from the local card game.

"Who's that toss-pot?" Nobby asked as the beaming Piggy McClaren took his large frame back to the cab of the second truck.

"Piggy. He's a replacement Jock and right old poor excuse for a man," Robert answered; he kind of pitied the poor bugger and anyone unlucky enough to be saddled with him for more than five minutes.

"Want me to teach him some respect for the regiment Bobby?" Mooro asked, punching one glove into another.

"Don't worry, Mooro, he's a sad little coward, I can handle his type," Robert replied.

"You weren't so handy with your fists when we got into bother with those navy poofs in Hong Kong, were you?" Nobby stated, with a grin on his cold face.

"Blimey Nobby, there was twenty of 'em!" Mooro pleaded. "Anyway, thingy is the better part of valour."

"What, pegging it as fast as your size ten army boots can carry you?" Ray said doubling up laughing.

"Be a man, Bobby, be a man, that's what my old dad always tells me," Robert said proudly.

"No Bob, your dad said 'be a coalman, be a coalman Robert'!" joked Robbo and the whole group cracked up.

The arrival of the captain, lieutenant and Sergeant Kim soon dampened their spirits, because Private London knew it was time to leave his friends again. The captain beckoned London with a friendly, but commanding wave.

"Right, I better go lads. See ya on the way back, all right." Private Robert London turned to go.

"Be careful Bob, and don't volunteer for any more stupid missions eh," were Nobby's words for his departing friend.

"Keep those Yanks in check," said Mooro.

"See ya Bobby," Ray simply said.

"Bye mate," was Robbo's farewell.

"Back soon," Robert called and jogged off to his truck and climbed in, just at the same time as Sergeant Kim and Captain Woodholme-Browne. The engine started second time and he pulled the beast of a truck around to face the road north.

"Sergeant Kim, what's the Korean word for drive?" the captain asked the small, silent South Korean soldier.

"Unjon," nodded the sergeant with a smile.

"Then unjon on, Private London," the captain ordered.

"Yes, sir." And with a quick look out of his window at his mates, Robert London drove off towards the grey clouds and brown hills and mountains ahead.

An hour after leaving Taechon the sky ahead through the windscreen had taken on a strange yellow-grey colour. Clouds of various shades of grey covered the sky, the tall mountains loomed closer. They had driven across a ford in a trickling river, where ice had formed on the water's edges. The dirt track-cum-road began to rise and they realised they were on the lower slopes of the brown hills that had seemed so distant this morning.

Bare trees began to line the road and after half an hour the trees were the only thing that could be seen on either side of the ascending track. The canopy of the trees and small shower of hailstones had darkened the road ahead considerably. Private London cursed his luck being in the lead truck in the convoy, his headlights were on, but driving was becoming increasingly difficult.

Sergeant Kim advised that the road would fork soon. North would lead all the way into red China and west would take them where the convoy wanted to go. It was nearly pitch black by the time they had found the fork. The road west widened to two lanes for some reason, yet the road became a bumpy and unforgiving dirt track.

"Least it's stopped hailing," half-joked the captain, as Private London squinted to see the road ahead. The track was on an even keel now, neither ascending nor descending, but a whole battalion of North Koreans could be hiding in the woods either side of the road.

"We cannot be far away from our destination," Sergeant Kim said, breaking the silence in the cab.

"Not going to drive off a cliff are we, Sergeant?" Private London turned towards the R.O.K. soldier worriedly.

"Look out man!" the captain suddenly cried aloud.

Robert London looked back at the road in terror as he saw a large dog-like animal run across the road right in front of the truck. Instinct took over and Robert London swerved right away from this animal and stamped his foot on the brake. The truck skidded off the road and its right front wheel bashed into a long fallen log. The deuce and a half came to a sudden halt, a couple of inches before a large fir tree.

Chapter 5

No Man's Land

The two other trucks managed to brake and keep themselves on the road. After a second of silence, all hell broke loose. RSM McConnell grabbed his Sten gun and Sergeant Dempsey his M1 Carbine and jumped swiftly out of the last truck.

The lead truck lay ten feet off the road, just before a large fir tree, upright, but it had skidded sideways for a few feet.

RSM McConnell's instincts took over as he scanned the darkness for enemy soldiers. Had it been a mine? Because he hadn't heard an explosion.

"McClaren, grab your rifle you useless lump of lard," the RSM bellowed at the shaken private.

"Erm, Sergeant Major McConnell, you and your man guard the trucks, Sergeant Dempsey bring your men," the lieutenant spluttered, stumbling around in the dark.

Sergeant Dempsey was already half-way to the lead truck anyway. Corporal Baker wasn't a slouch either and the lieutenant ended up following his men to the lead truck, finally remembering to un-holster his Colt .45 pistol.

The passenger door of the crashed truck flew wide open and Captain Woodholme-Browne jumped out, rubbing his right ear. Sergeant Kim with his rifle ready, jumped out next.

Private Hartnell and P.F.C. Perez made their way to the driver's door and wrenched it open.

"You okay, boy?" came Hartnell's mid-western tones.

Private London pulled himself off the steering wheel and rubbed at his ribs. Lucky he'd been wearing so much clothing because of the cold. "I think so." He felt a throbbing in his scar, and knew a headache was coming on. "Did you see it?"

"See what?" asked Perez from behind Hartnell.

"Animal. It ran across in front of the truck. It was big like a dog, or a fox with snakes biting its behind," Robert London murmured.

"He must have hit his head," offered Perez.

"Come on, Tommy, let's get you down from that cab," Hartnell said in gentle tones and Private London let himself be pulled from the driver's seat.

"Irish, check the wheels and chassis, Baker go and check under the hood," Sergeant Dempsey ordered.

"Yes Sergeant," and both jumped to jobs they were used to doing.

Back on the road the two Argylls scanned the trees for movement. Piggy could see nothing but dark trees and darker shadows. The RSM's veteran eyes saw no enemies either, but the hair on the back of his neck was standing on end. His instincts told him something was out there watching them, instincts that had kept him alive from El Alamein to Berlin during the last war.

He ignored his feelings and looked across at the first truck, all three of its occupants were walking and talking, so that was a relief.

Lightening his grip on his Sten gun, he followed the headlight beams of the second truck to examine the skid marks of the lead vehicle.

There were no mine or bomb craters, just the skid marks of the truck, that went off to the right where it finally came to rest. The RSM returned to where Private McClaren was standing, his rifle pointed into the darkness.

"See anything, Sergeant Major?" the nervous soldier spoke; this being the first time he had raised his rifle anywhere apart from the firing range.

"No, laddie, but keep ya peepers peeled anyway." The RSM turned to see the captain, the Korean sergeant and Private London being led back up towards the two idling trucks.

"What happened, sir?" the RSM asked as the shaken driver and passengers of the first truck returned to the roadside.

"Some animal ran across the road right in front of us," the captain explained, "it was bloody huge like a bear or something."

"The Private did well to avoid it," Sergeant Kim added.

"Oh my head," Private London stated, rubbing at his scar.

"Where are we, Sergeant Kim? Anywhere near our destination?" Lieutenant Samuels asked looking around at the enclosing forest that lined the dirt road.

"Sorry, it is hard to tell exactly," the sergeant bowed again, "yet I estimate we are one quarter of an hour away from the rope bridge, along this stretch of road." The sergeant's words were near-perfect Queen's English.

"Left-tenant Samuels, take the RSM here and Sergeant Kim in the second truck and scout out ahead until you find the rope bridge," the captain ordered, "then report back here on the double." The three men hurried off to the truck.

"Sergeant Dempsey," the captain continued to the US engineer, "how long will repairs on the truck take?"

"Well, fifteen minutes to change the wheel, another two hours to fix the engine and repair the oil leak," the sergeant replied, looking back at the crashed truck.

"Okay, then we'll make camp here for the night." The captain paused as the second truck roared off up the track, leaving them with only one working truck. "Private London, are you all right now?"

"Yes, sir." The private saluted and snapped to attention for good measure.

"At ease," the captain smiled in the dark. "You and Private McClaren will stand guard 'til the RSM returns, understood?"

"Yes, sir," they both replied in unison.

"One of you will be up here with the last truck, the other down by the first truck! Sergeant Dempsey, let's use the remaining truck to tow the crashed one back on the road and make repairs."

"Yes, Captain," the sergeant nodded and sloped off down the incline to the crashed vehicle and his men.

"And Sergeant?" the captain called after him. The US sergeant stopped and turned back. "Get one of your chaps to get a fire going and some chow on, because I, for one, am famished."

Only thirty minutes had passed when Lieutenant Samuels' party returned in the second truck. The first truck had been towed up the slight incline and back on to the road where some of the US engineers were working away on it. The knackered wheel had been replaced and they were well into repairing the problems with the engine.

The RSM was aghast as he parked up; the Americans had set up an empty gasoline barrel next to the fallen log and had a blazing fire going. He noted that the mouthy corporal and the flame-haired Irish-American-sounding soldier were mooching around preparing food at a very leisurely pace.

The short sergeant was supervising the two remaining engineers as they worked on the damaged truck. It was lit by a bulb clamped on the top of the bonnet, run off the idling battery of number three truck. This is where the captain sat, knees on the dashboard writing a diary or a report of the journey. The weather was bitter, yet thankfully dry: the threatening snow had so far held off.

The RSM was glad that his two privates were at least acting like soldiers. Piggy McClaren was patrolling by the cooking drum, trying to catch any of its warmth, but staying well out of the Yanks' way. Private London was in the semi-shadows leaning against a tree, his rifle up half balanced on a bough. He was scanning the woods like his life depended on it, and it well could.

The RSM exchanged glances with Sergeant Kim; apart from London, the rest of the group were sitting ducks for any Gook attack.

"Lieutenant Samuels, with your permission I would greatly like to scout the perimeter of the camp?" the South Korean soldier asked, deeming it a necessary evil and probably safer than being in the well-lit camp.

"Fine by me," the lieutenant said as he walked off to report that they had found the rope-bridge and plateau to the captain.

"Do you want one of my lads to go with ya?" RSM McConnell asked with respect for the sergeant's bravery and knowledge.

"Not necessary, Sergeant Major," he smiled, "my boots are not as heavy as your British Army ones."

The RSM laughed and patted the Korean on the shoulder. "Off ya go then, but report back to me if you sniff out any danger."

"I will, Regimental Sergeant Major McConnell." The Korean sergeant pulled his American rifle off his shoulder and edged off the road and soon merged into the dark woods that lined the road and camp.

The RSM looked at Private London, then moved off to order Private McClaren away from the fire and food and into the shadows a bit more.

"I see da Loo-tenant, the Gook and the hairy faced Limey are back," Corporal Baker commented, as he watched the lieutenant march down to the third truck to report to the captain.

"Well let's hope he ain't found da bridge, I just wanna get the fuck outta here," Private O'Keefe stated, moving his hands over the fire to warm them.

"I know whatcha mean, Irish, the war is practically over and we're here out on a fucking camping trip in some boondocks shithole close to Gook lines," the corporal complained, like it was his own private religion. "I'm a freakin' qualified US Engineer. I should be in some rear-echelon whore-house, selling off stolen whiskey and stoggies, not in the Korean version of the fucking Rockies," the corporal crowed, the heat from the drum fire only inches away did not penetrate his icy-cold bones.

"Ya hit the fuckin' nail right square on the head there, Teddy," Liam O'Keefe agreed as he always did, to whatever his corporal said.

"You okay there, boy?" Private Hartnell asked as he walked past the English soldier on guard near the trucks.

"Be better with a cuppa tea, sitting next to the fire, Yank," Private London said from the semi-shadows of the tree line.

"My name is John, not Yank. Private John Hartnell from Guildford, Idaho, pleased to make your acquaintance." The young soldier moved closer to the trees and Private London.

"Blimey, that's weird," the Englishman muttered.

"What's weird, boy?" the American asked.

"My name is Robert, Private Robert James London from Guildford, Surrey: in England," he added for good measure.

"Shoot bo-, Robert that is weird," the private whistled through his teeth, "that's co-ince-e-dence with a capital C, wouldn't you say?"

Robert smiled, this Yank seemed almost human compared with his comrades. The way Private Hartnell half-sang his longer words was quite endearing.

"It's nice to have something in common with one of you Yan...Americans." Private London lowered his rifle and moved nearer the Yank engineer.

"Yeah, well not all of us are like Baker and O'Keefe, hell Perez is a good old boy even if he is from the wrong side of the Rio Grande." The young American spoke in soft tones; Robert London liked the Yank, mainly because he sounded like a cowboy from all those Westerns he and Nobby used to watch at the ABC cinema back home.

"How's the truck coming?" London asked, with an occasional glance back at the woods.

"The deuce, she's nearly done," Hartnell smiled in the cold darkness.

"Good, the sooner we get out of this place the better," Robert London looked around his surroundings, "this place gives me the willies."

"I ain't sure what you said, but this is certainly no place to be on Halloween night."

In the inky blackness a figure crept forward, silently moving through the trees like he belonged there. The woods were silent also, which worried him, no birds or animals were present and it was not just the winter that had caused their absence. The whole hillside forest felt empty, just waiting for something to occur.

Sergeant Kim sniffed the air, he thought he had caught a brief scent for a second, yet it was gone again like a nasal will-o'-the-wisp. Something apart from the freezing cold was making the hairs on his head stand on end. Ignoring his primeval fear and praying for a blessing from his forefathers, he pressed on into the night.

Inside the camp food was being served, officers and NCOs to the right of the fire, other ranks to the left.

"So where's Sergeant Gook, eating worms outta the forest floor?" Private O'Keefe whispered to his fellow grunts and two starving Tommies.

Corporal Baker looked up from his mess tin of already cooling food. "Out with his Gook pals setting up an ambush."

"You reckon?" Private Hartnell asked, then wished he hadn't.

"Sure as eggs is eggs, boy!" the corporal mocked, tucking into his chow again.

"Don't worry, Yank, I'll protect your back!" Private McClaren sneered, rubbing the length of his rifle.

"Gee thanks," Baker sneered back and wolfed his food as quickly as possible.

"So what are you guys gonna do after the war?" P.F.C Perez asked, trying to defuse the tension a little in such an already chilly place.

"Run a whore-house in New Mexico, I hear your sisters are cheap," Baker shot back swiftly and with ease.

O'Keefe burst into rapturous fawning laughter, even Hartnell and McClaren smiled. London looked on dispassionately, if he'd been with his platoon he would have laughed also.

"Fuck you, Baker!" Perez spat back.

"That's what your eldest sister said to me!" Baker continued, laughing at his own jokes.

"Keep it down you guys, this ain't Summer Camp," Sergeant Dempsey called over from where he was sitting next to RSM McConnell.

"So, RSM, what should we do about sleeping arrangements?" Captain Woodholme-Browne broke off his conversation with Lieutenant Samuels and looked dubiously at the frozen ground.

"I have a plan, sir, if you'll follow me." The RSM stood up and the officers and Sergeant Dempsey followed him over to the three trucks.

The RSM pointed from the front to the last truck. "Officers, NCOs and other ranks."

"Hardly the Ritz, RSM," the captain replied, wishing he was back in a warmer Pusan bed.

"A bit draughty, but it's off the ground and that cold earth will sap the warmth out of your bones, gentlemen," the RSM explained. Dempsey nodded, he'd thought along similar lines earlier.

"Needs must, eh, Edward?" The captain clapped the lieutenant on the back, who was surprised at being called by his Christian name.

"I'm sure we'll manage," the lieutenant smiled, his thoughts far away from their mission or war.

"I thought, sir, as we have three NCOs we could have three watches headed by a sergeant, with two enlisted men as guards," the RSM explained as the captain climbed up into the first truck to examine his cramped sleeping quarters for the night.

"Very snug," the captain said to himself.

"The guard duty, sir?" RSM McConnell pressed for a response.

"Sounds like a good plan, carry on, Sergeant Major," the captain replied, not showing too much military interest at the moment.

"Yes, sir." The RSM saluted and walked off down the line of trucks with Sergeant Dempsey as company.

"So, Lieutenant Samuels, do you want the right or left side of the bed?" The captain looked down at his fellow engineering officer.

The lieutenant laughed, but had a good idea of where he wanted to sleep tonight.

"So how long do we get on guard duty?" Dempsey asked as they checked out the other deuces.

"Three hours each watch," the RSM explained, "split our lads up, what do you think?"

"Yeah if you take O'Keefe, I'll take Baker. Then hopefully we should have a peaceful night," the sergeant joked, knowing his men well.

"I thought Sergeant Kim should get first watch, then me and then you." The RSM and sergeant headed back to the fire to tell the men.

"Where the hell is our guide?" Dempsey asked.

"He's been gone a while too long for my liking." McConnell looked around the cold, dark, encroaching woods for any sign of life. "London, grab your rifle, we are going for a little jaunt," the RSM ordered as the two sergeants approached the rest of the men.

McConnell collected his Sten gun and headed off towards the trucks. Private London jumped up, grabbed his rifle and followed the RSM up the incline to the road.

"Where are we going, Sergeant Major?" Private London jogged a little to catch up with the short, broad Scotsman.

"To find Sergeant Kim," the RSM explained, checking his Sten gun was in full working order.

"Stupid Gook got lost eh? And he's supposed to be our bleedin' guide!" London quipped. A few months ago he had never even heard of Korea or their war and he really wasn't sure what a communist was either.

"Laddie," the RSM turned and stopped him with a powerful arm. "That 'Stupid Gook' is an allied South Korean Sergeant, a rank you will never attain. You will treat him with respect and follow his orders, do you understand, Private?"

"Yes, Regimental Sergeant Major." The RSM's harsh words had taken him aback a little.

"If we get into a fucking fire-fight who's gonna be more use covering your backside, a South Korean veteran or a bloody Yank mechanic?"

"I understand," London nodded. He was a man, but still growing into his adult mind and body day by day. Being in combat had hastened that process, by at least two years.

"Come on," the RSM ordered and tightening their grip on their weapons of war, they passed the trucks and headed for the dark woods.

"Can I help you, Regimental Sergeant Major McConnell?" came a Korean-accented voice from behind a large tree trunk.

The two British soldiers had raised their weapons before their brains realised who it was.

"Sergeant Kim, we were getting worried about you," the RSM explained as all three of them lowered their weapons.

"Were you?" the South Korean sergeant asked, staring at Private London.

"Yes, now get some food, you have first watch with Private Hartnell and young London here," the RSM explained.

Sergeant Kim nodded and headed back to the fire and food.

"Do you think 'e heard me?" Private London asked the RSM, as they watched him walk away.

"I'm not your aunty, London; I don't care if he runs you over with a truck and uses you as a bed spread. Let's get back to the camp." The RSM marched off, and, with one look at the eerie woods, Private London followed swiftly after.

"Time for bed I think," yawned Captain Woodholme-Browne. "What do you think Left-tenant?"

"Yes, sir," the lieutenant nodded, "we have a lot of work to do tomorrow."

"Come on, men," Sergeant Dempsey rose, "those not on sentry duty, hit the hay."

The American engineers and one Scottish soldier rose from their log seats by the camp fire and trudged off to the even colder confines of the trucks.

Private Hartnell noticed that Baker and O'Keefe were moaning and bitching as usual as they walked back to their deuces.

"Remember, any trouble rouse us in the second truck first Sergeant Kim," RSM said, wincing as he picked up his icy cold Sten gun with his bare right hand.

The South Korean sergeant nodded and the two other NCOs slowly walked off towards the trucks. The officers were already in their truck and Lieutenant Samuels was tying up the canvas flaps at the back.

"Your Captain could be in for an interesting night," Sergeant Dempsey told the RSM quietly as they slowly walked up the slope to the road.

"Why's that, Dempsey?" the RSM asked, intrigued.

"Well, back in Japan, before all this kicked off, me and a couple of the depot sergeants took a little trip to the local fun part of town, if you get my meaning," the sergeant said, leaning closer.

The RSM nodded, he'd been prone to a couple of these trips himself during his long army career.

"Things go well, we have a lot of fun at a place called 'Leaky Sue's'. I'd had my jollies and something I ate musta disagreed with my guts 'cause I was feeling as sick as a hound dog," the sergeant whispered, rubbing at his middle.

"Not the twenty beers you'd sunk then?" the RSM smiled as they reached their truck and scrambled inside.

"Who do I spy down the alley but Loo-tenant Samuels getting sucked off by one of the local geisha girls," Sergeant Dempsey continued as the RSM tied up the flaps of the truck.

The engineering, surveying and bridge equipment had been stacked and rearranged so two bedrolls could just about fit side-by-side in the space.

"So as I watch the fun, they swap over: and get fucking this, the girl has a dick!" the sergeant exclaimed as he made up his bed.

"What did your Left-ten-ant do?" the RSM asked, having heard of such lady-boy types in Hong Kong.

"Without a word L.T. gets down and starts blowing the geisha's dick!"

"Bloody hell and I thought only our officers were queer as Frenchmen!" the RSM laughed, deep and rolling.

Dempsey laughed too, glad to know that armies all over the world were the same. The officers were queer and clueless and the sergeants really ran the show.

Private London watched all the others troop off to their beds, feeling a little awkward, left with two soldiers from different countries that he hardly knew. At least he had the best watch, three hours on and then six hours continuous kip. The middle watch was the worst, your sleep being interrupted. The company could have been a lot worse; he was glad to avoid the ginger and mouthy Yanks and Piggy also.

"It's colder than a witch's tit at dawn," he said, rubbing his gloved hands together, his rifle over his shoulder.

"You can say that again!" Private Hartnell smiled, in spite of the lowering temperature, even if he didn't understand the whole phrase.

"It's All Hallow's Eve and we've got guard duty in a dark, spooky wood," London mumbled on, the cold numbing his brain.

"Sheet, it's Halloween, got any apples to bob?" Hartnell asked jokingly.

"What is this Halloweed you speak of?" Sergeant Kim asked. He spoke and taught English, but accents and dialects are hard to pick up.

"Halloween, Sergeant, it's when witches fly through the sky at midnight, the dead rise from their graves, scary stories get told," Private Hartnell tried to explain, but even to him it sounded childish and silly.

"I did not think America and Great Britain, two great industrial nations had such superstitions still." Sergeant Kim had started to enjoy himself; the first rule of being a teacher is that you never stop learning.

"We could tell some ghost stories to help pass the time," Private London suggested.

"This is agreeable," the sergeant nodded; men together, telling stories, was more the Korean way.

"So who's got a doozy of a story then?" Hartnell asked in his usual happy way.

"I do," said London.

"Okay, boy, let's hear it." Hartnell sat putting his Garland rifle on his knees.

Chapter 6

London's All Hallows Eve Story

"Well it begins like this," started Private London, "it's all about an old widowed schoolmistress, who lives alone in a small cottage."

The young man looked up at the windows of the quaint cottage and flinched as the rain pelted down onto his upturned face.

"There has to be an easier way to earn a crust?" he whispered to himself as he looked around the isolated archetypal chocolate-box cottage. David flicked his lank, wet hair out of his eyes and rubbed his hand down his face and sniffed the raindrops from the top of his nose.

"Well, in for a penny, in for a pound." With that he dodged the puddles and approached the front door, with its peeling green paint.

David pulled down the lapels of his demob suit, and looked around for a doorbell. There wasn't one, so his hand reached for the knocker.

With a quick glance over his left and right shoulders, he gave the door knocker three sharp raps. David stood back a step, flicked his wet hair out of his eyes and adjusted his sodden suit again. Twenty long seconds passed, which, to David, felt like an eternity. Despondency began to creep over him, as the realisation came that nobody might be in.

He was just about to turn around and head back to the railway station, when he heard movement behind the door. Shuffled footsteps approached and then stopped dead. David hopped quickly from one foot to the other, as he heard a bolt being drawn back and a lock being turned. The door was then opened inwards four inches and the right half of an elderly woman's wrinkled face appeared. He could see from where her white haired head poked out from behind the door that she was barely five feet tall.

"Yes...can I help you?" asked the old woman, in a frail, faltering voice.

"Hello, Mrs Tyler, don't you remember me?" smiled David sweetly, as he bent down to converse with her.

"No, sorry, who are you?" scowled the pensioner trying to work out what the handsome young man wanted.

"I'm a friend of your grandson, we used to go to school together, remember?" David gave his best politician's smile. "You used to give us sweets and fings."

"You were a friend of my Keith's?" asked the old woman almost to herself, the scowl on her face just normal age wrinkles now.

"Yeah you remember me, Keith and the other lads used to play football in your garden." David nodded an imaginary ball and kicked his foot out pretending he was an outside right.

"I remember those days, Keith and his mob coming in for sweets and drinks. Mucky devils, always covered in mud and soaking wet." The old dear wasn't looking at David; her eyes were focused on pre-war days gone by.

"Not much change now, eh?" David laughed, pulling at his sopping wet trousers.

"So you are, dear, isn't the weather awful today." The suspicion had left the old woman's voice and motherly concern registered on her rosy red cheeks.

"Terrible innit, in fact the whole week's been a right old washout. Worse than in Germany, I've just been demobbed see. First thing I wanted to do when I got back to England was to look up me old mate Keith. But I ain't got a clue where he is, so I thought to myself, his gran will know, and here I am." Quickly David raised a finger and then fished about in his jacket pocket.

"I've just remembered I brought these for you." Out of his dry-ish pocket came a bag of strawberry bonbons.

"Oh dear, you shouldn't have." The old lady took them lovingly into her warm hands. "Come inside, get out of the rain and warm yourself up, while I dig out Keith's address." The woman shuffled backwards, the door opening to let David inside. "I'll make us a pot of tea and then we can have one of your sweets afterwards."

"That sounds just lovely," smiled David as he stepped inside the cottage, wiping his shoes on the mat as he did. Ahead of him was a carpeted stairway heading upwards, to the left a large kitchen and to his right, a closed door.

The old woman shut the front door and showed David through the closed door into a comfy and busy living room.

"You're wet through, now go and warm yourself by the fire while I put the kettle on to boil." The kindly widow shuffled off to the kitchen as David made a bee-line for the roaring open fire.

David decided that, on this wet and ghastly morning, he really could do with a cuppa, to warm him up before he got down to the purpose of his visit.

David took off his jacket and put it on the back of one of the chairs. A small table was squashed tight against the only window in the room. Only two hard looking chairs with worn seats were pushed in, on opposite sides of the old table. Dave plonked himself down in an old, but surprisingly comfortable, armchair in one corner of the room. With a roaring open log fire next to him, he felt warm for the first time that morning. The other wall comprised of the door and a huge sideboard loaded up with seventy-five years of bric-a-brac, worthless except to the owner's memory. Next to the door was a large radio on a wooden pedestal, another armchair with a set of occasional tables, overloaded with women's weeklies.

David exhaled loudly and once again combed his wet hair out of his eyes with his left hand, his Brylcreem long since washed down the back of his shirt collar. He looked around the dirty brown walls, his eyes finally settling on the huge sideboard. He scoped the pictures on the walls, then his eyes swept up to the net curtains and something caught his eye. Something hand-sized and pink hanging down from the cobwebbed pelmet, twirled in the slight breeze from the old window.

Born, in his mother's opinion, with ten times too much curiosity, David stood up for a better look. Hanging from the pelmet, by a piece of ancient fishing line was the effigy of a witch on a broomstick. The crude-shaped thing dressed in pink tattered cloth, a draft from the windows blew it slowly around until it faced David.

"I see you've noticed my witch," commented the old lady from the doorway as she entered the room with a tray full of tea things.

"Yes," David replied looking from the tatty witch to the old woman.

"I bought her off a gypsy fifty years ago. My husband John thought I was soft in the head to waste my money on it," the old woman remembered. "The old gypsy woman said, put it up and it will protect your house and valuables." Keith's grandmother came over and put the tray down with a wobble onto the table underneath the window.

"I don't really believe in superstitions and curses, not after the war; only real life matters," David stated honestly to the old woman.

"Me neither, deary, but saying that I've never been burgled. So I'll keep it up there, just in case. It used to be bright green but the sun's faded it over the years," she said, putting out the tea things.

"I suppose you've amounted a lot of treasures and valuables over the years. This place couldn't hold them all; you must have them all in your castle in Scotland, eh?" wisecracked the ex-soldier.

"Oh I wish, dear," laughed the old woman, "no me and my things all fit in these four walls. Everything me and my Jack worked for is here, waiting for Keith when I die." The dry lips of the woman formed into a relaxed smile. David reciprocated, yet with an extra gleam in his cold blue eyes.

Just then their very different daydreams were interrupted by a long whistling sound coming from the kitchen. Keith's grandmother moved off to see to the kettle.

"I'll be back in a jiffy," she stated as she shuffled off quite sprightly to the kitchen.

As soon as she was out of sight, David jumped into action. He dashed across the room to the huge five foot wide sideboard and began to slowly and silently open the drawers and doors. His hands expertly rooting through the contents, searching for anything remotely worth stealing.

The old woman came shuffling back into the room. David grabbed the nearest picture off the sideboard and spun around trying to obscure the open door hidden behind his back.

"Is this your Jack?" David asked quickly, his brain acting on pure self-preservation.

"Oh you're over there now, always got itchy feet you youngsters." The old lady moved a bit closer, her eyes peering at the old black and white photo of a young man in an army uniform.

"No that's my younger brother Norman. He died in 1912 fighting the Germans. He was only twenty-seven, no age, no age at all to die. Now what did I come back for?" A frown deepened the lines on her world weary face. "Ah, I'll be forgetting my head next: the teapot!" She moved over to the table, picked up the teapot with both hands and turned to leave the room. "Now sit yourself down and I'll be back in a moment, dear."

David smiled broadly 'til the 'daft old cow' left the room, then exhaled loudly. He quickly closed the drawer and put down the photo. He went over to sit at the small table by the window, glad that his luck was still holding out.

His bored eyes wandered up to the witch that was dangling above him. The thing wasn't turning anymore; in fact it seemed to him, that it was pointing the end of its little broomstick directly at the defiled sideboard.

Just then he heard the old lady return from the kitchen once again and turned to see her coming through the doorway with the teapot. David jumped up and took the hot and heavy teapot from her and placed it on a mat on the table.

"Thank you," she smiled and moved to the other side of the table as David sat by the door again.

"Now I've put the water and tea in, it just needs a little brew." She sat down awkwardly and popped a gaudy knitted tea cosy on the pot.

"Would you like a biscuit, dear?" asked the old lady kindly, her hand reaching for the biscuit tin.

"A biscuit would be lovely." David twitched a little in his seat. "Erm, I couldn't possibly take advantage of your W.C. could I?"

"Of course, dear, it's a bit wet for the outside one, so use the bathroom upstairs, dear."

David got up with fake embarrassment on his face. "Up the stairs is it?"

"Yes, door second on the left, do you want me to show you?" the kindly grandmother asked, beginning to rise.

"No don't worry, I'll find it." David put his hand gently on her shoulder and set off out of the living room.

"I'll not pour the tea 'til you return, to keep it warm," she cried after him.

"Thank you," he called back from the foot of the stairs. Once upstairs he closed the bathroom door loudly, but he wasn't inside it, instead he crept into the old woman's bedroom. He went straight into a kneeling position next to the double bed, his hands thrusting under the mattress in search of hidden stashes of cash. The heavy weight of the mattress and bedclothes hampered his efforts, yet in the end he gave it up as a bad job. He turned his attention to the bedside cabinet now and with all the gentleness he could muster, he eased open the dark mahogany door in near silence.

Keith's grandmother stood by the window table. She put the palm of her hand against the tea cosy and pulled it away quick.

"Still hot." Her hand moved down to the table and something caught in the top edge of her peripheral vision. Looking up she saw that the witch, her witch, was spinning around and around like an out of control merry-go-round. Then without any warning or outside interference the witch stopped dead.

"Oh my!" exclaimed the old woman as she realised the witch's broomstick now impossibly pointed upwards, in a direct line up to where her bedroom was located. With a confused mind and not really comprehending it, she bustled off towards the stairs, to tell her young visitor.

"Bingo!" hissed David under his breath, for his hands had uncovered what he'd been looking for. He moved the heavy Household Encyclopaedia out the way and underneath was a surprisingly new strongbox. David reached in and pulled the heavy box out of the bedside cabinet and onto the bed.

"What are you doing in my bedroom, young man?" shrieked the old woman standing in the doorway of the bedroom, blocking off his only escape exit. He had been so overjoyed with his find, that her approach had caught him totally unawares.

David shot to his feet and spun around grabbing the strongbox in both hands.

"What are you doing? That's my money!" the old woman screamed at him.

"Calm down, erm," David faltered, he couldn't talk his way out of this one. It was like Cock-Robin lay dead at his feet, with an arrow in its side and he held the bow.

"Get out of my house. I'll call the police: help!" she screamed like a wailing banshee.

"Get out of my way!" he shouted back at her as he approached the old woman with menace.

"I won't, give me my strongbox!" she stated without a hint of fear. David could see she was getting the upper hand and he was the craven coward.

"Have it then!" With an angry swipe David smashed the sharp edge of the strongbox into the old woman's face with all his might.

Without a cry or gasp she fell lifeless to the floor with a thud. David lowered the strongbox and looked down in cold-sweated shock at the dead woman. The impact of the blow had shattered one eye socket, and scraped one bloodshot eyeball to lie against her squashed nose. Blood was everywhere. David swallowed back his bile and jumped over the corpse onto the landing.

Something like a bullet out of a gun shot up the stairs. The gypsy witch flew directly for his face and all David could do was scream as it imbedded its broomstick deep into his right eye.

David screeched and dropped the strongbox onto his foot, breaking it. His hands went up to his blinded eye, blood and other nastier liquids were running through his fingers. It felt like the witch had flown right out of the back of his skull, so intense was the agony.

Yet even in his marred state he knew he had to get out of this cottage and find a doctor. With his limited eyesight and broken foot he hobbled to the top of the stairs. David prayed to God to save him, yet he should have known: God doesn't help those who help themselves.

David's foot made it to the top step when he heard a rushing sound behind him. He turned his head to see what was coming after him on instinct. Out of the bedroom door flew the vengeful witch, aiming directly at David's remaining eye.

With the last of his life's luck, he managed to catch the witch effigy in both hands just in front of his face.

Yet the momentum caused him to take an involuntary step backwards onto his broken foot, which gave way beneath him. He fell base-over-apex down the hard stairs and was dead before his body hit the bottom step.

The police only found one baffling piece of evidence at the murder scene. An effigy of a green witch on a broomstick, affixed to a pelmet in the living room; its clothes and broomstick were covered in blood.

"What do you think?" Private London asked his companions around the fire.

"Good," Sergeant Kim nodded, deep in thought about the story's macabre meaning.

"It was, but I got a better one," Private Hartnell stated.

"Go for it then, Yank." London held out his hand for the American to begin.

"It kinda goes like this…" Private Hartnell began and the others moved closer to the fire to keep out the night's chill.

Chapter 7

Hartnell's Halloween Story

Around a hundred years ago, in the state of Virginia, there was a great plantation, run and owned for a hundred years by the Chesterton family. William Chesterton had been a big man around town and had been the local mayor on two separate occasions. He was rich, successful and had slaves and servants aplenty.

The only thing he was unlucky in, and which money could not alter, was love. His first wife, a distant English relative, had died five years after they had wed, in childbirth. Neither his pale English rose of a wife nor their son had survived.

William was devastated and became a drinker and threw himself into his business and mayoral duties. So it was a surprise when five years later at the age of thirty-five he tied the knot again.

His wife this time was Susanna, twelve years his junior and like as chalk and cheese to his first wife Anne. She had been a tall, thin, pale faced woman, from well bred English aristocracy. Susanna was a wild, curvier woman of the world; her father had been a local businessman, her mother from a local Indian tribe.

Now Susanna made him happy, no mistake, especially in the marital bed. His face softened again and the red blotches of booze abuse faded away. Yet three years of marriage and endless trying they were still without a child and heir. He loved Susanna to his very core, but he still yearned for the son he had lost with his first wife.

Susanna began to sense this too and came up with a plan. She persuaded her husband to visit her mother's tribe and make a vacation out of it. William was very fond of his servants and creature comforts and took much persuading.

Finally, in their seventh year of marriage with no pregnancy on the horizon, William relented. Even William surprised himself and enjoyed the fishing and hunting. Yet Susanna had visited with other ideas in mind; she consulted the wise old witch-doctor of the tribe. He gave her a draught to give her husband and advised a special place for their marital union.

That night Susanna slipped the draught into his drink and with the flimsiest dresses led him to an ancient and sacred burial hill nearby. Here were burnt the greatest warriors, the wisest chiefs and sage like witch-doctors of the tribe. Here the very earth was made up of their ashes and essences.

That night they made love on that hill with a passion and virility William had never felt before. All night they grappled and grinded naked in the dust, till dawn when they were both spent.

Nine months later a daughter was born to William and Susanna Chesterton. Any disappointment on the child not being a son and heir evaporated when William saw his beautiful baby girl. Never did a father dote on a child more and Lydia Susanna Chesterton had a wonderful childhood, with two loving parents and a whole plantation as her playground.

Even the Civil War, which caused some hardships, did not break up this happy home. William, a major in the Confederate Army, survived the war without a scratch, only to die two years later falling out of an apple tree while playing with his beloved Lydia.

Lydia was devastated and, as she grew into a beautiful young woman, she realised no suitor could ever match up to her lost father. More disaster struck as her mother died in the winter of her eighteenth year; leaving her the wealthiest and most desirable woman in the whole state of Virginia. Now William and Susanna Chesterton raised not a fool for a daughter and she stepped into running the plantation, as if she were born a man.

Her spirit inherited from her mother's side and strength from her father, made her more than a match for any local businessman. She built homes for the former slaves on the plantation and a European style factory and cotton mill as well. By the age of twenty-two a shoe factory was added, and the former plantation became a town within a town.

She was chased by the rich and the poor, the old and the young, but none could break the wall around her heart. There were rumours she used some of her workers as lovers, but Lydia Chesterton reached her thirtieth year a social and marital virgin.

Now the suitors had, well, given up on her, a strange thing happened. A travelling artist with a hint of Indian blood in him came to town and Lydia employed him to paint several portraits of her. His name was 'Luckless' Joe Jenkins and he had the charm and charisma to match his floppy locked looks. His passion was painting and he painted her in her work clothes, then in her riding gear, and then cajoled her into painting her in a beautiful blue evening dress, one that belonged to her mother, as Lydia dressed as much like a man as her full figure could allow.

When the painting was shown to her she fell in love with it. She realised that under the muck and brass she still retained her inherited feminine good looks.

So she employed Jenkins to paint a set of new private paintings that brought out her womanly side. The first painting showed her as a Parisian dancing girl, with tight bodice and feathers, the next as a Greek slave girl with a revealing toga, her hair in curls and obligatory Greek urn. The last he suggested one night in midsummer as they sat on the veranda drinking lemonade: Lady Godiva, naked aside her favourite thoroughbred, a suggestion her wild mother's side jumped at. The setting of the painting led Jenkins to join her buck naked in the nearby river and then her bedroom that night.

Their engagement caused a storm of gossip, excitement and envy throughout the town and most of Southern Virginia. They married on the 5th September that same year at the plantation, which the whole town turned up to. Lydia even gave every one of her workers a week off, paid, as she and her husband headed to Europe for a six month honeymoon, to take in all the culture and art galleries the continent could offer.

In fact, it wasn't 'til April the following year that they returned. Lydia returned to her business empire and Luckless sat about painting the sights and sounds of the Plantation.

Yet Lydia's happy marriage would soon falter. After a business trip to New York, Lydia came home early to find her husband of a year in bed with two of her thirteen-year-old Negro workers. The girls under Luckless' charming sway backed up his every word when poor Lydia was found at the bottom of the grand staircase: her neck broken. A loose piece of stair carpet and a broken shoe heel were blamed and Luckless Jenkins inherited the whole of the plantation and factories. Not that Luckless cared much for the running of his late wife's business. Card games, drinking parties and every woman in town with a pulse became his business.

One by one, as his gambling debts rose too high, a business was sold off until only a year after she died, Lydia's legacy, the Plantation, was the only thing left. Yet as in life, in death Lydia Chesterton had been busy.

A month after her burial: a month which had seen the fiercest of storms to batter Virginia in living memory, a worm found its way through the cheap rotted wood of Lydia's sodden coffin.

Up her once pretty nose it crawled, deeper and deeper burying itself deep into her brain, where it gorged itself on the grey matter inside. A week later it emerged, just different: this worm had turned. So on that day it began its long journey from the family crypt in the grounds towards the grand house. A year it took to make its long, wiggling journey, with so many near misses of feet, birds and other such dangers.

Two days it had waited hidden at the back of Luckless Jenkins' pillow, waiting, sensing, 'till at last the drunken debauchee and his latest whore fell onto the bed in a whisky induced slumber.

Even then the worm patiently waited a quarter of an hour before crawling over the pillow and into Luckless Jenkins' ear. With a vicious, unearthly fury, it began to bury its way deep inside, which was full of wax: enough for a birthday candle. Deeper still the worm burrowed, until wax turned to eardrum and eardrum to gristle.

Luckless Jenkins sat bolt upright in fright. A nightmare about his ex-wife's ghost standing over him, with a blood-dripping axe had shaken him from his deep alcoholic slumber.

He wiped the sweat from his face with the bedcovers and then tasted the dryness of his booze and cigar coated tongue. His splitting headache from ear to ear was just part of his partying territory.

"You ruined my family business," a spiteful feminine voice whispered in his left ear.

"Wha!" Luckless' head shot left in terror, even in the dark gloom of the bedroom, he could see that no one was present.

"It must be the bourbon and remnants of the dream," he thought, the pain and blood pounding in his brain.

"This is no dream, my beloved; this is your wife Lydia." The voice seemed so close to his ear.

Luckless turned to his sleeping companion, who lay naked on her front, all covers crumpled around her legs. She was snoring like some old lush vagabond three times her age; it wasn't her whispering.

"I'm here to kill you," the voice hissed deep inside his brain.

"Argh!" Luckless yelled and smacked the plump rump of his bed companion with all his terrified might.

The woman moaned, swore, then turned over and lapsed back into her boozy dreams.

The pain in Luckless' ear was increasing and he noticed the thick uncomfortable feeling was coming from his left ear.

"I'm in Hell waiting for you, Joe!" the voice in his left ear bellowed loudly this time.

Luckless Joe Jenkins bounded out of bed, dressed only in his shirt and nothing else. He shook his head trying to clear his thoughts, his fingers going to his left ear.

His ear was wet; something was oozing out of his ear hole. His little finger probed gingerly inside, deeper and deeper 'til its tip touched something alien, something that moved of its own accord deep inside his eardrum.

"Boo!" screamed his wife's voice in his ear.

Luckless screamed like a girl of five and ran from the bedroom onto the lit landing of the house. There was blood and brown crud on his shoulder; his words now had descended into 'Mer' sounds. Deeper he tried to probe, but his finger was too big to delve any further.

"Can't get rid of me 'til I get rid of you, Luckless," the Lydia worm hissed in his ear driving him to distraction. His whole head felt alive with pain. He had to get it, her, out, once and for all. An addled notion came to mind, one he would have rationally dismissed.

He ran to Susannah's old sewing room and searched through a cupboard to find the thing he was after.

"You're gonna join me in purgatory soon, Joe!" the voice in his ear laughed.

"No, no!" he laughed in return, yet his laugh was the laugh of the crazed and insane. Out of a sewing box, Luckless pulled out a large knitting needle; he smiled maniacally at his new solution and ran, crouching with pain back into the light of the landing.

Without an ounce of reason he stuck the knitting needle deep into his ear trying to get whatever was lodged inside, out.

"Deeper, Joe, deeper if you want rid of me," the voice hissed and laughed.

"Get out!" Joe screamed the needle going deeper and deeper, the pain from it just merged with the agony that screamed like a saw through the centre of his brain.

"What are you doing, Joe?" a female voice yawned behind him.

Luckless Joe Jenkins jumped out of his skin, tried to turn, but his balance was gone. He fell to his left, hitting his head hard against the balustrade of the grand staircase. It also sent the knitting needle right through the centre of poor old Luckless Joe Jenkins' addled brain.

The naked whore screamed in terror as the needle shot out of his right ear, preceded by a slime and blood covered worm.

Luckless Joe's body slumped to the floor, the voice and pain had suddenly eased. Looking up as his vision began to grow dark, he saw the six foot by four foot portrait he had painted of his late wife in her riding gear. The smile on her face now seemed to him a smirk, something the artist in him wanted to correct.

That was his last thought as his brain died and next to him the pierced worm perished also. Safe in the knowledge that she had got her revenge.

"Revenge," Private London nodded, "always good for a ghost story."

"What you think, Sergeant Kim? Do ya think you can do better?" asked Hartnell.

"I do have one story, my grandfather who lived not far from here used to tell me," the sergeant nodded, trying to recall all the details, in the correct order.

"Then tell away." Private Hartnell offered the South Korean the warmest part of the log, nearest the fire.

"I'm not sure it will scare you, but here it is," Sergeant Kim began.

Chapter 8

Kim's Kumiho Story

Many hundreds of years ago Korea was divided into three Kingdoms. To the north was the Koguryo Kingdom ruled by fair, but strong, Wang (or king in English).

He loved his people and loved the land, trees and mountains and was one of the first Buddhist friendly monarchs. The King and his Queen had three sons and one daughter.

Because he had three heirs that vied for the heirship of the throne, the King doted on his daughter. She gave him only love and wanted nothing further in return, unlike her older brothers. So for a Korean Princess she was given a lot of leeway and would often travel the countryside, visiting newly built Buddhist temples. She also had a love for flowers, especially the white ones that grew in the wooded hills north of the Sang (castle).

The beautiful Princess left the castle one spring morning, with her father's blessing, and headed north to the mountain woods in search of the snow white orchids she cherished. A botanist monk and two guards went as her bodyguards and guides, as the Koguryo Kingdom still had many wild parts to it.

After a lunch in a sunny glade, they continued in good spirits up the hill until they came to a cave. Growing at either side of the cave mouth were two swathes of snow orchids, like nature itself had designed a garden.

Yet nature had not, the dweller in the cave had and she was not pleased when the Princess and monk merrily began digging them up to transplant them to the Princess's royal garden.

Out of the cave sprang an evil spirit, long thought of as legend, even in these ancient times. The monk and Princess scrambled back in fright, as the two guards advanced to protect the princess drawing their swords.

That night as the Princess did not return home for the evening banquet, the Royal parents were worried. Even her squabbling brothers forgot their feuds for the time being, as each, like their father, doted on their younger sister. In fact, the King had to practically bar the gates to stop them riding off into the night to find her.

It could just be that her daughter wished to watch the stars or forgot the time and distance she had travelled, suggested the Queen.

Or it was a trap by the Southern Kingdoms to lure the King and Princess into an ambush, warned the King of Koguryo. Either way, she had the monk and guards to protect her, and they would begin their search at first light.

The youngest son would remain at the castle to protect the Queen and Kingdom, if this was indeed a trap to assassinate the King and his heirs. The eldest son would head east, the middle son west and the King and his men would head north.

For three days and nights they searched, but not even the slightest trace of her could be found. With heavy hearts they returned on the fourth day to the castle, the Queen broke down in tears and the youngest son, who had remained behind, wept openly. The Kingdom of Koguryo suddenly became a garden without any blooms or birdsong.

A week, then weeks, then a month went by with no news and the Royal family feared the worst. The King became desperate and sent personal pleas to the Kings of Shilla and Paekcha for information on his daughter's whereabouts. Just in case she had been kidnapped for ransoming. The Kings would normally be enraged by such suggested allegations, but both had daughters too and empathised with the other King's loss.

In an unprecedented act they swore an oath that if the Princess turned up in their Kingdoms, she would get a swift and safe escort home.

Another month passed without any news, so the desperate King ordered a proclamation to all corners of his realm. Any man who found his daughter alive would win his weight in gold and his daughter's hand in marriage.

Suddenly fifty percent of the male populace of the Kingdom was mobilised into finding the Princess. Most out of their love for the Princess and respect of the King, others out of lust and greed.

One such man, we shall call him Kunin, wanted the gold first and a beautiful wife second. His grandfather had been a general many years ago, yet an act of cowardice had blighted his once lofty career. He had grown too fond of his men and refused to send them into a battle, where he knew even a victory would mean the loss of two thirds of his men. His men were alive, but he was disgraced and his rank and lands taken away. His son bore the shame and the family had to become farmers to survive. When he was eighteen Kunin's father died working the land, his grandfather had already taken his own life many moons ago.

The day after his father's funeral, his mother found her son dressed in his grandfather's armour and weapons. She wept as he told her farming would not kill him. He would regain the family's wealth and honour and seek his fortune in the world. From that day his name was Kunin (soldier) and he travelled the three Kingdoms in search of employment as a mercenary.

He was twenty-one and scarred and hardened by battle when he heard of the King's proclamation. He swore he would be the one to find the Princess and regain his family's honour. Taking the gold and Princess from the King who stripped his family of its status, spurred him on further.

A month into his search he found himself in the mountains to the north of the Kingdom. It was midsummer and his horse trod lazily up the wooded slope. The sun shone in dapples through the tall trees and flies buzzed around the sweaty man and horse.

Both man and beast were hot and weary and Kunin decided to make an early camp at the next clearing. Ten minutes later they came to a gladed area and Kunin slid, almost fell, off his horse. He unsaddled his trusty animal and fed and watered it before himself.

So it was not until he sat cross-legged on the floor to eat, he noticed as he chewed the remains of a three month old camp fire. Suddenly, with renewed vigour he crawled around the glade on his hands and knees, searching for further evidence. He found a wooden bowl with the mark of the royal household on it by a small brook. Plus evidence of horses, a food sack and a brush and a latrine twenty or so feet away.

He found no evidence of a struggle, but this had been the luckiest and most significant clue to the Princess's whereabouts since he had begun. He knew of the Princess's love of plants, so he would camp here tonight then search for flowers in the morning. He may have a chance of finding out what happened to her in the cooler morning.

He and his mount awoke refreshed in the early morning light and after a hurried breakfast they set off. Kunin led his horse by a rope through the bridle so he could examine the ground and vegetation ahead for clues: without fear of his horse trampling them.

By midmorning they had come to a clearing, ahead was a shadowy cave mouth, with two swathes of almost cultivated · vegetation on either side of the cave. Kunin's farmer's upbringing knew these plants were the famous snow orchids by the foliage alone.

Tying his horse to a tree, Kunin drew his sword and crept slowly up to the cave's entrance. Peering in, he could see, not far in, a pile of bones with two skulls atop. Next to them were two sets of armour, but no weapons: most likely the remains of the two guard escort.

Suddenly from deep within the cave came a roar and Kunin back-pedalled as a tall, furious, white-furred bear came towards him out of the darkness. Kunin heard his horse scream in fright and pull at her rope as the bear attacked the lone warrior. Kunin had little time for thought as the tall bear bore down on him. Kunin lifted his blade above his head and with both hands pushed the sword into the bear's snarling mouth. The keen steel went up through the palate of the bear's mouth, slicing through its brain and out the top of its skull.

Kunin only winded himself as he dove and rolled from under the dying beast, as its bulky frame crashed to the ground, dead.

He was bent, his boot on the bear's head, retrieving his weapon, when a figure ran out of the cave. Kunin raised his bloody blade and then lowered it in shock as the Princess ran into his arms.

"You saved me from the beast, it killed my escort and kept me prisoner three very long months!"

Kunin could not help but be taken with the Princess's beauty and all thoughts of gold and revenge temporarily left his mind.

"You're safe now, come let me take you home."

Yet they had to walk as Kunin's mount had bolted during the fight with the white bear and was never seen again.

Three days later Kunin proudly walked through the gates of the castle with the beautiful Princess at his side. Happy crowds gathered at the roadside and followed their progress.

Ahead stood the smiling King, Queen and Princes, overjoyed at their daughter's/sister's safe return.

"I love you," whispered Kunin to the Princess as they approached the royal family.

"Do you?" the Princess questioned. "Then promise to love me no matter what."

"I promise with all my heart." The lone warrior smiled as they reached the royal entourage.

The Princess rushed into her family's arms and a great cheer went up around the castle.

Presently the King came up to Kunin and laid a hand on his shoulder, "Thank you for rescuing my only daughter, so you shall have your weight in gold and more precious, my daughter's hand in marriage."

Kunin smiled, his family honour was now restored, he was rich and to marry the most beautiful woman in all Korea. That should be our happy ending to this tale, but it isn't.

The wedding of the Royal Princess and Kunin lasted all day and when the new wedded pair were finally alone in their marital bed chamber they felt exhausted. Kunin fell upon the bed full of joy, rice wine and food, watching his beautiful bride approach the low bed.

"Do you remember you promised with your heart to love me, no matter what?" the Princess asked, slowly disrobing from her ceremonial clothes.

"I do," said Kunin and smiled at the Princess's love talk.

"Then let us see if you are a man of honour," the Princess grinned, but with an unvirginal twinkle in her brown irises.

The Princess let her final wrapping of silk flutter to the floor and stood before her new husband naked.

Kunin's smiling lips dropped open to form a stunned O shape. It wasn't the dowdy hair that spread up like brown fur from her vagina, that paralysed him with shock, but the three sets of small, perky breasts that covered her chest, abdomen and tummy.

"Love me, Kunin," the Princess creature spoke in a raspy whisper.

"No!" Kunin wailed and grabbed his ceremonial dagger which still hung at his bejewelled belt and stabbed the creature in the side as it lent over him.

Kunin turned and scrambled over to the other side of the bed, but was not quick enough to escape the clawing attack on his back. Kunin fell to the floor, his wedding clothes on his back in shreds, blood running from the wounds.

"Help!" he screamed as the Princess creature rounded the bed. Yet it was not the Princess whom he had wed, but a creature born out of primeval nightmares. The Princess's beautiful face had gone, replaced by that of a vixen fox, her body entirely covered in browny-ginger and white fur. Yet this five foot fox had not one but many tails, that undulated like snakes behind her.

"Kumiho," Kunin whispered as the nine-tailed fox bore down on him.

"Yes," the Kumiho hissed and brought one powerful hind leg down on the warrior's left leg, breaking it with ease.

Kunin screamed in agony as the creature laughed. Suddenly the door flew open and in entered the King and his sons armed with swords, fearing some ill had befallen their daughter/sister. Seeing it was outnumbered and out of its usual safe habitat, the injured Kumiho crashed through the nearest window and bounded with inhuman agility, from wall to wall until it had fled the castle.

The duped husband's wounds were tended and the King made him draw a map of where the Kumiho's cave was. Kunin begged to go with them, but with his injuries he could not get out of bed.

That night the King, his three sons and a troop of guards galloped from the castle, making all haste for the Kumiho's lair. Kunin lay in his bed on his side and wept; he had brought the creature to the castle: what fate would befall him on the King's return?

By morning the King's troops had reached the camp that both his daughter had stayed at and Kunin had later found. A low-lying mist enveloped the hilly forest as he, his sons and his men dismounted. Leaving two men to guard the horses, they proceeded on foot through the mist.

At last they came to the clearing and the entrance to the cave. They were about to enter, when a wailing moan was heard from inside and a female figure rushed out. She was naked, yet covered in dark mud and bits of fur, her fingers like talons reached out before her and her face was that of the Princess.

"Kumiho!" shouted the youngest Prince in fear as it ran towards the King, its eyes wild with madness. With a swift strike the King sliced off the mad creature's head, before it could attack him.

The King and his entourage lit some torches and plunged into the dark cave. They passed the bones and armour of his daughter's guards. Further and deeper into the cave they crept until they came to the Kumiho's lair. The place was piled high with human remains and treasures they had once possessed.

In an antechamber they found four posts imbedded deep into the floor. Two were empty, one had rope hanging from it, but the last had a pale occupant on its knees in filth, tied to it.

It was the monk and he was still alive, yet very malnourished and thin.

"Where is my daughter?" the King demanded not too gently.

"She gnawed through her bonds, have you not seen her? She has only just escaped," spoke the Buddhist monk.

The King fell to his knees in anguish. "What have I done?" he wailed: which echoed through the Kumiho's cave.

The opening of his chamber door woke Kunin from his slumber. As his eyes cleared he saw the Queen standing at his bed chamber door, a strange startled look on her worried face.

Suddenly her head whipped violently around with a sickening crack, until she could look at her own back. Pain racked his body as he sat up in bed, as the Queen's body fell to the floor dead. Into the room stepped his bride, once more in her almost human form.

Without a glance she stepped over the twitching corpse and moved next to the bed. A beautiful and serene look on her delicate face.

"What do you want, spirit?" the warrior asked in mortal fear.

"What rightfully belongs to me." The Princess/Kumiho smiled and plunged her hand through her husband's ribcage and plucked out his heart.

The last image Kunin ever saw was the unimaginable sight of the Kumiho devouring his still-beating heart.

"Bloody hell," Private London stated, "that was good."

"Good one, Sarge," Private Hartnell nodded in agreement.

"Look at the time," Sergeant Kim glanced at his watch, "our watch ended ten minutes ago."

"Time flies when you're being scared witless." London forced a smile; the cold was biting at his spine like a bitch.

"I will wake Regimental Sergeant Major McConnell." Sergeant Kim Jun Ho rose and headed for the trucks.

"A-Men to that." Private Hartnell rose stiffly and stretched his back.

"I just hope I sleep now and don't wake up with the screaming abdabs," Private Robert London said to himself, scanning the dark surrounding woods.

Chapter 9

The Bridge

The cold night passed much slower for RSM McConnell's and Sergeant Dempsey's guard duties. The day dawned even colder still, if that were possible and Private McClaren, who had been on the last guard duty, found his personal water bottle frozen near solid.

Dempsey raised the first and second watches from their slumbers in the trucks and set them about building up the fire and cooking a hot breakfast: plus coffee.

He wrapped on the tailgate of the first (officers') truck with the butt of his M1 carbine.

Captain Woodholme-Browne's head poked around the canopy flap. "Morning Sergeant Dempsey, cold one eh?" he smiled.

"Yes, Captain," the sergeant nodded politely, "did you sleep ok, sir?"

"Splendidly, Sergeant," the captain nodded and an awkward silence followed.

"I better check the other trucks," Sergeant Dempsey said, just to say anything at all.

"Good show," the captain nodded, "we'll be out for breakfast in a jiffy."

The captain's head disappeared into the truck again, as the sergeant trudged off wondering which planet officers really come from.

The men were fed, packed up and ready to roll by 08:00 hours. The smiling captain gave the word and Private London put the lead truck into gear and led the convoy onwards and upwards along the dirt road. Fourteen minutes later the three US army trucks came to a circular clearing near a rocky outcrop. At the other side of the ridgeway masked, by a few trees, was the rickety looking rope bridge.

The men quickly vacated the trucks, carrying their weapons.

"Now gather around, men," Captain Woodholme-Browne called to his United Nations troops. Grumbling from the icy winds that cut across the exposed hillside, the men made a semi-circle around the captain

"Now men, we have two main objectives: to check out the state of the rope bridge and evaluate the possibility of replacing it with something more military-friendly." The captain pointed across the dirt road towards the rope bridge.

"Secondly once we have made our initial survey we will proceed onto the plateau itself. With Sergeant Kim's help try and locate a similar bridge, connecting the plateau in a north-westerly direction with our forces, is the next objective."

"What happens after dat?" Corporal Baker asked from the middle of the huddle.

"Once we have surveyed the second bridge we'll retrace our steps and report back to HQ," the captain answered succinctly.

"Any questions?" Lieutenant Samuels asked clapping his cold, gloved hands together.

Nobody answered.

"Okay, let's get to work!" Sergeant Dempsey led his men back to the trucks, to unload their equipment.

"What shall we do, sir?" The RSM asked, pointing to Sergeant Kim and the two British drivers.

"Erm, I suggest we have someone to guard the trucks and others at the rope bridge to deal with any possible hostile incursions: how does that sound?" the captain suggested. He didn't really want to be bothered with military protocol now there was some proper engineering work to be done.

"Like a proper officer, sir," the RSM replied with a deadpan face.

The captain thought for a second as the RSM saluted and marched off to talk to his men. He wasn't sure if he had just been insulted or praised. Captain Woodholme-Browne shrugged it off; he was in his element now and hurried over to the trees to find Lieutenant Samuels.

"What do you think, Sergeant Kim?" the RSM asked, surveying the site with a military, not mechanical eye.

"Not a good position," the sergeant stated, pointing at the evergreen covered rocky outcrop.

"Aye I agree, laddie, the enemy could get at us from all points of the compass." The RSM shook his head.

"Very exposed," the sergeant added.

"Okay, take London here and set up a look-out position on that ridge." The RSM pointed up the rocky outcrop. "You should be able to see anyone coming up the roads or hill before we do up there."

The sergeant hesitated, he would rather be alone up there, but he had at least made a connection with the western man during their ghost story session last night.

"Problem, Sergeant?" the RSM asked, watching the South Korean soldier intently.

"No, Regimental Sergeant Major Mac-Connell," the sergeant bowed quickly, to show his compliance with the order.

"McClaren will guard the trucks, while I keep an eye on the engineers' backs. Everyone clear on what to do?"

"Yes, Sergeant Major, or Regimental Sergeant Major," the three men replied.

"Oh, Sergeant Kim, get Sergeant Dempsey to kit you out with one of those yank hand-held walkie-talkies before you leave."

"I will," bowed the South Korean sergeant again.

"Right then girls, to yer posts now!" the RSM ordered and the four infantry men headed off in different directions, as ordered.

It took fifteen minutes for Kim and London to climb up and around to their position. It was a great observation position, with views of the road each way, the survey site and was clear of any vegetation leading up to the ridge. Which also meant it was even colder than the road below.

The two soldiers settled in as best they could with some rocks breaking the icy winds from the sides, but not from behind. Private London had his pixie-hat over his helmet, a body warmer, a pullover, his combat jacket, shirt and vest underneath, mittens that you could flip off your fingers quickly to fire your rifle. Yet it was your legs that were more exposed with only long johns and fatigue trousers, that was where he lost his warmth.

Old snow, turned to solid ice, clung to rocky outcrops of the ridge, as the two men kept a watchful eye.

Sergeant Kim scanned the plateau with his borrowed US Military issue binoculars, his rifle propped up on the rocks close at hand. A pack with the walkie-talkie on top divided him from Private London, who clung to his No 5 .303 rifle like it was a portable radiator.

Apart from the US engineers busy at work with theodolites and poles, there was no movement on the brown hills.

The plateau itself seemed evergreen and lush through the binoculars. Its elevation sloped downwards from the other end of the rope bridge, so nothing but the green canopy of trees could be seen, even from the ridge's higher position.

Down by the rope bridge, Captain Ashley Woodholme-Browne had a wide smile of satisfaction on his face. The face of the hill and the plateau across the span of the rope bridge were solid rock and they had already identified a place where a steel sapper bridge could be built.

The US engineers had tested and pulled at the rope bridge, which only lost one plank as a result. Now they had to put a man across.

"Right then, Lieutenant, I think it's time for a little stroll," the captain said, gathering up his nerve to cross the old rope and plank bridge.

"Maybe I should cross first, sir, to recce out the other side?" RSM McConnell rushed over to his superior, Sten gun at the ready.

"Lucky I'm armed also," the captain stated pulling his Enfield revolver from its leather holster and walking towards the first rung.

"Are you sure you want to go first, Ashley?" asked Lieutenant Samuels, who was standing next to the posts that the bridge was secured too.

"Quite sure," the captain smiled and put one foot on the bridge, which swiftly sunk a foot lower as he put his full weight upon it.

He went forward another five steps; the wind and his weight made the thing creak and wobble. The captain quickly holstered his revolver again, he needed both hands for this job and, grabbing both sets of guide ropes, on either side of him, he proceeded.

The dip once you got to the middle was so pronounced that the other half of his crossing was quite a calf-aching struggle. Then, feeling exhilarated and cold from the icy North Korean winds, he was across.

Captain Woodholme-Browne drew his revolver again and beckoned for the RSM to come over. He watched as the stout Scottish Argyll stomped across the bridge, Sten gun in one hand, the other on the rope rail.

What the captain had failed to realise was that he was the first western man ever to set foot on the Yŏu plateau.

The RSM was now across and moved forward to reconnoitre the surrounding area. A path opened up twenty feet away, which suddenly fell away to a dell fifteen feet down a slope.

The RSM approached the slope, but could not see anything but the path, trees and bushes; the air was deathly quiet.

"Right, Sergeant Dempsey, send a couple of chaps across to make sure the bridge and supports this end are up to the job!" the captain shouted across the chasm, his voice slightly broken by the wind.

RSM McConnell frowned at the captain's back, his echoed call across the chasm would have alerted any enemy soldiers to their position.

Privates Perez and O'Keefe came across next, encumbered with heavy packs of equipment and extra rope to secure the rope bridge.

"Right then, RSM McConnell, we better sort out how to proceed with the next part of our little expedition." The captain stretched out his back and clapped his gloved hands together.

"Yes, sir," the RSM nodded, intrigued as to how the captain intended on proceeding.

"I want an officers' and NCOs' meeting in twenty minutes. Get Private Hartnell to haul his radio up to the ridge, relieve Sergeant Kim and have him send the first coded message," the captain ordered, remembering every detail of his orders.

"Yes, sir." The RSM walked back across the bridge, impressed so far with the Royal Engineer captain's orders.

"Everything okay Sergeant Major McConnell?" Lieutenant Samuels asked as the RSM returned from across the bridge.

"Aye, sir, peachy." He then proceeded to relay the captain's orders to the lieutenant and let him order his own men about.

"Hey, son, you look colder than an Eskimo in Alaska eating a Popsicle in winter," Private Hartnell stated to the shivering London as he replaced Sergeant Kim on the ridge; his Garland rifle and radio slung over his back.

"If I'm an ice lolly, who are you then, the seventh cavalry?" Private London retorted in a friendly manner through chattering teeth.

"I'm just the Good Samaritan sent to freeze with you," Hartnell smiled unslinging his rifle and taking the radio off his back.

"If you were such a Good Samaritan, cowboy, you'd have brought up a steaming mug of Rosie-Lee and a bacon sarnie," London joked, putting down the binoculars on the ground next to him.

"Hell, London, if I could understand what you were gabbing about, I might have!" Hartnell shivered and put down the large green canvas-covered radio carefully on a flat outcrop.

Private London laughed in spite of the numbness of his feet and Private Hartnell joined in.

"So what's going on down there and when am I going to be relieved?" London asked, flapping his gloved hands onto his arms to keep warm.

"We are going across the bridge I guess," Hartnell shrugged. "Anyway I gotta send the message for the Captain ASAP."

London took up his binoculars to scan the area again, as Hartnell set up his radio and antenna.

A hiss and a whistle caused London to put down his field glasses again and watch the engineer cum radioman at work. Hartnell crouched next to his large radio, a pair of earphones on and a mic to his lips.

"This is Centurion calling Rome, Centurion calling Rome, are you receiving? Over," Private Hartnell spoke the expedition's call sign and the HQ's into the mic.

"This is Centurion calling Rome, come in Rome." he continued.

"This is Rome, proceed with you message Centurion we can hear you loud and clear," the radio operator at the US 24th Division's Forward HQ in Sinanju replied.

"Roger that, Rome. We have found the picnic table and chair one is in good order; I repeat we have found the picnic table and chair one is in good order, over."

"Message received, Centurion. Now proceed with caution with all the cutlery to chair two, over."

"Message received and understood, Rome. I will inform the head waiter immediately, over. This is Centurion signing off, over."

"Roger that, Centurion, and good luck. Rome out."

Hartnell turned off the radio set and took off his earphones.

"What does that all mean?" London asked, the thought of tables and cutlery made his stomach rumble.

"I think it means we are going for a long walk across that there bridge," Hartnell replied pulling a packet of smokes from his breast coat pocket. He offered one to London, who flipped off his left glove to take a cigarette.

"Not off a short plank then?" London half asked, leaning forward with cupped hands so Hartnell could light his fag, with a wind-stuttering lighter.

"Nope, whatever you said in Limey speak," Hartnell replied bemused.

"Suppose you have no idea what Shanks's pony means then?" Private London puffed on his cigarette, which felt so good in the cold.

"I know you're English, London. But do you ever speak English?" Hartnell guffawed in a jovial way, as he lit up his cigarette.

"Pardon!" London laughed loudly and Hartnell joined in.

"Righty-ho, we have received the order to proceed with all available men across the Yoŭ plateau and find that second bridge," Captain Woodholme-Browne explained to Lieutenant Samuels and the three sergeants present.

"Begging your pardon, surely we will be leaving two or three to guard the trucks, sir?" RSM McConnell interjected.

"Normally I would, RSM, but we are not even up to platoon strength here and if we ran into trouble on the plateau or the three guarding the trucks were attacked with any strength, we'd all be up the swannie," the captain thoughtfully replied with authority.

The RSM nodded, the situation was far from ideal.

"We just have to camouflage the trucks as best we can," Lieutenant Samuels said.

"I spotted a deep gully beside the road not far back. We could back the deuces into there and fell some trees to camouflage them," suggested Sergeant Dempsey, thumbing back along the road.

"Sounds like a plan," Lieutenant Samuels nodded and clapped Dempsey on the shoulder.

"Right then, it's 11:00 now, so we need to off-load the ammo, gear and supplies we need for our trip. Lieutenant, you're in charge of that. Sergeant Dempsey, RSM McConnell and the other drivers will then hide the trucks as best they can. Meanwhile we'll get lunch going early and head off at say 12:30," the captain explained his orders.

"Sergeant Kim, I want you to scout out the immediate area across the bridge. You have one hour, I want you back here at twelve hundred hours for lunch, understood?"

"Sonsaengnim," the South Korean sergeant bowed and un-slung his Garland rifle.

"Any questions?" the captain asked, looking around at his men, no one replied. "Right then, let's get to work."

The soldiers split up, with everyone heading in various directions. The captain pulled his scarf up over his mouth and headed over to the bridge.

Like military clockwork the truck detail and Sergeant Kim returned to camp near on 12:00 hours. The engineers had rustled up a warm meal, probably their last for a day or so. Sergeant Kim reported no sign of enemy activity during his reconnoitre, in fact no sign of life at all. There was a path, but it was very overgrown and no one had seemed to have trod it in a long time.

At 12:30 hours they carefully crossed the rope bridge one by one, carrying packs, tents, a theodolite and other equipment, including the radio. The wind whipped across the chasm, its wind chill factor sending the temperature on the bridge to fifteen degrees below freezing. It was hair-raising to the men who had a thing about heights, but all crossed safely onto the Yŏu plateau without major incident.

Sergeant Kim took the lead with RSM McConnell, Captain Woodholme-Browne and Lieutenant Samuels following. Private McClaren with his rifle at the ready, walked in the middle of the pack-laden engineers while the veteran Sergeant Dempsey and Private London brought up the rear.

Once down the slope and into the dell, they all felt fifteen degrees warmer as the dense evergreen trees and bushes kept out the icy North Korean wind.

Even though they were glad to get the wind off their backs, all chatter stopped. Even Baker and O'Keefe's joking and bitching ended, the mission had entered its most dangerous stage. They were deep into no man's land now and who knew if all of them would make it back from the Yŏu plateau.

Chapter 10

The Temple

Sergeant Kim led the way, sometimes having to use his bayonet to clear the overgrown path he was leading them on. This, even for Kim Jun Ho, was uncharted territory; his village had been at the bottom of the brown hills. His family had left it when he was twelve years old, a year into the Second World War. They had moved south to look for warmer winters and work for his father. They had always meant to return one day, but at the end of the war the country had been divided in two.

Kim had never expected to see his old homeland again, but here he was in a place of superstitious rumour, that everyone nearby and for miles around shunned. He was a man now, an educated one, once a teacher of English, now a sergeant in the Republic of Korea army. What he did notice and kept to himself was the lack of birds and beasts, but that was because it was winter, wasn't it?

They soon reached the edge of where his scouting mission had led him. The terrain had slightly sloped ahead of them, but the dense evergreen and scrubs kept the way ahead secret until you were twenty feet or so away.

Still they followed the path, which according to the aerial photos, was leading them across the plateau towards the site of the second bridge.

Ten minutes later Sergeant Kim noticed the trees ahead were thinning out and more sky could be seen through the canopy above.

He raised his hand to halt those behind him, only the RSM followed at a distance as Sergeant Kim advanced to check out the terrain ahead.

The tree line ahead was thinning out and another tree line further ahead could be seen. Something didn't feel or look right to his keen eyes; it was not until he reached the edge of the tree line that he could see the reason.

A large dell the size of a football pitch, yet round like a bowl, like Buddha himself had come down and scooped away the earth with his hand, sat in the woods before him. Evergreen trees and conifers had been grown on purpose, it seemed, near horizontally at the rim of the dell. They ringed the sides and seemed to act as an ancient camouflage to protect the dell from aerial inspection.

A path three yards across led circling downwards. A noise behind caused Kim Jun Ho to spin round, his American made rifle at the ready.

Yet it was only the British RSM, holding a position at the tree line, his Sten gun at the ready. The RSM signalled that he was going to hold position with a hand signal and knelt next to a tree.

Kim nodded and began to move down the path to see what the overhanging trees and foliage covered. It only took him a few steps before he could see, hidden away from the world, a grey stone temple. It looked ancient and had seen better days as some of the structure was in ruins.

The further he descended into the dell, the stranger the place got. At the bottom of the path, another circular path led up the other side. Where both parts levelled out to the bottom of the dell, there stood some astounding carved stones.

Astounding to Kim because they were Tolharubang (grandfather) stones, carved out of black volcanic rock. Yet there was no such rock for hundreds of miles, they, unlike the stone temple, had weathered the years considerably better.

Kim looked from the fat stone guardians to the ground before the temple. He raised his rifle to his shoulder. The ground had been cultivated and some vegetable shoots still could be seen and the square patches of earth and bamboo canes.

A trimmed and lush green grass path led to the steps of the temple. Which itself seemed from another time or place; it had touches of various religions and cultures about it. Not a Buddhist temple, yet it had some carvings of Buddha in the walls, not quite the wooden pagoda structure or even a Confucian look about it. It seemed older than both religions and Sergeant Kim felt like he was walking into a dream somehow. It had spiral towers at each corner and the main and more maintained part of the temple was round, with a spire roof unlike any religious building he had ever seen in Korea.

The steps were well trodden and led up to an open entrance, where two fierce looking long-toothed warriors were carved, in a dance fight with long swords.

Kim looked up the path he had come to see RSM McConnell, followed by the English captain, Private London, Sergeant Dempsey and PFC Perez armed with his Browning Automatic Rifle (BAR).

Dempsey and Perez took up positions across the dell beside the other Tolharubang stone.

"I thought you might need a little covering fire," smiled the tall, handsome captain, his revolver held up at his right cheek.

"What is this place?" Private London whispered, gazing at the ancient temple.

"I think there may be someone inside," Sergeant Kim said to the captain and RSM.

"Have you seen anyone?" McConnell asked, scanning the rim of the bowl for an enemy ambush.

"No, but the garden is well tended and there is a smell of burning incense in the breeze," Kim explained.

"Well it's your show, Sergeant Kim, as it's a Korean place of religion, what is the plan?" Captain Woodholme-Browne said thoughtfully, he was here to scout out a bridge, not desecrate ancient Korean temples.

"With your permission, Captain, I will scout the temple out, if you would cover me from here." Kim pointed at the two positions by the volcanic carved stones.

The captain, RSM and private smiled, warming to the brave little South Korean sergeant.

"Go ahead, Sergeant Kim," the captain ordered and aimed his revolver at the temple, marvelling at its structure and design.

Kim hugged his Garland rifle to his stomach and ran towards the temple in a crouch, circling round from the right.

Meanwhile, Lieutenant Samuels, Corporal Baker and the rest of the party guarded the survey equipment at the tree line above the sunken temple.

Having drawn no enemy fire Sergeant Kim shouldered his rifle and climbed up the side of the temple onto a balcony. This avoided the steps that were visible from the entrance, but put him on the same level.

With his rifle back in his hands he moved swiftly forward to the wide open entrance itself. He peered around the corner and saw a long corridor ending in a circular room. The heart of the temple itself, Kim presumed.

Feeling his pulse thumping in his neck, Sergeant Kim took a deep breath and, leading with his rifle, entered the shadowy confines of the mysterious temple. The walls of the stone corridor were covered with copper sheets; beaten into pictures depicting battles between men, women and evil spirits.

The smell of the incense made his nose wrinkle as he slowly proceeded, step, by silent step into the shadows. The temple felt so warm compared to the biting cold outside; ahead now in the circular temple was candlelight and the sudden movement of a figure.

Sergeant Kim Jun Ho raised his rifle and almost let off a shot. He steadied his nerves and his combat experience came to the fore again. Surely an enemy would have opened fire on him by now, so he took a brave decision.

"Noogoo-seyo (Who's there)?" he called in Korean, moving forward, his rifle ready at his shoulder.

"Chom-needa (it's me)," came a woman's voice from the temple's core.

"Who is that (Noogoo got-eemneekko)?" Sergeant Kim followed up in Korean, his army boots entering the threshold of the circular inner temple.

"The last Mudang of this temple," spoke a Korean woman in her sixties, dressed in white, as she stepped from behind a statue.

"Are you the only Shaman here?" asked Kim in his native tongue, as he looked around at the strange idols and strips of white cloth that hung from the ceiling.

"Yes," spoke the Mudang, banging a large drum next to her. "Welcome Kim Jun Ho."

"How do you know my name and what are you doing here, on this plateau?" Kim asked, his Buddhist hackles raising a little, Mudangs were the lowest form of religion to him.

The little old woman cackled, "You look at me like something an ox shits from its arse, but you'll need my help soon, soldier."

"Stay here, witch." Sergeant Kim pointed his rifle at her, and then retreated back up the corridor onto the temple's outside balcony.

Seeing the sergeant was all right, Captain Woodholme-Browne and the rest of his men moved forward, guns raised but feeling a little more relaxed.

"Any signs of life, old chap?" the captain asked, moving up the steps to meet the South Korean Sergeant.

"Just a mad old woman, she says she's alone and I've not seen anyone else," the sergeant reported.

"What's she doing alone out here?" the captain quizzed.

"She is a Mudang, what your culture would call a fortune teller I suppose. No harm in her, she's just a shaman who talks to the spirits; I don't have much time for them myself," Sergeant Kim explained, but not the reasons why he had a deep felt hatred of Shamanism and Mudangs.

"What shall we do with her then?" the RSM asked both Sergeant Kim and the captain.

"Well we cannot take her with us, what do you suggest Sergeant Kim?" the captain asked for an opinion.

"I think we should search the temple, just in case and then leave her here to die of old age." The sergeant lifted up his rifle and went back inside to question the Mudang again.

"What's got his goat?" Private London said aloud.

"I dunno, but those gypsy fortune tellers out on Connie Island give me da creeps too," Sergeant Dempsey stated and followed Kim into the temple.

"Private Perez, better tell Left-tenant Samuels and the rest of the men to join us down here, off you go," the captain ordered.

The New Mexico born engineer saluted and hurried off to tell his lieutenant.

"Right then, RSM, let's explore this beautiful temple." The captain moved to touch the old stone with his hand.

"Beautiful?" McConnell looked around at the falling down structure, with strange carved figurines and statues. "If you say so, sir."

"What are you doing here?" Sergeant Kim asked the Mudang in Korean.

"Ha, I should be asking you that, you are the trespasser here, soldier boy," the old woman cackled, as she lit a set of candles.

Captain Woodholme-Browne and Lieutenant Samuels watched on as the two Koreans spoke. The captain loved the rhythms and cadences of different languages being spoken. English seemed such a slow and languid language compared to the fast, almost snapping bite of Korean.

"Just tell me who you are and what you and your temple are doing here and we will leave you in peace." Sergeant Kim tried to reason with the evasive woman.

"Peace, pah!" She actually spat on the floor. "I will only have peace after death." The shaman walked over to the first set of white cloth hanging from the brass hooks in the ceiling.

"There is a war on; the North Korean Army won't treat you as well as us," Sergeant Kim tried to explain, hoping to get some sense out of her.

Standing under the first hanging length of cloth she grabbed each bottom corner with her hands and ripped the entire length of the cloth into two pieces.

"Why is she doing that?" Lieutenant Samuels asked; this was wasting mission time.

"It means someone is about to die, so the shaman believe. She's just doing it to try and scare us off, I think," Sergeant Kim explained to the two officers.

"The North Korean Army have more sense than to come here. You and the other foreigners should leave before you cross the boundaries into her domain. She kills to live." The Mudang ripped another strip of cloth that hung from the ceiling.

"And who is she?"

"The evil she spirit trapped on this ancient plateau long ago. Don't you remember the legends of your village Kim Jun Ho?" She smiled and moved to rip another cloth.

"Will you stop that?" Sergeant Kim pleaded; the tearing sound was unnerving him.

"Deaths won't stop because of me, young man; you will seek me out in the end, as did your sister."

To the captain's and Lieutenant's horror, Sergeant Kim smacked the old woman across the face with the back of his hand, sending her sprawling to the floor.

"Sergeant Kim, restrain yourself!" the captain shouted, pulling the sergeant away from the fallen woman.

Lieutenant Samuels helped the Mudang to her feet as blood trickled from a nose bleed onto her white robes.

"We do not attack civilians, get out, we are leaving. Left-tenant, get him out of here and get the men ready to move out. We've wasted enough time already," Captain Woodholme-Browne shouted angrily.

"Yes, sir," Lieutenant Samuels replied and showed the shamed sergeant from the temple.

"You will be back Jun Ho, begging for help, that I promise. Do not pass the warning signs. You will only find death!" the old woman called after the retreating sergeant.

The captain stood before the old woman and bowed. "I'm so sorry about that, he will be on a charge when we return to base."

The Mudang looked at him sadly, her eyes sad and moist with tears. She grabbed the captain's right hand in both of hers and pleaded in Korean, "Twe-dawra-gada, ul choshimhada Kumiho! (Go back, beware of Kumiho!)"

"I am so sorry he hit you."

"Twe-dawra-gada!"

"I cannot understand you," the captain pulled his hand free, "I am sorry."

The captain turned on his heel and left the Mudang screeching after him, her wailing voice echoing up the corridor that led to the entrance of the temple.

"Kumiho!" was her last wailing cry, before she beat at her breasts and fell to the temple floor in an exhausted, emotional heap.

"Sergeant Major McConnell, let's get moving, I want to get to that bridge by nightfall."

"Yes, sir," RSM McConnell turned to the men, "move ya fat lazy arses, come on!"

Sergeant Kim stood at the bottom of the path leading up and out of the bowl the temple sat in. He glared at the Grandfather stones, with disgust, thinking about the shame his family had endured when his sister had left to become a Mudang. The shame that caused his father to uproot them from their family village and head south to escape the mocking laughs. How many beatings had his school friends measured out on him, because of his shaman older sister?

"Sergeant Kim, a word please?" Captain Woodholme-Browne asked, swimming with rage as he approached the South Korean sergeant. "Can you please explain to me why you struck an unarmed female civilian back there?"

Sergeant Kim looked up at the tall captain with shame on his face. "I am so sorry, Captain, it will not happen again." The sergeant lowered his eyes in subjugation, hoping that that would bring the matter to a close.

"I should hope not," scalded the captain, "but why did you do it?"

"She…" Kim looked up into the captain's blue eyes, "she insulted the Republic of Korea and my manhood," he lied.

"I see." The captain nodded. "Well I'm watching you, Kim, and I might put you on a charge, do you understand?"

"Yes, sir, thank you, sir." Kim was relieved the incident was over.

"Now move out, we've wasted precious daylight here." The captain pointed to the path; behind him, the rest of the men followed.

From the heart of the temple the Mudang stood and stared at her handiwork; out of the eleven white sheets which hung from the ceiling, four were ripped precisely in half.

Chapter 11

Warning Signs

Lieutenant Samuels looked worriedly at his watch: they had only two hours of light left at most.

"Do you think we'll reach the other bridge before dark?" Samuels asked his fellow officer as they trekked side-by-side through the cold damp woods.

"I should think so; this plateau cannot be too large," Captain Woodholme-Browne answered.

"I think I'll move up and ask Sergeant Kim, with your permission, sir?" Samuels asked, his Colt .45 ready in his left hand.

"Off you hop then, Edward," the captain smiled, and the lieutenant did so with a spring in his step.

Lieutenant Samuels found both RSM McConnell and Sergeant Kim in stationary positions up the path ahead. Samuels was about to ask what the hold-up was when he saw what the two sergeants were looking at.

"Ugly buggers aren't they!" RSM McConnell turned as the American lieutenant approached.

Standing eight feet high on each side of the path, were two carved wooden totem poles. Foliage and leaves covered parts of their length, which consisted of poles with Korean letters carved into them, with the last two feet having grotesque, wide grinning heads on top.

"What are they?" Lieutenant Samuels asked Sergeant Kim, as the rest of the expedition force caught up to their position.

"Shaman poles. They are placed here to stand guard and prevent evil spirits passing this point," Kim explained.

"Hey Perez, your mama and sister are here!" joked Corporal Baker to the New-Mexican soldier behind him.

"Funny," Perez sniffed, but bit his tongue.

"Cut it out yous guys," Sergeant Dempsey warned, moving forward to get a better view.

"Well let's brave the evil ghosties then, move out Sergeant Kim!" the captain ordered. The poles were well carved, but they had little time to delay after their unforeseen stop at the hidden temple.

"Yes, sir." With a deep breath, Sergeant Kim reluctantly passed between the poles, gripping his rifle a little harder as he did so. He hoped their journey would not get any more interesting. He, like the others, had an uneasy feeling as they traversed the strange, isolated world of the Yŏu plateau.

Sergeant Kim led the way silently; with RSM McConnell about ten yards behind, the rest of the party followed eight yards after him. The mood had become silent and sullen again: no one joked or even lit a smoke; this was the serious part of their mission.

The cold forest of trees seemed never ending, yet in fact they were only forty-five minutes trek from their destination now.

Up ahead, Sergeant Kim Jun Ho's senses were strained to the point, he felt like a headache was coming on. One missed sign from him could mean death for all eleven of them.

His acute awareness was rewarded when he noticed something different about the path or foliage ahead. He raised his hand to stop the column from moving forward, then closed his fist and pulled it down.

The RSM copied the arm action and the rest of the party stopped and knelt down, packs unslung: weapons at the ready. At the rear, Private London and Sergeant Dempsey turned and aimed their rifles back up the trail they had just come down.

Keeping low to the ground and off the beaten track in case of mines or booby-traps, Sergeant Kim moved forward to a dense clump of bushes and trees just off the path. The object that had stuck out from the green foliage could now be seen, it was a brown boot.

The sergeant was in desperate need of a swig of water from his canteen: his mouth felt dry, despite the cold wetness around him. Moving his Garland rifle to his shoulder he inched slowly forward to find prone legs attached to the boots. Another step brought another shock as another unseen body lay in a T-shape away from the first one, so ensuring it was not seen from the path.

The smell of blood filled his nostrils as he finally advanced around the side of the trees that hid the two obviously dead bodies. The toe of his boot kicked a rifle lying in the grass and weeds next to the first bloody body. It was a Russian made Simonov SKS 7.62 Carbine, as supplied to their communist allies, the North Koreans.

Kim moved closer to the bodies, they had suffered terrible trauma to the face, chest and arms. Blood was pooled around them, frozen in the cold. There was something wrong here: the wounds looked like slashing knife attack wounds, not penetrating bullet wounds.

He moved onto the path, pointed only at the British RSM and waved him forward. The rest of the party remained where they were on tenterhooks, as the RSM moved forward to join Sergeant Kim. Before the British veteran arrived, Kim noticed there were no tracks on the path ahead. Meaning that these soldiers had approached not from the path or the bridge it led to, but another direction.

The dead soldiers' bloodied winter uniforms bothered Kim also; he had never seen North Korean soldiers dressed like this. Their faces were too disfigured and blood-splattered to be of any help.

RSM McConnell whistled softly as he approached Sergeant Kim standing over the two corpses, his Sten gun in his arms before him.

"Any sign of anymore?" the RSM whispered to his South Korean ally.

"No." Sergeant Kim pointed off into the forest. "They seem to have come from the north."

"They seem dressed funny for North Koreans?" the sergeant major pondered, and then bent down to rifle through their pockets for I.D.

"I thought that," Kim nodded, and then scanned the surrounding area for enemies or more clues.

"There ya go." McConnell pulled a folded piece of paper from a breast pocket and handed it to Kim to translate.

Kim unfolded the paper and gasped. "I cannot read this Regimental Sergeant Major McConnell."

"Why not, is it in code or something?" the RSM stood up.

"No, it is written in Chinese. These are Chinese soldiers; that's why we did not recognise the uniforms."

"If the Chinks are here, helping the North Koreans, then we are up shit creek without a canoe!"

"We better inform the Captain."

"Too right, laddie, and HQ as well; if the Chinese have joined the fight, this war will not be over by Christmas, mark my words."

"You've found what?!" Captain Woodholme-Browne exclaimed as RSM McConnell reported back to the party.

"Two recently killed Chink soldiers, sir. Sergeant Kim thinks they have come from the north of the plateau."

"Move the men forward Left-tenant Samuels and make sure everyone's alert." Captain Woodholme-Browne followed the RSM forward, his revolver out of its holster now.

Sergeant Kim had retraced the dead soldiers' steps for twenty yards, the ground was frozen solid, so no tracks could be seen. He had found a winter hat with flaps, yet there was no insignia on it.

As he approached the two corpses, the two officers and RSM McConnell were standing over them.

"Ah, there you are, Kim, now are you sure these are Chinese soldiers?" the captain asked, bemused by this turn of events.

"The pamphlet one of them had was in Chinese, which I cannot read. And, what I can see of the faces, they look Chinese." Sergeant Kim stood at the foot of the corpses, his rifle in his arms.

"This is a bit of a mystery," the captain said mentally and physically scratching his head: he was an engineer, not an intelligence officer.

"That is only one mystery, Captain; there is an even more pressing problem to solve," Kim said looking from man to man.

"What's that, Sergeant?" Lieutenant Samuels asked, looking a little green around the gills, having never seen a dead body before.

"Who killed them and are they our friend or foe?" the South Korean sergeant pondered.

"Bloody hell, he's right." The RSM looked around him, things were getting decidedly odd.

Captain Woodholme-Browne looked from man to man, his stomach churning inside. He was out of his depth here and racked his brain to decide on how best to proceed. Then it came to him in a flash, *when in doubt, ask for help!*

"Left-tenant, get Hartnell up here with the radio and let's see what HQ wants us to do."

"Right away sir." The lieutenant saluted and gladly walked away from the corpses to find Private Hartnell.

The captain's good idea was short-lived as Private Hartnell could not get through to HQ or receive any United Nations' signals.

"The plateau here is lower than the hills where we crossed the rope bridge; I need to get to higher ground to make contact," Private Hartnell explained to the despondent captain.

"We have to get this message through, if the Chinese attack by surprise our chaps will be in all sorts of trouble." The captain exhaled, not sure what to do next; he still had a mission to complete.

"We better decide what to do quickly, Ashley, we don't have much more than an hour's light left," Lieutenant Samuels warned, he was all for abandoning the mission and retreating back to HQ ASAFP.

Yet something of the general's genes kicked in and Captain Woodholme-Browne of the 55th Field Squadron Royal Engineers of Her Majesty's British Army suddenly resolved what to do.

"Sergeant Dempsey, I want you, Hartnell here and erm Private London to head back to the ridge above the temple and try and get a signal through to HQ," the captain ordered. "The rest of us will continue on to the second rope bridge and quickly complete our mission," he finished.

"Whadda we do if we can't get the message through to HQ, sir?" Dempsey asked, silently glad to be retreating from the danger ahead.

"Return to the trucks and try again, then wait for us there. Even if you get a signal at the temple it would be best to do that also," the captain expanded on his orders for the American 3rd Engineering Battalion sergeant.

"What if we don't return?" Lieutenant Samuels asked the captain and NCOs present.

"Then Sergeant Dempsey can use his discretion. If you don't hear a peep from us in 48 hours, you are to take one of those trucks and return to base. The same goes if you come under enemy fire, is that understood, Sergeant?"

"Crystal clear, sir." The sergeant saluted and went off to inform Hartnell and London.

"Lieutenant Samuels, get the men ready to move in five minutes."

The NCOs moved off as ordered to get the men ready to go.

Captain Woodholme-Browne glanced down at the corpses one more time. "I hope I'm right, General," he whispered to himself.

"Good luck, Sergeant." The captain bade farewell to the three soldiers with a vigorous handshake.

"Yous toos, sir," the sergeant replied. He moved off back down the path, unhappy to be leaving his lieutenant and men behind.

"Stay alert, laddie," the RSM warned Private London as he turned to follow the American sergeant. Private Robert London just nodded grimly in return and walked past Private McClaren as he went.

"Donie get yor-self killed, ya Sassenach bastard!" were Piggy McClaren's kind words of farewell.

"If you see the enemy, Piggy, just show them that pale Jock arse of yours; that'll scare the buggers away." London smiled and McClaren replied with a deep bellied laugh.

Private Hartnell just patted PFC Perez on the shoulder and moved off with the others. It was a show of sympathy, knowing the New Mexican was stuck with O'Keefe and Baker.

Captain Woodholme-Browne had a sick feeling in the pit of his stomach as he watched them go. Was this a mistake? Only time and the history books would tell.

"Sergeant Kim, lead the way please." Captain Woodholme-Browne gripped his revolver and followed as the South Korean sergeant took point. Lieutenant Samuels followed close behind, with Corporal Baker and Private O'Keefe side-by-side behind. Private First-Class Perez, with his heavy Browning Automatic Rifle (BAR) at the ready and Private McClaren nervously holding his rifle, followed. Regimental Sergeant Major McConnell brought up the rear, his Sten gun pointing this way and that.

Chapter 12

Going to Hell in a Hand Basket

Captain Woodholme-Browne of the Royal Engineers lowered his field glasses and sucked at his stiff upper lip. He looked down from the Yŏu plateau over to the hills and mountains surrounding the enemy-held town of Kusang.

The rope bridge looked secure and in a better state than the bridge that had led them onto the plateau. The forest had ended some forty yards back and gave way to rocks and boulders. The bridge accessed by a man-made zigzag of paths, thirty feet below their current position. This cutting of paths into the cliff had obviously been done to connect the bridge to the lower hill that faced this side of the plateau. The path was rocky and looked treacherous and was badly exposed from all sides.

Sergeant Kim had volunteered to scout out the bridge below, while above him Lieutenant Samuels took photographs of all the relevant topographical places of interest. RSM McConnell crouched next to them, watching the other side of the bridge for enemy movement. PFC Perez had his BAR resting on a rock aimed at the bridge as well.

Further back and to the right, nearer the tree line were Corporal Baker, Private O'Keefe and Private McClaren. They were guarding the equipment and watching the forest and rocky outcrops to the north-east. The light was fading fast, as was the temperature on the wind exposed ridge and plateau edge.

Sergeant Kim rounded the last bend of the path as it zigzagged down to their objective: the second rope bridge over the plateau. He gripped his rifle as hard as his numb gloved hands would allow. A mist seemed to hang over the chasm below and the hills opposite. With the fading light and dark rocky outcrops, it made this place seem eerie and silent. He approached the bridge, looking from left to right.

A sound like the sudden spit of a venomous snake rang out of the silence. An impact like a hard kick to his stomach happened, exploding his rifle and spinning him round like a child's spinning top. His boots lost all traction and he fell, sliding down the hard biting rock face of the plateau into the misty depths of the plateau below.

RSM McConnell readied his Sten gun in shock as a sharp football referee's whistle was heard.

"Jaap Gick!" came a cry in Chinese from the furthest outcrops and forest to the north-east of their positions.

"Return fire!" RSM McConnell, the World War II veteran took command of the situation, as he and PFC Perez let rip at the advancing hordes of Chinese solider dressed like Michelin men.

"Fucking hell in a hand basket!" Corporal Teddy Baker exclaimed as the Chinese rushed towards his position.

"Fucking fire, Yank!" Private McClaren screamed as shots began to ricochet off the rocks they were hiding behind. McClaren aimed and felled an enemy with his first shot. He pulled back his bolt, expelled the empty shell and loaded another bullet into the breach and fired again. Corporal Baker put his Garland over his head leaning on the rock above and fired off his entire clip wildly, which ejected onto the ground beside him.

"We gotta get outta here, Teddy!" screamed Private Liam O'Keefe, clutching to his rifle like it was his comfort blanket.

"Liam, get down!"

The right side of Private O'Keefe's face exploded in a shower of blood and bones and he fell dead before even hearing the warning.

"Liam!" Teddy screamed in terror.

"We have to retreat, sir!" RSM McConnell called over the fire fight; the Chinese soldiers had gone to cover, but were advancing swiftly to encircle them.

Captain Woodholme-Browne fired his revolver halting a communist soldier in his battle rage charge. He pushed the walkie-talkie into Lieutenant Samuels' hands. "Get the men to safety!"

"I won't leave you!" Lieutenant Samuels cried.

"Sir, we have to retreat, come on Perez, move." RSM McConnell grabbed at Lieutenant Samuels and pulled the young lieutenant with him towards Baker and McClaren's position. Yells: covering revolver fire, ricochets, the earth dancing with bullet impacts, running, falling, bee-like whizzes of traced flashing before the eyes.

"Come on, you bastards!" McClaren screamed, his rifle, once untried, now a deadly weapon in his hands. Another charging soldier fell, blood jetting from a neck wound, his Burp gun chattering rounds into the sky.

"I gotta go!" Corporal Baker jumped up and ran for the tree line like the cowardly bully he had always been. He made it ten feet in before he came to a standing stop three feet from a young looking Chinese volunteer.

Teddy Baker pulled his trigger but nothing happened; in his terror he had forgotten to reload his rifle.

"Wait!"

The young chon-shih (private) speared the American with his bayonet, deep into Teddy Baker's guts, then again and again, 'til the US engineer fell to the forest floor dying.

The RSM had managed to drag the lieutenant half-way to McClaren's now lone position, Perez crouching and somehow firing was nearly there. He looked behind; Captain Woodholme-Browne had left his position and was following them. When two Chinese soldiers rounded on his position he raised his revolver to fire, but it clicked empty.

The second Chinese soldier, Fu P'ai-Chang Mai (Sergeant Mai), brought the stock of his 7.62mm Burp gun down on the captain's cap, knocking him lifeless to the floor.

"Damn it!" the RSM spat as a bullet exploded through his right kneecap as he pushed the young American lieutenant behind the semi-circle of rocks McClaren had bravely held single handedly.

"You're hit, Sergeant Major!" Lieutenant Samuels squealed; this was a nightmare to the young engineer. Death was staring into all their faces. Ashley was gone, his men were dying around him and he hadn't even fired a single shot from his pistol yet in the fire fight.

"Left-tenant, listen to me," McConnell grunted with pain, "I only have two grenades, I will throw both at the woods. When they explode I want you, Perez and McClaren here to run for your lives, all guns blazing. Understand?"

The young lieutenant pulled the scarf from his neck and wrapped it like a bandage around the RSM's knee; the cacophony of noise around him ignored as he worked on this one task.

PFC Perez jammed another twenty round clip into the underside of his light machinegun and switched positions to fire on the Chinese soldiers in the captain's overrun position. Its 0.30 calibre bullets nearly decapitated a helpless Chinese soldier, as he sat up too high above his cover to fire.

"Did you hear me?" the RSM grabbed the lieutenant's coat collar and pulled him up to growl through the pain into his face.

"What about Ashley?" the lieutenant asked with tears glinting in his eyes, ducking as a bullet clipped off the rock above his head.

"He's had it, now you've gotta run laddie, warn HQ: now move it, sir!" The RSM pushed him towards where Private McClaren was showing his true worth as a soldier.

"What about you, Sarge?" Private McClaren yelled above the noise of the battle.

"I'll cover your retreat, now go!" The RSM pulled both pins on his only two grenades and with his large hand, lobbed them one second apart into the nearby tree line.

Two simultaneous shrapnel sending explosions rocked the trees and a cut-short cry of pain was unmistakeably heard.

"Go!" the RSM screamed and, putting all his weight onto his good knee, sat up and sprayed his entire Sten clip into various enemy positions.

McClaren looked round to see the lieutenant running past him and followed, with Perez only a footstep behind. They had no time for tactical retreat, fire and run scenarios, they just had to peg it for their lives to the tree line.

The bullets zipped past them and impacted into the trees as they made it to the comparative safety of the evergreens. McClaren let himself have one glance back at RSM 'Jock'

McConnell, as he reloaded his Sten gun, as the Chinese forces advanced onto his position from three sides.

A burst from Perez's BAR felled an enemy grenade injured victim, who got in the way of their flight. Samuels, a sprinter in the Harvard track team was leading the retreat, tears for the captain and his lost men blurring his vision.

The lieutenant didn't even notice that he had run into an enemy position, the Chinese soldiers put here to cut off the UN forces' retreat were also surprised. A burst of automatic fire would have surely killed McClaren if he had not tripped over the dead body of Corporal Baker.

Perez fired a deadly burst of bullets that felled one of the enemy next to Lieutenant Samuels, then he hid behind a tree to reload with another clip.

Of the two remaining Chinese soldiers, one fired at McClaren, while a young seventeen-year-old chan-shih (private), rose his bayoneted rifle and pointed it at the young American lieutenant. Their eyes met, both locking in fear for the briefest of seconds. Lieutenant Samuels heard the shot like a fire-cracker poked in each ear. He and the young Chinese soldier were still locked in a fearful exchange. Until the Chinese youth fell backwards, a bullet hole in his heart, onto his fellow soldier.

McClaren saw this, and jumped to his feet. As the Chinese soldier tried to free himself from the deadweight on top of him, McClaren raced up and put a round into his left temple.

Perez moved up to join them, as Lieutenant Samuels stared down at his smoking pistol and the death he had brought with it.

"We gotta keep going!" McClaren shouted at the American officer.

"I–" Lieutenant Samuels was interrupted as McClaren's body twisted and turned in agony as several rounds of automatic fire thudded into his back and arms. He was dead before his body hit the frozen forest floor!

An enraged Samuels emptied his remaining six rounds from his Colt .45 into the Michelin man standing behind McClaren's fallen body, killing him.

"Run sir!" Perez grabbed the lieutenant's arm and together they ran, as fast as their lungs would allow, away from the combat zone.

A burst from his Sten gun saw two more Chinese soldiers fall wounded or dying. The remaining rounds saw the enemy, to his right now, dive for cover. As he brought up another magazine to slam in, a bullet hit the top of his left shoulder, sending him flying onto his back, the Sten gun left behind on the rocky cover.

The pain from his shoulder and knee, coupled with blood-loss caused his vision to be darkened around the edges. Yet still his military training would not leave him as his life ebbed away. It had been his life, his saviour, his marriage: slowly his bloodied fingers pulled his Webley revolver from its holster on his webbing belt.

Three shadows appeared in his failing vision standing above him; he raised his revolver and fired. One of the shadows fell backwards with a cry; he managed to get off one more shot before the Chinese bullets and death caught him. He died as he had always wanted: in a battle, saving others.

P'ai-Chang Kong spat on the RSM's lifeless body, he had killed many of his brave communist volunteers.

"Shall we pursue them?" asked Fu P'ai-Chang Mai as their captain approached from the rear, holstering his TT-33 Russian made pistol.

"No, we have their Commanding Officer; we will take him back to the village for interrogation," Lien-Chang Wu ordered the remainder of his men.

"Do you think these Capitalist soldiers killed our other men?" P'ai-Chang Kong asked his captain quietly.

"Of course, what else could have?" Lien-Chang Wu replied, and it was not a rhetorical question.

"But our men were slashed to pieces, sir, surely it was something else?" Fu P'ai-Chang Mai ventured, at thirty-seven he was the oldest man in the 12th Chinese Field Army.

"Enough of your peasant superstitions, Sergeant, grab the prisoner and get the men ready to move in five minutes," the stern Lien-Chang Wu ordered.

"What about the wounded, sir?" asked Pan-Chang Han, who also doubled as their field medic.

"If they are not fit to walk, shoot them, Corporal Han!" the ruthless Lien-Chang ordered and strode off, with his adjutant following closely behind. In the new Communist Republic of China, everyone was supposed to be equal; some like the captain were more equal than others.

Only one shot rang out before the remaining fourteen members of the once thirty strong Tiger Company moved out. With them, being dragged by the burliest soldiers from Yut and Yee platoons, was Captain Woodholme-Browne.

Now halfway back to the hidden temple, the exhausted Samuels and Perez risked taking the path again. The lieutenant and PFC finally stopped to reload and drink from their canteens, before trudging on back to link up with Sergeant Dempsey's group.

From the misty chasm between the Yŏu Plateau and enemy held territory, came a faint moan, like that of a departed spirit.

From the trees north of the fire fight, animal nostrils flared at the smell of blood. Feral eyes surveyed the bodies of the men who had fought here, on her plateau. Men from the north she recognised, others with wide eyes and pink pale skin, were far from home.

Then she was running back to her lair, faster than any other land mammal. Avoiding the large group of men and their yellow-haired prisoner, she headed for home ground, so she could wait in ambush.

Chapter 13

Flee or Fight

Sergeant Kim Jun Ho groaned and opened his eyes, but all he could see was white mist. Had he died and joined his ancestors in Buddha's loving embrace?

A movement of his left hand, and the pain that flared there and in other parts of his battered body, told him that he was still suffering on this mortal coil. His eyes cleared a little and he found that he was wedged on a three foot ledge, down the side of the plateau. The remains of a tree growing from under the ledge had prevented him falling to his death. Yet with the pain that rocked his body, he wasn't sure if he was totally alive.

His right hand was still gripping the butt of his American made and supplied rifle like a vice. He looked down his body and found the butt; trigger and trigger guard were all that was left of his Garland rifle. He let go of it and pushed himself up on his elbows with a grunt of pain to his arms, joints and back. He hurt all over, but pain meant one sure thing, he was still alive.

He sat up, then had to grab an outcrop of rock to steady himself as his head felt like it was spinning round on his shoulders. A quick test of his arms and legs, as his vision slowed to a stop, reported back to his brain that nothing, miraculously, seemed to be broken. Chipped, pulled, sprained and bruised, well that was a different kettle of fish.

The nausea and spinning of his head had subsided now, leaving only a stab of pain on the left side of his head above the ear. A quick examination with his left hand, found a little dried blood and an almighty bump.

Pulling his legs up and ignoring the stings of cuts and grazes, he had the opportunity to evaluate his predicament.

He had been very lucky indeed; the ledge, only two inches wider than his body, would not have saved him if the tree stump had not wedged him in. He thanked Buddha for that, but became increasingly worried about the silence above his precarious position. Why weren't the British and American forces aiding him? Did they think he had fallen to his death?

"Ch'ongssori!" he exclaimed, suddenly recalling that he had been shot, before falling off the plateau. He looked down at the remains of his rifle which had taken the brunt of the bullet. He checked his abdomen; it felt a little tender, yet there were no wounds. His hands were scratched and cut, but still in working order.

If he had been shot, what of the rest of the survey expedition: were they all dead? He would get no answers here; somehow he had to climb up the side of the plateau to safety. It was only twelve feet or so, but if he fell again, would the ledge catch him this time?

"Try the walkie-talkie, sir," PFC Perez ventured after they had finished their brief rest on the path back to the temple.

Lieutenant Edward Samuels nodded back at the soldier. He realised he knew little about the man from New Mexico. He had never really shone and always kept himself to himself. A man of few words, too many others in his Engineering Company had louder, but not wiser, voices. He had shown himself to be a true soldier and if they got out of this mess, he would recommend him for a medal.

Samuels raised the walkie-talkie he had carried from the battle and swore to the God almighty, Jesus and the Holy Ghost. A hole the size of a dime passed through the lower part of the chunky walkie-talkie. He tried to turn it on, but it was useless; angrily he threw it as far as he could into the forest.

"So much for the walkie-talkie eh, Perez?" Samuels said, standing up straight. "Come on, let's move out."

"Yes, sir." Perez looked back down the forest path, checking for movement as they set off. The light had all but gone from the day. The temperature was falling rapidly; it would be night before they reached the temple again.

Sergeant Kim Jun Ho felt very small, like an insect crawling up a wall. He grunted and stabbed his bayonet five, six, seven times, 'til it wedged into a crack in the rock just above his head. Night had fallen and the bitter winds cut through his clothing like it was rice paper.

Apart from his belly which rumbled, the rest of his body felt numb with the cold. The only soothing effect was that he couldn't feel all his aches, pains and cuts. He blinked away the tears the wind had whipped into his eyes and pulled himself up. On he struggled, trusting two numbed-to-the-bone hands and icy booted feet. He toiled upwards, knowing any rest would be the end of him. If he stopped now the winter's night had fallen below zero, he would never start again.

His boot pushed up on the bayonet wedged into the side of the plateau and he pulled and heaved himself up, reaching up now to grab the underside supports of the rope bridge. With one final effort he pulled himself back on to the Yŏu Plateau again.

His back felt like it was breaking, but he crawled up the zigzag path, fearing the icy winds might topple him over the side. The tears in his eyes from the cold wind, plus the darkness of a November night, meant his vision was severely impaired.

He crawled onwards through the rocks, outcrops and boulders, heading as best he could for where his allies had been positioned.

Suddenly the rock beneath his outstretched right hand sunk a little and fluid covered his hand. This wasn't rock; it felt like...felt like a body. Kim withdrew his hand with a revolted hiss and wiped the bodily fluids onto the earth.

Taking a risk he reached down to his webbing belt and detached his L-shaped torch and clicked on it. In front of him lay a soldier of oriental descent in a puffed up pale green uniform. He had several bullet wounds to the stomach and chest areas: and was not in any shape or form a North or South Korean soldier.

"Chungguk soram," he whispered aloud, not believing his own words as he heard them. This was a Chinese Communist soldier in North Korea. Not only that, but combat had taken place here, the Chinese had taken casualties: had his friends and allies also?

He clicked off his torch and waited in the dark, he heard nothing but the wind through the trees, bringing the smell of blood and cordite to his nostrils. Seeing, or more accurately, hearing, no reaction to his torchlight, he turned it on again and moved amongst the combat zone.

At first he was delighted to find only Chinese corpses; the rest of the company had put up stiff resistance.

The he found him...the hairy faced Scottish Regimental Sergeant Major. He was peppered with bullet holes, his revolver still in his hand. An enemy corpse lay right next to him. Sergeant Kim knelt down and closed the RSM's bloodshot eyes for the last time and said a little personal prayer.

Moving on a little way across from the RSM lay the ginger haired American engineer; he was only identifiable by his hair, as most of his face was missing.

Kim knelt down and retrieved the American's Garland rifle. Sergeant Kim checked it over and it was in good working order, in fact it had never been fired. The young ROK sergeant took some extra ammo from the dead New Yorker and slung the rifle over his shoulder.

Moving into the forest now he found more signs of battle, grenade damage to the trees, plus more corpses. Among the five dead Chinese he also found the bodies of the loudmouth Corporal Baker and the chubby British soldier called McClaren.

He could not find the captain, the lieutenant and another of the American engineers. Searching around the trees he could find no clues, so returned to the rocky combat zone. He found no trace of the missing men, had they been captured or escaped?

Something caught Kim's eye, next to a Chinese corpse was a British issue revolver. On examination all the rounds had been fired and on the rock cover were spare rounds for it. Kim took them both and put them in his backpack, hopefully to return to the captain at a later stage. The two officers and engineer must have been taken prisoner.

Moving through the combat zone and into the forest again to the north-east, he easily found the many booted trail leading away from the battle.

Unslinging his borrowed Garland, he turned off his torch, he waited for his eyes to adjust to the darkness and headed off into the forest after the Chinese forces and captured allies.

"This is Centurion calling Rome. Centurion calling Rome, are you receiving me? Over." Private Hartnell called into the radio handset for the umpteenth time since they had made it back to the ridge above the temple.

The earth was too frozen to dig in, so they sheltered behind a large fallen maple tree. Private London was eating something that had once been a farm animal squashed into a tin of his C7 rations. Sergeant Dempsey had his M1 Carbine resting on the log, scanning the dark trees and temple for signs of movement. The cold night and trees reminded him of the Arden, and the night before the 'Battle of the Bulge'. He had been a skinny teenager rifleman then and the fear of that time had never left his subconscious.

His older brother had bought it in Holland and his girl had sent him a 'Dear John' letter soon after. His parents were both dead and he had no real job or adult life to return to after the war ended. So he stayed in but transferred to the engineers, he and his brother Mike had always been tinkering with automobiles. This way he got to stay in the life he knew, but stayed away from combat, *So much for dat frickin' plan*, he thought.

"It's no god-damn good Sarge." Hartnell pulled off his headset. "I can't raise squat on this here thing."

"What about the Captain or the Loo-tenant?"

"Nothing."

"Okay, pack it up and get some chow inside ya, Hartnell." Sergeant Dempsey saw a faint glow from the confines of the temple, but only because their defence position was just to the left of the path leading downwards. Normally he would have investigated, but he didn't have the men and, besides, the old woman gave him the heebie-jeebies.

"Are we going to retrace our steps back to the trucks now, Sergeant?" asked London's rough English tones.

"It's dark and I don't wanna be crossing that sorry assed excuse for a bridge at night. We'll hole up here 'til first light."

Private London sat on his upturned helmet to keep the cold from his backside, and ate from his tin. He really liked Hartnell, and Dempsey was okay in his way, yet his list of people he missed was increasing day by day.

He kinda missed Sergeant Kim, RSM McConnell and Captain Woodholme-Browne; he felt safer in their company. Then he got to thinking of Nobby and Ray and the rest of his 'Die-Hard' mates from D-Company. He was glad he had seen them all on the way up to the plateau. Now he knew he could slip back into his old platoon and not feel like some new replacement.

In turn, his wounding in action had brought him in contact with Lillian in Japan, and oh how he yearned to see her again. Lastly, but definitely not least, he missed his parents, the coal yard, home and cricket.

"Did you hear that?" Hartnell cried as a muffled sound like thunder echoed from the distance.

"Ssh!" the Sergeant hissed, his cold ears straining as the dark fell about them. The icy wind was blowing from the south-west, so it made it hard to hear anything from the path where they had left the rest of the expedition.

Dempsey was sure he could hear small arms fire, but it was just elusive to his ears. The odd noise could be heard, but not substantiated for the next ten minutes: then nothing.

The freezing forest atop of the Yŏu Plateau returned to relative silence again. Only the trees swaying in the breeze could be heard.

"Okay boys, get your helmets on and rifles at the ready, this could be a long night." Ten seconds after Sergeant Dempsey's order, a No5 .303 rifle and a Garland rifle appeared at the ready either side of his Carbine.

That old Arden feeling of fear gnawed at Dempsey's cold bones once again. He had joined the 3rd Engineering Battalion to escape the horrors of combat. Maybe God had seen through that bluff and knew inside he was a combat soldier. Maybe it was his destiny to fight again, and face up to the fears that he had long hidden in engines and the bottom of a bourbon bottle.

Dempsey wondered what the hell had gone on, had the rest of the company found more Chinks? He only had two hours to wait to get his answer.

A pistol shot only two hundred yards ahead caused Sergeant Kim to dive for cover. He had heard nothing, but the sound of the wind whistling through the trees since he had started after the enemy.

He heard a loud voice ahead bark orders in Chinese, which he could not catch. Even if he did, he only knew about ten words of Chinese anyway.

He lay still on the hard frozen earth and waited, no sounds of pursuit or weapons' fire followed. Maybe the pistol shot had not been aimed in his direction at all, then a colder feeling hit his bladder. Maybe the Chinese forces had executed one of the prisoners.

Fear and rage suddenly burned in his heart and standing to a crouch, he crept forward to see what he could see. He moved through the trees to the left of the path, which gave him the best cover. With his rifle at his shoulder he deliberately moved forward step by step towards the area the pistol shot had come from.

By the time he edged to the right area he could see very little, the Chinese Company had moved out.

Then he spotted it, a body, sitting up against a tree, his arms at his side, head lolling to the right. Kim checked the way the enemy had left and could hear the odd sound of movement along the path ahead. Keeping his borrowed rifle trained down that path, he approached the body. He felt with his right hand the body and uniform of the dead soldier.

Blood from a leg wound wet the South Korean's hand and Kim was relieved to find the dead soldier, from his uniform, was Chinese. Sergeant Kim lifted the poor soldier's head and could just about see the wet slickness of blood from his forehead.

Kim wiped his hand on the Chinese soldier's arm and stepped away from the dead man. He felt rage and sickness once again: this poor unfortunate had been wounded in the leg and obviously had been slowing the company up, so the bastards had killed him there and then, even though they could have carried him.

Sergeant Kim took a quick piss nearby and hurried on after the enemy. If they could do this to one of their own men, what would they not do to the prisoners?

An hour later Sergeant Kim was forced to halt again. Thirty yards ahead, just out of the tree line in a semi-circular clearing, stood the Chinese Company.

Rocks and boulders littered the clearing, but unlike the bridge area where they had attacked, this was not the northern edge of the plateau. The trees continued on, surrounding the small clearing.

Kim could make out a dozen or more men with weapons in the dark, but could not tell who was who. A torch flicked on up ahead and Kim could faintly see it was being carried by a Chinese officer. He seemed to have two soldiers with him, but the rest of the men remained as darker shadows.

The torch was sweeping back and forth between the trees, underbrush and rocks. Kim was glad the torch wasn't aimed in his direction, but what were they looking for: supplies or weapons?

The officer gave a happy sort of cry and he and the two men moved forward to move some bamboo and underbrush apart. The rest of the Chinese began to move now and hope returned to Kim's heart as a prisoner, over a foot taller than his captors, was pulled to his feet.

Sergeant Kim watched as the Company moved through the underbrush, between a crack in two huge boulders and disappeared. Five minutes later the whole Chinese Company had disappeared, like some Arabian fable, into the rocks. The bamboo and underbrush had sprung back and the torch glow had faded into darkness again.

Sergeant Kim rose from his hiding place and moved slowly forward towards the boulder and clearing. There must be a gully or cave mouth somewhere behind the foliage and between the rocks, he mused.

"You got 'em?" Sergeant Dempsey hissed softly.

"Yes," Private London replied, his rifle end moving slightly in the dark.

"Got who?" Private Hartnell whispered, he could see nothing new about the cold woods and black shadows of the night.

"Ssh!" was the sergeant's only reply as his and London's weapons followed the two shadowy figures emerging from across the bowl that the temple was hidden in.

Suddenly Hartnell noticed the movement as the two armed figures began to descend the western path down to where the Tolharubang stones guarded the way.

Down the figures warily moved, then Sergeant Dempsey recognised the weapon the smaller of the two figures was carrying. He reached down into a trouser thigh pocket and pulled out his torch. He aimed it towards the gully and flicked it off and on once.

The two men froze and sought cover behind the Grandfather stones. Then after a tense twenty second wait, two flashes replied to Sergeant Dempsey's one.

The sergeant stood up and waved his lit torch above his head for a few seconds. In reply, the two soldiers below made their way up the nearest slope to the path that led back to the first bridge.

Private London kept his rifle aimed like any good soldier should, as his American compatriots rose from the safety of their cover. The log was about twenty yards away from the path, in the cover of a copse of trees.

"Over here Loo-tenant," the sergeant spoke, his voice carrying on the icy wind.

"Sergeant Dempsey, I'm so relieved to hear your voice," the ieutenant enthused in a weary voice as he and Perez approached their defensive position.

Private London finally let down his guard and stood up, trying to get some warmth into his frozen extremities.

"Hey, Miguel, that you boy?" Hartnell's voice lifted the tension a little, as he went to embrace PFC Perez.

"Where's everyone else?" London asked the question that was in the forefront of Dempsey's and Hartnell's minds also.

"We were ambushed by superior Chinese forces by the bridge. Baker, O'Keefe, McClaren and Sergeant Kim are dead." Lieutenant Samuels relayed the encounter sadly.

"What about the Captain and the RSM?" London butted in, hardly believing that poor old Piggy McClaren and Sergeant Kim had bought it.

"Either captured or killed I'm afraid. Perez and I only just made it back alive." Lieutenant Samuels looked down at the cold dark forest floor, an empty feeling in the pit of his stomach.

"You left them, sir?" Sergeant Dempsey asked, thinking about his dead men.

"The Captain ordered us to," the lieutenant's voice had a whiney edge to it now, "he ordered me to inform HQ about the Chinese."

"Your Sergeant Major covered our retreat; he is a brave man, Private London," PFC Perez explained to the young British National Serviceman.

"Wadda we gonna do now, Loo-tenant?" Sergeant Dempsey asked. He had a few ideas, but he had nine years' military training behind him, and had to bow to college puke with only one.

"The radio!" the lieutenant whispered to himself.

"Sir?" Dempsey replied.

"Did you get through on the radio, Private Hartnell?"

"No, sir, no dice," Hartnell replied.

"Ain't we going to go back for 'em Left-tenant?" asked London, feeling, as the only British soldier left, that he had to speak up for the captain and RSM.

The lieutenant took off his helmet and rubbed at his thumping temple. "I need to think...it's so damn cold here."

Dempsey looked around at the rest of the enlisted men. They, like him, were worried that the lieutenant was losing the plot.

"If you're cold Loo-tenant, there is one place we could go to warm up." Hartnell pointed towards the dim light coming from the entrance to the temple below.

It took Sergeant Kim longer to find the hidden entrance than he first thought it would. The Chinese officer had the advantage of using a torch and he had obviously found it before.

A trip in the end showed him the way. His foot caught on a rock and he fell through a section of thickly bunched bamboo, lucky not to discharge his rifle as he did so.

Rubbing at his aches and bruises he edged along in near absolute darkness. Cold and rough stone was not too far away on either side of him as the passage or valley began to descend gradually in front of him.

No light shone from below and no sounds could be heard as he followed the secret way downwards. He'd thought he had come to a dead end at one stage, as he could feel only hard rock in front of him. The darkness had tricked him as he felt with his hands the passage turned, did a one-eighty and headed even more steeply downwards.

Down he traversed and the passage zigzagged twice more, before he felt a cold breeze on his face. The dark ahead had become slightly less umbral; he must be getting to the end of the passage and whatever lay beyond.

He took the captain's revolver from its bag and loaded it in the dark. Then he proceeded down again, his rifle slung, but revolver at the ready. He could use his left hand to feel his way along, while gripping the revolver in his right.

Suddenly the rock to his left hand side was gone and he ducked down behind some ancient masonry. He peeked out from behind the ancient carved rock and gasped at the scene that he beheld.

Sergeant Dempsey and Private London took the lead, with Hartnell and the lieutenant behind and Perez bringing up the rear of the party. They trod step-by-step into the temple along the long passageway.

They edged their way along until they stood at the entrance to the large inner temple. London noticed that some of the long white banners that hung from the temple ceiling had been ripped or cut upwards in two.

Ahead in front of a raging brazier of fire knelt the old woman who they had met earlier; she seemed oblivious to their presence for the moment.

Sergeant Dempsey motioned for London to go left and thumbed that he would go right. They moved off as Lieutenant Samuels and Private Hartnell entered the circular inner temple. PFC Perez crossed himself and waited in the passage, guarding the way back with his BAR.

Lieutenant Samuels looked from Dempsey and London, then raised his leather gloved fist and coughed loudly.

The Mudang remained motionless, her behind resting on her heels she stared into the orange and yellow flames.

"Erm, excuse me?" he started, "we need a place to stay."

Sergeant Dempsey tipped back his helmet and rubbed across his eyebrows, they were at war here, no time for Harvard tea dance pleasantries.

Slowly the Mudang rose and turned to face the intruders. She walked past the lieutenant and right up to Private London, well his lower chest anyway.

"Yŏngguk namja," she said to the Englishman and beckoned him over to an ornate wooden desk, with parchment, quill pens and ink.

London looked at Lieutenant Samuels for help, whom nodded and waved to him to follow.

Deftly she picked up the quill in her bony fingers and began to draw. Robert London sniffed and slung his rifle over his back and watched the picture evolve before his eyes.

Robert liked to draw himself, but was amazed at the swiftness and delicate accuracy of each stroke.

"It's a picture of the Captain!" he exclaimed to the rest of the US engineers present.

"Do you know where he is?" Lieutenant Samuels asked, walking up to stand beside the English private.

The Mudang smiled with what was left of her teeth and started another picture. Dempsey inched forward this time as the ink began to flow again.

The old lady seemed to shiver, like someone had passed over her grave, as she completed the next picture. It showed the captain held by each arm by a Chinese soldier; behind him a temple or buildings could be seen.

"Looks like da Chinks do have him," Dempsey drawled in his New Jersey accent.

"How do you know all this?" the lieutenant asked in slow deliberate English.

The old shaman woman did not answer; she just took up another piece of parchment and began to draw a map. They quickly realised it was a map of the plateau, with the two bridges first to be drawn, the first bridge to the south of the plateau and the second to the north-west. She drew the hidden temple and the path they had followed across the plateau. Then the map got really interesting.

Top centre on the northern curve of the plateau she drew a little temple and a few huts around it. Then she immediately drew over it with little trees until they were hidden.

"This place, is it hidden like the temple?" the lieutenant asked, his eyes bright with hope.

The woman pointed at the hidden temple and village and said, "Chunggugui."

"Is the Captain held prisoner by the Chinks there?" Private London asked, wishing Sergeant Kim was here to translate.

The old Mudang pointed at the drawings of the captain, and then pointed at the hidden northern village on the map.

"How the hell does she know all this, sir?" Sergeant Dempsey's voice of reason piped up.

The Mudang did not even look at the American sergeant; she just went back to her map and drew two parallel dotted lines from her temple to the other hidden temple/village.

She then walked towards the north curve of the inner temple, to a statue of a fierce bear creature in a semi-circular alcove.

Private Hartnell walked across the temple and raised his rifle a little, just in case this was a trick.

The Mudang cackled and pulled at one of the man-bear's arms, which swivelled downwards and a grating stone sound echoed from the wall next to the alcove. The old lady, using wiry strength, pushed a door sized section of the wall inward two inches.

"Kach'I oda." She smiled and beckoned the soldiers forward with her left hand.

"Well I'll be a whore's drawers!" Hartnell exclaimed, from where he was standing it looked like some sort of secret passage.

"Blimey," London stated as he tagged on behind the lieutenant and sergeant, as they followed the old woman's beckoning.

"Milgi?" the woman asked, making a pushing motion with both hands, towards the secret door.

"Dempsey, London, help the lady out," the lieutenant ordered as they approached.

"Gimme a break," Sergeant Dempsey muttered under his breath, then, standing next to the British soldier, they both began to push.

With a little effort, and silent praise for the old woman's strength, they pushed the secret stone doorway inwards.

Sergeant Dempsey whipped out his torch and shone it down the dark passageway that the secret door had revealed. Steps led down only a little way and the stone-sided passage led on straight into the darkness.

"Get the men ready to move, Sergeant, we are going to surprise those Chinese bastards and rescue the Captain." Lieutenant Samuels took out his pistol again, a grim look on his young face.

"We're gonna do what, sir?" was the sergeant's surprised reply.

"Take this passage like the map says and attack the Chinese position by stealth, Sergeant Dempsey. Is that clear?"

"But Loo-tenant, apart from London here we are engineers attacking a superior force of Chinese soldiers in a fortifiable position." Dempsey tried to reason with the greenhorn lieutenant.

"Ah yes, but we will have the element of surprise, Sergeant." The lieutenant puffed up his pigeon chest and stuck out his chin, to make himself look bigger.

"What about the Captain's orders to inform HQ of the Chinks?" Suddenly the mild-mannered lieutenant had gone from engineer to General Patton, in the space of one fire fight.

"We can still inform Colonel Yorke, once we have rescued the Captain and got off this God-forsaken plateau," Lieutenant Samuels insisted. He knew in his heart that Ashley was still alive and would risk anything to save him.

"This fortune-teller ain't playing wid a full deck, what if we run into an ambush?" Dempsey pleaded; he didn't want to lose any more men.

"You have your orders, Sergeant Dempsey," Lieutenant Samuels barked.

Sergeant Dempsey looked from the lieutenant, to the crazy Korean woman, to the men, and backed down.

The Mudang grabbed a flaming torch from the wall next to the secret passageway and descended the five steps in front of her. The lieutenant followed quickly behind, Dempsey nodded for Private London to follow.

Robert London liked the brash American Sergeant, but wanted to save Captain Woodholme-Browne if he could.

"Perez, get your ass in here, we're moving out," the sergeant bellowed across the inner temple, "Hartnell, you too!"

Private Hartnell moved past the sergeant as PFC Perez entered the temple and made his way towards the sergeant.

"In there?" he questioned as Hartnell descended the stone steps.

"Aha," the sergeant nodded in affirmative.

Private First Class Miguel Perez looked to the heavens, crossed himself and entered the cold, dank passageway.

Sergeant Dempsey looked around and crossed himself too, "Ace, King, Queen, Jack," he whispered and was last to enter the secret passageway.

Chapter 14

The Village

Captain Ashley Woodholme-Browne found himself tied to the most rickety wooden chair his bum had had the misfortune to sit upon. His head ached like hell and he wished to God, he could scratch the itchy dried blood from his face and neck.

He was alone for the time being, alone in a dark wooden hut he had been hauled into an hour ago. His head was fuzzy about all the facts, but he was sure he'd been dragged down into some subterranean village.

The Chinese soldiers had been the only people he had seen, so he assumed the place had been deserted for some time.

Ashley wondered if anyone had escaped the Chinese ambush apart from him. At least Sergeant Dempsey's trio could raise the alarm back at Divisional HQ.

A rickety door, which seemed to have been woven, rather than nailed, together, was pulled abruptly open and the light from an oil lantern flooded the tiny one room hut.

Three Chinese soldiers entered the room, two volunteer soldiers and then a rather cruel looking fellow officer. One of the soldiers hung the lantern above Ashley's head, on a low rafter, then stepped back to stand to attention next to the chair. The other soldier held his Burp gun in his hands, as he stood in front of the door guarding it.

The officer then moved to stand in front of Captain Woodholme-Browne, his legs slightly apart, just eyeing up the young British Officer. The enemy captain sniffed and then slowly took off his pair of fur lined brown leather gloves. The Chinese officer neatly folded them away in a coat pocket and just stood and stared at Woodholme-Browne for a minute.

Captain Woodholme-Browne had sort of expected punches to vital areas and shouted interrogations, but the Chinese officer's silent treatment was far more unnerving.

"What is your name?" the oily toned officer spoke in near perfect English.

Ashley raised his eyebrows in mild shock, trying to remember the articles of the Geneva Convention on the treatment of prisoners of war.

"Let's make it easier for you; my name is Captain Wu Pin Lu of the 12th Chinese Field Army, advanced scout company." The Chinese captain began to circle the English captain's chair. "Who are you and what are you doing on this plateau?" Wu Pin Li continued to walk slowly around the prisoner, knowing when he went out of vision it would put the British captain's hackles up.

"Woodholme-Browne, Captain, serial number one, two, two, four, zero, zero, six, eight," the captain replied crisply and with as much British stiff upper lip as he could muster.

"See that was not too difficult was it, Captain Woodho-Browne?" Captain Wu stopped pacing in front of the prisoner once again. "Now what are you and your American friends doing on the Yŏu Plateau? There are no North Korean soldiers here to fight."

"Looking for a good picnic spot for General McArthur's victory tea party, what about you?" Captain Woodholme-Browne replied bravely, staring right back at Wu's cold brown eyes.

If he was expecting a rebuke of the fist variety, he didn't get one: the Chinese captain tittered politely.

"Tea eh? That's something our nations have in common, as well as Hong Kong. Why side with the capitalist pig Trueman and his fellow countrymen when our countries have allied in the past?"

"I'm a soldier in His Majesty's British Army; not a politician. But some tea would be nice, if it's forthcoming." Captain Woodholme-Browne smiled and Captain Wu smiled back, but his eyes said something different.

"You are putting on a very brave face, Captain Woodho-Browne, but I would not be smiling if all the men under my command were slaughtered."

Captain Wu's words had the desired effect and the smile dropped from the Royal Engineers officer's lips.

"Now the niceties end, Captain, what unit are you from and what American Division do you report to?" The Chinese captain's words were more shrill and louder now.

"Woodholme-Browne, Captain, serial number one, two, two, four, zero, zero, six, eight." He gritted his teeth and pushed out his chest for effect.

"Why are you on this plateau?" Captain Wu shouted.

"Woodholme-Browne, Captain, serial number one, two, two, four, zero, zero, six, eight."

"Fu-Pan-Chang Shi." Captain Wu nodded at the Chinese lance corporal standing next to the chair, who bowed at his captain and balled his fists.

Sergeant Kim Jun Ho crawled slowly and painfully on his belly, behind the masonry of a fallen archway to his left where there was more rock cover.

An ancient looking stone walled hut lay only twenty feet from his original position and two Chinese soldiers were using it as a guard room. Luckily rock falls and masonry debris littered the slopes and rock face where the entrance to the forgotten village was.

Sergeant Kim held his position and peeked out from under a large man-carved piece of rock. One of the two guards was trying to light a fire in the hut, while the other chatted to him from outside.

To the left of the small hut leading from the rubble where the entrance came out was the remains of a cobbled road. The road led between the remains and ruins of a village with stone walled huts with wooden, bamboo or some sort of thatched roofs. Some huts were small, others family sized, a few were still usable, but the majority were half collapsed.

What the road led to, through the hidden village, was a golden temple which seemed to have been carved out of the surrounding rock face. It must have taken decades to carve it out and then overlay it with gold. It was sixty feet high and fifty feet across. It seemed to Sergeant Kim that it looked a little like the Mudang temple they had found, but it had three pagoda style towers that led up from a more oblong base. Two huge statues of beasts Kim could not recognise stood at the bottom of golden steps that led up to the dark temple entrance.

Yet that was not the most shocking aspect of the ruins, temple and village. The whole place was below ground in a titanic cavern. To the far right beyond the village was an opening out on to the side of the plateau, maybe fifty feet or so below the plateau's edge. A five foot stone wall covered the bottom edge. While trailing plants on a ledge that traversed the length of the top of the opening, ensured it was hidden from outside view.

The temple and the village were perfectly hidden and it looked like it had been for many generations of his forefathers.

Sergeant Kim could see other Chinese soldiers moving about the ruins, carrying flaming brands. Two were far away across the vast cavern exploring the great opening and wall. A couple more could be seen exploring the village and torchlight shone from the temple and some of the more intact huts.

The guard on the road went inside his hut and Sergeant Kim swiftly moved on through the rubble and rocks away from the soldiers. The side of the cavern to the left of the dissecting road was obviously darker and less of the village huts seemed intact. Only a larger hut, three times that of any of the others seemed habitable; In fact it looked well looked after, more so than the fallen down hovels nearest to it.

Sergeant Kim decided to keep to the darker end of the cavern and keep to the rocky slopes. One hut, with only half its stone walls left, was very close to his position and it was there he would make for.

He had not seen hide-nor-hair of any prisoners yet, but in the dark cavern at night it was understandable. They were probably being held in one of the smaller habitable huts nearer the great opening, or in the shining gold temple itself.

He wondered as he crept from rock to shadow, how the Chinese forces had stumbled on this place. He had lived in this area as a young boy; he had heard many myths and legends about the Yŏu Plateau, but never of a hidden village and a temple of gold.

Maybe that's what the Maoist soldiers were after, gold to fund the Communist war in Korea. That seemed the logical answer, but everything about the Yŏu Plateau defied natural logic. This was the last vestige of an ancient era, hidden away from the mechanical and industrial destruction of the mid-twentieth century.

The plateau, like the two temples and this hidden cavern, belonged to an ancient and more mystical era. Where dragons, heroes and magic were commonplace and that scared his analytical school teacher mind to death.

The Mudang temple, the Tolharubang stones, the shaman poles, were all here to stop something escaping from this place. Who or what dwelt here, he wondered, and could he rescue the prisoners before it or they showed themselves?

The secret passage from the inner temple had led for sixty or so yards before coming to a halt, at a rusty looking iron door.

The Mudang looked back with another toothy grin of reassurance and pulled a brass key from the folds of her robes.

The remaining men of the Engineering expedition raised their weapons in readiness, just in case it was a North Korean trap.

The old woman turned the key in the lock and pulled the door inwards, with three jarring tugs. It looked like the door had not been opened in a good many years.

Even though it was dark outside and inside, the area through the door seemed colder and more naturally illuminated.

The Mudang wrapped her white robes around herself and moved through the doorway. Lieutenant Samuels raised his Colt .45 and followed her through. He had to duck as the walls and ceiling became earth and ends of roots. Ahead of him the Mudang squeezed past a large dark object blocking the passageway ahead.

It was the rough bark of a large tree and as he squeezed around it, a wet icy breeze assaulted his face and neck. A push with his legs and he was outside, in a ditch or valley which led onward. Snow was falling and easily settling on the frozen earth. Trees and bushes lined the top edges of the trench, which were seven or so feet below the tree line.

Lieutenant Samuels moved forward to give Private London space to squeeze past the tree. He moved closer to the Mudang, who stood, her face up to the snowy heavens, letting it fall on her aged countenance.

Soon the whole party were through the gap and they set off through the now heavy swirling snow: following the Mudang along the trench that stretched ahead of them.

Captain Woodholme-Browne was worried; he hadn't felt the last two punches to his face and head. He wondered if he was going to pass out as the blood dripped from cuts on his cheek, nose, mouth and above his left eye.

"Gau La!" ordered Captain Wu loudly to his lance corporal.

The Fu-Pan-Chang stepped backwards and began to rub his bruised and bloodied fist.

"Now, Captain Woodho-Browne, are you ready to talk?" The Chinese Lien-Chang crouched down and looked at the once handsome face, now bloodied and bruised.

"What unit are you from, Captain?" the Chinese captain asked again, "What is your mission here?"

"Bollocks to you!" the British captain spat, sending blood flying on to the Chinese captain's trousers. He knew being in the company of lower ranks would pay off sometime.

"Do!" the captain shouted at the guard by the door, and held out his hand waiting.

The surprised guard fumbled around his belt and pulled a four inch bladed knife from its sheath.

"Now you will answer my questions." Captain Wu waved the knife in front of the captive Englishman's eyes for effect. "What shall we cut off first? An ear? An eyelid? Or something lower?" the captain sneered in his low throaty voice.

Captain Woodholme-Browne knew the game was up and any second now he would blab.

"Lien Chang!" cried another Chinese officer as he burst through the flimsy door.

The Chinese captain stood up and threw the knife into the floor, his face incandescent with rage at his subordinate's interruption.

Grabbing his P'ai-Chang by the shoulder of his winter coat, he pushed him back through the door, into the cold darkness of the subterranean village.

"How dare you interrupt me, Second Lieutenant Kong!" the Chinese captain raged in his native tongue, "This better be important."

The young second lieutenant was glad of the darkness so his tyrannical commanding officer could not see the tears of fear welling around his eyes. "We've captured someone in the village, in the larger building over there sir." The P'ai-Chang pointed to the darkest end of the cavern.

"Wait here!" the captain barked, yet a little less abrasively.

Lien-Chang Wu turned on his heel and re-entered the hut where the British captain was being held captive. "I will let you have time to think now, Captain Woodho-Browne." The cruel Chinese captain smiled. "When I return I will expect answers. Or as your Shakespeare puts it, your pound of flesh."

The Royal Engineer could do nothing but stare back at the Chinese captain, his face a mask of pain.

The Chinese officer left after barking orders to the two remaining guards. Captain Woodholme-Browne closed his puffy eyelids and wondered, what had been so important to interrupt his interrogation? Had the Chinese caught up with Sergeant Dempsey and his men? If so the whole of the United Nations northern front could be in mortal danger.

"So who have you captured?" Lien-Chang Wu asked his P'ai-Chang as they crossed the road towards the largest hut in the cavern.

"Erm, it's easier if you just see, sir," the young officer stammered.

"A surprise, Kong, good for you boy for showing a little backbone for once," the captain smiled wickedly.

They approached the large hut, which seemed to be three round huts built together.

Fu P'ai-Chang Mai stood outside the hut's entrance waiting for the officers, whom he bowed to as they approached.

"I hear we have another prisoner, Sergeant?" the captain asked, intrigued by his men's sense of mystery and suspense.

"This way, Captain." The Fu P'ai-Chang opened a thick wooden door, which let light stream out.

The Lien-Chang walked past his Fu P'ai-Chang who held the door open for him. The light from a lantern and an open fire made his eyes wince, then the overpowering warmth hit him.

"Blessed warmth," the captain purred, "how is it so hot in here?"

"The fire heats a patchwork of clay pipes that are laid beneath the floorboards. They run the length of the building, Captain," the veteran sergeant explained.

The captain closed his eyes and let the warmth caress his heavily clothed body; it had been over a month since he had felt such heat.

The sergeant, meanwhile, had moved forward to open the next connecting door, which was crafted from pine. The place made Wu Pin Li feel uneasy and it wasn't just the stifling heat.

This hut seemed to have an old Roman heating system; it had solid almost European designed doors and just did not sit right in the ancient subterranean cavern.

He moved through the threshold, and then stopped dead in his tracks, like instant rigor mortis had set in.

Before him, stood in between two of his soldiers, with bayonet fixed rifles at the ready, was the most beautiful young Korean woman the captain had ever seen. She was dressed in a yellow and brown hanbok which flowed down to cloth wrapped and showing ankles. Her hands were clasped together at her abdomen, covered by long cuffed sleeves.

Lien-Chang Wu reckoned she must be about nineteen years of age, her hair, long and black, was braided down her back. The Chinese Captain was captivated by her beauty and bemused by her sole presence here in the village.

"Have you questioned her, Second Lieutenant Kong?" he asked his P'ai-Chang, turning his head slightly his way, but unable to take his eyes off the girl.

"I've tried a little, Captain, but I don't think she speaks any Cantonese or Mandarin," Kong replied looking at his Lien-Chang, yet his eyes kept flicking to the Korean girl every second or so.

"Sergeant Mai, you know a little Korean, see if you can get any information out of her."

Fu P'ai-Chang Mai Pai Tiao moved up, just in advance of his Lien-Chang.

"Eerumee otdok owe-seemneekka?" the sergeant asked for her name in Korean.

The girl raised her right hand and placed her open palm over her mouth. Either she couldn't speak or was refusing to speak.

She let her hand drop and hid it under the folds of her sleeve again; her eyes never left the Lien-Chang's eyes. The Chinese captain blinked, he felt he was losing himself in her red painted lips.

"She could be a spy, dressed as a girl," offered P'ai-Chang Kong in his native Cantonese.

"Oh my poor innocent Shuo Tiao, what do they teach young officers these days?" Lien-Chang Wu chuckled.

"Sergeant Mai, prove to the Second Lieutenant that this is a real woman," Lien-Chang Wu ordered politely.

"Captain?" Fu P'ai-Chang Mai questioned the order.

"Do it!" the Lien-Chang hissed with menace.

The Fu P'ai-Chang did not hesitate this time; he walked up to the Korean woman and firmly yanked apart her robes just enough to expose the tops of her small breasts.

"Satisfied now Kong?" Lien-Chang Wu asked the young officer sarcastically as the girl covered up her exposed body again.

"Yes, Captain." The young P'ai-Chang bowed with embarrassment.

"Leave me and the prisoner alone now, I will question her myself," the smirking Lien-Chang ordered.

"What about the British officer?" P'ai-Chang Kong asked.

"I will deal with him later Kong," Lien-Chang Wu replied, noticing the low bed and pillows around the sides of the room for the first time. "I want you to search the entire village and temple again." Lien-Chang unbuttoned his coat as his men left the room. "Oh and Kong, I do not want to be disturbed, even if you capture General MacArthur himself: is that understood?"

"Perfectly, Captain." P'ai-Chang Kong understood all too well what the Lien-Chang meant.

P'ai-Chang Kong stationed two men to guard the only door into the building and he and Fu P'ai-Chang walked silently towards the temple to organise another search of the cavern. The air seemed ten times colder now that they had experienced the warmth of the large hut.

The Korean girl smiled lustfully at the Chinese captain and opened the front of her dress to expose her breasts again.

With hungry eyes she walked towards the Chinese captain, who immediately slapped her hard across her left cheek. Wu Pin Li continued to unbutton his winter coat as the girl crashed to the floor.

He smiled smugly as she looked up at him, her eyes wild and feral, yet a concupiscent smile still on her bloodied lips.

She crawled towards him again as he let his coat fall back down his shoulders and onto the warm floorboards behind him. The brazen girl rubbed her head up the side of his left leg, and then her long delicate fingers reached upwards to unbutton his army trousers.

Sergeant Kim Jun Ho felt sure as eggs is eggs, that his hiding place was about to be discovered. He had heard loud Chinese voices in the next room for the last fifteen minutes or so. He had waited behind an upturned table, his Garland at the ready to shoot anyone who burst through the wooden door: but nobody had come!

He had managed to slip into the largest of the huts over half an hour ago, by sheer damn luck!

The hut had been slightly raised off its stone foundations and he had found a trapdoor covered with dirt only by accident, when he felt it give under his boots, as he crept around the hut. He cleared the dirt away, lifted it up and then had to plunge inside sharpishly to avoid a Chinese patrol. It was overwhelmingly hot under the hut, with clay pipes too hot to touch. A trapdoor overhead had led him into the back room of the three round roomed dwelling.

Only light through the doorframe of the next room provided any illumination. It must be a dining area: it had a square table, two chairs and chests and shelves full of scrolls and books. They looked very ancient but the light was not sufficient to make out any titles.

A crash of an opening door, shouts in Chinese and a woman's unmistakeable wail, made him freeze in his tracks.

He moved out of his paralysis and headed silently to the door. The door and frame had been warped by damp and the years, so a crack of opportunity could be seen.

Some kind of curtain blocked his view, so he followed the crackdown until he was on all fours. A gap where the curtain had not been fully drawn across gave him a view of the lantern and candle lit room beyond.

He could see one Chinese soldier plain as day, holding his bayonet fixed Carbine towards the body of a young Korean woman. Sergeant Kim blinked; the bright light was such a contrast to the darkness of the cavern that his peeking eye was weeping.

When more Chinese troops entered the room, he retreated to the end of his darkened room and slowly and silently upturned the thick wooden table to crouch behind.

Now after no troops had come to break down the hidden door, he crept forward once more. His right eye going to the low crack between the door and its frame.

"Kwa sŏnggyohada," he swore under his breath as he watched the willing Korean girl tug down a Chinese officer's combat trousers: and greedily go to work on his small erect penis.

The Mudang stopped and shivered. Either side of the now deep trench were two Totem poles identical to the ones they had passed on the path during the day.

The snow was like a blizzard above their heads; being in the trench protected them from the freezing winds, but not from the heavy snowfall. All of the soldiers' helmets, shoulders and packs were covered white.

Private London caught some snow on his gloved hand and after a minute, ate some to relieve his thirst.

"You okay?" Lieutenant Samuels asked the old woman as she began to sing a chant in Korean.

Samuels looked back at Private Hartnell, who just gave an *I don't know* shrug back.

The Mudang clapped her thin ungloved hands together. "Suhoja!" she cried, and then carried on past the shaman poles.

"This is giving me the screaming abdabs," Private London muttered as they set off again, following the old Korean woman.

"I know what you mean," ventured PFC Perez behind him, "this place is unholy."

"Reminds me of a creek back home the old prospectors said was the devil's playground," added Private Hartnell from in front of London.

"Cut the crap guys," Sergeant Dempsey said from the rear, "and the talking."

The small band of United Nations soldiers trudged through the deepening snow after the Mudang. Dressed in her white robes she was nearly invisible in the darkness against the snowy backdrop.

Lieutenant Samuels stifled a yawn at the same time as his stomach rumbled. He'd not walked so far since officer's training, but the thought of Captain Woodholme-Browne being held captive by the enemy spurred him on.

Chapter 15

Lien-Chang Wu's Last Stand

Captain Woodholme-Browne awoke from his groggy sleep, his face smarting like he had washed with a stinging nettle flannel. As his eyes refocused he noticed that only one guard remained at the door: looking exceedingly bored.

Ashley Woodholme-Browne kept his head at a loll; his eyes only open as slits. If he was going to get out of this alive he would have to do something soon, before the vicious Captain Wu returned.

He tested the rope around his wrists, tied behind the chair: but they wouldn't budge. Around him, rope was wrapped around his waist, only his legs were free. Maybe he could rush at the guard and get a lucky shoulder barge on the Chinese volunteer.

Just then the young Chinese soldier turned and saw the British captain was slyly looking at him. He raised his rifle and pointed it at the Royal Engineer's head.

"Ju-ee!" he stated loudly, hatred in his communist eyes.

"I get the message," Captain Ashley Woodholme-Browne croaked from his blood-tinged lips. His escape plan would have to wait a while, at least.

Lien-Chang Wu's shirt followed his combat blouse on to the floor. He was nearly naked as he pulled down his trousers, his boots and socks were still on.

The Korean girl was still on her knees before him in supplication, fellating his rigid penis like it was an ice popsicle. Wu grabbed her hair roughly with both hands and grinded his pubic hair into her face, his cock thrust past her tonsils.

Wu Pin Li smiled broadly, this night was getting better and better for the cruel Chinese Lien-Chang. The successful attack on the capitalist forces makes him twist fistfuls of the Korean girl's hair round in his fist. The smell, cries, noise of battle and especially the deaths had given him a steely erection during combat. The thought of it made his penis feel like a steel bayonet protruding from his loins.

His mind wondered over the corpses of battle and he applied the coup de grace to his own injured soldier. All the while his vile thoughts replayed themselves on his unfortunate sexual victim. She hardly had time to gasp for any air and he viciously thrust into her throat, again and again.

One more image of killing his second wounded soldier that could not keep up, was enough for Wu. With a savage grunt and thrust, he ejaculated deep into the girl's throat, his legs trembling with ecstasy.

He held her deep, not caring about her suffering, having experienced the greatest orgasm of his life. Then, as the feeling ebbed away, he finally let her slip from his grasp to the floor. She gasped for air, rivulets of Wu's semen dribbling from each corner of her battered mouth.

Wu breathed deeply and ran his own hands over his taut and hairless chest and abdomen. The coughs and splutters of his victim only excited him more. He looked down and was surprised and pleased to see that his erection showed no signs of wilting.

"Ngor surng yeeu dor dee!" he mocked his victim in Chinese, but she did not understand his statement that he wanted more.

Sergeant Kim had thankfully not seen the last throws of the Chinese officer's savagery. He had carefully reopened the trapdoor, without too much noise and had eased himself beneath the hot pipes underneath the large dwelling again.

He dragged himself to the outer trapdoor and listened, but his escape plans were quickly dashed. Loud Chinese voices could be heard above him, their voices muffled by the wood of the trapdoor.

He decided to wait there in the enveloping womb of heat and wait until the voices went go away. The warmth of the pipes were making him sleepy and with his bruises, wounds and lack of food, a little nauseous as well. Add to that the cramped confines of the tunnel, he knew he could not stay at the trapdoor for longer than another five minutes tops.

If the Chinese guards did not leave he would have to make a decision. Either to exit the tunnel all guns blazing or retreat back to the dark room again and be trapped in comfort at least.

Wu Pin Li was in his full naked glory, his boots, trousers and underwear lay on top of the rest of his army clothes. He had given the girl a boot to the thigh and stepped on her left hand before he had made her take them off of course. She was quite a compliant little bitch, taking her punishment well. The Korean girl had wailed, cried and grunted in pain at all the right places.

Yet still she came back for more abuse. Wu's mission, men, thoughts of his English captive, had been blown away by this beautiful and darkly lustful Korean girl.

He stood above her in total domination, his penis still hard and not since his teens had an erection that lasted so long. She was on all fours in front of him, her backside and feet towards his naked and toasty warm feet. She looked back at him over her naked shoulder and smiled wantonly, blood and semen dried on her lips and chin.

She slowly lifted her bruised left hand and squeezed her left breast hard, her nails digging into her tender flesh.

Wu lifted his eyebrows in surprise and his hand slipped down to rub his erection. She was unlike any girl he had ever been with before, most had been crying for their mothers by now. He had initially thought that he would despatch her with a bullet to the back of the head, while buggering her to death.

Now his thoughts had changed, he would take her as a trophy of war. Ideas of dog collars and leading her about on a chain were bouncing around his sadistic mind.

The girl's hand had reached back to the folds of her dress and she began to hitch up the material. She slowly pulled it up her legs and over her naked behind. She did so with both legs, so the dress was bunched up on her back: her naked thighs, round bottom and moist cunt exposed to him.

Wu didn't even hit her this time; he sunk to his knees, pulled her vaginal lips apart with his left hand, while his right hand guided his cock to her wet, warm opening. Once half an inch in, he moved his hands to her hips and looked deep into her dark eyes: as he thrust his entire length deep inside her. The look of shock and pain in her eyes, matched his initial painful thrust as her vaginal walls pulled back his foreskin as he roughly entered her.

With each subsequent thrust the pain in her eyes and his penis subsided. Soon both cunt and invading cock were lubricated with desire and their fucking began in earnest.

Sergeant Kim swallowed some bile and decided it was time to retreat back to the dark room. Even if he got back outside, he felt sick and dizzy and would be shot in an instant.

He shuffled back past the hot pipes, breathing hard, and went back into the room, with its cooler darkness, and re-closed the trapdoor. He fumbled for his canteen and took three small sips of water.

Then poured some water into his palm and splashed it over his face. Feeling a little better, he sat on a chair, his canteen at his feet, and his rifle on his lap.

Lien-Chang Wu thrust away, as he and the Korean girl rutted like dogs on heat. He was building up a nice sweat as he fucked her hard. He would take his girl back to China as his sex slave. He had been promised a promotion to Ying-Chang and his own battalion if he completed his mission successfully, and all the honour and trappings that it would bring. His mission was to find the golden temple of the Yŏu plateau, before the United Nations forces did.

The communists were after its gold. They knew that you cannot fight a war without money. Wu recalled that the Roman Cicero had said the very same thing nearly two centuries ago. The remains of his British education in Hong Kong were still in the back of his communist mind: which bore his early hatred for the British, because two drunken Royal Navy sailors had raped and beaten his mother to death. A scene he had witnessed aged only five and which made him the man he was today.

Rage took him and he smacked the palm of his right hand repeatedly against her thighs and buttocks and thrust deep inside her. When he noticed she was squealing with delight, a swift punch to the back of her head showed her not to enjoy it more than he was.

Her head bowed now to the floor in supplication as he built up again to shoot his seed deep inside her. Maybe she would get pregnant, oh what fun he could have with her then, he thought evilly.

Lieutenant Samuels blinked at the snow that had stuck to his eyelashes. The darkness and the blizzard conditions made keeping his eyes fixed on the old woman dressed in white ahead a difficult task.

It wasn't until he nearly bumped into her back, that he realised she had stopped. The rest of the men approached behind him, huddled up for any kind of warmth. There was not a toe, foot, hand, finger or face between them that was not numb with cold.

The Mudang tugged at his left hand which was holding his switched off torch.

Lieutenant Samuels's numb thumb eventually flicked on the torch switch and everyone squinted against the intruding glare. Extending his arm the torch shone past the Mudang's pointing finger towards a round, snow covered stone. The trench had come to a dead end and the obviously man carved stone circle, which was about six feet in diameter, blocked the way.

"Tonol," the Mudang spat through the snow that flew into her mouth.

"Tunnel," Lieutenant Samuels repeated, glad that one word out of a million sounded the same in both English and Korean.

He pointed a leather gloved finger at the snow covered stone and the old Mudang nodded in return.

"Annyonghi," The Korean Mudang said and bowed towards the young American officer. Then with a sprightly step that belayed her years, she was away. She was past London, Hartnell and Perez before Lieutenant Samuels could even cry out, "Stop her!"

Sergeant Dempsey made a grab for the old shaman woman, but as he did the blizzard seemed to quadruple in intensity between her and the American engineer. Even in the darkness Dempsey's eyes were temporarily blinded by the dense swirling snow in front of him. When it died down a few seconds later the Mudang had vanished. She left no footprint or sign in the snow covered trench.

Dempsey trudged/ran on a few steps down the deep ditch, but she, in her white garb was nowhere to be seen.

"Shit," he cursed to himself, "I've lost her, sir."

"What we gonna do now?" Private Hartnell despaired to no one in particular. The snow and the freezing, below zero, temperatures were even getting to his cheery disposition.

"You, Hartnell and London are going to help me open this tunnel," Lieutenant Samuels said. "Now snap to it!"

The two soldiers hurried forward to help their superior officer, who was dusting off a two inch layer of snow from the top half of the wheel shaped stone.

"I don't fucking like diss Loo-tenant," Sergeant Dempsey warned, moving closer. "This could be a god-damn Chink trap."

"Noted Sergeant," was Samuels' only reply. "Now push, men."

With much effort and Perez's late help, they pushed the round, carved rock into a before hidden groove in the trench wall: revealing a dark tunnel entrance.

Lieutenant Samuels' torch pierced the darkness of the tunnel; it had stone sides and columns to support its roof and the world above.

"Let's go!" Samuels said and plunged into the tunnel, which sloped downwards after four steps. London, Hartnell and then Perez followed him inside.

"What else ya gonna do, Joseph Dempsey," he chided himself, "sit out here and freeze to fucking death?"

Wiping the snow off his Carbine, he pulled out his torch and followed the rest of the men into the dark, dank tunnel.

Down the snow covered trench the Mudang watched the foreign soldiers enter the tunnel with interest. She began to trudge back to her temple, singing a shaman protection song against the evil fox spirit Kumiho.

Lien-Chang Wu Pin Li lay on his back, his sweaty arms behind his head, exhausted from another prolonged sex session.

The Korean girl, whose stamina seemed to be unbound, pulled herself off his shrinking post-ejaculative cock. His manhood wet with mixed post-coital juices, audibly 'plopped' out, and fell onto his sweat-shiny groin.

He watched her red-slapped behind rise, the red puffiness of her vaginal lips and the streaks of semen down her inner thighs made him smile with rare satisfaction.

He liked that fact that she still wore her dress like some symbol of her lost virtue. Her shoulders, with bite marks, were exposed, as well as her breasts which he had slapped and squeezed 'til they were bruised. Her dress was folded up and tucked into her waistband to expose her thighs and her slightest of ankles.

He breathed in deeply through his nose then out again slowly. He could really do with a good eight hours' sleep, but the girl had other ideas. She reached up to a shelf and pulled down an earthenware jar. She removed a cork stopper and turned to face the Chinese Lien-Chang again.

'What next?' his controlling sex addled mind wondered. The girl answered by pouring a clear shiny liquid into the palm of her left hand and proceeded to rub it into her perky, yet tender breasts.

Wu felt a twitch of interest in his flaccid manhood, like a caught fish giving its final flip of escape on the quayside. The girl smiled deeply and moved to kneel at his feet. He lifted his head with interest as the girl poured more sesame oil into her left hand, set down the jar, then rubbed her long fingered hands together.

Wu watched on as the girl began to massage the oil into his feet and toes, it felt exquisite after all the cold weather marching he had done recently. Her gentle touch on his toes nearly outstripped the feeling he had got from the vile and degrading sex acts he had performed on her over the last two hours.

The girl troubled him, after all the pain he had inflicted on her, she still came back for more. Maybe she had a master here, the temple protector; maybe this was the only life she knew? Yet her soul and spirit seemed strong and intact, maybe she was unbreakable: maybe he was the one to break her.

Wu smiled, the girl smiled, her thoughts her own, and rubbed more oil into his feet and ankles.

Sergeant Kim was feeling a lot less light-headed now, so crawled silently forward again to the low crack in the doorframe, to see what was going on.

Things had swung the other way in the room beyond. The Chinese officer seemed to be supplicant and the Korean girl had taken the lead. The Chinese captain was on all fours now, sideways on to Kim voyeur's eyes, peeking through the gap between door and lower frame. He couldn't see the Chinaman's head or shoulders; only the lower half of his body and all of the beautiful Korean girl's many charms. Kim felt a pang of cowardice, letting this vileness continue. He hid behind his ideology, that she was North Korean, an enemy civilian, or was it his fear of death? Any attempt to free the girl would bring the rest of the Chinese forces swiftly down on them. Then they would both be killed for certain, not an improvement in the situation for either of them. Where there was life, there was hope, he had taught his senior English students, which seemed an age ago.

There was something else that kept his eye at the crack, something his honour would never admit. The sight of two glistening bodies, hot from many acts of sex and the anticipation of more to follow, was appealing to a deeper, baser side of him. He watched on.

Lieutenant Samuels led his men on silently through the man-made ancient stone tunnel. Every last one of them was fatigued, but glad at least to be out of the freezing snow and icy winds above ground.

The tunnel they had been following for an hour had been dead straight at all times with only a slight, near unnoticeable, incline downwards. Samuels' mind was impressed with the workmanship that could engineer such a straight, even dimensioned tunnel, through solid rock for such a length.

On they walked, the only sounds were that of weapons' straps, belts and webbing moving against their forward motion.

"Halt," Samuels hissed to his following band of soldiers.

Up ahead, he was unsure how far, was the faintest of glows.

"Lights off," he ordered and within seconds they were in total darkness. Yet ahead, maybe a hundred and fifty yards or so, was some sort of natural light.

The Korean girl flicked her jet black hair from her face as her tongue darted out to lick the tip of his penis. He was still on all fours covered in oil. She had her forearm on the floor, her head bent round his left leg and under his abdomen.

Lien-Chang Wu moaned with pleasure, never had a woman bewitched him so with her love arts. The girl's long tongue licked along the underneath and tenderest part of his shaft. Then, like a cat lapping at milk, she licked and licked at the end of his manhood. Wu felt a quiver of delight, or was it a muscle spasm down the side of his right thigh? Then he felt her strong left hand replace her rasping tongue.

She moved to a position behind his naked behind, her hand making slow, pulling motions on his erection. Her tongue came from her luscious lips to lick at his salty tasting testicles. She sniffed in deep the musk of his hot groin and licked up his ball sack to his anus.

The feel of her hand tugging at his slightly red and overused penis and the feel of her tongue probing his sphincter, sent waves of ecstasy through his body. She was in total control now, willingly doing things only he had forced upon other women before her.

Kim Jun Ho watched on spellbound, his full-bladdered erection like a steel bayonet beneath his fatigue trousers. He watched as the girl sucked deep on her forefinger then pushed it deep into the Chinese officer's back passage. Kim wondered what that would feel like, his hand reaching down to grip his erection through his trousers, to stop the frustrated pain there.

Two fingers had replaced one and Wu felt no pain, the sweat and the oil had lubricated both her fingers and his anus. In and out she worked them, all the while slowly wanking his cock with the other.

Two fingers painfully became four, but the pleasure side still vastly outweighed the pain side for Wu. Deeper into his anus her hand probed and when the pain outranked the pleasure, a faster tossing of his erection regained the sexual balance. Never had a woman gone so far, or taken his body beyond the extremes of sexual gratification.

Sergeant Kim could not turn his eyes away, he had never imagined such sexual practices existed or were physically possible. His hand pressed down on his penis now, something had to happen soon, whether it was ejaculation or he pissed himself.

He watched on aghast as the girl's entire fist worked its way inside the Chinese officer's colon. Then he noticed something wrong, subtly, at first something about the girl did not seem right. Her dress had slung lower as she fisted the enemy officer hard.

Kim gasped, his erection dying in his grip. Underneath the girl's small breasts, was another pair of slightly smaller breasts.

Wu felt an uncomfortable feeling like a stomach ache now and the deep thrusting of her fist was getting too painful.

"Stop," he whispered in Chinese.

A tight pain in his guts made him turn his head round to make her stop, then he saw her chests.

She laughed as he saw her dress was wide open now to reveal not one, but three sets of breasts running down from her chest to her taut stomach.

His eyes widened in horror as her entire arm thrust deep into his anus, through his bowels like they were jelly, and grabbed hold of his liver. Blood burst from his mouth concealing any screams. Then she pulled out her blood and crud covered arm, her hand holding most of his liver. A cold feeling raced from his groin to his head: the icy rush of death.

His eyes glazed over as the last image he saw was the girl, saturated with his blood, taking a deep bite of his liver. His body collapsed to the floor as the smiling girl chewed on his internal organs.

Sergeant Kim scrambled back from the door on his backside, shaking uncontrollably. His left hand fumbling to grab his rifle strap to drag it with him, backwards, into the room's darker shadows.

Cold fear twitched every muscle in his body, his stomach churning, his thoughts caught in a maelstrom of terror. His instinct took over and his body, on autopilot, scrambled and pushed him back to the hut's wall. There he cowered in a foetal position, hugging his borrowed Garland rifle for dear life. Childhood fear pushed away his teacher's intellect and soldier's training. He knew what was really on the other side of the door: a malevolent spirit from ancient fables. Both his sister and he had been told them as children, as a warning not to wander off alone: lest the Kumiho caught you.

Then his ears heard what his tightly shut eyes could not bear to witness. The connecting door between the centre room and his opened, and light and shadows flooded over his prone body. His ears heard the dreaded sound of heavy footfall approaching where he cowered. Sergeant Kim could not stand it any longer; his eyes flew open to see what neared him.

His primal screams echoed through the hidden cavern, as the Kumiho entered the room. Her face no longer human, but that of a fox. Upright she walked and he saw her ancient lithe haired body in all its evil majesty. Her three sets of downy hair covered breasts, her cunt open and oozing, like the saliva from the Kumiho's sharp fanged mouth. Her gait balanced and steadied by the eight tails that withered and flowed behind her like fur covered serpents.

Outside the door of the hut the two Chinese guards exchanged shocked looks and, ignoring their officer's orders, rushed inside with their rifles raised.

In his hut Captain Woodholme-Browne and his guard also heard the scream. The young Chinese volunteer turned to look out the door without thinking.

This was all Ashley Woodholme-Browne had been waiting for. He hoped the general would be proud of his engineer son now, as he ran at the guard, bent nearly double, the chair tied fast to his back and hands.

Lieutenant Samuels led his small band of men along the ledge the tunnel had come out on to. They passed through a vegetation covered chiasmic opening in the side of the plateau. Then, crouched down in a ridge of rocks and old masonry, he deployed his fighting force as best he could. His eyes, both adjusting to the darkness of the cavern in front of them and to its contents.

A shout of warning suddenly went up in Chinese, from an eagle eyed Chan-Shih near a ruined hut nearest to the side of where they entered. Followed, an instant later, by a fainter scream of such mortal terror.

P'ai-Chang Kong heard both cries and ran down the steps of the golden temple, cocking his TT33 pistol as he did so. Fu P'ai-Chang Mai and two Chan-Shihs followed at his heels, Burp guns ready to fire.

Chapter 16

Internecine

The two Chinese Chan-Shih guards entered the hut at haste, their bayonets raised and fixed in place. They hurried through the first room and kicked open the connecting door and hurried into the room beyond.

The first soldier nearly slipped over in the blood that the floor was awash with. His comrade managed to steady him and they both looked down at the mutilated naked corpse of their commanding officer.

It reminded the Chan-Shih who had slipped of when a fox had gotten into the chicken coop at home. Blood was oozing out of places where it clearly shouldn't. The cruel eyes of their Lien-Chang stared at them, bringing fear into their hearts even after death.

Movement through a door ahead, which had been hidden before by drapery, forced their eyes upwards. Another figure lay on the floor, over it towered something tall and awkward looking to the eyes. It turned, loping towards them on paws, rather than feet, a human-sized fox walking on hind legs, with eight tails swishing and twisting behind it.

The Chinese soldiers, who believed in only the evils of man, and had no place in their minds for fairy tales and gods, fired their rifles. They emptied six rounds each into the torso of the advancing beast.

The young guard turned his head, but forgot to bring his rifle round to bear, as the English captain shoulder charged into him. The Chinese guard was pushed back against the wall of the hut. He tried to raise and free his rifle from between the two of them, but the captain butted up with the top of his head into the young Chinaman's jaw. The Chan-Shih yelped in pain as it had caused him to involuntarily bite into his own tongue.

Seizing on any small advantage, Ashley head butted the short combatant on the bridge of the nose.

Captain Woodholme-Browne, hands still tied to the chair, roped to his back, kicked hard through the shocked soldier's ankles. This took the poor fellow by surprise and down he fell onto the floor, clutching at his broken nose.

As he did, Ashley aimed his chair and took a light backward jump towards the head of his enemy. There was a sickening sound as the chair and eleven stone of Englishman hit home. One of the legs had penetrated deep into the Chinese soldier's left eye socket, killing him without a cry and only a violent twitch of his entire body.

Ashley Woodholme-Browne refused to look down at what he had done; instead he eyed the bayonet-fixed rifle and pondered how he could cut his bonds with it. Outside he heard the opening salvos of small arms fire and the unmistakeable short bursts of the American made Browning Automatic Rifle (BAR).

Pan-Chang Han joined P'ai-Chang Kong's squad of men as they rushed in a crouched fashion towards the retorts of weapon fire. Four huts formed a line diagonally across the cavern nearest the opening and enemy attack.

The hut furthest to the left of him was where the British captain was being held. The hut furthest to the right had no roof and parts of the walls were missing. From here Fu-Pan-Chang Shi and a Chan-Shih were exchanging weapons' fire with several enemies, dug in around the rocks and ruins of the vast vegetation-covered opening.

P'ai-Chang Kong took Pan-Chang Han and one Chang-Shih with him and directed Fu P'ai-Chang Mai and another man to each take up defence positions behind the central huts. With two further men back guarding the main way into the hidden cavern, Kong thought he had done well in such a hectic situation.

He ordered his men to lay down suppressing fire to keep the invading forces pinned down to their cover and wait for Lien-Chang Wu to arrive and advise him further.

P.F.C Perez had found excellent cover between some V-shaped masonry, which provided a great field of fire across the cavern floor. Sergeant Dempsey and Private London were dug in to his left and Lieutenant Samuels and Private Hartnell to his right.

"Here, take this!" Sergeant Dempsey offered and pushed his own Colt .45 pistol into Perez's gut.

"Thanks, Sergeant," Perez accepted and put the pistol down on a rock next to his knee. Dempsey knew Perez's one 20 round clip would not last him long, even if it was used sparingly on its slowest cycle rate.

Out of the four huts ahead of them in a rough line, only rifle and automatic weapons' fire was coming from the ruined hut to Lieutenant Samuels' right. Even the green lieutenant engineer knew that they would need to force any opening and attack. He had not the men or ammo to stay under cover for too long.

A burst of BAR fire caused a cry of pain from behind the enemy-held hut, and the level of fire from that position dropped by half.

"Great shot, Miguel!" whooped Hartnell as he fired off a round towards the same enemy position.

"Shut the fuck up, Hartnell, and mark your men, we ain't out shooting rabbits with your cousins on the farm now!" Dempsey berated the young private, because he didn't want the kid to give away his position and get shot.

"Sergeant, I want Perez to give covering fire then the rest of us will attack that position." The lieutenant pointed towards the ruined hut, where the enemy was coming from.

"We better–" Dempsey ducked and the rest of the men flung themselves down behind cover as heavy fire suddenly erupted from the central two huts below. The bullets ricocheted and exploded chunks of stone and masonry all around their positions.

Dempsey listened intently while the rest of the men tried to make themselves as small as possible behind their cover. They were under three, maybe four, automatic weapons' fire, plus rifle fire from at least three or four positions now. Things were turning out for the worst and they were well and truly pinned down now.

The shadows and darkness were a help, they had sides of huts to aim at, and the Chinese had to aim for muzzle flashes. Yet dawn would not be more than an hour off and then, with the light flooding through the opening, they would be in trouble.

Sergeant Kim watched as a silent spectator as the Chinese soldiers fired into the Kumiho from only four yards away. Seizing the initiative, he scrambled on his belly with his rifle to the trap door and pushed himself through it. Not wanting to see who would come out as victors, because whoever won would spell the end for him.

The Kumiho wavered, her vixen head bowed looking at the wounds and blood on her breasts and belly. Then slowly she raised her head, her ears pointing ceiling-wards in furious anger. One Chan-Shih managed to fire another round before the fox spirit was on him, her sharp teeth ripping out his throat with a swift bite.

Gargling blood, the soldier dropped his rifle and fell to his knees dying, his free hands trying to stem the precious flow of life blood from his torn neck. Seeing bullets were having no effect, the remaining soldier bayoneted the Kumiho deep into her flanks with all his strength. The beast gave a mewling howl then, turning her body like no human could, bit down deep into the poor soldier's left wrist.

The shocked man let go of his rifle which slipped out of the Kumiho's side, as the vixen-spirit's teeth ground and sawed at his bones.

Unfortunately, he could not keep on his feet and he slipped backwards on to the blood covered floor. The fox spirit now loomed over him, and then something heavy and wet fell onto his chest.

Looking down in rising terror, he saw that it was his own severed left hand. The Chan-Shih turned to his side and tried to crawl away. A cold swish of the Kumiho's paw sent an instant of pain to his right leg. He was on his front now, crawling for his life, the butchered stump of his left hand always in his teary vision. Blood flew and his back arched in agony as the Kumiho's paw and extended claws shredded the clothes and nine layers of skin on his back.

"Mo chun!" he cried out. When the clarity of death strikes, ideology and theology fall, the young Chinese private called for his mother.

Blood poured from his wrist stump, leg and back as the Kumiho danced like a kitten over him, playing with him like one of her lesser feline cousins might do with a mouse.

The Chan-Shih had reached the doorway and was dragging himself through, his life-blood draining away, his body temperature and blood pressure crashing.

It had been many a decade since the Kumiho had had such sport. She pounced and poked at her victim, remembering centuries ago when her sisters and she had done the same.

On his elbows, the Chinese soldier pulled himself along, his movements slowing from feet moved, to mere inches. He coughed and struggled to move forward again, but his body was shutting down. His heart no longer had enough blood left in its veins to keep pumping. With no gasps or memorable last words, he just expired. A mutilated, bloodied mess, his short life brought to a sudden end, not by enemy bullets, but ancient, undying evil.

His right leg spasmed and the Kumiho pounced upon it with her teeth, but it brought about no reaction. The Kumiho moved forward and prodded the man's head with a paw, his head moved back and stopped.

Seeing her sport was finished she looked back into the farthest room to see that her Korean man had escaped. This didn't matter, the hunt was on and her bloodlust was up and, more than that, somewhere inside the hidden cavern was one of the special men.

She could feel his presence and had done so before he had even crossed the bridge to her plateau: her prison. Something in his very make-up and blood surged with an ancient trace of her beginnings. Only eight such men she had found in over a century and a half. This man would be her ultimate mate, a coupling that would bring about her last and ninth tail. The curse on her bloodline would finally be broken and she could leave her prison/plateau: fully a woman, whole and deadly beautiful.

Sergeant Kim's mind was a whirl of panic, a fox spirit from ancient legends behind, the thunderous echo of gunfire ahead. His mind not his own, he turned and twisted on the spot and when he stopped, the golden temple was in front of him. He rushed up the steps and into the cavernous entrance and the welcoming glow of brazier's fire.

Try as he might, Captain Ashley Woodholme-Browne could not get the dead guard's bayonet or his hands in any kind of position to cut his bonds and free himself.

He was cursing his luck when automatic fire hit and penetrated the roof above his head. He would have ducked if he had had the time, or the chance, as he was in a semi-crouch position anyway. He had to go now, like this and try and make his way to friendly positions.

Stretching and turning his neck Captain Woodholme-Browne bit into the handle of the door with his teeth and pulled it slowly backwards far enough to get a foot in the door. He crept out of the hut, down an awkward stone step into the gloom of the cavern once again. Tracer fire immediately showed where the Chinese forces were positioned. If they had not been concentrating their eyes and weapons forward, he would have been stopped straight away. He ran as fast as his crouched body allowed him, around the back of the hut and safe from enemy eyes and guns.

Rounding the hut from the left hand side, with the vast cavern opening to his left, he took stock of the situation. Both sets of forces were in fixed positions with adequate cover. The enemy had superior numbers and most likely better stocks of ammunition.

If he waited here, dawn would soon arrive and lower his chances of a concealed escape. He had to go now, hugging the darkness that clung to shadows below the rim of the opening. A burst of BAR fire caused the Chinese forces to duck for cover. This was Captain Woodholme-Browne's starter pistol, if you like, and he headed left into the coverless shadow under the vast vegetation camouflaged openings. His back ached terribly as he moved along at a slow crouch, praying to God to be invisible to the enemy.

The two Chinese soldiers put to guard the entrance to the cavern were in a military quandary. Should they join their fellows in battle, or should they investigate the screams and gunfire from the large hut behind them and nearer the temple?

Then one Chan-Shih broke ranks, he had to join up with his fellow communist soldiers to crush the western oppressors, and off he ran to join the melee. The other Chan-Shih dithered on the path that led to the temple, but then he saw a figure run up the temple steps and vanish inside the entrance. Being more curious than communist for the moment, he jogged up the cobbled path, his Burp gun at the ready. *Who had entered the temple, was it Lien-Chang Wu?*

He would never find out, because as he neared the temple something flew out of the darkness and tore off his head. His dying eyes caught sight of two glowing eyes and fangs, then the lack of oxygen and blood to the brain made his rolling head see no more.

Captain Woodholme-Browne was nearly three quarters of the way to rejoining his men, when shots began to zero in on him. He picked up his heels as much as he could and began to run as fast as the chair tied to his back would allow him.

The United Nations contingent noticed a sudden swing of enemy fire from them to a position near the rim of the cavern opening. Someone was running towards them, at a crouch with something large attached to their back.

"COVERING FIRE!" Lieutenant Samuels roared as he realised what was happening and whom the fired upon runner was. He moved down the rocks and masonry as the BAR barked its deadly 0.30 inch rounds at the enemy positions.

Private Hartnell shot off eight rapid rounds from his Garland, the clip pinging out of the top of the rifle to clatter on the rocks near him. Private London rose a little, his rapid movement of his bolt-action .303 rifle firing wildly at the Chinese lines. He could now see the captain rushing towards them, bullets hitting the floor and rocks around him.

Sergeant Dempsey gritted his nicotine stained teeth and fired his M1 Carbine, they had to forget accuracy and concentrate on suppressing fire to give the captain a chance of escape.

Lieutenant Samuels fired his Colt .45 as he reached the lower boulders and rocks on the cavern floor. He could now see Ashley's face, contorted in pain as he ran only ten yards from safety now. A final burst from the BAR emptied into Fu P'ai-Chang Mai's position, causing him to duck back for safety. Then he was out again, his Russian made sub-machine gun trained on the fleeing prisoner.

P.F.C Perez pulled the twenty round box from the underside of the BAR, his probing fingers told him what he already knew; it was empty. A weapon without any ammo was basically just a 20 lb club. Effectively for the moment, at this range, he was out of action.

It wasn't dawn yet, but the opening that took up the whole of the right side of Private London and the rest of the UN forces' position, gave off a lesser blue dark. The whole of his right arm ached from firing: his trigger finger, his palm from using the bolt action and pull on his arm muscles when he fired. He saw the captain was only seven yards from safety now and fired again in the enemy's general direction, half an eye glued on his commanding officer's progress.

"Come on, Ashley!" yelled Lieutenant Samuels, he was no longer even bothering to fire his pistol. The combat, his men, the enemy and even the war were forgotten, as he watched Captain Woodholme-Browne stumble to his knees.

Lieutenant Samuels went to aid him, but a hail of automatic fire forced him to throw himself onto his back, behind the cover of a large outcrop of rock.

Ashley gave a yelp of pain as a round hit the chair, penetrating through and grazing past his lower back.

Sergeant Dempsey had come down to a firing position, just above Lieutenant Samuels, trying to pin down the enemy fire with his M1 Carbine.

Captain Ashley Woodholme-Browne forced his aching limbs up and, ignoring the blood running down his left flank, he pushed on, only yards from safety.

"Edward!" he cried out to the American lieutenant, his body only five yards from the young officer's position.

"Come on!" Lieutenant Edward Samuels shouted over the din of weapons' fire. He reached out for the Royal Engineer captain, but a bullet ricocheted off the rocks, through his clothes, across the skin of his forearms. He ducked backwards again, in shock rather than pain.

"I'm hit," he said to himself and looked from his arm to Ashley's face – he was nearly home.

Captain Ashley Woodholme-Browne's handsome but slightly pained face exploded into an eruption of flesh, blood, brains and bone. He fell swiftly to the cavern floor, dead. Only two yards from safety.

Lieutenant Samuels grabbed his injured arm and stared in shock, the man he had come to admire and respect was gone. Going from a living and breathing man to a casualty of war in the blink of an eye.

"Bastards!" Sergeant Dempsey fired his Carbine from one enemy position to the next in anger.

P.F.C Perez crossed himself and said a silent prayer. Then he picked up the sergeant's loaded Colt .45, a grim, determined look on his face.

Private Hartnell of the 3rd Engineering Battalion, 24th Division, kept on firing his rifle: he hadn't noticed what had happened yet.

Private London stopped firing altogether, tears rolled down his cheeks like a salty eye dam had burst. He turned and sat behind his cover, his back to the action, cradling his rifle to his chest. His rifle was called Betty II, the first he had lost on 'Middlesex Hill'; they were named after Betty Davis.

He had lost two men he looked up to in twenty-four hours, was his number up next?

"Keep firing!" yelled Sergeant Dempsey in his thick New Jersey accent.

Private Robert James London, last British survivor of the expeditionary force, bit his bottom lip, turned around and began to fire again. If he was gonna die in combat like his brothers in the Second World War he was damn-right fucking sure he was going to take a few enemy soldiers with him.

Fui P'ai-Chang Mai lowered his weapon; the rounds he had fired had downed the escaping British prisoner. He should be elated, but he wasn't. This wasn't the Communist doctrine he had signed up to and took, like a new religion, into his soul. He just wanted to be back on his farm, with his family, doing his bit for his country, everyone equal and happy. Soon everyone here would be equal, the greatest equaliser of all: death.

A squeal of fear from the rear of his position caused his thoughts to fly away. He turned to find that his forces were under attack from the rear.

He rose and moved to his left, towards another hut, where the P'ai-Chang and two men had been positioned.

A body appeared from the dark and landed at his feet, causing him to fall to his knees to stop himself losing all balance. Weapons' fire had caused the roof of a hut, just behind their forward line, to catch fire. It was burning wildly now, so he could see clearly the eviscerated body of Pan-Chang Han Jue Mu. His clothes and skin had been sliced open from groin to neck, blood and inner organs, steaming because of the cold, were everywhere. No small arms could have done this, only artillery shells could do this kind of damage.

He grabbed his weapon and ran closer to the next hut.

"Bong!" came the cry of help, as he rounded the hut.

Before him, stood over the P'ai-Chang, was some sort of beast. The P'ai-Chang lay sprawled against the hut, unconscious, with the fox like creature ready for the kill.

One of his Chan-Shihs appeared at the creature's side and fired every round of his rifle into the many tailed abomination of nature.

Fu P'ai-Chang followed suit with his automatic weapon, the creature, standing erect like a man, threw its paws into the air, looked up and wailed in pain and anger.

Both Chinese soldiers' weapons clicked empty within a second of each other, sending both the Fu P'ai-Chang and the Chan-Shih reaching for a new drum and clip respectively.

The rounds seemed to have no effect on the fox-faced beast and it sprang upon the unfortunate Chan-Shih before he had located a new ammunition clip.

The Kumiho landed on the Chinese soldier's chest, its sharp teeth biting repeatedly at the poor man's throat. As it did, the clawed paws of the Kumiho dug into the upper arms of the soldier and pulled them both out of their socket and flung them behind her. It took the Chan-Shih another seven seconds after that to expire.

Fu P'ai-Chang Mai, even as a veteran of other wars, had seen enough. He fled back from the front line, back through the village towards the golden temple.

Sergeant Dempsey looked up from watching Lieutenant Samuels put a field dressing on his arm, back to the combat in hand.

Something odd was going on, the enemy field of fire had halved and the intensity also. Whereas a few minutes ago, half a dozen or so weapons had been firing onto their positions, now it was down to two rifles and one Burp gun. Some intense fire-fight had happened near a burning hut; then those positions had gone silent. It didn't make sense, unless someone else was attacking the Chinks.

"Loo-tenant," he called, and again until the dazed young officer turned to look up at him. "Loo-tenant, ammo's getting low, we got to either haul our asses outta here now or go on the offensive."

"Get the men ready, Sergeant, we are going to charge that far hut with everything we have." The lieutenant finished his bandaging and picked up his Colt .45 from where it had fallen onto the rocks.

"Are you sure about dat, Loo-tenant?" Sergeant Dempsey ventured. The young officer's mind must be in la-la land at the moment, after seeing the British captain die right in front of him.

Lieutenant Edward Samuels wiped the cold tears from his colder cheeks with his free gloved hand.

"Fix bayonets!" he ordered, ignoring his sergeant, his eyes on his fallen captain.

"I never wanted to reach forty anyways," Sergeant Dempsey muttered under his breath, "okay men, fix bayonets and get ready to run."

"Fix it to what, Sarge?" P.F.C Perez asked, looking down at his borrowed Colt .45.

"Your pecker, Perez, but if that ain't hard enough just hold it, okays?" Sergeant Dempsey joked, why not? It could be his last chance: ever.

Hartnell tittered and climbed down to the sergeant's lower position, clapping London on the back on the way.

"You coming, Limey Guildford man?" Private Hartnell asked as he moved past.

"I'm coming, Yankee Guildford man!" Private London fired off a shot then made his way down the rocks and rubble to join the others.

Fu P'ai-Chang Mai Pei Tiao ran up the golden steps, passing between the two golden guardians of the temple. Each held a fiery brazier in their hands/paws to light the way. Once through the initial passage, the temple opened up into a room the size of a palace ballroom. Columns and arches and entrances to dark tunnels led off this main area. The centre had to be avoided as there were many four by four feet deep, square holes in the floor. Each had a sliding gold covered plate on each side, but even closed they left a hole an unwary foot could fall into.

Fu P'ai-Chang Mai edged around the left hand side of the inner courtyard area, this too glowed with the fiery blaze of braziers that hung high on chains from the tall shadowy ceiling.

The Chinese sergeant moved forward, aiming for the dark confines of the archway and passage ahead. There he would wait in the dark for the fox beast to sniff him out. Maybe the grenade in his pocket or a shot to the eyes would slow this fox spirit down.

"Jimwei hu," he whispered, suddenly recalling the name of the beast from his grandmother's fables.

"Kumiho!" said a startling Korean voice from the dark passage he had been heading for.

A Korean soldier emerged from the shadows, his rifle aimed high at Mai's head, before he could raise his automatic weapon.

Fu P'ai-Chang Mai lowered his weapon, as the scared Korean sergeant advanced on him.

"Kumiho," Mai whispered and nodded, the Nine Tailed Fox was deep rooted in both their countries' legends.

"It is killing my men," Fu P'ai-Chang Mai said in hesitant Korean.

"I've seen it also; it slaughtered your Captain like a herd animal," Sergeant Kim spoke.

"Then I have a choice to die by your hands or the beast's, not good options." Mai laughed, which echoed around the vast temple hall. Sergeant Kim laughed with him, but just hoped he could stop.

"Or we could fight it as brothers, men against the dark?" Sergeant Kim offered, lowering the muzzle of his rifle to aim at the Chinaman's chest.

"What would your American allies say?"

"They are here?" Sergeant Kim gasped, the fighting, the noise, it all made sense now, to his now less addled mind.

Lieutenant Samuels crouched down beside the corpse of Captain Ashley Woodholme-Browne and touched his bloodstained blond locks.

"We gotta go, Loo-tenant!" Sergeant Dempsey screamed through the gunfire that whistled past the lieutenant.

"Goodbye, Ashley." Samuels rose as he spoke, and then smeared the blood of his dead captain on each of his cheeks like Red Indian war paint.

"Charge!" he bellowed and ran at the enemy positions behind the last hut to his attacking left.

Dempsey, Perez, London and Hartnell ran from their cover after the young warrior, screaming like banshees from hell!

Chan-Shih Tan Hui Rui lent into the side wall of his cover and fired his rifle towards the oncoming enemy.

A scream made him twist his neck to the left and the next hut. In the light of the fire raging behind him, he could see what was happening to his comrade, with aghast horror.

Some tall, thin beast of an animal was clamped onto the Chan-Shih's back, biting hard into the back of his neck. Dark liquid, which could only be blood, jetted from the poor soldier's neck like a high pressure hose.

Chan-Shih Tan ignored the bullets that hit near the wall he used as cover and staggered back towards the cobbled road in terror.

He looked right to see Fu-Pan-Chang Shu Bai Rui, lifted off his feet as a round took him in the shoulder. Another round hit his stomach as he fell bleeding. The charging enemy forces were close now.

Chan-Shih Tan dropped his rifle and fled, this was far too much for the ex-fisherman's mind to bear. He ran at full pelt, down the old cobbled road for the golden temple, hoping it would be his sanctuary.

Samuels' men fired as best they could as they ran, with rounds flying past them from the enemy positions, then suddenly most of the firing ceased.

Private Hartnell's shot lifted the Chinese lance corporal from his feet, while Lieutenant Samuels' 0.45 inch round hit him in the gut as he fell. Samuels jumped over the dying Chinese soldier, his eyes enraged and hunting for death and revenge.

He fired at a retreating enemy soldier, then a dark shadow loomed over him, and a thump to the back of the head sent him down for the count, unconscious.

The rest of the men rounded the collapsed hut to see the lieutenant fall. A large animal of some kind, with many tails and a mouth full of sharp teeth roared at them.

Sergeant Dempsey and P.F.C Perez, who were nearest to the strange animal, fired their weapons. Privates Hartnell and London held back in horror, this could only be the creature from Sergeant Kim's story, the Kumiho.

Dempsey and Perez emptied fifteen and six rounds into the raging beast respectively, enough lead to put down a charging rhino. It had no effect, except to make the animal angrier; it leapt at the two American soldiers bowling Sergeant Dempsey over: his head hitting the side of the hut and keeping him down.

Poor P.F.C Miguel Perez took the full brunt of the Kumiho's attack, as it bit off the whole front of his face.

"Run!" Private London cried, grabbing his American friend's webbing and pulling him towards the cobbled road.

The Kumiho ignored the terrified yells and concentrated on her meal. A moan from the dying Chinese soldier made her look up and sniff. She let the bloody corpse of Private First Class Perez fall to the cold earth and trotted slowly over to the Chinese lance corporal, the smell of his blood intoxicating her nostrils.

"Where the fuck we going, boy?" Hartnell asked as they ran.

"I dunno mate," London puffed, "just fucking run!"

The temple steps loomed in front of them, and up they ran into the golden temple to join the remains of both human forces, who had bigger concerns now than a war.

Fu P'ai-Chang Mai held the shaking Chan-Shih Tan in his arms, trying to comfort him. Army rank, communist, country had all gone out the window now; they were just two men from simple backgrounds, scared witless.

Sergeant Kim stood at the archway, the two Chinese soldiers behind him. His rifle at his shoulder, he heard a noise at the temple entrance, then footsteps. It wasn't the Kumiho; it was the sound of two pairs of army boots. He heard a stumble and a curse and smiled widely.

"Fuck my old boots!" Robert London cursed loudly as one of his boots half fell in a hole and he stumbled.

"So much for the silent approach," John Hartnell commented, as it was his turn to pull at his friend's webbing to keep him upright.

"We meet again," came an accented voice from the far side of the vast temple hall. Two rifles swung up to point at Sergeant Kim Jun Ho of the Republic of Korea army.

"First monsters, now I'm seeing ghosts," Private Hartnell stated in disbelief.

"We thought you were 'brown-bread', Sergeant?" London inquired, glad to see a friendly face.

"Bread. Ghosts. What a strange language English really is," said the sergeant moving to greet them.

"We've seen it!" Hartnell exclaimed.

"That bleedin' fox thing from your story," London added, breathing hard from running.

"Is there anyone else left alive?" Sergeant Kim asked the two men.

"I don't think so." Private London shook his head in guilt.

"We just ran, Sarge," Private Hartnell added, feeling guilty about running away from a fight.

"You could not have done anymore; bullets do not seem to harm it." Sergeant Kim frowned; they were no more cowards than him or the Chinese soldiers.

In the dark passageway, the Chinese private let out a sob of despair.

"Who's that?" Private London asked as he and Hartnell raised their rifles once more, towards the shadowy passage.

"New allies," Sergeant Kim said quickly. "They are hunted by the Kumiho also, so we fight it together."

Fu P'ai-Chang Mai appeared weapon-less at the entrance of the passage, his arms raised above his head.

The American and British soldiers stiffened, their fingers on the triggers of their rifles. Images of the dead Captain Woodholme-Browne filled both their heads, killed by Chinese fire and here was one right in front of them.

"Please, this is Sergeant Mai," Kim stated, stepping in front of their rifles, "we need him if we are to stop the Kumiho!"

"What was that?" Hartnell asked, breaking the tension a little. All of them had heard a grating noise, like stone rubbing against stone, somewhere deep inside the temple.

The braziers above their heads fizzed and crackled: the flames turning black for an instant.

"I don't frigging like this," London murmured, as a dark mist began to creep from the empty passageways and unseen holes behind hideous statues.

Chan-Shih Tan Hui Rui fell into the hall and crashed to the floor unconscious.

"Cover your mouths!" Sergeant Kim warned, putting his hand over his lips. Hartnell and London had scarves they put to their mouths as the dark almost alive mist engulfed their legs. It had the consistency of smoke, but bore no smell at all. Mai fell halfway towards helping his comrade.

Sergeant Kim fell next and London and Hartnell stared at each other with wide uncomprehending eyes. Hartnell fell into the enveloping black mist and Private London was alone with his fear: until he too fell a second later.

As soon as the English soldier fell unconscious to the floor, the black fog began to evaporate. Not swirl, blow away, or sink into the temple floor, it just dissipated leaving the hall clear again.

The Kumiho appeared at the entrance to the inner temple on all fours, dragging a lifeless body in its teeth.

Chapter 17

Gusul

Lieutenant Samuels awoke first. The throbbing pain from the bruise the size of a golf ball had dragged his unconscious mind into the waking world. His head was on his left side, his cheek resting on something cold and metal. Pins and needles began to surge up his bent legs for some reason.

His eyes flickered open, but all his blurry vision could see was floor in a place he'd never even been before, unless it had been some primal nightmare. He was confused, his head was on the floor but his body wasn't; it was below him, below ground level. Red tinged fires high above his head lit the large room; an entrance was in the centre of the wall ahead of him. Faint natural light, not the darkness of the combat, crept into the entrance passage.

Where the hell was he?

Where were his men?

He tried to rise, but couldn't. Something stopped his shoulders from rising upwards.

He was suddenly aware that he was squashed down into a hole, with only his neck and head at floor level. Looking down he saw, and realised for the first time his predicament. His body was in some sort of man-made shaft in the floor, about four feet square. Across the hole, from either side, a brass plate with a semicircular hole on either side had been slid across around his neck. The now round hole held his neck loosely in position, with solid looking iron bolts slid across the face and length of both plates to keep them secure. He tried to heave up with all the remaining strength he had, but the plates holding him there never budged a quarter inch. His body felt weak and his head woozy and the pins and needles in his legs didn't help either.

He was trapped like a rat in a drainpipe; the Chinese must have captured him last night. A groan to his right caused him to look round as best he could and then his morning got even worse. To his right, in the same neck trap as him, was Sergeant Dempsey. He was coming to, dried blood on his scalp and face where he'd bashed his head against the hut.

Lieutenant Samuels found he could turn his whole body underneath the neck plates and looked behind him. Another six helmet-less heads protruded from similar bonds in a square area in the centre of the room.

The first he noticed was a bit of a shock; it was Sergeant Kim, whom he thought had died at the second bridge ambush. His small eyelids were firmly shut, but next to him was an even bigger shock. It was the head of a Chinese soldier, also with a head wound like him and Dempsey, and next to him another sleeping Chinese soldier. Another Chinese soldier was on the right back row, with Private Hartnell next to him in the centre: both were asleep.

There were twelve traps, three feet wide and four feet deep set in the floor. Samuels noticed that P.F.C. Perez's and Private London's heads were nowhere to be seen.

If the Chinese were prisoners too, who had imprisoned them and whose side were they on?

"Sergeant–" Lieutenant Samuels coughed to get his weak words out, "Sergeant Dempsey?"

"Wha!" groaned the short New Jersey man, the metallic taste of blood in his mouth.

Behind Samuels, the middle Chinese soldier began to stir, his eyes flicking suddenly awake.

"Ngor day yee ga hai bin do a?" P'ai-Chang Kong Shuo Tiao cried out in shock, wanting to know where he was.

"Shut the fuck up you, Chink bastard, I gotta dousey of a headache," Sergeant Dempsey shouted from his pit, looking around at the Chinese second lieutenant, then back to his own lieutenant.

"What happened? Where are we?" he asked his platoon commander, his headache loud and painful in his ears.

"I have no idea, Sergeant, but it's happened to the Chinese forces as well." Samuels had to speak loudly over the indignant jabbering of the Chinese officer.

215

"It was an animal, it attacked you and then it must have got me," Dempsey painfully remembered, wishing he could get a hand out to scratch his itchy scalp.

"Who does this animal belong to and who put us in here?" Samuels asked, looking back at the rest of the sleeping prisoners. Only the three soldiers with head trauma had come to so far.

"Sergeant Kim, wake up!" Dempsey shouted behind him, "Hey Hartnell! You guys wake the hell up right now!"

The three sleeping soldiers didn't even stir, nor did the other two Chinese soldiers.

"Maybe they've been drugged?" Samuels ventured as he watched the Chinese officer bark at his men also with no effect.

"Ngor mun ming?" Kong said to the Americans, but they could not understand that he was saying he didn't understand either.

A change in the amount of light coming through the entrance in front of them caused the three lucid men to look around.

Through the entrance tunnel from outside the temple came the Kumiho in all its fox shaped glory. It moved forward on all fours and stopped a few feet away from Lieutenant Samuels and sniffed the air.

Sergeant Dempsey was shocked to see that there was not a mark or bullet wound on the sleek long form of the beast. The Kumiho padded forward, between the traps of Dempsey and Samuels, sniffing from side to side as it went. She was searching for a special man she knew was among them, the smell of blood, sweat and piss was affecting her olfactory senses.

The two American engineers turned their heads as much as they dared, not wanting to attract any undue attention from the large fox. It padded in between Kim and P'ai-Chang Kong; it ignored the Chinese officer, but gave the sleeping/unconscious R.O.K sergeant a long, close sniff.

Then she was off again up past two empty traps, past the Chinese private and turned right to sniff the back of Hartnell's head.

"What's it doing?" hissed Sergeant Dempsey to his lieutenant.

"I have no idea," Samuels replied, but he did. Deep down, he hoped it wasn't true that the human sized fox was sniffing out its next meal.

The Kumiho moved on past Hartnell and down the next isle, she passed next to Mai and stuck her nose into his hair and sniffed hard.

The Chinese officer had lost it now big time, he was screaming and crying and trying with no luck to escape.

The Kumiho sniffed Fu P'ai-Chang Mai quickly then moved to stand to the right of P'ai-Chang Kong. The two US soldiers twisted their heads round to watch in impertinent fear. The fox-beast looked at the Chinese second lieutenant, moved forward and licked the man's cheek.

Kong had stopped jabbering now; fear in his eyes and in his combat trousers. The Kumiho suddenly stretched its mouth nature-defiantly wide and clamped the whole of Kong Shuo Tiao's head inside.

Dempsey and Samuels looked on in horror as the jaws slowly began to close together. Kong screamed as the vixen's teeth punctured deep into the skin of his jaw. Then the blood ran everywhere, the two US soldiers turned away in disgust as the skull began to crack under the bite of the beast.

Both squeezed their eyes shut and wished to hell this was a nightmare that they would soon wake up from.

One last piercing scream erupted from Kong's broken jaw before his entire skull was crushed together like it was a flimsy chicken egg. His brain exploded inside the beast's mouth and she greedily sucked in all its knowledge and savoured the taste.

Lieutenant Samuels nearly vomited, managing somehow to swallow back the bile as the Kumiho crunched the enemy officer's skull. The salacious slavering continued for a minute or so, but felt like an hour to the two conscious US engineers. They could do nothing, their bodies were cramped up in holes and their heads exposed to the evil fox spirit.

Sergeant Dempsey tried hard to picture his house back in the States, his wife, his boy and girl. Yet the images would not come, fear and their mortal peril banished them.

The Kumiho had obviously finished its feast and trotted off once again around the conscious and unconscious entrapped soldiers.

Joe Dempsey opened his eyes and glanced to his left to look at the young Lieutenant Samuels who was whispering the Lord's Prayer through snot and tears. The young lieutenant really did look like a scared teenager now. What was he, twenty-one?

No age to die, no age to see such death and horror. The world was a cruel mistress his dad had once told him, and Jesus H. Christ, he had been right.

Both soldiers stiffened, as the beast moved behind them; Joe Dempsey could hear its footfalls and breathing. Its long, lithe, short haired body went slowly past the back of the sergeant's head, until it stopped behind the lieutenant.

Lieutenant Samuels was drooling from terror, a long constant murmur of fear emitting from his trembling lips. The Kumiho sniffed at Edward Samuels' neck, then drew back, its jaw opening wide over him. Lieutenant Samuels could feel the hot putrid breath of the animal on the back of his cold neck. His bladder let go and his cold body went rigid with the fear of imminent death.

Lieutenant Samuels blacked out at this point, his fate would befall him unawares, like the rest of the captured soldiers.

"Leave him alone, you stinking fox bitch!" Sergeant Dempsey bellowed at the Kumiho. If he was next, he wanted to go out shouting like a man, not whimpering like an adolescent girl.

The Kumiho turned her head towards the sergeant with hatred in her eyes.

"Fetch!" Sergeant Joseph Dempsey snarled at the Kumiho, a mocking grin on his weathered, stubbled jaw. It was his last act in a long line of small to large heroisms.

The creature pounced!

Robert London dreamt of being chased. He looked behind him, in the swirling dark confines of his mind. He knew what was after him. This dream he had had a hundred times as a young boy. The vicious black guard dog his dad kept at the coal yard had broken its chain and was after him.

This dream hadn't bothered him for ten years or so now, so why had it come back to haunt him? He turned in his sleep and something soft and warm tickled at his nostrils and cheek. His body stretched and more warm soft comforting fur caressed his naked body.

He breathed in deeply and out and a pleasant smell like dried fruit entered his nose and mouth. His hand fell from its naked flank on to the soft fur in front of him. His eyes flicked awake, his body tensing up, as his mind searched his memory for any connections on where he was, to where he had been.

He was not in the temple hall; maybe it was another part of the building. This room seemed warm and cosy: fur pelts lined the floor where he lay. The light was tinged red and cast extravagant shadows across the wall that he could see.

He sat up and discovered many things in one short second. His senses took in everything he saw, smelt and felt, but took a lot longer to comprehend. He was in a smallish ten by ten foot room, with black lacquered wooden panels adorning three of the four walls. The other had many panelled screen against it. The floor was of mats, with the centre of the room covered in furs and pelts, including that of a snow tiger. A small, low wooden table sat against one wall, with incense burning in a small copper brazier. Two jugs of poor earthenware design stood on either side of the incense, with two wooden cups next to the right hand side jug.

The red light came from lanterns hung two on each wall. Each wall's lantern had red glass and orange glass to give the warm room an even rosier glow.

"I'm stark bollock naked," he said to himself, sitting up into a cross-legged position.

Then he noticed a person shaped shadow cast against the wall, behind the long unfolded screen. He looked around for his rifle or bayonet, but no weapons nor any signs of his clothes could be found. He pulled a pelt over his privates and stood up, feeling very nervous and nineteen. The shadow moved along behind the screen, as he wondered who was coming and why he seemed so scared. His memory felt like that night out in Hong Kong, whole parts of it were foggy and lost in a booze addled mist.

"Who's there?" he stammered, as the shadow reached the end of the screen, it seemed tall and menacing.

Then from behind the screen slipped a most beautiful Korean girl of around his age. She was about five foot six and she was dressed in pale pink robes that seemed to flow as she walked towards him. An odd little pink, crepe paperish hat seemed to sit somehow atop of her long silky black hair, which hung down over the front of her shoulders and back.

"Where am I, miss?" he whispered, not sure that his words were even audible to the girl.

Then she smiled, her teeth perfect and white, a dainty, shy smile.

Robert London smiled back, but more of a dopey, bashful, smile of a teenage virgin.

"Anjuseyo," she spoke in a soothing, rich voice and made lowering motions with her hands.

"You want me to sit?" he asked, nearly dropping the pelt covering his wedding tackle, which caused the shy, but sensuous girl to giggle.

Robert's cheeks and chest flushed red with embarrassment, so he swiftly sat down again on the warm, comfortable furs. The girl, meanwhile, walked, or seemed to shuffle in her pink dress, towards the small table.

"Don't 'appen to know where me togs are do you?" Robert asked, for asking sake. The only Korean word he learnt in the war so far was 'maektchu' which meant 'beer'.

The girl knelt down before the small table and bowed, then proceeded to pour a liquid into the wooden cups from the right hand jug.

"I wish Kim was here to translate for me."

Images suddenly shot back into his addled memory. Something about a wild animal, smoke and a fire-fight. Where were Kim and Hartnell?

"Where are the rest of," Robert London fired a pretend gun, "the soldiers?"

The girl frowned and shook her head; turning on her knees she offered him one of the wooden cups.

She lifted her wooden cup and said, "Anae," then took the other and offered it to Robert London and said, "mam-pyon."

Robert London rubbed his forehead; this wasn't getting him anywhere, yet it wasn't the lovely Korean girl's fault. So he took the cup from her and drank deeply, because his mouth had a funny oily taste to it for some reason.

He looked down at the drink then finished off all that was left. The girl smiled wickedly behind her own cup and then finished her drink also.

"That's lovely." Then he pointed inside the cup. "What is it?"

"Seek-he," she said as she bowed forward to kiss his fingers and take the cup from his hands.

"That tastes better than your first cuppa in the morning and that after work, first light and mild, all rolled into one." He smiled widely, all thoughts of his comrades in arms, war and death, had retreated back into the foggy depths of his brain.

The girl placed the wooden cups down on the table, then reached out for the other jug.

"What's next then?" Robert London asked, the smell of the incense and the looks of the girl were intoxicating.

"Shinhon yohaeng," she purred, the wedding had been short and sweet, now it was time for the honeymoon. The girl placed the jug between them, as she shuffled on her knees closer to her new and ninth husband. She then proceeded to unwrap the thin dress from around her body. First her slender arms were revealed, then her shoulders, until she had a long green sari like train of thin, gossamer like material in her hands. She placed this behind her. Now her top half was only covered by a darker green waistcoat type bodice. This revealed a slight showing of cleavage, but kept her torso fully under wraps.

Smiling, she put both palms of her hands together like she was in a prayer and lowered them into the jug between them. When she pulled them out again, they were covered with nutty fragranced oil.

"What's that then?" he asked intrigued, if not a little nervously.

"Sogyu," she smiled, moving towards him, her mouth slightly open, her tongue running along the underside of her top teeth. She shuffled closer and put her oiled hands onto his broad muscular shoulders. His legs were youthful and skinny, but his upper body was quite wiry from working at the coalmongers and his cricket bowling.

The oil was body temperature and as soon as her small hands began to work on his shoulders, any virgin teenage tension or nagging doubts ebbed away. His eyes closed as she squeezed and pulled at his taut young skin; he hadn't felt so relaxed since Lillian had taken care of him in hospital.

He went rigid, his eyes flew open and he found he was holding the Korean girl's wrists, too tightly, one in each of his hands away from his shoulders. The Korean girl looked shocked, and it seemed to him that the irises of her brown eyes had turned oval in shape and orange for a briefest of seconds. He blinked a bemused look frowned upon his countenance now, it must have been a trick of the light. He had no idea what he was doing, but saw the pained expression on the girl's face and instantly let her wrists go.

"Sorry, I don't know what came over me," he said to her hurt brown eyes. Lillian's existence had vanished back to his nagging subconscious.

The girl shook her head and smiled, her long lush hair flowing from shoulder to shoulder. She moved her hands to her waistcoat and one by one, using both hands to hold and lift, pulled her breasts out of the garment. Both, slightly squeezed together because of her garment's neckline, rested on the material for Robert to admire.

Robert London swallowed; these were the first pair of breasts he had ever seen in the flesh. She grinned and he grinned gormlessly back.

Reaching down into the jug again, she once more oiled her hands. She brought them up and slowly began to massage the oil into her own pert breasts. Robert wished he'd grabbed a larger fur pelt as the blood pumped hard into his manhood, making it feel like an iron rod attached to his groin. Her hands caressed her chest in slow circular motions, her dark brown nipples becoming hard and prominent.

The girl smiled seductively at him, knowing she had his full attention again. She reached out and took his large hand in hers, oiling it slowly finger by finger, as Robert watched in a daze.

She gently pulled his right hand towards her small left breast and held his hand to it with hers.

Her oiled skin and the soft pliable feel of her breast were un-duplicable. He ran a thumb over her engorged nipple, the feel of his skin on her sensitive puckered skin made her shiver and gasp.

They looked up into each other's eyes and somewhere their souls connected. Then she reached out to touch his face, a look of longing and also of sadness in her eyes.

Then, putting both hands onto his shoulders, she tried to push him down, backwards.

"Nupitta," she said to him and a giggle formed on her soft lips, her hair falling forward over her face. He resisted at first, like a baby once you had the breast, nothing else was any substitute.

He finally twigged that 'nupitta' was Korean for 'lie down', and laid back, his finger tips last to caress her erect nipples. He laid back, his arms going over his head, to rest the back of his head on his hands. He smiled broadly, the fur pelt slipping aside, his smooth long penis now in full view.

Her eyes were drawn to it, but then flicked up to his face; she could not stop her nature and licked her lips in a circular motion.

"Twich'ok-kkorida!" she ordered pointing with her finger and her head, in a nodding, turning finger motion.

"Oh," he replied, a little disappointed, but turned over anyway. She was in charge, an exotic, erotic, dark skinned female, with obviously more experience than him. He wiggled himself into some sort of comfortable position, his erection prodded into his belly a bit.

More green material flew across the room, and he looked back to see the girl was naked from the waist down. Her dark green waistcoat was enough to act as a mini-skirt: but it didn't stop Robert catching a glimpse of dark pubic hair as she sat down.

She gently pushed his legs apart and shuffled her bare legs into the gap he provided. She moved the jug closer and to the outside of Robert London's naked hairy right leg. Dipping her hands into the oil again, she then placed her oiled hands on his left ankle. Then she rubbed up the entire length of his calf and upper thigh. This she repeated for his right leg. This felt so good to Robert, he didn't know whether to come or cry.

He breathed in deeply now, the incense filling the gaps in his memory with images of her. He felt the oil and her warm hands on the small of his back now. Then felt the gentle brush of her breasts on his buttocks as she stretched across his back, her oiled hands reaching his shoulders and neck. There her hands worked, un-knotting his neck and shoulder muscles. All tensions, fears and bad memories had faded away like they were children's fairytales now.

As her hands pushed along his skin, she breathed in deeply of his musky man scent. She hoped this, her ninth marriage, would last and that she could make him stay with her forever. Her other husbands had broken that marital trust and lost what she had given over to them. Now this man from a distant island would be her last husband, her life as a normal wife would soon begin. Once the honeymoon was over she could have everything she ever dreamed of long ago. To leave the Yŏu plateau with her new husband and start a real life together and have offspring to suckle at her teats.

She pulled her hands down his spine and each hand caressed a buttock. He murmured in excitement as her long tongue licked down the crevice between his cheeks. The tip of her tongue wiggled round at his hole there, then sucked at his balls and the root of his cock.

Robert couldn't stand anymore; he turned on his side, then fully onto his back. His hard erection vibrated inches from her face now. His foreskin had pulled back a little as he lay on it, his opening dribbling with pre-cum.

Her passions, like his, were rising and her small right hand grabbed his wobbling erection at the base to steady it.

Robert London gasped; he had wanted her to touch him for so long. She opened her small delicate mouth; her tongue came out over her teeth and licked at the dribbling juices at the head of his penis. She licked around the opening of his foreskin and lapped up all the pre-cum. Robert's eyes crossed in delight, he had never known such sensations.

Her hand stroked the length of his cock as she gently pushed down his foreskin with her closed lips, to reveal his deep red end. Her mouth opened wide and her hand slipped down to the base of his rock-hard erection.

Robert sat up on his elbows and watched in amazement and lust as her head lowered onto his penis and the whole of his length was swallowed up inside her warm mouth and throat. A cold feeling then seemed to creep into the inside of his penis, like the sperm inside were freezing solid inside him.

As her head rose up, he was relieved to see that his hard member was still intact and he hadn't spoilt anything by ejaculating yet. It had felt so close a second ago, now the sap had fallen a bit, but his erection remained.

The Korean girl raised herself onto her knees again and reached out with both hands, arms fully extended towards the young soldier. Robert took her hands in his and helped her pull him up into a sitting position, with the help of his strong back muscles.

The vivacious girl then put her left leg over his right and her right over his left leg, straddling him. Robert looked down and saw the black pubic hair between her legs parted now, his erection seemed to be pointing the way to her vagina. The girl pressed herself against him now, her oiled breasts into his face, which he greedily suckled. Her left hand reached down to grab his manhood, as she hovered over it, trying to get both their sexual organs in alignment. Robert felt hard pressure on the end of his helmet, then her hand was free and she slid slowly down the length of his cock. Robert's hands went to her smooth round backside to steady himself, his virginity gone and life changed forever.

Her arms went under his armpits, up his back so she could grab onto the back of his shoulders. Then she started to pull herself up on him, then lower herself down, sending warm, wet sensations all along the base of his manhood.

Robert began to breathe heavier and the Korean girl gasped every time she lowered herself onto him, his penis buried deep inside her. Robert squeezed her behind as the girl began to ride his cock like a jockey with five furlongs to go.

The intensity and emotional volcano he felt was unparalleled, only being in combat did his adrenaline pump around his body faster. In battle, his emotional state and senses were at their peak, here too he felt that plateau of emotions; yet lust and the tactility of love making were definitely the better of the two experiences.

Deeper she forced him into her, their bodies merging as one sexual entity. He felt the icy feeling in the core of his shaft melting and knew ejaculation was near. She too felt the tug of orgasm to her loins and knew it was time.

The Korean girl moved her hands down his back then up to cup his face between them, tenderly. Her bouncing decreased to a pelvic wiggle that slowed, but did not end, their mutual pleasure. Then her deep brown eyes stared into his and Robert felt like he was falling into her very soul.

She lowered her face to his and kissed him ever so tenderly on the lips, her mouth wetting his drier lips. Then he responded by kissing her hard on the lips, her hands went into his hair, entwining her fingers in it.

She slowed his kisses down by licking first his top, then his bottom lip with her tongue. Both breathed hard through their noses, as she continued her friction movements on his ready to pop penis.

Delicately she used her top and bottom lips as a jack, to open his mouth slightly and slipped her tongue inside his mouth. Being a quick learner his mouth parted wider and his tongue bypassed her tongue to explore her mouth cavity.

Now they were fused together at mouth and groin, two souls experiencing that oneness of carnal knowledge.

Robert was enjoying the French kissing even more than the penetrative sex, their lips locked, tongues exploring each other. There seemed to be a taste of metal in their mouths, like an electric storm overhead. The hair on the back of his neck stood on end and it seemed to him she gave a slight hiccup in the back of her throat. Then he felt round and hard next to her teeth, something small like a warm marble.

He explored it with his tongue, then felt her push it with her tongue into his mouth. Her tongue rolled it around inside his mouth as her pelvis intensified its momentum again. Images flashed into his mind as the girl rode his cock and explored his mouth with her tongue. His late brothers appeared in his mind's eye, then the marble slipped back into her mouth and images of chasing Roman Legionnaires came from somewhere.

Then the marble was in his mouth again, tasting of her and his body gave an involuntary shake, as he replayed the time he had been wounded on the head on 'Middlesex Hill'.

He thrust the marble back deep into her mouth, not wanting that image, his sperm pulsing up his inner penis. Then it was her again, with a man dressed in splendid Samurai armour, walking hand in hand through cherry blossomed trees.

Then the marble stopped, between each of their lips, he saw a large fox running through a green forest its head snapped quickly to the left and morphed into the Korean girl's face that he was passionately bonded: lastly he saw the caring face of Nurse Lillian White.

The intensity and lust of the moment could not be held and he came hard inside her and she shuddered wildly, her body wracked with orgasm. He opened his mouth to cry out in pleasure, and before he knew it the marble had gone into his throat and he had swallowed it down easily to avoid choking on it. He continued to pump his semen into her for a full twenty seconds and she clung onto his neck, head next to his scar, as her waves of ecstasy subsided.

The images had vanished like the end of a reel of cinema images and finally he was spent. Breathlessly they clung to each other's perspiring bodies for a full five minutes afterwards; neither had felt such intensity of sensations in their lives.

He was the first to pull away, his cock still rigid inside her small frame. He touched his bruised lips and hiccupped once.

"What was that?" he pointed inside of his mouth.

"Gusul," she smiled sweetly, her hair a crazy mess over the front of her face now. Then she swiftly slid sideways off his finally melting member. Their juices instantly dribbling out of her slightly agape vagina.

"Nupitta." She patted the furs next to her and he lay down facing her, glad to get his legs moving again.

She pulled himself close to him, her exposed breasts touching his torso, snuggling closer. Robert felt emotionally drained and fatigued from his exertions, so he pulled one of the big tiger furs across them both.

Both fell easily into dreamless sleep, their bodies entwined in post-coital bliss. An hour later she turned away from him in her sleep. Robert London did not stir or reach out for her in the night: so did not get to feel the soft touch of her fur-covered body.

Chapter 18

Escape to the Temple

"Lillian," he murmured and his eyes flicked straight from sleep to cold reality in less than a second. He sat up on the fur covered floor and wiped at the saliva on his cheek and chin where he had been drooling.

His nose was stuffy and he sniffed as he looked around the small room again. The girl was nowhere to be seen.

The candles were unlit stubs and the lanterns flickered as they grew low on fuel. Images of Nurse White and his duty as a British and UN soldier faded back into the world of dreams again.

He had to find the Korean girl again: she had taken his virginity and enslaved his heart. Standing up he soon realised he had an overly full bladder and a large aching erection. Even his bewitched mind had to capitulate to his bodily functions.

He looked around the room and saw no obvious toilet facilities, only the jugs; but pissing in your new lover's oil and drinking jugs would be a tad rude.

Rubbing his full lower abdomen he made for the screen that covered one wall. Pulling it away from the wall and pushing it closed so it half concertinaed up revealed two things. Firstly his boots, trousers, shirt, battledress and the rest of his garb and secondly the outlines of a black lacquered wooden doorway.

He dressed hurriedly, every time he bent his full bladder twinged irritably from his bollocks to his belly button. Finally half dressed, his boots on but laces undone and his winter army coat and webbing belts over his left arm, he moved to the door.

There was no lock or door handles on the door, so he put both palms on the top half of the door and pushed. The door gave a small click and swung outwards, pushing against some kind of black curtain. As he pushed the door further open, the curtain billowed out to the right hand side to reveal another, larger room.

Leaving the door ajar just in case he had to get back in, he pushed past the dark curtain into the large, and considerably colder, stone clad room. It was like stepping from your cosy fire lit parlour out into a winter's morning in your garden.

Robert London pulled on his winter coat, but left it unbuttoned, his only thoughts and desires were to find somewhere to pee, before he did himself some internal damage.

Quickly he spotted a large urn in the corner nearest to him and the curtain covered door. He hobbled towards it; thankfully his erection had subsided now. He freed his John-Thomas and started the long process of relieving himself into the thigh-high urn.

He closed his eyes and sighed with relief as his urine made a tumbling sound against the china urn. It took over two minutes to empty his bladder, his whole body slumped with relief as his muscles could relax again.

He exhaled and dressed properly again, then turned around to fully take in the room he found himself in. The covering he had thought had been a curtain, was in fact a large black tapestry that hung from a golden ten foot rod affixed to the stone ceiling. Bright red tightly painted Korean script covered the centre of the black material.

The wall opposite the tapestry had a huge eight foot high statue, set in a semi-circular alcove. Standing betwixt two large round shield-shaped braziers of orange fire, was a repulsive chimera of a figure. Half was a nude human woman, half some dog-like animal: the creature had two heads fused together at the back of the skull, but shared the same half skin, half fur covered body.

Robert London turned away from the grotesque carved image and noticed the wall in between the statue and the tapestry had an open passageway leading from it. After buttoning up his battledress and lacing up his boots he headed for the passageway, desperate to find his exotic lover again. Also glad to get away from that statue and the slight pong of his own piss.

Down in a secret place beneath the statue laid the woman that Robert London was seeking. Yet here, in the utter darkness of her lair, he would not have recognised her. The roughly hewn walls of the room had clay pipes running through them. Moss and fungi clung to the walls and floor in places. The floor, if it had been visible was covered with bones, skulls, parchment like skin and fur; not laying strewn about, but fashioned into a round doughnut-shaped nest, in which she lay. She? Because she was female, but not altogether human: not yet!

Her body moved and rippled, showing sometimes skin, sometimes fox fur and she writhed in a semi-aware state. Her whole body was undertaking her ninth post nuptial, Gusul giving, transformation. Her three sets of breasts ached like it was the bloodletting cycle of the month. Her nipples, sometimes teats, felt like needles were being stabbed into them. Her back ached, but her tail bone itched and sometimes gave her shooting lances of pure agony.

She knew the process was harsh; it was getting worse every time, yet this would be the last time for her. The familiar itch meant a new tail was growing and soon she would have nine, after countless centuries. Then she could be a real woman, whole and able at last to leave her plateau prison.

Her thoughts, angered by pain, went to the Mudang and what vengeance she would avail upon her and her temple before she left. Agony wracked her changing body again, but very soon she would be free.

The dark passage turned right, as Robert London felt along with his left hand. As it did, faint light could be seen up ahead. As he got closer, he saw, from the way the light and shadows lay, that the passage ahead turned a corner to the left.

He wanted to call out for his lover, but did not speak her language or even at this time know her name. That they would remedy in time, as they lived out their remaining days together. As Robert London turned the corner he saw the passage ended ten feet ahead, opening up into a large room. The air seemed cooler now and a rank smell filled his nostrils.

Something lay ahead on the floor of the huge room ahead, he could see round objects ahead. His heart quickened and his befuddled mind raced for understanding.

It was not until he entered the cavernous room that he realised what the round shapes could only be. Artificial light came from above and strangely natural light came through a passageway that he recognised. He had been here before, with men, comrades: his fellow soldiers.

The fog lifted from his love-addled mind as he stared at the human heads protruding from the floor and the sight of blood. He suddenly recalled everything: who he was, the war, his comrades and the true nature of the girl that he had copulated with last night. She had given across more than she had ever intended and he knew that he must escape now, before her new invincible self awoke.

He rushed forward to the nearest head, trapped at floor level in some devilish pit. It was a Chinese face he did not recognise, but the one directly to the left he did: it was Hartnell.

He dashed over and fell to his knees in front of his American friend; Hartnell's white face was leaning to one side, his head trapped between two metal plates.

"Hartnell," London said in an agonised voice, how could he have forgotten his comrades, the battle, and the bloody war!

Getting no response, London pulled up and slid back the bolts that locked the two plates in place. Putting his right hand against the American's neck, he used his other hand to push aside the plate. He had to bash the plate three times with his palm to get it fully out of the way. Holding Hartnell's head as best he could, he pulled the other plate away. Hartnell's head slipped out of his grip and slouched backwards, to bang against the back of the pit edge.

"Ow!" Hartnell awoke, the pain jolting him out of an uneasy dream.

"Fuckin' 'ell, you're still alive then?" Private London exclaimed, as Private Hartnell's eyes focused on him.

The Englishman reached his arms under his American friend and pulled him out of the trap, so now Hartnell was sitting on the floor, with only his stiff legs still in the hole.

John Hartnell shook his sleepy head and gazed around the vast temple hall, at the torturous scenes around him.

"What on God's good earth is going on here, friend?" Hartnell asked rubbing at his legs, which had grown stiff from confinement.

"I wish I knew," Robert London replied as guilt flooded his body. He had spent the night making love to God-knows-what of a girl and betraying his beloved Lillian. He knew the lust of last night would send his soul into the arms of Lucifer if he did not make amends: that he would do, by helping his comrades escape this murderous plateau.

"Come on, let's get the others free." Private Hartnell woke London from his thoughts, with two slaps to the Englishman's right knee.

Robert London reached out a strong hand, which John Hartnell gratefully took in his, and the Middlesex Regiment man pulled him from the trap.

London moved forward to the next empty line of three traps; one unknown to him had been his.

"What about this guy?" Hartnell asked, pointing back to the Chinese soldier in the next trap, as Private London turned round to answer.

"Let's get our blokes out first, eh?"

Hartnell, the engineer, conceded to London, the soldier, that it made sense to get their men out first, before their once enemies. There were no creatures about now and who knows how they were going to react.

Private London breathed in hard when they reached the next trio of traps, all were occupied: kind of!

At the far left hung the head of a Chinese soldier, to the right was Sergeant Kim's bowed head, but in the middle, only blood, bone and part of a neck protruded. In the row directly ahead of the bloody mess was the young lieutenant's ashen pale face, and next to him was Sergeant Dempsey's head, slumped down to the chin in his hole.

"I'll get Dempsey, you rescue Kim," Private London said taking charge, not by rank, but by natural inherent leadership.

"Good as done, Bobby," Hartnell replied, moving across to free the R.O.K sergeant's bolts.

London moved to Dempsey now, he was looking at the cold natural light coming from the entrance to the temple. He did not notice the blood that soaked into his army greens as he knelt.

London pulled back his bolts and then gripped the locks to pull the plates aside. Behind him Hartnell slid back his plates with ease, causing Sergeant Kim to slump forward and let out a moan.

"Soon have you out, Sarge," London said, through gritted teeth, as he pushed one of the stiff plates to the side. The workings seemed gummed up with some sort of rust, as he put all his upper body strength into it.

It resisted for two seconds then suddenly slid all the way across in one swift movement, causing Sergeant Dempsey's head to tilt sideways. As Private London moved to hold him up, the head toppled sideways off the remaining plate and fell decapitated and severed at the neck into the pit to join his body.

Robert London screamed higher than any pitch since he had been eleven and in the church choir. He scrambled a few feet away from the traps and threw up a yellow slick of watery vomit.

"Oh my God," Hartnell exclaimed, not quite believing what he had just seen.

"Wae?" mumbled Sergeant Kim in Korean, as he came to his senses.

"Come on, Sarge, we need you." Hartnell, with tears in his red eyes, focused on the job in hand and tried to blank out the image of Dempsey's falling head.

Robert London felt cold all over now, as he shivered on his hands and knees, spitting bile on to the floor. He looked down through tear filled eyes and dry heaved on seeing the puddle of vomit before him.

Something caught his eye: in the mostly wet internal liquid lay a marble sized ball, not covered in sick. It pulsed white, with blue and coral coloured milky swirls in it. Without thinking clearly Robert grabbed it and thrust it deep into his army coat pocket.

He got up and moved to the side of the room to lean against the cold wall.

"You okay, London?" Hartnell asked, pulling the South Korean sergeant from his pit trap.

Robert London just waved his hand above his left shoulder, without turning around. He wondered when this nightmare mission would end, and if anyone would escape its horrors.

Ahead in an alcove, something caught his eye. He moved forward, his mind glad to have something to concentrate on.

In the centre of the room, Hartnell and Kim crawled towards the protruding head of Lieutenant Samuels, scared of what they might find. The young engineering officer looked deathly pale and cold to boot.

Sergeant Kim reached out a shaking hand, two fingers going to the officer's neck, searching for heat and a pulse.

"He is alive." The relieved South Korean army sergeant exhaled, his fingers sensing a faint pulse.

Kim held his neck as Hartnell freed Lieutenant Samuels from the plates. They pulled his still unconscious body halfway out of the pit.

"Loo-tenant Samuels, wake up, we got to go." Private Hartnell shook the officer as he spoke loudly in his ear.

"We have to hasten." The sergeant moved forward and slapped the young unconscious officer hard on each pale cheek. The reddened cheeked officer stirred, his eyes flickering awake.

"I'm glad you did that, I'd be on a charge for hitting an officer if I'd done it!" Hartnell exclaimed, holding his commanding officer in his arms as he slowly gathered his wits about him.

"Then it is a good thing I am not in your army," Sergeant Kim said and moved off on shaky feet to free the Chinese sergeant.

Meanwhile, Private London had found a weapons haul in an alcove in one corner of the great temple hall. The only problem was they had been smashed to splinters of wood and all the barrels or stocks had been bent or broken off.

Private London was sorting through the debris to see if any of the weapons were at all salvageable. By the time he had finished, Lieutenant Samuels and the Chinese private were sitting with their backs to the nearby wall, recovering.

Hartnell, Mai and Kim were anxiously standing behind him; they wanted weapons, but they wanted to leave the carnal temple more.

"What have you got, Private?" Lieutenant Samuels asked, feeling uncertain of the alliance with the Chinese soldiers.

"All the rifles and machine guns have had it, apart from the BAR which we have no ammo for," Private London explained, some pistols lay next to the BAR in front of him.

"What do we have?" Sergeant Kim asked the British soldier.

"One Chinese pistol with one clip; two colt .45s with two and a half clips; and one Enfield revolver with four rounds," Private London explained to his small audience.

"I believe the Lieutenant and I have the Colts, London the revolver and Mai the TT33 pistol," the South Korean sergeant suggested.

"Is it wise to arm the Chinese?" Lieutenant Samuels coughed into his hand repeatedly.

"What about me?" Hartnell asked feeling naked now without a firearm.

"I've got four asserted bayonets for you and the Chink John," London added, "probably more use than the bullets against that thing anyway!"

London handed one bayonet each to Hartnell and the Chinese soldier named Tan. He pocketed the other one and handed the last to Sergeant Kim.

Without looking at Samuels, Kim handed the TT33 pistol and the last bayonet to Mai. Fu P'ai-Chang Mai bowed and took the weapons, then bent down to pull up his comrade.

Private Hartnell reached out a hand to his fellow American and pulled the young lieutenant onto his unsteady feet. With Kim leading the way, they walked out of the hellish temple, back outside onto the temple steps. Hartnell aiding Samuels followed, with Mai and Tan behind and London at the rear: revolver at the ready.

He looked back at the golden temple wondering where she was. Would she come after him? The intense passion he had felt last night had vanished in the cold morning light. It felt like one of his early teen wet erotic dreams now: with the lust gone, only guilt remained.

They walked as quickly as possible down the steps, nothing came to stop them. Up the cobbled road they all traversed, eyes darting this way and that anxiously. There was no sign of the Kumiho and only their footfalls made any sound in the eerie surrounding silence.

Sergeant Kim led the way, holding the Colt .45 firmly, he couldn't help but notice the distinct lack of bodies. Or any signs of conflict come to that, only the burnt out shell of a hut sat as a reminder of the bloody internecine battle that had raged here last night.

Sergeant Kim Jun Ho made for the rocky path that would zigzag its way up a passage to the plateau above, the Chinese followed him.

"This way, Sergeant Kim," Lieutenant Samuels ordered, stepping off the road under his own steam, with Hartnell and London following him.

Sergeant Kim turned full around to see that his UN allies were walking off in another direction, towards the opening in the cavern.

"I came this way, sir." The sergeant pointed up towards the path between the rocks.

"Really?" Samuels mused. "We are going back this way, it heads right back to the other temple."

"What about the Chinese soldiers, sir?" he asked as Mai looked at him quizzically.

"If they come back with us, Sergeant Kim, they will do so as prisoners of war." Lieutenant Samuels stood his ground facing the South Korean sergeant, "I'm an Engineer not a MP."

Sergeant Kim pointed to the Chinese then their escape route, then to him and the others' different way to go.

"An-nyong-ee keseyo," Sergeant Kim said goodbye in Korean and bowed.

"An-nyong-li kyeseyo," Fu P'ai-Chang Mai Pei Tiao replied with the correct Korean farewell. Both he and Chang-Shih Tan Hui Rui bowed low and hurried off into the rocks.

"Come on, let's hurry." Private London took point as he knew the way, and Kim the rear as he didn't.

They hurried past the burnt out hut now, scouring the area for signs of Chinese dead and the body of Private-First-Class Miguel Perez. They found nothing as they rushed across the battlefield, only the night before they had bayonet-charged across. They found the odd empty bullet casing, but nothing more.

Finally they reached their incursion point where Captain Ashley Woodholme-Browne, their mission C.O. had fallen. His, like the other corpses, was gone, not even the chair he had been tied to was there. It was quite bright now as they were so close to the opening, it seemed a sunny, but cold, 2nd November morning.

Each looked back as they reached the secret passage that led out of the cavern; each had their own private horrors to recall; and each mourned for the men they had lost.

Deep inside the temple a three foot square stone slab shot out of the floor by an ancient alcoved statue. The slab flew five feet through the air and exploded into many pieces as it came back to earth again on the hard stone floor. Up out of the hole, bare feet walking on roughly hewn steps, she strode purposefully.

She wore no garments, her naked body exposed to the elements. Her waistcoat and Hanbok no longer required to hide her bipolar body. She was complete and as beautiful as a human woman as any mother's womb could produce. She stopped, her palms feeling down over her large breasts, down over her now flat torso and stomach. After all the centuries she had lost the last fox vestiges from her human form. She had gained her ninth tail and so much more, power was hers, she would never age, she could bear children and at last she could escape her prison.

Her last husband had gone, she could sense him leaving through the shared Gusul he carried with him. She entered the great hall and walked past the headless corpses that remained, corpses held no interest to her now: she craved only the living.

On the steps of the temple she stood, surveying the cavern and old village that had once held her many worshippers. They had all perished decades ago, now she would see the wonders of the world beyond the plateau and be worshipped once more.

She walked along the road towards the end, where the two sets of armies and allies had parted. She sniffed the air, each of the survivors' scents, bringing an image of those men into her inner eye.

The woman looked left then ahead, and then moved off after one set of masculine odours.

As he led the way along the dark tunnel, Robert London shivered, *like someone had walked over his grave.* He shook his head and pressed on through the endless darkness. He had the unnerving feeling that his Kumiho bride had just woken up from her post-nuptial slumber.

Mai and Tan were out of the accursed cavern now, shivering in the cold morning light. Through the snow covered woods they marched, their inadequate footwear and trousers already wet through.

Fu P'ai-Chang Mai wasn't exactly sure if they were still on the path, but they kept near to the plateau's edge, so they must reach the bridge to safety within the hour.

Tan Hui Rui was labouring a little in the deep snow, so Mai Pei Tiao turned around to give his fellow man a hand.

That's when he saw her!

Walking naked through the snow and freezing temperatures, she strode out of the woods towards them. Fu-P'ai-Chang Mai raised his pistol at her and he and Chan-Shih Tan watched her steady approach.

"Jau hoy," Mai warned her to leave them alone, but the captivating beauty only walked closer towards them.

Mai adjusted his stance and cocked the hammer of the Russian made pistol and took aim; Tan next to him readied his bayonet: still she approached.

A shot broke the muteness of the morning and a red hole appeared in the Korean girl's perfect torso.

"Tan jau!" Fu P'ai-Chang Mai pushed his comrade into action, "jau."

The girl looked at her stomach and just wiped away the blood and the bullet hole had miraculously vanished.

Tan Hui Rui had seen enough and ran for his life, Mai Pei Tiao fired two more shots as the Kumiho woman got closer. One missed, the other hit her thigh, and she just turned to Mai and smiled.

He stumbled back as she ran at him, another shot wildly missing her, then he fell back over a snow hidden fallen branch. He raised his pistol to fire as he lay in the snow awaiting death, but she ignored him and ran past after Tan.

Mai struggled and slipped in the snow and rose to a steady kneeling position, firing off another bullet at the back of the woman. She staggered as it punctured her spine, her stride slowed; then she was off again to catch up with Tan again.

Mai slipped as he tried to rise again, then once over the branch, went after the Kumiho woman as fast as he could manage.

Tan Hui Rui ran for his life, but the snow seemed not to affect the chasing woman. A glance behind saw that she was near; he turned to run harder when she sprang. She was light, but her weight on his back knocked him into a tree trunk. Pain seared his right breast and he spun in a daze and fell with his back slumped against the tree.

Chan-Shih Tan Hui Rui stared at the rising, smiling woman, then saw the bayonet he had been holding, protruding from his right chest area. As he had hit the tree it had wedged his bayonet carrying hand in between it and his body and now it was sunk to the hilt inside him.

He knew his life was over at only twenty years of age, blubbering he looked from the bayonet to the evil woman: a coppery taste in his mouth. Shock, internal damage and fear, caused his life to end forever, three seconds later.

Running with tears in his eyes, Mai Pei Tiao saw the head of his last remaining comrade slump forward in death. The Kumiho woman turned and grinned wildly at him.

He fired causing part of her hair and skull to fly off behind her; she was twelve feet away. She paused to turn and stare at it as it lay, staining the snow, then walked slowly closer.

Another shot at nine feet made a temporary mess of her left breast, still she approached. Mai had a desperate choice now as only one round remained in the TT-33 pistol.

"Mm hai," he said, shaking his head as she got within seven feet. The pistol went to his temple and he blew out his brains.

The Korean woman watched the brave man fall into the snow and bowed at him. Then she was off running at great speed through the wintery woods to catch her next group of prey.

Private Robert London had been anxious to the point of throwing a wobbly in the long dark tunnel. It had been claustrophobic, the only sounds being of boots on stone and the puffing breaths of the exhausted soldiers.

Now they were outside again, free from the tunnel's dark confinement, but Robert wasn't sure if they were any better off. It had stopped snowing, but it lay in deep drifts along the dell. The sky was blue with a few white clouds high above the stark canopy of trees. It was hard going through the snow and the freezing cold bit at the helmetless soldiers as they trudged along. London had found his Middlesex beret in his battledress tunic pocket and given it to the lieutenant to wear. Not because of rank, but because he seemed to be in a worse state than the rest of the other remaining men in the expedition.

The legs of all the men ached around the calves and thighs as they had to high step their way through the knee level snow.

Private Hartnell led the way now, with Sergeant Kim aiding the lieutenant and London bringing up the rear. He gazed back along the white-washed length of the dell, but already the tunnel opening was out of sight. The huge stone was too heavy to move in their condition so they left it and hoped for the best.

If the Kumiho did come after them, he was sure she could have rolled aside the stone with ease anyway. Their tracks through the snow filled trench would not be hard to follow either.

Turning his head forward again his foot hit a snow buried rock and he fell forward into the soft, cushioning snow.

"You okay, boy?" Hartnell asked as he and the others turned around.

"Just tripped, I'm fine," Private London replied quickly, getting up and dusting off the snow from his coat.

"Let's keep moving, men," the lieutenant urged in a drawn voice.

Sergeant Kim rubbed at his cold watery eyes and helped the lieutenant trudge on. He hated this small trench they were painfully and slowly traversing: it was an ambush alley.

On she ran with a girlish whoop of excitement. The cold air on her skin, the feel of the snow between her toes as she ran, was somehow new. She was like a newborn child in some respects, a new species even and she felt enthused with power.

Whether as a fox or in her near-human form, she always had to keep a low profile, to the shadowy dens of the earth. Now she would be free to roam, to dominate mankind, to rule as the world's undying queen. She had learnt much of the new world, its wars and its languages, from the soldiers she had killed. English, Cantonese (Chinese) and modern Korean, she had added to the ancient Korean, Greek and Latin she already knew.

With her new husband once again under her sway, she would suck the knowledge from the learned scholars of the world. He would give pleasures to her new human form and offspring, all her centuries old dreams would come to bare.

A branch whipped across her cheek, drawing blood: the lick of pain she savoured like ice cream sundae.

On she ran, a smile constant on her parted lips, the scent of her mate was in her nostrils. The mental tug of the shared Gusul was like a mini-compass in her frontal lobes. She hunted him and his weak fellow soldiers; they were heading for the sanctuary of the Mudang's temple not knowing its powers of protection from her were waning.

"We're getting there!" Robert London looked up at the two ugly faced totem poles, as Hartnell passed through them, ahead of Samuels and Kim.

Hartnell wasn't too fond of the totem poles; the ones back home near the farm had also given him bad dreams. Yet it showed they were making progress, but the sun shining on the snow covered trench was making his eyes ache.

The temple would give them protection from the Kumiho he hoped, and at the least warmth and maybe the odd morsel of food.

Kim's belly rumbled loudly as he and Samuels passed between the poles. He too hoped the Mudang had food and felt more open minded to her advice since his last visit.

London felt a tug at his coat pocket as he went to walk through the totem poles. He turned to see what his coat had snagged on, but saw nothing. He turned, a frown on his cold lips, then made to step forward. He felt resistance like he was walking into a gale force wind for a second; then he was through. He eyed the totem poles suspiciously as he followed the others; they had not noticed his hesitation.

The woman jumped gracefully down onto bended knees into the snow-ladened dell. She sniffed at the dark tunnel entrance behind her, and then headed off in the other direction. The direction the soldiers who had escaped earlier had followed.

The soldiers' progress had slowed the further along the dell their exhausted bodies and minds had traversed. They rested, not because they wanted to but, because fatigue had finally overcome them. They knew stopping was dangerous, because they might not start up again; or the Kumiho might come after them.

"One more minute, then we head out," ordered Lieutenant Samuels weakly, he was feeling the worst out of the four of them.

While the soldiers had stumbled along slowly, the Kumiho had flown along the dell at full pelt. Ahead she saw something that slowed her to a dead stop and old anxieties returned to haunt her new outlook on life.

Four yards ahead, heavily dusted with snow were two totem poles. They had been the bane of her existence, protecting the Mudangs and their cursed temple from her vengeance. The totem poles had kept her from roaming too far from her cavern lair, while the Tolharubang (Grandfather) stones and the Mudang's prayers had kept her from leaving the plateau.

She breathed in a lung-full of cold air, her cold erect nipples moving up and down as she did.

"I am new," she whispered in her husband's tongue and moved closer to the right hand poles. Then her small frail looking fist punched at the bottom of the pole. A large splintered dent appeared as the result of the punch. Then with furious combinations she punched left then right handed into the base of the pole. A crack appeared in the old weather worn pole, which quickly ran three feet up its length. She smiled now, ignoring the blood that ran from her fingers, to stain the snow beneath. More punches caused the crack to widen and then the wooden pole split in two halves. One piece falling into the snow, the other still erect, its heads now ruined.

The Kumiho kicked at the remaining half now and with her second connection it fell also, beside its other half.

Laughing with gleeful delight, she just grabbed the remaining pole with bloodless healed hands and just pulled at it with her increased might.

It took five seconds to break off halfway down and she threw it down upon the remains of its paired pole.

Then, even though she had a woman's form, she was no lady and her feral behaviour got the better of her. She stood astride the two fallen poles of imprisonment, squatted slightly, then let forth a stream of steaming piss all over them. Leaving the ruined poles lying in red and yellow stained snow behind her, she walked along the dell. Her prey were close now, she could almost taste them.

"Hurry," Sergeant Kim hissed as they had all heard the loud cracking of wood echoing along the winding small valley.

The tree was up ahead now and behind it would be the secret door to the temple passage. They hurdled-ran as best they could, but the drifts near the tree seemed deeper than in the rest of the long dell.

Private Hartnell, the sprightliest amongst them, made it to the thick trunk of the tree first. He began to burrow through the four foot snow drift that had covered the gap they needed to squeeze through to reach the inner door.

Private London was soon next to him, pulling at the snow with his hands to clear the opening next to the tree.

Sergeant Kim and Lieutenant Samuels stood side by side behind them, pistols raised in outstretched arms down the dell. They waited.

The very air seemed frozen around them, the silence deafening, but there was no sign of pursuit.

London and Hartnell looked at each other, the way was now clear of snow.

"Go on," Robert London nodded for the American to go first.

John Hartnell winked and pushed himself through the tight gap, crouching down as he did. He soon felt the cold iron door in front of him and searched in the darkness for a handle.

Hartnell felt movement behind him and saw London silhouetted against the snowy gap, then move into the small tunnel behind him.

"Having trouble?" Robert London enquired, moving next to his friend.

"Buddy, if I could see it would help," John Hartnell replied, his gloved hands feeling around the door.

Then illumination from a petrol lighter held in London's hand, showed parts of the door.

"Don't have a crowbar in ya pants pocket too do ya, Bobby?" Hartnell could now see a large iron ring was fixed to the centre of the door, but no handle to the lock was visible.

"Only thing in my pants is me meat and two veg, Johnny boy," replied London, bemused by the question and not knowing that 'pants' had two different transatlantic garment meanings.

"What?" John Hartnell asked, equally confused by their shared language. What had food got to do with crowbars?

"Is it open yet?" Sergeant Kim called down the hole.

"No," was the joint Anglo-American reply.

"Go and help them, Sergeant," ordered the lieutenant, his Colt .45 trembling in his cold and frightened hand.

"Sir?" Sergeant Kim looked down the still empty dell to his superior.

"Are you still here? Go and help them: that's an order Sergeant!" the lieutenant said loudly through gritted teeth and with a touch of anger.

"Sonsaengnim." The sergeant bowed and then saluted his commanding officer, then headed for the hole.

"Let's give it a shove, mate," Private London suggested, putting his shoulder to the door.

"Shove?" John Hartnell was learning new English words every minute, but he got the gist and put his shoulder to the door also.

"One, two, three, push," London said and together Hartnell and he pushed at the rusty iron door. The door swung in three feet then juddered to a halt. They heaved again as Sergeant Kim entered the now cramped passage behind the two privates.

The door was open wide enough to let them pass now, so London went through, relighting his hot metal lighter as he did.

"Go through." Kim patted Hartnell on the shoulder, "I will inform the Lieutenant." Private Hartnell did not have to be asked twice and followed London in to the secret temple passage, proper.

Sergeant Kim moved out of the passageway into the cold harsh Korean winter again.

Robert London meanwhile, had pulled an ancient looking torch from its rusty wall holder and was trying to light its end.

"Let me try." Hartnell approached and gently took the torch and lighter off him; instantly they were plunged into darkness.

"Oh good plan, Yank," London exclaimed to where he hoped Hartnell was standing.

A few seconds went by and London was by now tapping his numb footed boot on the cold stone flagstones.

There was a spark then the lighter lit again, held under the torch, which now caught fire and spluttered into life.

"Good old US ingenuity, my friend," Hartnell smiled, handing back the hot lighter.

"How'd you get it to light?"

"I poured most of your gas from your lighter onto it." Hartnell beamed in the torchlight.

"You wasted my lighter petrol?" London frowned, but was just jealous that he hadn't thought of it.

Just then, Sergeant Kim appeared at the doorway with Lieutenant Samuels in the small earthy passage behind him. Kim went through to join the others and Samuels went to follow; then heard movement outside somewhere along the dell. Quickly Samuels reached around the door and grabbed the key, which the Mudang had left in the lock. Grabbing the ring on his side of the door he pulled the door closed, bracing a foot against the door frame to aid him.

As he heard startled cries from behind the door, his fingers found the lock, wobbled the key in and locked it. Then, pulling with what strength adrenaline was giving him, he broke the key inside the lock and tossed the end he had into the darkness.

He swallowed hard, gathered his nerves and pushed himself past the tree trunk, back into the snowy dell. He took off his long officer's coat and threw it onto the side of the trench and checked his magazine and then pushed it back into the Colt .45.

He looked up and exhaled a billowing icy breath before him and said a silent prayer. Then she was there, fifty yards away at the bend of the dell.

He stood whey-face, his legs physically shaking with fear. He adjusted the width of his stance and raised his pistol at the slowly advancing Korean girl.

Then he frowned, realising that she was completely naked, the first nude woman he had ever seen, and his last.

He fired his first shot while she was still forty-five yards away; it missed by the breadth of a barn door. He steadied his shaking right pistol arm, with his left holding it steady at the wrist. He fired again and this time he was rewarded, his bullet hit high on her upper left arm, causing the girl to spin slightly and stop her in her tracks.

He lowered his pistol to look at her; she stared at him and smiled widely. Then her right hand went to her bleeding wound and just wiped the blood and damage away: flicking it onto the crisp white snow.

Then she ran at him from a standing start, arms pumping, her face a grotesque mixture of fox and female human features.

Another shot disappeared into the snowy bank to the side of her, the next in quick succession hit her stomach; she didn't even seem to flinch this time.

Twenty yards now and shots to her chest and then stomach again, slowed her little. With blood oozing from various wounds she ran at the man, ready to inflict death.

At thirteen yards his round hit her in the solar-plexus, rendering a wound that Samuels could see fragments of bone protruding through.

At ten yards he pulled the trigger of his Colt .45 again, but it just clicked empty.

He lowered the now empty and useless weapon and stared at his own form of death closing in on him.

"I'm coming, Ashley," were the last words of Lieutenant Edward David Samuels of the 3rd Engineering Battalion of the 24th Division, United States Army. The Kumiho hit him like a tsunami and tore his mortal body to pieces.

Inside the temple passageway, three men stood in the flickering torchlight, ears straining to hear beyond the iron door. They had initially tried to smash at the lock and, when that failed, pull at the door with their combined might. It did not budge and the first faint pistol shot from outside, ceased all fruitless efforts.

They, to-a-man, stood in silence and counted the rounds go off one by one. After the seventh shot there were three seconds of silence, then a scream of pain.

The three men from different countries looked at each other with a shared sense of utter despair.

"Why did he do it?" Private London whispered.

"To buy us time to escape maybe?" Private Hartnell said, not sure of his C.O.'s reasons for sacrificing himself.

"Then we must use the time wisely," Sergeant Kim stated, "and retreat to the temple."

With sad hearts they nodded in agreement and turned to go. Ahead of them in the dark shadows that the torchlight could not illuminate, stood a female shape.

The trio of soldiers raised whatever weapons they had as the shadowy figure advanced on their position.

"Kach'I oda," said the Mudang, now visible in her flowing white robes, beckoning for them to follow her.

The small band of soldiers looked at each other in apprehension. Then a pounding on the outside of the iron door behind them pushed their army boots into action. They followed the swiftly moving Mudang along the secret passageway and into the warmer, comparative safety, of the hidden temple.

Once back inside the inner temple the shaman woman pushed the bear spirit statue's left paw upwards. The secret doorway into the passageway they had all just exited closed slowly, with a reverberating bang. The Mudang then moved sideways and pushed up the right paw of the statue.

There was a loud rumble and an almighty crash from behind the secret door that made the temple floor shake under their feet. Behind the secret door a five tonne block of stone had fallen from the ceiling, blocking the passageway, both ways, forever.

The Mudang turned and smiled her toothy grin at the soldiers and said, "Umshik?"

"Wadda she say, Sarge?" Hartnell asked the new leader of their diminished expedition.

"She has food for us," Sergeant Kim answered as the Mudang beckoned for them to follow her.

Chapter 19

Three Phials

The soldiers ducked under the ripped hanging white banners of cloth and followed the old shaman woman. Sergeant Kim could not help notice that of the eleven lengths of cloth only three remained whole and intact.

The Mudang led them along a narrow, bending passageway into a small room, which must act as her living quarters. White freshly washed robes hung from strings to dry across one wall. A small cot with filthy looking covers stood low to the ground in one corner, a fireplace (with burning coals) stood in another. The Mudang moved to a large pot that was suspended over the flames and stirred the contents with a wooden spoon.

"Annta," she said, motioning with open palms pushing down.

Even the Englishman and the American knew that she wanted them to sit, but they still looked at the sergeant for guidance.

He nodded; his face a poker player would be proud of, unreadable. All three of them sat down cross-legged like they were at infant/kindergarten/yuch'iwon school.

The Mudang put down her spoon and poured the three soldiers a wooden cup of water, giving them all to Kim to pass along.

When Robert took his, he had a sudden flashback to last night and the Kumiho girl doing the same thing. His head swam for a moment and his body felt like gravity had deserted him for a second.

"You okay, London?" Hartnell asked, concerned for his friend.

"Yeah," Robert took a sip of the cool water, "just tired that's all."

"You and me both," Hartnell replied, rubbing at his tired eyes.

The water refreshed Robert London's head, as he watched the Mudang fill four wooden bowls with rice and vegetables. These she passed along also and Kim handed the bowls round.

"What's for dinner then Sarge?" Hartnell asked, sniffing at the exotic steaming food in his hands.

"Rice and a few winter vegetables," Sergeant Kim looked at him bemused.

"Oh," Hartnell sniffed again, he'd been in Korea for three months and had only ever eaten US Army rations and chow.

"It's like rice pudding," London explained between gobfuls of rice, "but without the milk and sugar, of course."

"What's rice pud-ding?" Hartnell asked London, still bemused.

"Eat it, Private Hartnell, it will fill your ever rumbling belly," Kim stated, his fingers scooping the rice into his hungry mouth.

Looking from side to side as his companions feasted and seeing that no cutlery was forthcoming, Hartnell pushed his fingers into the rice and began eating.

The Mudang smiled, and then ate her food slower than the ravenous soldiers. She eyed them one by one, wondering if they each had the strength to attempt the task the spirits had forced upon them.

When they had finished second helpings of the rice meal, the Mudang poured a thicker golden drink into their drained empty cups.

Hartnell sniffed at it first, then London; while Sergeant Kim quaffed down the amber drink in five gulps.

"What you think?" Hartnell asked London as he tentatively sipped at the drink.

"It's Sagwa-Chasu, it's good." Sergeant Kim forced a smile to reassure them.

"It's scrumpy," London said elated and gulped down the refreshing drink.

Hartnell tried his drink. "That's apple cider," he said and drank some more.

251

"What are we gonna do now, Sarge?" Hartnell asked after they had finished their meal.

Sergeant Kim watched the Mudang clear away the bowls; he had been thinking the same thing.

"We have to get back and warn HQ about the Chinks, don't we?" London queried, feeling drowsy after his meal.

"To understand your destination in life, first you have to understand the journey," Kim Jun Ho replied to the young private enigmatically.

Robert London looked at the R.O.K sergeant bemused. Even though he had the body, strength and courage of a man, he was still a teenager who had left school at fourteen to work in his dad's coal yard.

"You will understand one day, my friend, now I must speak to the Mudang, if you will excuse me."

Hartnell and London exchanged young mystified glances, but then again nothing on this mission had made any sense.

"Shaman, I humbly beg forgiveness for my words and actions at our previous encounter," Kim said in his native tongue, bowing before her.

"I told you, next time we met you would beg for my help." She cackled and stood up to him.

"Are we safe here?" he asked, they felt warm and safe, but those feelings could lead to their complacent deaths.

"For the moment," she nodded, "the Grandfather stones keep the Kumiho from entering the temple area."

"How long have we got?"

"You must leave within the hour, I will hold her off as long as I can, but her powers are strengthening."

"Why?" Kim asked.

The Mudang looked at the foreign soldier, and then beckoned Kim to follow her. "Just you," she added.

The two privates rose to follow them, but Kim motioned for them to sit back down with his left hand. Kim followed the shuffling feet and the swishing garmented figure of the Mudang. They returned up the narrow passageway into the inner Mudang temple.

"One of your warriors has mated with the beast. She has gotten her ninth tail and gained human immortality," the Mudang explained, a resigned look upon her face.

"I've seen it!" he said aloud. "But I thought it was just a story that my grandmother told my sister and I to stop us from wandering too far from our village."

"Stories, myths, legends: just because these things happened before paper and writing were invented and were told from generation to generation, does not mean they are not true." The Mudang looked even older and smaller now as she sat down on the side of a plinth.

"What do we do? How can it be stopped?" Kim asked, pacing up and down.

"The Kumiho is powerful now and grows stronger with every second. Her looks now can beguile most men, her strength is that of twenty warriors, no spear, arrow, or bullet can harm her."

"Then we have no hope?"

"Ha," the Mudang cackled, "if you have breath in your lungs then there is always hope."

"Can you kill her?" Kim turned and asked quickly.

"No." The old shaman woman sighed. "I am the last guardian here; the Mudang temple was built as a prison only; if we could have killed that evil spirit we would have done so generations ago. There is only a legend of three warriors from different lands, that will band together in friendship at the last to battle the Kumiho, with the fate of mankind at stake." The Mudang looked up, as her words sunk home in the sergeant's mind.

"It is time we summoned your fellow warriors here, I have something to show you all."

Meanwhile the two privates and now fast friends sat back, smoking two of Robert's thin roll-ups, as Hartnell had lost his cigarettes. That wasn't the only thing that had gone missing in the cavern: the radio set, his helmet and his C7 rations had all vanished.

"What do you think they're talking about?" Hartnell asked, just for something to say.

"Dunno, cowboy," London replied, his roll-up permanently stuck to his bottom lip as he spoke.

"I ain't a cowboy, Bobby; I live on a farm in Idaho," the young American engineer tried to explain to the British National Serviceman.

"You got any horses on your farm?" Robert asked, his geography of the United States was only learnt from trips to the local cinema.

"Three, why?"

"Do you have cows on your farm?"

"Yes," Hartnell replied slowly, half knowing where this was leading.

"Then to me, you're a fucking cowboy." Somehow, from somewhere, they both cracked up in fits of laughter. It wasn't because they had felt jovial, it was just a blessed relief from the horrors they had both just witnessed.

"Shoot, Limey, when it comes to US geography, you got shit-for-brains," Hartnell retorted and they laughed harder.

"I know what America looks like," London boasted.

"Really?" Hartnell was far from convinced.

London raised his left hand, "You have your New York here, full of mobsters." London then raised his right hand. "You got Hollywood over here, full of movie stars. Then in between, them both–"

"–Cowboys!" Hartnell interjected.

"–Cowboys!" London nodded, "See, easy-peasy."

"Easy-peasy," Hartnell repeated and frowned, the word sounded like something a kid from kindergarten would come up with.

Just then Sergeant Kim reappeared into the room and the two privates scrambled to their feet.

"Follow me," was all he said. So the two men stubbed out their smokes, gathered what little gear they had left and followed him.

Two minutes later they were standing behind Sergeant Kim, as the Mudang knelt before the plinth of a statue. She raised the white sheet that covered the stone beneath, to reveal three golden handles. They were attached to three round golden plates set into the stone.

"Kkonaeda," she urged the three soldiers, then spoke quickly again in Korean to Kim.

"She says we must each choose a drawer to pull out and carefully," Sergeant Kim translated to the other two.

Each golden circular plate was four inches apart from the other, so the three men knelt down as a unit and grabbed one of the cold golden handles each.

Sergeant Kim pulled on the left handle, Hartnell on the right, leaving London in the centre. The drawers were heavy, but slowly they pulled out inch by inch with a grating noise.

The tubular drawers extended to reveal a near solid golden base, with just a square hole sunk in the middle. Inside this cut-out was a black lacquered box, inlaid with leaves of exquisite jade work and opal flowers.

All three soldiers looked at the Mudang for permission to pick it up and she readily goaded them with beckoning hand motions.

Each man reached into the drawers and retrieved a black box.

"Choshimsuropkka," the Korean woman warned in a hushed voice and Kim passed on the message to handle it with care.

The three warriors foretold in the Mudang legends of old, rose up, the boxes carefully held in both hands: like a just caught, wicket taking, cricket ball.

The Mudang went to Kim first and used her fingers to push his forefingers into a certain place on the side of the box. There was a tiny click and the lid slowly opened upwards to reveal what lay inside.

There inside, cushioned by surrounding red velvet, was a teardrop shaped glass phial containing a clear red liquid.

The Mudang then went to London and helped him open his box to reveal a similar phial of blue liquid. Hartnell was last and his box opened to reveal a phial containing a yellow liquid.

"What are they for?" Kim asked the Mudang. "What do they do?"

"If the Kumiho catches you up and you have no other means of escape, throw this at her advancing feet."

"Will it kill her?" Kim asked in Korean again.

"Kill her, maybe?" The Mudang shrugged, "Aid your escape, definitely. Stop her possibly."

"That does not seem very encouraging," Kim spat back, his old Buddhist heckles rising again.

"What is life? What is death? We are mortals, we do not live in absolutes, both are journeys of faith. The Kumiho has evolved now into a form no spirit on earth has obtained for over a millennia," the Mudang tried to explain, a tired look on her haggard face.

"Yesterday I was the Kumiho's keeper, today we are equals, tomorrow I will be dead and she will rise beyond my powers." The Mudang patted his arm and shuffled towards the way out of the inner temple.

"Now it is time for you to leave together, but my inner sight fears you will each face the Kumiho alone." The Mudang stood by the passageway that led out onto the snow covered real world beyond.

"What did she say?" London asked, looking from his phial to the R.O.K sergeant.

"Yeah, what gives, Sarge?" Hartnell added.

"It is time for us to go; we must warn our forces of the Chinese presence. Keep the phials safe and if you're caught by the Kumiho, throw the phial at her feet, it will give you time to escape."

Hartnell and London looked down at the coloured phials and closed the lids together. Kim followed suit, then each of them put the boxes into their coat pockets for safety.

They pulled up their collars and grabbed whatever little gear they had and walked towards the temple's passageway that led outside.

London led the way, revolver in hand, saluting the Mudang as he passed, which caused her to smile in spite of the dire situation.

Hartnell nodded at her as he passed and she bowed in response.

Kim bowed low before her and went to follow his two comrades out of the temple. The Mudang reached out and caught his arm in a vice-like grip. "Your sister is alive and safe, and far away from this war, Jun Ho," the Mudang imparted a final piece of information.

"Where is she?" Kim asked, his heart beating fast with renewed hope.

"Far from here across many seas in a country whose name I do not know. She has her mission in life too, warrior. Now you must hurry from here, I just hope these words add fire to your heart." The Mudang turned her back on him and walked slowly towards the drawers to close and conceal them again.

Kim Jun Ho had many more questions to ask, but he would get no more answers here. He and his fellow warriors had to escape to warn of the Chinese army's surprise attack. Yet now he had another reason to escape the plateau: to find his sister.

The cold hit them instantly as they hurried down the hidden temple steps into the bowl it was situated in. Each touched the grandfather (Tolharubang) stones as they passed for good luck then trudged up the rising path to the top of the concealed bowl of land. Each took one look back at the hidden temple, trying to take a mental picture of it for their memories.

Then, led by Sergeant Kim, Privates Hartnell and London headed back into the trees that covered most of the Yŏu Plateau and back along the snow covered path, from whence they came.

The Mudang stood in her temple and began to sing and move: beginning a Kut ceremony to ward off the evil fox spirit as long as her old body could manage.

The Kumiho had been forced to retrace her steps after the secret passageway into the temple had been blocked. She stood in all her proud naked glory on a snow covered path, with another set of shaman totem poles blocking her way.

This time one punch and one well aimed kick had felled these ancient poles of protection. Her strength and powers were increasing every hour she lived in her new immortal human form. She couldn't wait to be with her new and last husband again and to populate the world with her cubs. Then she would use the human race as slaves to do her bidding and she would be the alpha female: with domination over all.

Firstly she had the old Mudang woman to deal with and that would be a slow, long-thought-out death. The Kumiho smiled and bounded off through the snow, towards the hidden shaman temple.

Chapter 20

Pursuit

The snow and lack of rest slowed them down, but finally they climbed up the slope to find the bridge they had crossed only twenty-four hours ago. It seemed so much longer, because so much had happened to them and changed their lives forever.

They hurried across the bridge, each of the three soldiers thinking of the eight comrades who would never escape the horrors of the Yõu Plateau.

"The bridge." Private London looked back after they had crossed, "We should get rid of it."

"Good thinking, Private London," Sergeant Kim said taking out his bayonet. Hartnell followed suit and both men began to cut at the nearest thick ropes supporting the bridge.

"What about me?" Robert London asked, standing behind them. "Can I do anything?"

Sergeant Kim turned his head towards the Englishman as he cut, "You can go and get the trucks ready."

"Right-ho," London ran off, "I'll see you blokes in a jiffy."

"Keep your eyes open, Bobby," Hartnell warned, concerned that his friend would be all alone for a while.

Robert London just waved to acknowledge his American friend and hurried off to where they had stashed the three trucks. It felt good to be off that infernal plateau at last and back to the real world: shame the real world was a war zone. It took Robert London ten minutes to get back to the gully where they had hidden and camouflaged the trucks. Luckily for him the overhanging rocks and the wind direction of the snow meant the hidden trucks were only lightly dusted with snow.

He began the task of dragging away the evergreen branches that had covered the front of the first truck. This was the worst for snow and he hoped the radiator had not frozen solid.

It wasn't until they had cut the third rope that the bridge began to buckle, flip over and look on its last legs. They had both moved to cut the last rope when the bridge, all by itself, gave way at their end. It swept like a swing across the abyss to crash into the other side. Half of the planks came loose and fell downwards; the bridge was well-and-truly-out-of-action.

The two soldiers smiled at each other and hurried down the mountain road to help London.

The Mudang in her temple stopped dead and turned around. She walked briskly out of the temple and stood on top of the steps looking down.

Across the hidden bowl, before the Grandfather stones stood the Kumiho in her human form. The game was up now and she stared death in the face. No more amounts of chanting and ceremonies could save her now.

The Mudang watched with interest as the Kumiho raised her arms aloft before the two Grandfather stones. With her legs in a wide apart stance, the Kumiho, in human guise closed her eyes and focussed her mind.

The Mudang watched as the snow on top of the Grandfather stones began to vibrate and then fall from their great domed heads. Soon all the snow had been shaken off, followed by small splinters of the volcanic rock they were hewn from. An audible crack was heard across the bowl as large splits appeared in both of the guardian stones.

The shaman woman winced, as the ancient stones exploded in all directions sending a brief cloud of fine snow into the air. When it cleared the nude Kumiho/woman stood untouched by the flying debris. A large smile now stretched across the countenance of the nine tailed fox spirit.

The Mudang had seen enough; she turned on her heels and hurried back inside her temple. The ancient protection had now gone, leaving now just an empty ruin from a forgotten time.

She knelt in the centre of the inner temple room. She grabbed the hem of her white robes and ripped a large tear all the way up to her shift.

Behind her, entering the guardian temple for the first time, came the Kumiho. The temple's power, though failing stripped the nine tailed fox of her human appearance. On hind paws she walked up behind the praying figure of the old Mudang. Saliva dripped from her widening jaws as she prepared to enact her millennia planned revenge on her Mudang guardians. Her claws reached down to grab the old woman's arms, to pull them from their sockets. As her paw touched the Mudang's shoulder, the white robed woman fell sideward, dead.

The Kumiho stared at the ancient heavily lined face and saw that long rent in her robes and howled with disappointment. The wizened old bitch had died of old age and in doing so had robbed the Kumiho of her revenge. The nine tailed fox tore at the corpse in a rage, ripping the body to pieces and coating the temple with blood and gore.

The Mudang had won only a tiny victory in her death, yet the whole world waited beyond the confines of her plateau prison and now no one could stop her. Stopping only to piss on the scattered steaming remains of the Mudang, the Kumiho strode from the temple.

As soon as the cold air had hit her, she saw that her human skin, so long in gaining, had returned. As she slipped down the temple steps, the two pillars at the temple entrance crumbled and fell. Behind her naked back the temple fell in on itself, its spires crashing down across it causing the roof to cave in.

Snow, dust and smoke billowed into the air as the temple decomposed into a mound of rubble in the Kumiho's wake, leaving only a spire, the steps and a mound of stone to act as the Mudang's mausoleum.

Private Robert London was glad he was alone for the moment, as he stood on the engine block with his penis exposed to the freezing winds. The radiator cap was off and he was pissing as best he could aim into the frozen up radiator.

The other two trucks were in better shape because they had been further down the gully and less exposed to the previous day's blizzard.

London pushed in, zipped up, pulled down his coat and jumped off the meaty engine. He fixed on the radiator cap, closed the bonnet and raced to the left side cab door. He got in, slamming the door behind him and realised not for the first time that this was an American left-hand drive truck and slid across the seats. Hoping the engine would start quickly to stop his piss freezing up, which it thankfully did. He had used the camouflage branches to wedge under the front and back wheels of the first truck and over the snow ahead. Private London revved up the engine to warm it up then shifted the 'deuce n a half' into gear.

The truck resisted for two seconds, like a tramp woken from a meths binge; then jerked forward onto the branches. Robert London gunned the engine for all its worth and the truck began to roll up the incline, back onto the snow covered dirt road. Once safely back on the near level track, he idled the engine and jumped out: hoping no Gooks or Chinks were in earshot.

Then he smiled, for trudging along the winding mountain track now came Kim and Hartnell.

"So why can't we all go in one truck, Sarge?" Hartnell asked as they fixed a tow rope from the first truck to the second one down the gully.

"The message about the Chinese army must get through at all costs," he explained, "If the enemy or the Kumiho gets one of us, it will give the others a chance to escape."

"What if we come up against any enemy in front of us?" London asked from his position next to the first truck.

"Then we plough through them without stopping, with luck one of us will get back to our lines," Sergeant Kim explained as he finished attaching the tow-rope.

"I don't like our odds much, boys," Hartnell said, to himself really.

"Let's just try our best, eh," London called down to them, and then got back up into the truck. Hartnell got into the second deuce and started her up, while Kim stood by with branches, by the wheels.

The Kumiho in womanly form raced up the steep incline to where the rope bridge stood. Or had once stood!

Only the posts were visible across the gap between the Yŏu plateau and the outside world. She moved forwards and looked down, what remained of the old rope bridge dangled downwards.

She turned and looked to the treetops, her feral eyes scanning left and right. No fallen bridge could keep her from her new husband and her new life.

She skipped across the snow to stand behind the thick ancient trunk of a hundred year old deciduous tree. She placed her small hands on the rough texture of the bark and began to push with inhuman strength. She could hear the spirit of the tree scream out in terror as the tree tipped/pitched forward, its thick roots erupting from the snow and earth beneath her feet. She stepped to the side of the tree, its length pointing at a thirty degree angle over the gorge.

Her fingernails dug deep into the bark now and she pulled the tree down, so its upper branches crashed onto the other side of the chasm.

She dusted off her hands at a job well done and hopped on to the tree trunk bridge with all the grace of a gymnast. She ran across the tree trunk now, her arms outstretched to either side for fun, rather than balance.

She hopped off the other side and landed with her legs apart ready to spring into action, but she didn't. She closed her eyes and savoured her moment of escape, then she pissed into the snow to mark her territory for good measure.

The three mixed sets of booted prints were easy to find in this weather. Like temporary markers in time, crushed into the snow that covered nearly everything.

She reached down and grabbed a handful of crushed snow from one of her mate's boot prints and put some in her open mouth, the rest she rubbed down her small chest and into her pubic hair. Her longing to be reunited with her husband grew to an insatiable urge and she bounded off down the mountain track to find him.

"Good luck," Private London said as he embraced Hartnell, then Kim in turn.

"See you on the other side, Limey," Hartnell said to his friend Robert London. This wasn't usual military behaviour, but they had just gotten out of a very non-military situation.

"Remember, stop for nothing, not even a friend, promise?" Sergeant Kim told them.

The two privates nodded and then saluted the R.O.K sergeant who bowed, feeling slightly embarrassed, but proud of their gesture.

They parted and each went to their idling trucks and climbed in.

Private London, the best driver, led the way in the first truck, with Sergeant Kim following and Private Hartnell at the rear. Hartnell being an engineer could drive most vehicles, Kim could drive a car, so had gotten some quick on-the-spot tips from London.

The three engines roared as they moved off, slowly at first, gaining speed as they went. Robert London didn't want to go too fast and slide off the snowy mountainside, nor did he want to dawdle, with the Kumiho somewhere behind them.

Soon they were going along at a safe steady, but not too slow, pace. Twenty minutes into their drive the circular clearing where they had told each other scary stories, flashed past.

All three of the remaining soldiers glanced at the snow covered area, as much as their driving skills allowed them. Then it was gone forever and their trucks rumbled on down the snow covered road into the brown hills of North Korea.

The Kumiho had reached the gully only a quarter of an hour after the three trucks had left. The smell of burnt petrol ran through her sensitive nostrils.

The only sign of their presence were lines of the trucks in the snow and one empty gas barrel.

Far from getting tiresome, she was enjoying her freedom and the hunt. It had been years uncounted since her sisters and she had once hunted men like this.

On she ran over the snow, her lungs full of cold air, and her legs never tiring.

The day wore on and the mountain tracks became hill roads, the snow was thinning the lower they drove.

Robert London nervously looked into his rear view mirror every couple of minutes just to make sure both trucks were still following him.

The snow had all but gone from the cold landscape now and the roads were level. Driving had become easier now, yet tiring to the arms and legs. The journey had obviously taken longer coming back than going because of the adverse conditions. Yet soon they would be returning to the Taechon village and the comparative safety of the British Middlesex Regiment.

The village held by his own regiment could not be more than fifteen minutes' drive away and he couldn't wait to see those ugly mugs of D-Company again.

Whereas the three trucks heading back to friendly lines had to follow the roads, the Kumiho could cut across frozen paddy fields in a straight line.

She just caught sight of the last of the three trucks on the road ahead, disappearing behind a small tree covered rise. Not far ahead she could see a village and her nostrils picked up the scent of many young men.

She smiled and began to follow them again. She pursued the three trucks, only a minute behind now, as they entered the outskirts of Taechon.

Robert London cut his speed in half now, as the small forms and outlying huts of Taechon went past his side windows. He wondered where the road block and sentries were, as he had seen no signs of his fellow countrymen so far.

At last, as he made his way towards the centre of the village, he could see a body of men ahead. A hut a little way back from the road was ablaze and the soldiers were standing over four or five dark shapes on the frozen earth.

At the sound of the approaching truck, the group of twenty or so men turned around. They raised their weapons in a bemused fashion; these had not been the vehicles they had been expecting.

Suddenly London realised the soldiers ahead wore padded jackets like 'Michelin Men' and they had raised their Russian built machine guns.

"Fuck my old boots!" he exclaimed and slammed his British army boot down on the accelerator.

The Chinese and a few North Korean soldiers scattered in all directions, fearing for their lives as the two and a half tonne truck came thundering at them.

Sergeant Kim saw the lead truck suddenly increase its speed and looked left to see twenty Chinese soldiers run from between some huts. Taechon had been recaptured by the enemy and the three US military trucks were driving straight into a Chinese hornet's nest.

Private Hartnell gunned his truck also as the enemy swarmed out of every bolt hole in the village to see what was going on.

The men London had scattered were rising from behind the villagers they had tortured to death for information on the enemy. The first truck had rounded a bend now, the second was after it, so by the time their guns blazed, only the last truck was a real target.

Then the cacophony of small arms fire rang out across the centre of Taechon village. Private Hartnell's driver's side window exploded as rounds began to hit his truck. He ducked as best he could and pushed the pedal to the metal. The Lord's Prayer came to mind and he muttered this to himself as the enemy bullets pinged off his vehicle.

Up in front, Private London could see the Chinese forces had kindly dismantled the former British roadblock. Only half a dozen soldiers stood around the only road in and out of Taechon; at ease because the enemy had left just before they had arrived.

London just ploughed through the unfortunate men like skittles and headed south away from enemy lines.

Two rounds entered Sergeant Kim's windscreen, sending cracks into the glass and leaving two coin sized holes in it. One of the Chinese soldiers London's truck had missed was up and firing.

Kim had ducked to avoid the attack and his truck had skidded right and clipped the firing enemy by sheer fluke. He thanked Buddha for aiding him today, and managed to reign in the truck before it went out of control and headed off after London's deuce.

Poor old Hartnell being the last had got the worst of the enemy machine gun fire. Not a window of his truck remained intact, even his wing mirrors had been shot to hell.

Luck or the Lord was on his side at the moment, because he drove on without a scratch. The end of the village was now in sight and Kim's deuce could be seen on the long southern road to safety.

A more experienced Pan-Chang lowered the aim of his Burp gun and fired at the last retreating vehicles wheels.

Both of Private Hartnell's two back left tyres exploded into nothing, the deuce and a half truck front left wheel went down into a frozen pothole. Suddenly Hartnell felt the whole truck start to tip as the momentum of his speed sent the truck sliding over on to its side. Hartnell gripped onto the wheel for grim death, ice and stones shot up into his face as the deuce continued to slide across the icy road, only stopping as it hit a bank on the right side of the road, just outside of town.

With a cheer the Chinese soldiers ran towards the crashed US truck, as a dazed Hartnell looked around the cab for his bayonet. He couldn't find it so crawled out the glassless windscreen and stumbled along down the south road.

Two hundred yards from the straight road out of Taechon, London looked into his rear view mirror and slowed his truck to a halt. Kim had to slam on his brakes and move parallel to London's truck to avoid a crash.

London was out of his cab in a flash, his revolver drawn, with a cursing sergeant behind him.

Hartnell looked up from his slow and painful escape. His leg hurt like hell and all he could manage to do was limp towards his comrades in arms.

He saw Robert standing behind his halted truck and smiled, he knew his English friend would come back for him. He saw his friend was shouting at him and now Kim stood beside him.

Four pairs of rough hands grabbed him and a wooden rifle stock crashed down on the side of his head. His vision faded and the Chinese soldiers dragged his limp form back to Taechon.

"Nooo!" Robert London bellowed and fired off a shot at more advancing enemy troops. Then Hartnell and his four captors were lost behind ten or more Chinese soldiers, who began to fire on his and Kim's position.

"We have to go!" Sergeant Kim ordered pulling at the distraught Englishman. The rounds were coming thick and fast now and one just hit the side of London's truck an inch above his head.

London knew there was nothing they could do and rushed back to his cab and Kim entered his. The two trucks sped off, with enemy fire in their wake.

Robert London could hardly see the road ahead because of the tears flooding from his eyes. When they were out of firing range Sergeant Kim dropped his truck back behind London's. Only then did he wipe a welling tear from the corner of his right eye.

The blow on Hartnell's head had only glanced off his skull, which his Momma always claimed had been fashioned out of lumber wood.

He was dazed and felt blood trickle down his jaw line to his chin. He let his captors drag him, and hoped that somehow he would find a way to escape.

When they moved along the road round a hut into the heart of the village something chaotic was occurring. The Chinese and North Korean soldiers were firing wildly in all directions, bemusing Hartnell and his captors. Had the US cavalry arrived to save him or had London and Kim come up with a rescue plan?

Then Hartnell saw what was happening and knew no one could save him now!

A female figure stood amidst a carnal scene of utter destruction. Her slim Korean body was covered from head to toe in blood. Around her lay at least twenty Chinese and North Korean soldiers, all dead.

The remaining soldiers of the advance enemy force were firing into her body causing flesh and blood to spray in all directions.

Then she pounced, springing forward twenty feet to punch through the head of a still firing soldier. Then she was on to the next two men, dashing their heads together; both exploded like two overripe water melons.

On and on the murderous scene continued. The Chinese soldiers had faith in their communist built machine guns and fired until death. The North Korean soldiers were rattled by local legends and fled the battle scene.

Private Hartnell was dumped to the floor as his captors brought their arms to bear on the she-creature.

Hartnell watched as the Kumiho, a perfect huntress, dispatched man after man to death's oblivion. Then he looked around and saw he was unguarded and forgotten during the one sided fight.

He scrambled up a bank on hands and knees and tumbled and rolled down the hard earth on the other side. A cultivated field of over-winter onions lay before him, and he rose to a crouch and ran.

He had gotten halfway along the field, when he realised all the rat-a-tat-tats of Burp guns had ceased. He was yards away from the road again and could see his wrecked deuce-and-a-half, not too far distant.

Suddenly the hairs on the back of his head stood on end and he realised he was not alone. He slowly turned his cold and tired body and there, standing not thirty feet behind him was the Kumiho!

She was perfect again, no blood or wounds showed on her flawless young skin. The fact that she was completely naked scared him more than anything. Because she held no weapons, wore no protection and had the eyes of a child, which chilled his already cold spine.

She smiled and walked forward a pace. Then he remembered the box and pulled it from a deep inside pocket. She was twenty feet away now as his cold fingers fumbled to open the secret catch.

Fifteen feet now and the box was open, he looked up to see her dainty feet tread gracefully between the onions.

Ten feet now and out of the box he pulled the phial of yellow clear liquid. He looked at it, suddenly conscious of the fact his life depended on something so small.

Eight feet away and the phial landed before her feet, breaking easily on the frost impacted earth. The liquid disappeared into the earth and both man and Kumiho stared at the spot.

Nothing happened!

The Kumiho smiled, went to step over it then hopped back in shock. From the earth below in a ten feet radius around her, small green shoots were pushing themselves up through the hard earth.

Hartnell shuffled backwards to avoid the fast growing plants. The shoots were green and knee high now and twisting and sprouting new side shoots every inch or so. The thicker-by-the-second stems were now turning brown and entwining the Kumiho in a living plant prison.

Higher the plants grew and thicker and browner the stems and shoots became. The Kumiho was covered now up to her breasts in these dark entwining vines.

Then she screamed, as she struggled to free herself, because out of the brown stems and shoots grew the sharpest hooked thorns Hartnell had ever seen in his young life.

The razor sharp thorns stopped her struggling as they bit into her perfect tan skin. The thorns were over her head now, and she had to close her mouth and eyes to stop the stems invading them.

At ten feet high the thorns ended their growth and Hartnell saw the Kumiho was well and truly trapped.

He gave a cocky little wave and headed off back towards his crashed truck. Rounding the vehicle he peered inside and saw his bayonet was imbedded in the passenger seat. He ducked inside the shattered vehicle and then wiggled it from side to side to free it from the upholstery.

Nothing else seemed of much use so he hauled himself out of the half-crushed cab. On the road right in front of his boots was a slick trail of blood.

A blood covered, fleshless hand clamped hard around his throat, crushing his Adam's apple. The near skeletal Kumiho woman had him in her vice-like grip. Her flesh had been flayed from her bones as she escaped and pulled herself from the ripping thorns.

Half her face and one eye was missing, her lips had been torn away, showing too much of her lower teeth. Her arms and thighs were almost skeletal in appearance with only strips of shredded muscle and flesh remaining. Her breasts had gone and her ribs had been exposed and Hartnell could see her black heart beating within.

The air in his lungs was gone, his vision blurred; he heard a sickening crack and then neither heard nor saw anything in his life again.

The Kumiho let the dead US engineer fall lifeless onto the road. Then she knelt as best her thorn ravaged body could manage and eviscerated Hartnell from neck to groin. Into his steaming remains her bony fingers invaded and grabbed at his liver. Bringing up to her lipless teeth she devoured it swiftly, followed quickly by his warm heart.

Standing up only a minute later, her flesh and naked body were whole and regenerated again. She waved at Hartnell's corpse and continued her pursuit of the remaining two trucks. Her whole-again feet pounded along the hard road surface as she ran at an incredible speed after her husband.

When the two remaining trucks reached a fork in the southern road, they saw it was marked by a burning twisted shell of a truck.

They rounded the burning vehicle, unsure of whose forces it had once belonged to. They continued onwards, seeing no signs of the enemy, yet no signs of friendly troops either.

The cold November day wore on and grey clouds above threatened snow.

All of a sudden Robert London's ears popped and an almighty explosion rocked his truck. He braked hard and looked in his rear view mirror and gasped. Kim's truck was slewed across the road, its back canopy aflame and both rear right wheels missing.

London opened his cab door and was about to jump out when he saw the Kumiho standing in her wifely form, barely twenty feet behind Sergeant Kim's truck.

He looked at the burning vehicle and saw a huge crater in the road: Kim's back wheels had set off a landmine. He looked for Kim, but could see no sign of him inside his cab.

The Kumiho began to walk towards him now and with no sign of whether the R.O.K sergeant had survived, he jumped back into his idling cab.

The gas tank of Kim's deuce exploded as London drove off, sending the Kumiho flying sideways off the road.

This gave London time to accelerate away; he looked back in his rear view mirror to see the whole of Kim's truck aflame now.

The Kumiho dusted herself off and was about to chase after her beloved husband, when she heard a groan of pain coming from the other side of the burning truck.

She skirted the flaming truck; the heat it gave off was a pleasant change from the relentless cold.

In a drainage ditch four feet from the edge of the road lay Sergeant Kim Jun Ho. He'd been by the open driver's door when the fuel tank had gone up sending him flying into the ditch.

His right leg was broken in two places; his face, left hand and arm were badly burned. Even in immense pain he had already pulled the black lacquered box from an inner pocket. He held the box as best he could with his burnt left hand and opened it with his right.

The Kumiho saw what he was doing and jumped down into the ditch on top of his injured body.

The Kumiho knocked away the box, but the red phial was already in Kim's right hand. Her tiny, but immensely strong hand closed like a vice around his wrist.

He pressed his burnt face into hers and said "Chuktta!"

With his last ounce of strength he crushed the phial in his fist and the red liquid inside ran down both their forearms. It fell onto his smouldering army coat and, with a whoosh of burning oxygen, a circle of intense flame shot up around them.

Both man and Kumiho cried out in agony as the flames burnt them. Kim thought of his sister and kept his eyes open as long as he could to watch the beast burn. Her hair was aflame like a candle, her skin tightening and blistering like his own.

His throat burnt as he tried in vain to draw oxygen into his air starved lungs. He could see all his clothes were ablaze now as well as the Kumiho.

272

He felt her burning hand grab his throat, but he could not see now, and a heartbeat later he felt no more pain ever again.

The Kumiho cried out in agony and dropped the lifeless man, to be cremated into the Korean earth. She suddenly shed her human skin and leapt from the flames, her fur on fire onto the frozen field beside the road. She rolled out her flames and patted down the rest with her paws. For the second time in a day, since her rebirth, she felt less than invincible.

She spat a hair-ball onto the frozen earth and transformed her appearance again, returning to her naked, but now un-burnt, Korean girl form.

With a quick glance at the Korean soldier's burning remains, she started to run down the road again. Her beloved mate wasn't too far ahead now and she would soon catch him up again.

Private Robert London had no more tears left to cry. He had lost every single one of his fellow expedition comrades. Captain Woodholme-Browne and RSM McConnell had been so good to him. He doubted if their bodies would ever be recovered from the Yŏu Plateau.

Now he was the last of the three warriors and the special bond he had with Kim and, even more so, Hartnell, was lost forever.

As his truck crossed over a small bridge, he was unaware that he was only a mile away from the safety of the British fall-back positions at Pakchon.

The truck bounced down the other side of the bridge, causing him to slump onto the steering wheel slightly. A sharp pain dug into his ribs, as the black box in his top pocket was wedged between him and the wheel.

Something else he kept safe in that pocket was his letter from Nurse White and he wanted to see her face again, so much.

Yet the face he saw was the Korean woman who'd taken his virginity, staring at him through the passenger window, as she clung to the running board. He grabbed his revolver from the passenger seat and shot her in the face through the glass.

The Kumiho, through shock rather than pain, fell from the side of the truck onto the road. Robert thrust the revolver into a large coat pocket and concentrated hard on his driving. As the deuce crested a small rise he could see the outlined houses of Pakchon ahead.

Hope rose in his heart, and then all hell broke loose. The remains of the passenger side window exploded inward and halfway through it came the Kumiho in full nine tailed fox form.

Robert London had nowhere to go so he pulled the steering wheel hard to the right, opened the driver's door and jumped out.

He landed on his feet, which buckled under him, and fell, rolling over and over, the wind knocked out of him.

The truck meanwhile slewed off the road into a line of trees that bordered the side of the road. The truck's back wheels lifted in the air and it spun completely around, smashing to a halt into the side of another tree.

Robert London lay on the cold road, his palms, knees and face stinging from the tiny stones that lacerated them; but more worrying was his lack of breath.

He struggled onto his hands and knees, gasping for air that just would not come into his lungs for some reason.

Then out of the wrecked truck she clambered gingerly and at last he let out a gasp of air. She walked towards him; but something was wrong, her left forearm seemed broken and pointing at an odd angle away from her slender body. She realised this, stopped and snapped her arm back into position with a loud crack.

Robert had managed to sit up on his knees now, but he had a stabbing pain down his right side. It felt like he'd cracked a rib or two during his jump from the speeding truck, but now those injuries were the least of his worries.

She stood only yards in front of him, both on the hard frozen road, with its potholes and puddles, saying nothing.

"What do you want?" he hissed, the act of speaking hurt his sides.

"You are my husband, my mate. I just want you, Robert, as any wife would." Her perfect English surprised Private London, well as much as he could be surprised anymore.

"But you killed everyone," he protested, but his memories of his friends and family were fading like the night before.

"Shush, you need no others but I, Robert. Together we and our children will rule over all others." Her words were so calming, so reassuring, how could he hate someone so beautiful and loving?

"But I..." he began, but forgot what he was going to say halfway through.

"I need you to throw away that phial you have on you," she coaxed gently. "Cast it aside and we can be lovers once more."

Images of their carnal entanglements of last night were the final straw and he reached inside his coat to open his bulging pocket and retrieve the small black box. His hand touched its smooth sides, but also something else there. He wracked his addled mind to remember what it was: then he remembered it was Lillian's note and all the Kumiho's spellbinding words drifted away like a sea mist.

He took out the box and gently opened it and the lid slowly swung up. He took the blue glass phial from its velvet and held it in the palm of his cut hand. He stared into its blueness; the words of Sergeant Kim came back to him.

To understand your destination in life, first you have to understand the journey.

Cutting through his mind like piano wire through cheese, only one destination came to mind above any other thought or emotion.

"Nooo!" cried the Kumiho as Robert threw the phial, which landed and broke apart on top of a frozen puddle before her feet.

Robert scrambled back as the puddle grew rapidly in size and depth. Down into the clear blue waters the Kumiho sank, her hands reaching out for Robert in desperation.

Tears rolled down both their pained faces as she sank into the pool up to her chest now. Her frightened eyes boring into his, her mouth open to speak as the water reached her chin.

"When you die, I will live again!" she cried, before her head sunk beneath the pool. He could see her for a while, but then she vanished from sight deep into the pool's magical depths.

Then, as the exhausted soldier watched, the pool began to shrink again, smaller and smaller, until only the original puddle remained.

Something felt hot inside his coat pocket and he reached inside and pulled out the Gusul.

It felt warm, and blue and pink hues floated in its opaqueness. A wave of nausea hit him and he dropped the Gusul into the black lacquered box and snapped it shut.

That's how his comrades from the Middlesex Regiment found him, sitting on his knees in the middle of the road. Their jeep pulled up and four soldiers bundled out, one went to investigate the crashed truck, as the others raced towards him.

They had to lift him to his feet to stop him staring at a frozen puddle in the middle of the road. They took the black box and popped it in his coat pocket and led him silently back to their jeep.

Chapter 21

Endings

As Robert London finished his extraordinary war story the coughing fit began.

"Granddad," Paul cried out with concern and moved forward to help his grandfather raise the oxygen mask to his face.

It took a full twenty minutes for the coughing fit to die down. To Paul, his grandfather looked more frail and withered in body than when he had arrived this morning. The grim story from his Korean War days had taken much out of him.

"Do you need anything?" Paul asked and Robert London sat slumped in his favourite chair, his yellow tinged eyes staring at his grandson.

Slowly he pulled the oxygen mask down to his white stubbled chin.

"I need you," he gasped, "to promise…to do something…for me." Robert London's words were shortened by the lack of air in his cancer riddled lungs.

"Anything, Granddad, you know that," Paul replied with a lump in his throat. Seeing his granddad like this he knew he would never smoke a cigarette in his life again.

"The Gusul," Robert swallowed, "in its box must be buried with me; the rest…is yours to keep." Since the Kumiho story had been told, all the day's earlier strength and life had left him.

"I promise, Granddad." Paul grasped the old man's large hand and smiled weakly. He wanted to add that his granddad wasn't about to die anytime soon, but such platitudes now seemed worthless.

"Can you help me into bed, son," Robert London asked, hating the fact he was a burden to anyone.

"No probs." Paul reached under his grandfather's arms and pulled them both to a standing position. Paul was shocked how light his once muscular fifteen stone grandparent had become.

Robert London was asleep only a minute after Paul had put him to bed. Paul Harvey watched his grandfather's, uneven breathing as he slept, wondering what to do.

After five minutes, he drew the curtains to the back bedroom and went into the living room again. He took a last peek at the strange opaque marble inside the black box, and then shut the lid.

Putting it back into the tin, he took it to the kitchen and found a sturdy plastic bag to put it in.

He left it on the small kitchen table and then he heard the front door go. He entered the hall, just as his mother came in through the front door: her key in hand.

"Paul," she smiled, "how's he been?" she asked closing the door behind her.

"Not too bad," Paul answered, "he's having a little sleep now."

"I better check in on him." Angela walked past her son, taking off her thick jacket as she did.

"I'll make you a tea if you want one?" Paul asked, following her up the long hallway.

"Bloody hell, who are you and what have you done with my son?" Angela half-joked and turned back to face her beloved Paul.

"It's Granddad, he has a good effect on me." Paul grinned, and then suddenly rushed into his mother's arms, sobbing his heart out.

"Oh, Paulie," she patted his back and shed a few tears herself.

The afternoon grew darker still and the rain came at four as Paul and his mum sat in Robert's front room watching television.

Angela popped her head round the corner of her father's bedroom door, on a trip back from the loo for the umpteenth time that afternoon. He was still sleeping, lying on his back, pillows propping up his back and head.

As soon as she closed the door slowly, a wind ruffled at the drawn curtains.

Robert London's eyes shot open and he was suddenly aware of a short shadowy figure standing at the end of his bed.

The room was in semi-darkness and Robert could hear the rain rattle his window, and his heart thumping in his chest.

A nude womanly figure started to crawl from the bottom of the bed, until her beautiful face was but inches from Robert's.

"You can't be here!" he hissed, the pain in his body now like a flame inside him.

"I can be many things, husband," she taunted in clear English. "Even imprisoned on the plateau I sent my image out to make your truck crash."

Robert London could feel her hot breath on his parched lips and the exotic perfume of her body.

"I have nothing to fear from you, Kumiho, I'm already dying." He managed to squeeze the words out of his tightening chest.

"I know," she smiled, "and when you die the Kumiho line will be reborn."

"I won't allow it."

"Allow it, husband? You can't stop it. Haven't you tried a thousand times to destroy or lose the Gusul, the symbol of our union? Hasn't it always come back? It's part of you as well as me and from it I will be reborn, Robert."

Fear suddenly hit his heart; at the end of his life he was helpless to stop the Kumiho. Maybe if the Gusul was buried deep with him, it might be the end for both of them.

"Didn't you always long for my body, Robert? One night was too short for our love." She grasped his head in her hands and kissed him passionately.

"I never loved you," he hissed turning his head away as his hand reached out for something on his bed stand. "I had a wife and I loved her with my heart. I pity you."

"Pity me, little man, why?" She drew back now, trying to fathom his thoughts.

"Love isn't fear," he said and pulled a framed photo of him and Lillian White on their wedding day towards him. "Real love makes you feel safe," he croaked and held the photo to his chest, smiled and closed his eyes.

When he opened them a second later, his bedroom was empty and all the pain in his body had gone.

"Coming Lil," he whispered to a corner of the dark bedroom, where nothing but an old chair stood. Yet he saw something, not the Kumiho and nothing he could ever tell another living soul. Robert London closed his eyes and let out his last earthly breath.

Lorna Da Silva ran up the garden path to the bungalow's front door. It was raining hard a second ago, but suddenly the rain had ceased and the dark clouds of a minute ago were blowing eastwards on a swift breeze.

Seeing the lights were on in the living room she rang the doorbell, rather than use her key. Robert's daughter Angela opened it and invited her in.

"Looks like the weather's changing again." Angela peered at the clearing skies, before she shut the front door.

"It was raining cats and dogs only a minute ago," Lorna commented walking up the hallway, "How's he been?"

"Paul says he's been in fine form today, telling stories and all sorts." Angela smiled, trying to gain any hope from this hopeless situation.

"He's in bed," Paul said to the nurse helpfully as he appeared at the living room door.

She smiled at Paul, not without a hint of 'God-your-attractive in it.

She imagined that Robert had once looked so young and handsome, as she headed for the bedroom door. The room was a bit dark so she turned on the bedside light as she entered. Then she stiffened; something beyond training and experience told her he had gone.

"Angela," she called behind her as her fingers reached for his neck to feel for a pulse. She knew before she double-checked on his wrist that Robert had passed away.

Angela entered the room, with Paul behind her and saw her un-breathing father lying on his death bed.

"I'm so sorry," Lorna said and stepped aside for the family.

"Dad!" Angela wailed in grief, falling to her knees beside her father's bed.

Paul stood behind her in shock, tears rolling down his cheeks.

"Do you think he suffered?" Angela turned to the Macmillan nurse. "He died all alone."

"Look," Lorna pointed to the wedding photo in Robert's hands, "I think he knew, and now he's not alone." Lorna Da Silva wiped a tear away from each eye as Paul bent down to hug his mother.

Chapter 22

Heroes and Villains

Colin Harvey made it to the bungalow to see the ambulance take his father-in-law's corpse off to the local hospital.

Angela rushed into his arms and sobbed her heart out. He reached out and grabbed his son's shoulder too, as he stood close by, his eyes red from crying.

"Come on let's get you two inside, have a cuppa or something," Colin suggested and all three went inside the bungalow.

"Do you need anything, Angela?" Lorna Da Silva asked once they were inside the hallway.

"No, Lorna, I know the procedure because of mum." Angela took Lorna's left hand in both of hers. "I wanted to thank you for what you did for dad and for us." Tears that had only just stopped rolled down her puffy cheeks again.

"He was a true gentleman," Lorna smiled, "it was a pleasure to help him."

"Thanks again," said Colin hugging his wife. "You fancy a cuppa or something stronger?"

"No I better get going: you have my number if you need any help, don't you Angela?"

"Yes," Angela managed to squeeze out of her throat.

"Well I'll be off then." She went to get her coat. Paul followed her down the hall to open the front door for her.

"Let me know when you've made the arrangements, I like to attend and say goodbye," Lorna said picking up her bag.

"I will," Paul nodded; he could only manage the odd couple of words before his voice became too quivery to speak.

"He was a brave man your granddad," Lorna patted his shoulder and smiled.

"Thanks," was all he could think of saying, as it was a struggle to say anything.

"We better gather all his valuables, cheque book, bank cards and things and lock up tight before we go," suggested Colin as they finished their tea, though Angela had hardly touched hers.

"Do we have to think of that now?" Paul asked, lines of sadness on his forehead.

"Best to, the place is gonna be empty for a while, we don't want some thieving toe rag nicking all his stuff, do we?"

"He's only just died for fuck's sake!" Angela shouted and jumped up and ran from the kitchen to the bathroom.

"Angela, I'm sorry," Colin called after her, standing up. "I didn't mean anything, I was trying to help."

"I know, dad, come on, I'll help you." Paul rose, putting one protective hand on the plastic bag as he did so.

"What you got there, mate?"

"Granddad gave them to me today, his old cricket things and war medals and stuff," Paul half explained.

"That was nice of him." Colin patted his son's back.

"Better check his bureau first, in the front room," Paul suggested.

"Sounds like a plan," Colin said and they walked out of the kitchen towards the living room.

"Right, we're off to the florists to sort the flowers out for Friday," Angela called from the hall to the living room.

Colin Harvey put down his newspaper and joined his wife and son in the hallway. It had been four days since Robert London had died and Angela had thrown herself into the funeral arrangements.

Colin had surprised even himself by how supportive he had been for his wife and son. He needed to be really, because he had been betting heavily the last three days and had lost a stack of cash. He owed Jonesey the bookie half a ton and the fat bastard was getting itchy for his dosh.

"Remember my —" she began.

"— Clothes are being delivered sometime this morning; I remember," he finished.

He kissed her cheek with a grin and rubbed Paul's arm as they left.

An hour later, he was trying to find a horse in the papers to give him a 100% mark up on the fifty quid in his pocket.

The doorbell rang and spoiled his concentration.

"Who the fuck could that be?" he huffed and put down his pen and newspaper on the arm of his favourite chair.

He got up and walked briskly to the front door and pulled it open.

"Sign here please," said an overweight delivery driver in shorts, thrusting a dress sized plastic wrapped package into his arms.

"Oh, right." Colin had forgotten the delivery, so intense were his present money worries. He put the clothes on the stairs and put his moniker on the delivery note.

"Thanks, bye," the delivery man said in a bored voice and headed off back to his white van.

"Must be great to have job satisfaction like that," Colin said to himself as he closed the front door.

Getting money out of Angela at this time would be darned near impossible and lower than he normally sank. He had to do something, so he thought he'd better take her clothes upstairs, to keep in her good books.

He put the plastic wrapped clothes on the double bed and wandered past Paul's old room. On his unmade bed was the plastic bag from his granddad's bungalow and a tin half showed inside.

Whistling to himself he pushed open the bedroom door and sat on his son's bed. He pulled out the tin and sat the large heavy old biscuit box on his knees.

He pulled the lid off and was immediately shocked by the first item he saw, a bloody handgun.

Colin picked it up and pointed it at a half naked girl on one of Paul's old posters.

"Go ahead punk, make my day!" He twisted his lip into a Clint Eastwood impression.

He put the revolver down gently on the bed, maybe he could off Jonesey the bookie and not worry about the money he owed, he jokingly thought.

He fingered the tip-toed over medals and envelopes until he grasped the black lacquered box in his sweaty palms. He tried to lift the lid, but it wouldn't budge.

"Must be a Chinese puzzle box," he mused, all those days watching 'Bargain Hunt' had come in handy.

It took him a full five minutes before, by complete accident, his forefinger made something click inside and slowly the lid opened.

Inside was an opaque pearl the size of a marble which seemed to shimmer with different hues as he watched it; Colin whistled loudly. He gingerly reached out a finger to touch it; it was solid enough, but not cold at all.

"This should pay off my debts, with a little left over to have fun at Sandown later in the month." Colin Harvey put the box back into the tin and went to his son's walk-in closet and opened the door. He knelt down and began to forage through the old board games, Lego and football boots.

After a five minute search through the toy life of his only child, he came up with what he was after. Paul was never willing to throw away a toy and Colin hadn't minded, he'd enjoyed years of playing game after game with his son.

Now in his hands was an old Tupperware box, blue and opaque. Colin pulled off the lid to reveal Paul's marble collection. Finding one the exact size and roughly the same-ish colour didn't take long. Soon the marble was in the black box, which was inside the tin and returned to its original position.

A minute later Colin had skipped downstairs, pulled on his jacket and was out the door before you could say 'corpse robbing bastard!'

Twenty minutes later he was in Bernie Shackleton's pawn shop off Turpin Road, showing the stolen 'Gusul' over a well-worn counter.

Bernie had a jewellery lens jammed in his left eye and was examining it closely.

"It was your father's?" Bernie asked tapping the strange marble sized ball on the counter and listening to the noise it made.

"Late father-in-law's late estate," Colin explained, "just need a little capital to help with funeral expenses," which was a barefaced lie. Robert London's funeral had been arranged years ago: he would be buried next to his beloved Lillian. A special death policy would cover all expenses and more.

"Wait here!" the bulky Bernie said and shuffled off to look at a book, he vaguely remembered from somewhere out the back.

Guilt hit Colin Harvey as he waited on restless legs; Paul would never forgive him. Colin decided there and then to take it back and sell something else to pay off his gambling debt.

Bernie shuffle back into the main shop, his dour poker face unchanged.

"I'll give you two grand for it," Bernie offered and watched Colin's surprise reaction. All thoughts of guilt and remorse had been blown away by cold hard cash.

"Deal," Colin smiled back at Bernie. "Cash only of course."

"Why of course," Bernie smiled back, knowing this rarest of balls was best sold in certain circles for several million pounds.

Colin left the pawn shop and headed into the main shopping centre, hoping to catch up with his family and treat them to a guilt-off-setting-lunch.

Paul stood outside the funeral directors, just gazing at the beautiful tombstone in the front window. He had the black box in his hand, stuffed into his coat pocket and waited.

What he was waiting for, he wasn't sure. A sign from the almighty, a lone white dove to land on his head. He wanted to get the 'Gusul' out to give it one last look, but that could be dangerous, so still undecided he stood watching the shop frontage.

Just then the door to the funeral directors opened and an old couple, helping a younger woman with a toddler, emerged. The older couple thanked the men at the door, while the young woman just picked up the child and wept.

Presently they moved off and Paul felt like a small stupid kid fearing the dentist, he sucked in a lungful of air and headed into the funeral directors.

Over three hundred people crammed into the Cathedral for Robert James London's funeral. Friends he had a countless number of: old soldiers, ex-cricketers, coal monger friends and old customers, paid their respects in droves.

The sun shone through the stained glass windows, which Paul vaguely saw through his tear-laden eyes. The service was hard, but the funeral itself in the graveyard was near unbearable. Paul felt great relief when it was all over and they headed back to the bungalow for the wake.

The Kumiho story was now over and buried deep with his grandfather, his small part of the tale was over too, so he could head back to Newcastle soon and continue his life.

"You 'ear about Bernie the bolt?" Tommy Harris said, placing four pints of courage best from a tray on to the pub table.

"No, what?" Colin asked, it being the only interesting thing Tommy had said since New Year's 2001.

"Got murdered, in his shop two nights ago." Tommy sat down grim-faced.

"Fuck off?!" Eddy Houghton exclaimed with a resonating burp.

"True mate," Tommy nodded, "my Kevin's boy is a copper ain't he."

Mike Daniels coughed and nodded for Tommy to continue his news item.

"Well the alarm's been strung so he and his mate goes to investigate and find old Bernie dead." Tommy looked around the table for effect, eyes wide open.

"What happened to him?" Colin asked; a cold shiver had nestled in the small of his back.

"He was cut up bad, by all accounts, and listen to this, had all his organs cut out!"

"What, like his dick?" Eddy Houghton asked with his usual aplomb.

"No, you knob, dick?" Tommy shook his head. "His heart and lungs and stuff."

"Who'd wanna do that?" Mike Daniels asked sipping on his bitter.

"Dunno, but nothing was nicked or anything, so I reckon he must have stiffed someone a bit too tasty," Tommy mused, trying to eke out every inch out of the grisly tale.

"Where you going, Colin?" Mike asked and Colin looked around to find he had stood up for some reason.

"Bog," Colin replied and wandered off to the gentlemen's to have a little think.

For the next week Colin Harvey was a little skittish and stayed at home a lot, helping his bemused, but grateful wife sort out the banks and things.

Robert had left the bungalow to Paul, to start him on the property ladder; his money, over a quarter of a million pounds, he had left to Angela.

Chapter 23

Full Circle

Paul had spent the first week of his return to University life locked in his room, catching up on work and essays he had missed.

He worked twelve hour days and when he felt like slacking, the thought of his late grandfather spurred him on.

After a week of intense writing and typing he had not only caught up, but was ahead in a few subjects. With only the occasional visit from Ruben he had not seen a soul and by the time Saturday came around he was more than ready to let his hair down.

With a few mates he headed into town and went to the loudest, girl-crammed club they could find. Paul wasn't in that frame of mind and turned down three eager looking girls with matching bottle blonde hair. He just wanted a drink and a laugh with his mates tonight. The thumping base sounds of the rhythmical music blasted any emotional thoughts from his mind.

The drink and the music were doing a good job of emptying his mind of essays and funerals and he smiled for the first time in a fortnight.

"You wanna dance?" a sweet female voice called in his ear.

He spun round to give a negative reply, and then stopped when he saw her. She was five foot five in high heels, a mini skirt, and a low cut purple top. Her hair was long and brown, her eyes pale grey and her body slightly tanned.

Paul had never seen such a beautiful woman in all his young life. She reached out a delicate long fingered hand, which Paul put down his beer and took.

She led him into the thronging masses of the boozed up clubbers and they began to move with the music. She slid up against him and slowly they began to dance to their own rhythm.

That night the rhythm moved on to Paul's bed, as the girl slid up and down on top of him.

"What is your name?" he asked, his hands mashing her breasts together as she grinded herself down on him.

"My name is Pok-Kku." She smiled and lay down to kiss him. Her tongue intertwined with his as their French kissing became more urgent and passionate.

Paul could feel the hairs on the back of his head stand up on end, as her lower rhythm also intensified.

Suddenly Paul stiffened, well stiffened more, because in between their wet tongues something hard, the size of a gob-stopper had formed.

THE END

Author's Note

How this book (and others) came about.

Every book to me is like a child; each one begins and evolves in different ways.

Kumiho didn't start out as a book at all; it was a personal research project into my family history. My father died of cancer in 1980 at the age of 48; I was only 11 at the time. He was, and always will be, my biggest hero. I knew he had been a soldier (National Serviceman) and he had fought in the Korean War. A war mainly forgotten as it came only 5 years after the Second World War and seemed to be merged into the Vietnam war for some minds.

He never spoke of it and never sent away for his campaign medals, something as I child I could not fathom. In our minds, bravery, heroism, medals and war deeds were things to boast about.

So in my late thirties, with two sons of my own I wanted to try and imagine what it would be like to be my 19-year-old father at war. His two years National Service began in 1949 and he was sent to BAOR (British Army On the Rhine) in 1950. When the Korean War broke out he and about a hundred other men were drafted into the 1st Battalion, the Middlesex Regiment (The Die-Hards). They were shipped off to Hong Kong and then Korea, put in an American truck and driven to the front line.

It's hard to imagine with easy foreign package holidays now, the culture shock these young men faced. The furthest they had probably been from home was the Isle of Wight. Now they had visited three countries in a few short months, been given a rifle and told to shoot an enemy, intent on their deaths.

So I read every book I could find on the British side of the conflict and I soon realised I had a wealth of knowledge of weapons, units, dates and battles in my mind. I recalled an old idea I had to set some sort of vampire novel into the recent Balkans conflict, so I reclaimed that idea and adapted it. So the joint UK/US forces expedition took root, set around Halloween.

The lost temple and a crazed priest arrived in my id; all I was missing was a monster. I didn't have to wait long for on the internet waited the Kumiho, ready to come from ancient Korean myths onto my desk.

So the story spawned from that, with chapters' titles written before the story was a quarter way through. I had done this before on the first (unpublished) book I ever wrote entitled *The Calling*. My first published novel, *Demon*, had chapter number, but no titles, why?

I wish I knew. It's just the way it happens; I have little control over why some of my books have chapter numbers and titles, where some don't. *Demon* stemmed from a long walk home on a cold winter's night from a pub to my old flat in Surbiton. It is a long road and takes ages to traverse. What would happen if a girl came running down that side road, with a demon after her? So *Demon* began and Dela Robinson came along, fully packaged, age, name, race, height and mannerisms all there. Some other characters need a little more time and effort. So I had a start and, on a holiday in Greece in 1999, the rest of the story just came to me.

On another (unpublished, in its box folder) fantasy 800-page plus epic called *The Eternals*, the process was different again. I had a hundred pages of notes and maps; individual character sheets for the heroes, setting out age, sex, favourite music, drinks, sports etc. This is helpful during a pub screen, but can restrict your imagination also. I've never done this since; now all these people are in my head, plus two other half-finished (aborted) novels and the next seven ready to transfer from my brain to the ink written page.

Enjoy, there is more to come.

Bibliography

The following books/articles I found very helpful when writing this novel:

The Illustrated Directory of 20th Century Guns by David Miller

KUMIHO "She's more than a Shapeshifter" by Frederick J Mayer

Kumiho by Charles La Shure

Fox Wives and Other Dangerous Woman by Heinz Insu Fenkl

The Middlesex Regiment 1919-1952 by Lieutenant-Commander P K Kemp

South Korea in Pictures – Visual Geography Series – Lerner Publications

The Die-Hards in Korea – editor Colonel J N Shipster CBE, DSO

Pluck Under Fire by John Pluck

Our Men in Korea by Eric Linklater

Culture Shock Korea by Sonja Vegdahl Hur & Ben Seunghwa Hur

Battleground Korea, The British in Korea by Charles Whitting

British Forces in the Korean War, edited by Ashley Cunningham-Boothe & Peter Farrar

Infantry Operations & Weapons Usage in Korea by S L A Marshall

The Korean War 1950-53 –Osprey Men-At-Arms Series

At War in Korea by George Forty

Korean & Chinese Translations

Korean	English
Korean	**English**
Ch'a	tea
Anio	no
Sonsaengnim	sir
Unjon	drive
Yŏu	fox
Noogo got-eemneeekko	
twe-dawra-gada ul	who is that
Choshimhada kumiho	go back, beware of Kumiho
Ch'ongssori	gunshot
Chingguk saram	Chinese (person)
Yongguk namja	British man
Chunggugui	Chinese
Kach 'I oda	come along
Milgi	pushing
Kwa songgyohada	having sex
Suhoja	protector
Tonal	tunnel
Annyonghi	goodbye
Anjuseyo	sit
Maektchu	beer
Anae	wife
Nam-p'yon	husband
Kaptta	pay back
Eerumee otdoke	
dwe-seemneekka	what is your name
Shinhon	honeymoon
Sogyu	oil
Nuptta	lie down
Twich ok-kkoride	turn over
Wae	why
An-nyong-ee keseyo	goodbye (to person going)
An-nyong-li-kyeseyo	goodbye (to person staying)
Kach'i oda	come along
Umshik	food
Annta	sit down

Yuch'inon	kindergarden
Saqwa-chusu	cider
Kkonaeda	take out
Choshimsuropkle	carefully
Chuktta	die
Seek-he	sweet rice drink
Pok-kku	restoration

Chinese

English

Jaap gick	Attack
Yut	one
Yee	two
Gau la	that's enough
Do	knife
Ju-ee	Stay
Ngor surng yeeu dor dee	I'd like some more
Mo chun	mother
Bong	help
Jinwei hu	Kumiho
Ngor day yee ga hai bin do a	Where are we
Ngor mm ming	I don't understand
Jau hoy	go away
Jau	leave
Mm hai	no